Tide of Terror

Terry Smith

This is a work of fiction. Most events described here are imaginary. The settings, and some history are factual but characters fictitious and not intended to represent specific persons. Nor too is it suggested the events described actually occurred.

TIDE OF TERROR

Book cover design by Martin Smith
Cover photo Courtesy : Marc Hill/Alamy
Photo modifications: Martin Smith

Acknowledgements

I am sincerely indebted to Mr. R.A. CARR, Pilotage Manager of the Port of LONDON Authority at Gravesend, Kent, for the most detailed literature provided on the Commerce Installations, Services ,locations and facilities along the banks of the River Thames from the outer reaches through to London. I take this opportunity to apologise for the liberties taken with the PLA's River Pilot's Service for the purpose of this story.

Thanks are also due to my friend, Book Sales Agent, Trevor Williams, for his humorous "corrections" to the original script and encouragement towards publication.

I should not forget the support and contributions from my wife Susan and daughter Donna to whom I dedicate this novel.

I am also particularly indebted to my son, Martin, for his time, perseverance and computer expertise in creating both a striking cover design for the novel and formatting for publication.

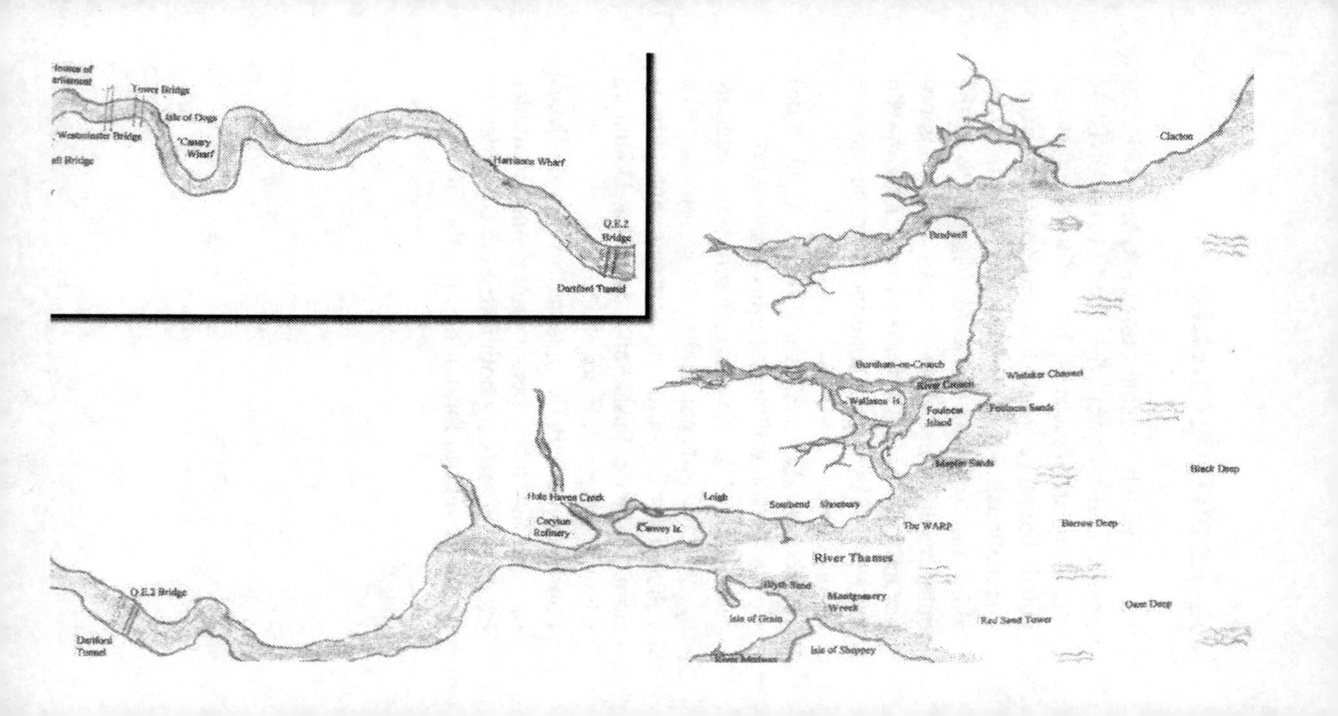
Tower Bridge
Isle of Dogs
Westminster Bridge
'Canary Wharf'
Q.E.2 Bridge
Dartford Tunnel
Clacton
Bradwell
Burnham-on-Crouch
Whitaker Channel
River Crouch
Wallasea Is.
Foulness Island
Foulness Sands
Maplin Sands
Black Deep
Hole Haven Creek
Leigh
Southend
Shoebury
Coryton Refinery
Canvey Is.
The WARP
Barrow Deep
River Thames
Blyth Sand
Montgomery Wreck
Oaze Deep
Isle of Grain
Red Sand Tower
Isle of Sheppey
Q.E.2 Bridge
Dartford Tunnel

PROLOGUE SPRING 1945

'Dunno what 'e 'ad to get 'isself bleedin shot down for, the war's nearly over,' mumbled Aircraftsman Henry Martin to himself while trying to see beyond the bow of Air Sea Rescue launch 271 bobbing comfortably in the passive swell and enshrouded in thick mist somewhere off the east coast of England.

Unfortunately for Martin, Captain (Pilot Officer) Read-Denny was gifted with acute hearing and clearly heard every word.

'For your information Martin, he, being Pilot Officer Gregson, was not shot down at all. His aircraft developed a mechanical problem that forced him to ditch. Instead of bemoaning your lot think of how he must be feeling at this moment - alone in a vast expanse of open sea - wondering if he has any chance of being found and rescued in this murk ! And, don't forget he could even be injured,' admonished the P.O.

Anxious to redeem himself, Henry, after a considered pause to appear suitably chastised, queried, 'Do you think the war will be over soon Sir ? My pal Nobby 'All - 'e's the Radio Op on Pilot Officer Ericsons boat - says 'Itlers 'ad it and it'll all be over before September.'

He knew his redemption was achieved when the Captain responded with a cheery, 'Let's hope he's right, I've lost too many good friends in this conflict. But, there's still a war on at the moment and poor old Gregson is somewhere out here in the drink. He's relying on us to get him back home safe. We've all survived the war so far so let's keep a sharp lookout, find him and get back to base.'

Careful not to repeat his earlier blunder, Henry pondered how anyone could keep any sort of lookout until the sea fog dissipated. Hopefully the Skipper's obvious superior hearing might pick up the sound of a whistle blowing, or they'd motor into a sign of oil or debris where the plane had gone down. Perhaps then the poor bugger in the water might have a chance. 'Don't give much for 'is chances otherwise.'

'Is the sky brightening a little, seems it's clearing ?' voiced the Captain to nobody in particular. It did appear the odd break in the mist's density was occurring with some frequency.

Feeling someone ought to respond, Coxswain and gunner Flight Sergeant Charles Murray piped up with a hopeful, 'Think you're right Sir. I thought I just spotted something off the starboard bow a minute ago,' although in truth he realised it was, probably, simply a hopeful figment of his imagination. But no, there it was again, fleetingly glimpsed through the swirling mist.

'There Sir, just over to the right, ….it's….it's..Christ it's a bloody floating mine! Don't move the boat! ' he screamed out.

Nobody said a word, all four deck watchers speechless and the only sound to be heard, that of the gentle purring of the boat's engines at idle and plash of water lapping the craft.

'It's o.k. Flight, it's drifted astern - no danger to us as we are. We'll turn and slowly follow the drift ; might give us a chance of finding the P.O. If he's managed to get into his dinghy he'll be behind us now.'

'Better take it easy had we Sir ?' queried Murray. 'Wouldn't want to catch up with that horny bastard and visibility's still not very good yet.'

'Quite so Flight. We'll motor at slowly for four or five minutes at a time and then idle and listen. We might get lucky - no good relying on the possibility of a sighting.'

The powerful engines responded immediately to the call for more power as the craft rapidly swung about and slowly increased speed, almost catching a daydreaming Henry unawares, only a lightning instinctive reaction of grabbing the Lewis gun mounting on the side of the wheel-house keeping him on his feet.

After a few moments slow motoring the Pilot Officer ordered, 'stop' on the engine telegraph. 'This is no good, this fog is hampering any serious search', he declared. 'Get us all a nice cup of tea Martin while we have a listen to see if we can hear any whistle. In fact Flight, give a few blasts on your whistle, see if we can invoke any response.'

Before either could respond to the Captain's orders, Aircraftsman Roger Cook, the acting medical orderly keeping a look-out to port, stopped everyone in their tracks with a questioning,'Can anyone else smell diesel fumes?'

Sniffing the air coxswain Murray confirmed, ' Now you mention it, I can. It's quite strong too. If it was petrol I'd say we were near to where the aircraft went down.'

Just then the little rescue launch drifted out of dense fog into a bright, almost clear, patch some five or six hundred metres wide.

'What the hell ? Look……,.'orderly Cook gasped open mouthed and suddenly struck speechless.

They were all already looking - wide eyed at the scene , albeit slightly enshrouded in mist, that met their eyes. The incredulous sight of a surfaced German U-Boat with a powerfully armed 'E' Boat just nosing up to the craft shocked everyone into silence.

Quickly pulling himself out of his stupor, Captain Read-Denny snapped, 'They haven't seen us yet Flight. Get the machine guns manned. I'll call Parish up from the engine room, Corporal Scammell can look after the motors himself !'

Sergeant Murray quickly dispatched Henry to man the rear deck 20mm Oerlikon, taking the starboard mounted Vickers .303 and mouthing 'Quiet' to the youngster Parish as he appeared on deck. 'Take the port Lewis gun,'he whispered.

Meanwhile the Captain had rung down to the engine room for 'dead slow astern', hoping to creep further back into the fog. 'We can't take this lot on, we're well outgunned,'he murmured. 'If we can avoid being spotted we can signal base and get some support out here; hopefully there's something a bit stronger than us in the near vicinity.'

They might have made it but for a terrified Keith Parish whose itchy, nervous, trigger finger involuntarily tightened to loose off an deafening chatter of red hot lead in the general direction of the German craft.

The puppet like contortions of some of the U-boat's deck crew would have seemed quite humorous to anyone who was unaware of the cause of their acrobatic display. But certainly not to the young marksman who threw up his hands aghast at his blunder, then threw up a spew of his recently consumed lunch all over his feet.

'Open fire, don't let them reach their guns!'screamed Read-Denny on witnessing Parish's *faux pas* and ,at the same time, attempting to swing round the nearest Lewis gun himself while still steering the high speed launch in reverse.

Unfortunately, apart from young Parish's remarkably accurate opening burst, the ASR crew's gunnery attempts - not helped by the Captain's erratic reversing - mainly failed to find their target, the exception being Henry's efforts with the Oerlikon. His see-saw spraying in the target's direction eventually resulted in the ammunition not being entirely wasted as, unbeknown to anyone other than the 'E' boat's crew, one burst stitched a neat line of holes from just below the waterline up to the foredeck, killing two engine room occupants.

The bravery of both the submarine and 'E' boat's crews could not, however, be thwarted by such inaccurate fire, most reaching their weapons unscathed.

Still some twenty metres short of the safety of the fog bank, Captain Read-Denny watched in fascination as the German gunners, obviously more experienced than his own, quickly found the range. Seemingly in slow motion, he saw a line of spurts *walk* across the water towards his wooden boat, culminating in a deck clearing slaughter of both gunner, Reg Clarke , who just disappeared straight over the side in a flurry of arms and legs - visibly no longer attached to his torso - and the hapless teenage Parish ,who was still staring at the vomited mess on his feet. Having not fired a single round since his *accidental* discharge, he was in the motion of bringing up his hands to cover his ears against the infernal din when the lethal fusillade caught him in its travels, taking his head with it from between his closing hands.

Shouting for full speed ahead to engineer Scammell, the Captain was surprised when his boat continued to reverse - especially as he had already started to turn for a forward dash into the thicker fog. As a result he suddenly found the craft presenting a larger target for the German crew as they swung back towards the U-boat.

'Flight see what 's going on below,'he shouted above the continuing noise of the battle. 'We need forward power at top speed to get out of range.'

Fortunately the unexpected manoeuvre had thrown the German gunners' aim and for a brief spell they were clear of the deadly barrage; giving Read-Denny the chance of a quick look back at the carnage on his decks.

'The engineer's dead Sir, that last straffing punctured the hull and poor old Scammell copped a couple in the chest,' puffed Murray re-emerging on deck. 'You've got forward power now but we're taking in a little water, must have caught one below the water line.

I don't think it's too bad, I can probably plug it once we're out of sight of those Kraut blighters !'

A loud report followed by a roaring sound overhead, and water splash just astern, interrupted the officers' conversation and caused the skipper to turn his boat back towards the densest fog and focus his attention on getting away from the heavier U-boat gun that was now joining in the attempted destruction of the rescue launch.

Apart from Henry Martin's stuttering Oerlikon, their other weapons remained silent while the German boats crew again opened up in earnest with everything they had; the crescendo of bangs, ratatat tats and whining bullets obliterating Read-Denny's shouted orders to medical orderly Cook and Flight Sergeant Murray to :'Get back on the guns!'

Not that the pair needed any such order, self-preservation and a need to revenge their dead shipmates was all the encouragement they required. Murray launched himself at the nearest Lewis gun and Cook dropped his lamentable first aid kit to scramble over to the Vickers machine gun.

Neither made it. The German machine gunners again found their mark, a scything spread catching Cook across his lower stomach and slamming him up against the starboard bulwark. And, although the anti-shrapnel padding around the cabin and wheelhouse absorbed most of the burst's remaining shells, one ricochet imbedded itself between Murray's shoulder blades, throwing him into the gun he was so anxious to get to.

The life-saving fog enveloped the boat and the Pilot Officer slewed the craft round in a sharp turn away from the withering fire still whining through the mist as the Germans sought to stop their prey from escaping.

Henry's Oerlikon ceased firing, seemingly obeying the same order presumably given to their adversary's crew : the deafening clamour suddenly died away.

The engines ,too, faltered to leave the battered launch wallowing helplessly in a rolling swell before coughing back to life as Read-Denny disengaged the powerful 500 bhp powerhouses to attend to his wounded crew.

'You alright Martin ?' he enquired on seeing the Aircraftsman staggering towards the wheelhouse. 'Not hit are you ? Help me with the

Flight Sergeant and have a look at the Medical Orderly.'

'I'm o.k. Sir , just feel a bit queasy. Cooky's had it: have you seen him - guts spilled out all over the deck ? I don't need to check him out any more; how's the coxswain ?'

'He's still breathing but he's passed out and we need to get him some proper attention urgently if we're to save him. I don't think our medical supplies are going to help much , even if we still had Cook.'

'Perhaps the engineer can help Sir, I'll get him up from below.'said Henry.

'Scammell's dead . There's just you , me, and poor Murray here,' replied the Captain. 'And, if that German 'E' Boat comes after us we'll all be for the chop. The engines are playing up; we're taking on water and nearly defenceless. Our position couldn't be worse. I didn't think I would be thankful for this fog,'he added forlornly.

'Perhaps,'......Henry started to say when he was cut off by a tremendous flash of light and explosion from somewhere just ahead of their boat. Their already ringing eardrums, having suffered the recent firefight clamour, and then the close violent thunderclap, were further assaulted with yet another loud - but muffled -

report ; followed by an increased rocking of their craft as a larger wave rolled by them.

'What on earth was that ?' enquired the dazed Aircraftsman. 'If only this damn fog would clear.'

'I think our enemy just blew up, or ,perhaps, was attacked by one of our craft Martin,' responded the Captain. 'Not likely it was one of ours though. This fog is still too thick to see far ,so it's much more likely that we either scored a lucky shot earlier or, judging by the force of that first explosion , that mine that passed us has proved to be our saviour. I'll see if we can creep over in that direction ; don't think there's much danger now,' he added nudging the controls to slow ahead.

Almost immediately one motor cut out and the other started to splutter, the boat barely getting under way. Not that it required much momentum , the sky suddenly lightening to quickly reveal a hazy sun and the sea fog thinning to permit much increased visibility.

'There Sir, over there !'screeched Henry. 'Bloody hell, look at that !'

Clearly discernible as the boat drifted into the mist free patch, less than a kilometre away, their eyes beheld the incredible sight of the shattered , upturned ,'E' boat slowly sinking by the stern, the bows briefly lifting clear of the rippling waves before slipping below the surface and revealing frantic activity on the deck of the U-boat.

It was obvious to Read-Denny that the submarine was also in serious trouble, a definite list to port and volumes of smoke pouring out of both the deck hatches and conning tower. So concerned were the crew as to their plight that the guns were unmanned , in fact the deck gun appeared to be missing.

The ASR launch remained undetected - or, if spotted, was considered no threat, tempting the Pilot Officer to order Henry back to the Oerlikon. But, in an instant, he realised his own craft was in no state to get back into battle and their little pop-gun not capable of subjecting the German *Unterseebootwaffe* to any serious damage other than clearing the crew off the deck.

It appeared that the submarine was actually under way as shortly it was stern on to the rescue launch .And, thought Read-Denny, was fading into the mist - unless the fog was again thickening.

Whatever; the Germans obviously had troubles of their own and showed no interest in their attacker , leaving their adversary to lick their own wounds.

'Keep an eye out Martin,' commanded the Captain, disappearing down the hatch. 'I'm going to have a look at the engines and damage we've sustained.'

His first impression was that of very little harm -the exception being the engineer's blood-stained corpse slumped in a seated stance against the port engine and immersed up to his waist in slopping oil-scummed water. Three rays of light streamed through ragged bullet holes to focus on poor Scammell's chest, highlighting the fatal wounds that ended his life.

As his eyes became more accustomed to the gloomy interior, still screened by a swirling smoke, he could clearly see a small bubbling ruffling the surface of the sloshing water in the area of the bow. Splashing up to the point, he quickly confirmed the source of the incoming flood, a single relatively small hole that could easily be plugged.

Turning his attention to the engines, which appeared undamaged, he was, at first, perplexed as to why they had failed. Then it became evident as he noticed a strong smell of petrol and spotted the severed fuel line. Fortunately the damaged line had actually been severely crushed, the volatile spirit hardly dribbling out to create a thin film over the bilge water.

Emerging on deck, he called out, 'Martin , Can you fix up the leak below - it's only minor - and put something under the leaking fuel pipe down there ? I'm afraid we won't be going anywhere under our own power so we'll have to pump out manually if necessary.'

'Fraid the radio's had it too Sir, look's though we're really up the creek without a paddle. Still, I'll soon block the leak so we won't sink. These wooden boats are double skinned and really tough and base will know where we are won't they ?'

'Only roughly , didn't have any time to radio our position once we were in combat and I don't even have a clue as to where we are exactly after all our meandering over the ocean,' responded Read-Denny.

Five minutes later Henry returned to state, 'All o.k. now Sir, stopped both leaks but can't do much about the water we've taken in . I'm a bit knackered, begging your pardon Sir, at moment but I'll give the hand pump a go as soon as I can.'

'Not to worry, it'll take more than that little drop to give us any trouble. At least that infernal fog seems to be disappearing altogether now. There's quite a bit of wreckage from that 'E'-boat drifting our way. Don't appear to be any survivors though ,'exclaimed the Pilot Officer.

'Guess we'll never know what really happened to sink it ?',voiced Henry, peering in the direction of the flotsam. 'Look, clinging to that carley float, I'm sure I saw an arm raised just then '

As the floating wreckage drew closer Henry's observation proved to be correct. There was, without doubt, a person weakly waving at them.

'What do we do Sir ? It looks as though he'll float past us unless we can move the boat.'

'I'm tempted to say let the bastard drown, but you had better see if you can throw him a life-line,' answered Read-Denny. 'He looks to be an Officer from what I can see of his uniform. I'm curious to know why an 'E'-boat should rendezvous with a U-boat in this part of the North Sea now that the war is obviously nearly over. Perhaps he'll come up with the answer.'

Henry's remarkably accurate thrown line fell almost on top of the float making it easy for the tiring swimmer to grab at the first attempt. The Aircraftsman dragged the German, still clinging to the float, alongside the launch and dropped a rescue rope ladder over the side. The oil-smeared face of the Officer looked up at his rescuer and coughed hoarsely in perfect English 'Help me Tommy, I have not the strength to climb.'

'Hang on mate, the name's 'Enry, not Tommy', retorted Henry while clambering over the side to assist the lone survivor .

It was all he could do to get the man on deck unassisted, little effort made by the Officer himself who appeared uninjured but completely exhausted. By the time Henry finally dragged him on to the foredeck and propped up against the hatch cover, he too collapsed gasping for breath.

The Captain appeared round the side of the wheelhouse to take a look at their captive and immediately ordered, 'Martin remove that side-arm he's wearing, we don't want to find ourselves held at gunpoint.'

Having recovered his breath the Aircraftsman crawled over to the slumped German , unclipped a leather holster and removed a Luger pistol before standing up and lounging back against the wheelhouse cabin.

'Who are you ?', barked Read-Denny to the prisoner. 'And what are you carrying in that briefcase ?', he questioned on suddenly noticing the valise chained to the Officer's wrist.

'I am *Konteradmiral* Karl Von Wohmoll of the German Kriegsmarine, and should afforded the respect and courtesy my superior rank demands,' he pompously declared in a much stronger voice than the earlier plea for help. 'The contents of my case are private papers and of no concern to you. I will not answer any more questions - I demand you take me to your Commanding Officer.'

'I remind you Sir, you are my prisoner and will be afforded every consideration but we are unable to start our engines and, YOU WILL do as I order . I will decide what or what not is of concern to me Rear Admiral !', roared the Pilot Officer mindfully struggling as to what such a high-ranking German Officer was doing on a small inshore craft.

'See what that case contains Martin. Perhaps that will provide some answers if our illustrious Admiral continues to be unco-operative.'

'Wait, I will show you ',Von Wohmoll suddenly volunteered, opening the clasps and reaching inside.

Two rapid reports echoed out as the German commander withdrew a second hand-gun and pulled the trigger in one smooth movement.

Read-Denny staggered back into Henry, a surprised look on his face as he stared down at two red blotches that appeared on the front of his tunic before falling forward and knocking back his killer as he was rising to his feet.

In death the Pilot Officer's involuntary tumble saved Henry's life, spoiling the aim of a third bullet intended for the unwary Aircraftsman who made a life-saving grab for the other pistol.

The two explosions were almost simultaneous as both adversaries raised their weapons and fired.

A fierce pain shot through Henry's left side as a violent impact threw him backwards on to the deck, only the low handrail stopping him going over the side. In what seemed like slow motion as he was propelled back, he noticed , with some satisfaction, a large red blossoming hole appear in the centre of the Rear Admiral's forehead.

'Aagh !,' he groaned levering himself back upright and turning to bend over his fallen Captain. 'You all right Sir ?' he queried. 'I've been hit but the bastard's dead.'

The lack of any response forced him, grunting in his own pain, to pull his colleague onto his front. 'No, you're not are you Sir?,'he murmured to himself on seeing the blood soaked jacket and blank ,lifeless, expression on the Captain's face.

A loud groan alarmed him until he realised it came not from the shot German but from the injured Flight Sergeant who he had almost forgotten during the rescue and subsequent events.

Stumbling back to Murray, Henry realised the he had again passed out although his breathing seemed steady, which was more than could be said for his own. Propping a lifejacket and rolled up sweater under the Coxswain's head the Aircraftsman tended to his own injury as best he could with the limited first aid equipment at his disposal.

Having stemmed the flow of his wound, Henry turned his attention to the German Officer whose actions had possibly killed them all.

'What's so important in your case that you didn't want us to see?,' he murmured feeling inside. A dozen or so sheets of typewritten German meant nothing so were left in situ but his hand withdrew clasping a package about the size of book.

Carefully unwrapping the parcel, he discovered a small metal, jewel-encrusted, box that reminded him of the type ladies used to keep their valuables in. By this time his curiosity almost made him forget the pain of his wound, fumbling fingers opening the lid to reveal a glittering array of diamond studded necklaces, earrings and loose stones that took his breath away.

Basically Henry was an o.k. guy, as honest as any law abiding citizen, his first reaction to replace the box and its contents back in the case.

'Phew,' he mouthed, 'I get it. That bastard was fleeing from our invading forces. I bet that sub was on it's way to South America or somewhere and this little lot was to provide the swine with a life of luxury.'

Prologue

The realisation that the jewels, if handed over to British authorities would never be likely to be returned to their rightful owner caused Henry to think in a less than usual honest fashion, his East End *Finders Keepers* upbringing coming to the fore and inducing a resolve to keep the find for himself.

He hadn't noticed before but it was beginning to get dark and, so it seemed to him, the fog was returning. Also his head was swimming and he realised the loss of blood from his wound was causing him to feel very weak.

'You're not in too healthy a state Martin,' he said as he stumbled into the wheelhouse for a drink and sipping a few mouthfuls before slipping into unconsciousness on the cabin floor.

He awoke in pitch darkness and instinctively fumbled around the cabin for the torch normally clamped to the wall by the radio. His fingers found the rubber cylinder handle and, mercifully, the lamp lit at the touch of the button to illuminate his surroundings.

It took a few moments for his mind to register exactly where he was and what had happened, his weak condition making every movement a painful experience.

Peering out of the cabin, only blackness met his gaze in whichever direction he looked , although he thought he briefly glimpsed a short - lived glitter just off the starboard side.

Where am I he wondered ? The boat has been drifting now for hours, surely I must be somewhere near land.

His musings were suddenly interrupted when the craft, to the sound of a harsh scraping alongside, gave a lurch and his quickly switched on torch beam showed up the upper works of a large ship.

Recognising the launch had collided with a foundered vessel, he summoned up the strength to pull himself up and tie a rope around a wire stay emerging from the water into the darkness. I must be near to land if I'm on a sandbank he reasoned. Perhaps when it gets light I'll be spotted.

With a possible rescue at hand his thoughts returned to the jewels and the dilemma of where to secrete them on the boat for a later return to collect them. He realised , in his weakened state, if rescued he would be whipped off to hospital and any possessions he had on him be removed, making it foolish to hide the diamonds anywhere in his clothing.

A sudden weak croak from the Flight Sergeant interrupted his ramblings about jewels and diamonds . Had the Coxswain heard ? No, it seemed, Murray remained comatose. An idea dawned on him. Pack them into some empty 20 mm shell cases, seal them in and tell his rescuers that he was keeping the cases as a memento of his ordeal. Surely then they would be returned to him.

The loose jewels proved no problem, soon secreted in the brass cases and sealed in with loose caulking, plenty of which was littering the deck, before being consigned to his jacket pocket.

Looking at the remaining jewellery, he closed the box lid while he contemplated how to break it up for easy concealment …..and promptly passed out again .

Dawn had broken when he awoke and peering over the bulwark he could see land on both sides. Forgetting his serious injury he attempted to get to his feet but found he was too weak to even pull himself fully upright. He could, however, see a launch approaching from the nearer coast, a few minutes more and they would be alongside.

Too late now to consider breaking up the other diamond pieces, his only thought was where to hide the box at his feet. Unable to move, he did the only thing possible - slid the necklaces and earrings down between the double hull skin alongside his head where the shattered wood gave him just enough space to drop the loose jewels in. The casket itself was too large to slip into the hole So, mindful that all the evidence of the jewels should be hidden to avoid awkward enquiries, he, against all natural instincts, tossed the jewelled box over the side…thinking, as he slid into a coma, I might be able to recover it later. Quickly sinking beneath the waves, the trinket box settled gently, with a puff of disturbed sand and sediment, on the sloping deck of the sunken SS Richard Montgomery.

Three oil-skin clad sailors boarded the shot-up launch , two immediately turning away to vomit over the side. The one made of sterner stuff growled, 'Oh my God ! Look at this charnel-house, is anyone alive ?'

Henry weakly waved an arm, 'Here mate,'he croaked.

'There's another alive here - just,' said another , now recovered, rescuer. 'We've got to get this pair ashore quickly to save them,' he added. 'They've both lost a lot of blood.'

The Aircraftsman remembered little of his trip ashore to hospital, fading in and out of consciousness, the last thing he heard being a whispered comment ,'I don't think this one is going to make it,' as his dimly seeing eyes registered only a white ceiling.

' Nurse, it's no use, I'm afraid he's gone,' said the Surgeon removing his mask. 'See that his mate - he is going to be okay - gets those two brass shells he kept on about. He seemed most concerned that they were not thrown away, kept mumbling that they were a souvenir of their only direct action of the war. Better give them to Murray now he's on the mend,' said the Doctor as he closed Henry's eyes and drew the sheet over his head.

1

The present day ...

Ryanair flight 332 gracefully settled on the run-way at Gatwick Airport to the obvious relief of the passengers who enjoyed a perfect flight from Dublin but, horrendous, turbulent descent through thick storm clouds. Many were sick and nearly all were white-faced and visibly shaken. All, that is, except the would-be macho men , exaggeratedly laughing and suffering a spate of verbal diarrhoea in a show of false bravado.

Saleem Hakimi ,deep in thought, remained seated until the cabin was nearly empty before suddenly realising he was being spoken to by an Air hostess.

'Are you alright Sir ?', the composed, calm, voice enquired. 'You're not sick I hope. Do you require assistance or a doctor?'

'No,no, I'm sorry, just waiting for the rest of the passengers to go first. I'm in no hurry and was just sitting here thinking of how bad I'm going to find the traffic on the M25 at this time of day', the lie slipping easily off his tongue. In fact his thoughts were on an entirely different subject - that of meeting his other three Islamic 'brothers' of his terrorist cell with the good news he had to share with them.

He was certain that his group were unknown to the authorities, or known only as the
Invisibles, the title given to terrorist cells who undoubtedly existed but about which nothing was known, especially when they were comprised of British Nationals. Searches for such groups also invariably centred on major cities, not out of the way places like Southend-on-Sea in Essex.

Saleem, the eldest at 28 years and leader of the illicit group, was the son of a wealthy industrialist who fled Iran when the Iranian authorities accused him of , 'collaborating with the Imperialist West and profiteering'. Fearing for the family's lives, his father used his influence and connections to escape to Europe , claiming political asylum and being granted permission to reside in England in 1977 with his English born wife and Saleem's elder brother Imad. Saleem was born less than a year later in Wembley where the family had settled.

Pale skinned, well spoken with very little accent , sporting smart western clothes and, without the obligatory moustache so often associated with Middle Eastern Muslims, Saleem easily passed as the English businessman his Southend neighbours assumed him to be. Careful never to meet with his fellow conspirators at his home in the quiet suburb street a stones throw from the famous resort's seafront, he carefully nurtured his anonymity by not becoming overly friendly with anyone in the road .In fact, he was known to neighbours only as Steven Hunter, the name he used to rent the house over six years earlier on moving out of the family home following the suicide of his parents.

'Thank you for a pleasant flight....except the last part,' he jokingly said to the hostess, rising from his seat, collecting his briefcase from the overhead rack and scurrying down the exit ramp after his fellow passengers.

Fortune favoured him at the luggage carousel where his small holdall case was among the first to appear and allowing him to beat the rush to the customs exit.

The customs official , a plump, red-faced, authoritarian figure, took an unusually long time studying his passport. Looking a little perplexed, he twice opened his mouth to say something before closing it in silence and taking yet another look at the document that he held in his hand. For a minute Saleem thought he had mistakenly handed over his other passport that he used for his onward journeys.

Finally the official could contain his curiosity no longer and blurted out, 'You're British are you Sir?', despite the passport clearly showing that was the case. Recognising he had made something of a fool of himself he quickly added, 'It's just that your name threw me for a moment there, certainly not Irish is it ?', he joked , quickly waving him through to cover his embarrassment.. Not that Saleem would be so foolish as to carry anything in his luggage that could bring him to the attention of anyone in authority….an important lesson of his early indoctrination to terrorism. His second passport was safely hidden inside a secure, cleverly disguised, pocket of his jacket. Breathing a sigh of relief, he lost no time in getting into the main concourse and transport back to his car.

With airport security so tight, especially following the London underground bombings that had occurred while he was in Ireland, and the abundance of surveillance cameras, he had specifically instructed the other cell members that he was not to be met by them. 'I will drive myself back to Southend,' he ordered before he left for the Emerald Isle. 'It is especially important now we are an active unit that we maintain the utmost care if our mission is to be successful.'

'What is the mission ?', Latif Amin had questioned. 'I am ready to blow up as many infidels as I can and am happy that I shall be rewarded in heaven.'

'Our targets have not yet been decided. I will be away for two weeks to arrange many things and will inform you of the decided plans on my return.' There was nothing to be gained by telling them more. What they didn't know - such as his destination beyond Ireland - they couldn't tell if anything went wrong.

His circuitous journeys, via Southern Ireland, France, Turkey and Iran, led him to Afghanistan where he met with leading terrorist masterminds in clandestine meetings arranged during an earlier ,fact-finding, trip to Pakistan. Operating a travel agency, Getaway Travel, provided him with every opportunity of unlimited journeys to virtually anywhere in the world with the perfect reasons.

Chapter 1

By the time he had got back to his car his thoughts switched from the euphoria of having arranged ample funding and ,on approval of a suitable target, provision of necessary explosives, to that of selecting the target that would produce the maximum disruption to the economy - a greater priority for him than the killing of innocent victims.

Saleem was no suicide bomber. He had agreed with his Islamic masters. 'You are a leader who can further our cause by continuing to plan and progress attacks throughout England. It is important that you remain undiscovered and leave any direct , suicidal, action to the *chosen ones*.'

Turning onto the M25 motorway and immediately getting snarled up in a lengthy jam gave the terrorist leader the first inkling of an idea that would, perhaps, achieve both maximum casualties - appeasing the Amin brothers - and create commercial and industrial mayhem. In fact, the more he thought about it the more he recognised the after effects of such an attack would be financially crippling for the country's commerce for years to come.

Pulling into the Clacket Lane Services for a break while the traffic cleared, a now excited Saleem parked and made a call to a London number using a public telephone. 'I already have a meeting place.' - the agreed coded notification of the intended target - he quietly whispered into the mouthpiece. The listener waited while he went on to name the site and request, ' Perhaps you can let me know tomorrow where and when I can pick up the customer , assuming he still wants to come ?' - another coded message concerning the acquisition of required arms and explosives, if his target was approved.

' I will get him to come into your business and make his own arrangements,'was the curt response as the line went dead.

Returning to his car with a plastic cup of coffee, Saleem withdrew a notebook from his briefcase and started to make a list of his requirements, commencing with a substantial sum of money. If he was to carry on his terrorist activities after a successful first strike it was, he realised, important that no unaccounted for monies were withdrawn from his personal or business accounts.

Thinking of the finances required to mount his proposed attack caused his mind to deviate and reflect on his father's misfortunes, the start of his own hatred of the Western, cut-throat, financial way of life. He was in no way a devout

Muslim, attending Mosques less frequently than he knew he should. But, following his parent's financial ruin when a few poor business decisions resulted in bankruptcy and the banks declined to help, leading to them taking their own lives, he turned to his temple for solace and became an easy convert to hatred of all things Western when others quickly recognised his need to find an outlet for his anger.

He still clearly remembered that day when he returned home from visiting a friend of his University days, Mohammad Sadat, to find a police car and ambulance outside his parents house. Instinctively he knew something bad had happened, a sympathetic Policewoman confirming his worst fears with 'I'm afraid there's been a terrible accident.'

It was, however, no accident. Stunned by the dreadful news Saleem was comforted by the family's neighbours who explained Mr and Mrs Hakimi had committed suicide by sealing themselves in their car with a hosepipe from the exhaust. It was the neighbour who alerted the authorities when he spotted smoke escaping from the locked garage and heard the running engine.

In his grief, from that day onward , Saleem vowed that he would, one day, revenge his parents deaths, 'a thousand times over.' He snapped out of his morbid reminiscence. That day was nearly to hand !

Realising that, until he finalised his plans, he didn't know exactly what munitions would be required he put the notebook away . 'I'll compile a list this evening before tomorrow's visitor,' he mouthed to himself.

The traffic appeared to have lessened, at least it was flowing freely - Saleem pulled back on to the road and motored sedately towards the Dartford Tunnel.

Twenty minutes later he was queuing at the tunnel's toll booth to pay his pound fee and staring up at the ,sixty five metre high, Queen Elizabeth 2 bridge, almost mesmerised by the engineering marvel that carried four lanes of continually flowing vehicles into Kent.

A tooting from behind jolted him out of his fascination and he quickly threw his pound coin into the basket to raise the automatic barrier into the tunnel.

As usual with just four lanes through the two tunnels, vehicles jostled for position, everyone's journeys seemingly more important than anyone else as they sought to get what amounted to just one car's length ahead.

Saleem smiled to himself as a sudden addition to his planned attack came into his head. Emerging from the tunnel's gaping mouth into Essex, he was glad to see the traffic was very light, giving him an equal choice as to whether to take the M25/A127 route, or the more direct A13 road back into Southend.

He chose the A13 on a snap decision that he would , to confirm an idea, make a slight diversion on his way home. Driving past the way into the massive Lakeside shopping complex he suddenly remembered he had told his Travel Agency manager that he would pick up some more wooden brochure racks from the Centre's Ikea Warehouse, the amount of Holiday literature available this year far exceeding his shop's display capacity.

Turning back at the Chafford Hundred roundabout, he returned and parked in the huge Ikea car park…..sitting in his car, brain racing as he toyed with a thought of a change of target.

The massive 120 acre Retail Park and Shopping Centre, with it's average 75,000 visitors a day, had the potential, Saleem realised, of a prime terrorist target for inflicting large numbers of casualties. But, already, he had seen two people carrying rucksacks approached by , he presumed, special security and led away. It was obvious that, following the London bombings, security at such places as major shopping centres had been stepped up and anyone carrying any sort of package was going to be stopped short of any large gathering of people. And, to make any significant impact on a place like Lakeside, a substantial number of operatives and great amounts of explosives would be required.

Entering the extensive Ikea store, he noticed that they too had employed extra security, a burly uniformed guard keeping a close eye on those entering. No, he thought, dismissing the idea and making his way to the required section for his purchases. The original idea has much to commend it and the eventual result could well be far more spectacular and, long-lasting, than a suicide bomber killing himself and limited numbers of *the enemy*.

In no hurry, he kept to the inside lane on leaving the Park and drove the fifteen miles along the A13 to the complex Sadler's Farm Roundabout at a modest speed, deep in thought for most of the time and almost forgetting his planned diversion on to Canvey Island.

Remembering, unlike ordinary roundabouts, he could turn right, he took the first right exit off the circular maze into the Canvey Way and increased speed down the long straight stretch on to the Island itself.

Making his way to Hole Haven creek, he parked up and clambered up the sea-wall from where he could see the spreading expanse of the Canvey Calor Gas terminal and Coryton Oil refinery, mentally noting the location of mooring jetties and the nearest storage tanks.

Not wishing to be seen to be overly interested, he quickly returned to his car and resumed his journey home, briefly pulling up on the Eastern Esplanade on Southend's seafront and gazing out towards the Kent coastline, again in deep thought. Before starting off for the final half a mile to his home, he walked along the promenade to a nearby telephone booth with the intention of calling Mohammad to inform him that he was back from his trip and make arrangements to see him and the Amin brothers the following evening. It was, he soon discovered, a waste of time, the vandalised box devoid of an actual telephone handset, the dangling cord testimony to some moron's show of strength.

He toyed with the idea of using his mobile but instantly dismissed the thought, remembering that others had unknowingly betrayed themselves - albeit after they had carried out their bombings. Saleem could not allow himself to make such a fundamental error of judgment. 'Better to leave the matter for now. It is not that important ,I should get home and consider the finer details of my plans.', he murmured angrily to himself.

Saleem lived alone, never having married, nor having any particular inclination to do so. A reasonably handsome man he, although not shy, tended to keep well away from anywhere large gatherings of women were to be found. He never visited nightclubs and had few friends to go out with or visit....other than his co-conspirators who, of late, he had met with at various locations at least two or three times a week to discuss the ways his group could cause the greatest atrocity in pursuit of their cause. Realising he was hungry he rang out for a take-away Indian meal before settling down to gather his thoughts and assimilate his ideas before finalising the plan. Loathe as he was to commit anything to paper, he quickly came to the conclusion that he would have to make some notes to ensure he had thought of everything before he met the others and give to his visitor the next day.

Unsure whether his Islamic leader contact had, in his brief telephone call at the motorway service station, fully understood his requirements, he listed the intended targets and, alongside, the armaments and explosives necessary to achieve success.

The London based leader was aware of the original target previously agreed but, Saleems' circuitous journey home had put an audacious idea for further targets into his head. Confident that, once notified, his al-Quaida go-between would readily agree to his new plan and provide the additional ordnance, he set about encrypting, using a previously agreed code of Canadian place names and grocery shopping , the full list of the sites to be attacked and total armaments requirements.

Just as he was giving the matter more thought the door-bell rang, alarming him like a sly schoolboy caught cheating in an exam and causing him to slam his notebook shut before realising it was, probably, only his meal delivery.

Still deep in thought he opened the front door and, without looking, beckoned the young delivery boy in. 'Put that down in the kitchen there for me,' he said indicating the way, 'while I get you your money.'

On his return his heart missed a beat when the youngster emerged back into the hallway,

recognising the young delivery lad from a Mosque visit he had made a few weeks ago. He quickly handed over his money with a small tip and speedily showed the boy out with a ,'Thank you young man,' just stopping himself from saying the youngster's name that he knew to be Ramzi.

He breathed a sigh of relief as the door shut, hopeful that he had not been recognised himself as he was aware that his next door neighbour often ordered home-delivery meals from the same take-away. What if he did remember him and mentioned it to his neighbour ? If that happened his carefully cultivated subterfuge would have been divulged and , in the current climate, he would certainly come under suspicion for disguising his true identity. Perhaps, even, his ungrounded behaviour would be reported to the police ?

Should I run after him, he asked himself ? No, if he hadn't been recognised that would be tantamount to giving the youngster another opportunity to recall having met him, and, more importantly, where. Best leave it and chance the brief Mosque encounter was only a problem in his own mind. If only he hadn't ordered the meal ?

As if to punish him for his unwitting mistake ,his appetite had disappeared , resulting in his just picking at the food and seeing most of it consigned to the dustbin.

Forget it , he told himself. Get back to deciding on the list of items required to put the plan into action. If the worst was to happen and he was asked awkward questions by his neighbour he would cross that bridge when, or if, it happened.

Returning to the task at hand he listed the requested armaments and supplies with a similar simple coded shopping list previously agreed with his contact controller, a method that made it unnecessary for them to actually meet. Such devious measures gave the terrorists confidence in their anonymity , the only weakness being the go-between link although ,even here, Saleem reflected he had never seen the same messenger twice.

After giving his requirements some thought he had made a shopping list of:
Garlic, **E**ggs (large, at least one dozen), **T**omatoes (3 lb), **D**oughnuts (4), **R**ed **L**eicester (1lb), **R**olls (5), **W**affles, **A**pple **T**art, **B**acon (2 lb), the first letter of each item relating to the predefined code - for example any listed item beginning with **B** defining Bombs, anything commencing with **D** referring to Detonators etc.

His request for Guns, a large quantity of Explosives, three Timers, four Detonators, a Rocket Launcher, four Rockets, a Wetsuit, an Air Tank and two Bombs would, he knew, be understood when his list was delivered, although the messenger would have no idea of the true content of the message.

Assuming that his targets and supplies would be approved by the British, Al Quaeda Commander, he had one more thing to do before retiring to bed - look in the local newspaper to see when the Waverley paddle steamer made it's evening trips up the Thames Estuary from Southend Pier to Tower Bridge. Discovering that the next scheduled river cruise was only a few days away he made himself a note to ensure he made a booking in the morning, perhaps, he mused, inviting Mohammad to join him.

Feeling tired from his travelling, Saleem made his way to bed and switched on the television set in the room to watch the news before going to sleep. Within minutes his eyelids were drooping as he fell into a light slumber, his subconscious mind suddenly snapping him wide awake as the Television Newscaster announced, ' London's Metropolitan Police today arrested another suspected terrorist involved in the July bombings following a late afternoon raid on premises in West Ham. No further details have yet been issued but it is understood that the suspect is a twenty seven year old Pakistan male associate of one of the failed , 21st July, bombers.'

No, it couldn't b……….the telephone shrilled on the bedside table interrupting his frightening thought and demanding his attention. Lifting the handset he held the instrument away from his head as a meaningless gabble erupted from the earpiece.

'Calm down, speak slower please,' he spoke into the phone with his mind racing as to who it was calling him at that time of night and suspecting that he already recognised the voice despite the incessant chatter.

'Have you got the television on ?' enquired a still agitated voice. ' Mohammad has been arrested, he'll tell them…….'. ' Hold it right there, who's speaking ?' interrupted Saleem, fearing that he already knew.

' It's Asif, Asif Amin, what shall we do, they'll come for us soon ?' answered the clearly shaken youngest member of the *Southend* cell.

'Now listen to me,' commanded Saleem. ' I have the television on. There is no indication that it is Mohammad. Just because he lives in the West Ham area does not mean he is the person arrested. He would have been at work in Stratford and, as far as I am aware, he did not know any of the London cell members involved in the bombings. I would have known of any connection. Now pull yourself together. You have been told that you must never contact me here directly. Your incredible stupidity could put our whole group at risk.'

' I'm sorry,' said a much calmer Asif. ' I did not think. When I heard it on the news I just panicked and thought I must telephone you immediately; although I was not certain you had returned from your trip to Ireland.'

Chapter 1

'Put the phone down NOW!' screamed Saleem. 'You have already said far too much over this open line. You will be contacted tomorrow.'

Violently slamming his own handset down on the cradle, he clasped his head in his hands in despair. 'Why have I got such an imbecile in the group, he'll kill us all !' he shouted at the television before remembering that his was a semi-detached house and that, on occasions ,he had been able to hear the sounds of his neighbour's love-making and raised voices through the dividing wall.

Now wide awake, mind racing at the sudden misfortunes of the evening, he put all attempts at sleeping aside. Turning off the television he lay back and contemplated the unexpected setbacks to his, and the cell's, security.

First, the possible misfortune of the take-away delivery boy. The more he thought about it the more certain he became that he was recognised. Would the youngster say anything to anyone about it? It was then that it hit him ! Recognition was the least of the worry, he had slammed the notebook shut but the sheet of notepaper had been left open to view. Ramzi must have seen it .What could he do about it now ?

He suddenly realised that he had no option but to *silence* the lad to protect his plan, false identity, and safety of his group. If such a course of action was to be pursued he recognised that it would be necessary to act quickly before the boy passed on the information to anyone else.

Glancing at his watch he noted it would be another hour before the Indian Take-Away restaurant closed and Ramzi finished his deliveries. Where does the greatest danger lie he pondered, committing murder or facing the inevitable questions as to why he was writing lists of weaponry and explosives, plus disguising his identity ? Given the current suspicion of anyone of the Islamic faith, hiding his true name could have been an excuse....but for the fact he had hidden it for many years and the list was tantamount to an admission of evil intent.

Mind made up he quickly dressed and quietly left the house by a side entrance to his garage. Walking swiftly up the road he soon made his way to his local railway station car park where he selected a nondescript Ford Escort car that he was certain would not be alarmed. A sharp backward elbow easily shattered the driver's window and confirmed the lack of any warning device. In one smooth movement he cleared the driver's seat of broken glass and slipped behind the wheel. Recalling his tutor's instructions on *hot wiring* a vehicle, part of the Afghanistan camp training, he wrenched the wires from the ignition and quickly identified those required to fire the engine into life.

The motor started at the first attempt and Saleem exited the car park less than two minutes from choosing a suitable vehicle for his intended purpose.

His timing was perfect, pulling into the kerb of the Shoebury road within sight of the Indian Take-Away premises from where his meal was delivered, less than five minutes after leaving the station car-park and just as the establishment was closing.

Ramzi came out of the doorway as the shop's lights were extinguished and walked off in the opposite direction. Saleem started the car and slowly followed, awaiting an opportunity to carry out his planned killing.

Ensuring his lights were off and pulling his rollneck pullover high up to cover the lower half of his face, in case any inquisitive late night walker became suspicious of his movements, he hung back until his quarry left the brighter lights of the major road and turned into a dimly lit side street.

As the young lad stepped off the pavement to cross the road. Saleem gunned the engine, pressed the accelerator hard into the floor, and swung the car directly at him like a lethal missile.

Startled by the roaring engine, Ramzi looked back just as vehicle reached him, but stood no chance of avoiding the impact which threw him high in the air and into the windscreen .His limp body rolled off the bonnet as Saleem braked violently and backed up to swiftly motor forward again over the inert boy.

Certain that he had *neutralized* the threat to his plans, he sped off in the direction of the seafront, turning the car's lights on at the end of the road to avoid the possibility of falling foul of any police night patrol.

Surprisingly, both headlights came on, neither having been damaged by the deliberate collision, testimony to his accurate driving skills in hitting the boy exactly central.

He was sure that he had not been seen but it was likely that the car's engine noise had alerted some of the inhabitants of the street where the boy lay, making discovery of the victim fairly certain within minutes of his speeding away. It was, therefore, vital that he dumped the car as quickly as possible and, not as he originally intended , drive it to some out of the way spot and set fire to it.

'I should not have acted so impulsively and thought things through better,'he muttered to himself. 'How would I have got back home if I had done that ? No, the police will think it's a hit and run accident by some joy-riders, especially when it is discovered the car was stolen. All I have to do is dump the vehicle a few miles away from the scene, ensure I've left no evidence of myself, and get home unseen.'

The solution suddenly jumped to mind - the best place to get rid of the vehicle was in another car park and he had just thought where to do so and avoid any chance encounter walking home in the dark.

He continued in the direction of the Shoeburyness seafront and on to the esplanade, driving a few hundred yards and turning into a large grassed car park. A few vehicles were parked near to the entrance so he drove to the far end close to some beach huts and coasted to a halt, waiting a few minutes to ascertain his movements had not attracted any attention before silently opening the door and slipping quietly out.

Keeping the parked car between himself and the seafront road, and crouching low, he quickly made his way between two huts onto the deserted beach. Certain that he had not been seen leaving the house earlier he had decided his best plan of action was not to return until early morning.

But, on the off chance that the stolen car had been reported and was spotted by an observant police patrol, he walked along the beach for a few hundred yards before carrying out the next part of his idea, that of breaking into a beach hut for the night.

Finding one with a single flimsy padlock he withdrew a heavy Swiss Army knife from his pocket and half a minute later he had gained a noiseless entry. There was little inside, the only items he could see in the dark being a rubber ring and folded up sun lounger.

Careful not to crash into anything he opened up the lounger and laid back closing his eyes before remembering to close the door and set the alarm on his wristwatch for six o'clock.

Chapter 1

With no feelings of remorse , fatigue soon overtook him and he drifted off into an untroubled sleep.

An incessant buzzing next to his ear brought him instantly alert, his usual sleepy awakening being replaced by an immediate recollection of the night's events and where he was.

Rising from his bed he edged the hut door slightly open, letting in the dim morning light, and peered out through the narrow gap. The beach, as far as he could see, was deserted.

'So far so good,' he murmured, folding up the lounger and replacing it against the hut wall before opening the door fully and stepping on to the beach.

There was nobody to be seen, just as he had hoped. Quickly closing the door and replacing the broken lock , he smoothed his clothing and hair before creeping between the huts and peeking over the sea wall.

The only person in sight was a heavy set man with a towel under his arm crossing the road a hundred ,yards away, heading in his direction. 'Surely not a swimmer at this time of the year,' he whispered to himself.

Saleem ducked back down behind the wall, sure he had not been spotted but certain to be so if the early morning swimmer continued in his direction. He dived beneath the nearest hut and listened as the man's footsteps got closer, suddenly aware that the hut he was under was only two away from steps leading to the beach.

If he comes down those he must see me. He held his breath, fearful that even inhaling and exhaling would give him away. The man walked on by and Saleem heaved a huge sigh of relief before crawling out from beneath the hut and again peering over the sea wall.

'All clear,' he gasped, quickly mounting the steps on to the pavement and setting off at a jog in the opposite direction to the swimmer.

Nearly two miles from his home he worked out his best route and soon turned up a side road off the seafront passing only one other person, an elderly ,well dressed gentleman - even at that time of morning wearing a shirt and tie - walking a small dog.

'Good morning,' he amiably called from across the road , requiring a response from Saleem who would rather have remained silent.

Anxious to appear perfectly normal , he cheerily waved back with a grunted, 'Another nice day coming up I think,' not stopping his easy jog to give the stranger any chance of studying his features. Thank goodness I had the foresight to go out last night in just a dark tracksuit, he thought and secretly pleased at the way his trained mind had automatically responded to the morning's events so far.

Stopping only at a Newsagent to purchase a Sunday newspaper, he soon reached the end of his street where he slowed to a walk, tucked the paper under his arm and strolled casually up to his door, a shrewd move as , surprisingly, his next door but one neighbour was just coming out of his gate.

'Hello Steve,'he greeted eyeing the newspaper. 'Didn't know you were an early riser. I thought you had your papers delivered.'

'Only the local Evening Echo. Can't get any-one to deliver just a Sunday paper. I
normally get one later on but I couldn't sleep so decided to take an early morning walk,' lied Saleem in case his neighbour became curious as to why he was up and about so unusually early on Sunday. 'Where you off to then, this early ?'

' A nice round of golf. Freddy Willis, you know the tall chap you were talking to at my barbecue last summer, is picking me up in a minute as the wife wants the car today while I'm , as she says, Playing boy's games.'

Opening his front door Saleem retorted, 'Might see you at the *nineteenth* later then.' Grateful to get inside, he slumped , sweating, in the nearest chair, dropped the newspaper, and contemplated his shaking hands as realisation of the enormity of the previous night's murderous action brought him back to reality.

'If only I had eaten at the Services I could have avoided all this. I just hope
I've not jeopardised the whole operation,' he thought. 'What about Asif and his panicky, un-thinking ,telephone call ? And, was it Mohammad who had been arrested ?' His mind was a turmoil ;' what to do ?'

'There's only one thing, I'll have to visit the Mosque today . There's bound to be gossip among the congregation and, maybe, the Amin brothers will be there. I should be able to see if they are being watched and, if not, slip them a note to meet me in the park, 'he considered.

He went into the bathroom, stripped off completely and showered before placing the discarded clothing in a black dustbin bag and dressing casually in smart lightweight beige slacks with open neck pale brown and white striped shirt .Picking up the bag he took it through to the garage and placed it in the boot of his car before returning to the kitchen in realisation that he was both hungry and thirsty after his night's exertions.

Keeping an eye on the time he breakfasted on muesli, toast and coffee before picking a light fawn coloured jacket off the back of a chair and going back outside to open the garage doors. A glance at his watch showed him it was now past nine thirty but his road was still empty of any activity and he met nobody on his way out.

They say a criminal often returns to the scene of his crime but Saleem had no such thoughts, turning out of his street in the opposite direction and sedately driving towards Southend where he left his car in a multi-storey car park, descending to ground level and walking over to the nearby taxi rank.

Disturbing a newspaper reading cabby, he opened the door and climbed in breezily issuing instructions as to his destination, a place a little way short of the Mosque but within an easy walk. The driver was obviously happy to have his boredom relieved by his unexpected customer, chatting non-stop throughout the journey about Southend United's football match the previous day.

Saleem , although not at all interested in football, quickly gathered that it was an important cup game and, according to the cabby, Southend 'should've walked it, ….but lost !'All he could do in response was sagely nod and murmur sympathetically until, somewhat relieved, he realised his *chauffeur* was saying, 'Ere we are Sir, that'll be four pounds twenty pence.'

Handing over a five pound note with a, 'Keep the change,' he signalled dismissal and stepped off towards the Mosque. He had deliberately avoided arriving any earlier, deciding he would not, on this visit, actually enter. Just as he approached the corner of the road the assembly started coming out of the nondescript building, some gathering in small groups to chat . Among one of these he spotted the Amin brothers but hung back on the corner awaiting dispersal of the gathering, not wishing to be seen directly speaking to the would-be terrorists.

Latif looked up, spotted him, and made to come over but Saleem shook his head to indicate no; nodding in the direction of the nearby park . Taking Asif by the arm Latif bade farewell to the others and walked away towards the recreation field.

Chapter 1

Saleem waited a few moments to ensure nobody followed them before joining them on a park bench.

'I am so sorry for my stupidity,' blurted out Asif before Saleem even sat down. 'I will never be so unthinking again, please do not dismiss me from the group. I will blow up a thousand infidels,' he exaggeratedly pleaded, the words coming out in a torrent.

Although still inwardly angry at the young man, Saleem, mindful of his own slip up, hissed, 'Be sure you are more careful in future or I will kill you myself. The operation I have spent a long time planning and co-ordinating is far too important to be jeopardised now by such inconsideration. Fortunately for you, you are important to the plan and cannot be readily replaced now matters have almost progressed to action.'

The elder Amin brother interjected, ' He begs your forgiveness Saleem. It was a silly mistake that will not be repeated. I have already found out that the person arrested in West Ham was not Mohammad. The newspapers say he is Raj Moffat who is an illegal immigrant. Are you here to tell us the plan and what we have to do ?'

'I have decided that this is not the right time to inform you of our targets just yet. I have a few details to discuss with Mohammad and am still awaiting authority from our leaders, which I expect to receive in the next few days,' replied Saleem. 'Today I just wished to confirm for myself that our cell had not been compromised by Asif's thoughtlessness. I am confident none of us are under any sort of observation or suspicion so perhaps one of you would be so kind as to call me a taxi to take me back to Southend. There is no sense in taking any chances by us being seen together in the same vehicle; there are so many security cameras around these days, better I take a taxi. We will meet at the usual place on Friday evening when your curiosity and patience will be rewarded.'

In response to Latif's call, a taxi drew up at the park gate just as Saleem's brisk stroll saw him arrive at the rendezvous at the same time. To his relief it was a different driver,
nowhere near as talkative during the return trip as his fellow driver, permitting him to pursue his own thoughts.

The Amin brothers remained seated following Saleem's departure, discussing the bombings in London, the first Al Qaeda attacks on British soil. ‘Our brothers willingly gave their lives for our cause’, exclaimed the young Asif. ‘Their sacrifice will help make Britain an Islamic state,’he enthused. ‘I have waited years for this chance; I hope our own attack is even better and we kill many more *unbelievers* with Saleem’s plan.’

Latif, less zealous than his nineteen year old brother, replied, ‘ Have patience Asif. Do not let your enthusiasm to become a martyr to the cause rule your actions. It is very important now that we act perfectly normal, just carry on with your daily activities in your usual manner. You had better get back to the shop, father will be expecting you. I will see you on Friday.’

Asif rose, put on his crash helmet, unlocked his moped from the nearby railings, wheeled it to the entrance and drove off; leaving his elder, twenty two year old, brother to contemplate his limited time left before his own martyrdom, and how he had become a conscript to the terrorist cause.

The Amin family actually came from Peshawar in northern Pakistan, close to the border of Afghanistan, only moving to Britain in the early nineties to join relatives in a business venture in Birmingham. At first the young brothers were homesick; a feeling aggravated by some abusive racialism from near neighbours. It was this fact more than any other that convinced their father and mother to move out of the Midlands and purchase a shop elsewhere.

A, too good to be true, business opportunity arose when the *Pakistani grapevine* led them to Southend -on -Sea in Essex to take over an already established good grocery business that had experienced no trouble in the five years it had been established.

The move, encouraged by the young boys' enthusiasm for the seaside, proved to be an astute business and personal decision. The family were readily accepted in the neighbourhood, the business continued to flourish and the youngsters quickly made many friends at both school and in the locality.

Encouraged to attend the local Mosque, the boys - as they got older - often found themselves inadvertently *brainwashed* by , not so much clerics of the Muslim faith, but *angry young men* of the congregation whose forthright opinions of Western dominance in Middle Eastern countries - imagined or factual - slowly but surely poisoned their minds, often causing friction with their own father.

Chapter 1

Thinking back, Latif could not recall any particular time or event that convinced him that the terrorist cause was either just or even the only way of pursuing Islamic goals, both he and his , more easily led, brother just drifting into thoughts of terrorism to achieve the political aims.

Asif still resided in the family home assisting in the business . But Latif, following a particularly nasty argument with his father, found himself *banished* and *disowned*, fortunately quickly setting himself up in a rented flat of a friend of Saleem who he had recently met at the Mosque gathering. Since that day he had only spoken to his father very occasionally, their feud never having been revoked.

He had, however, in recent years mellowed and become more thoughtful, his lessened Mosque attendances, away from some of the zealots undoubtedly weakening his earlier resolve towards terrorism. He was, nevertheless, not completely *cleansed* and remained determined not to let his cell brothers down - except in one respect……he had decided he did not want to be a Martyr.

'Asif should also not die. He has much to live for and is still so young,' he quietly uttered unthinkingly being in such a public place. Fortunately the nearest pedestrians were a good fifty yards away and he snapped out of his reverie before they approached closer. 'No, there is no need for anyone to die. I will speak to Saleem when I know of his plan.'

Looking at his watch he left the park bench and, with a spring in his step, made his way to where he had parked his , newly purchased , sports car; easing into the driving seat and, with a second look at his watch, setting off to pick up his girlfriend. Basically quite shy in the company of females ,he, although considered pretty good-looking, had been without a girlfriend for nearly a year before meeting Saisha. Now, he decided, he had strong feelings for her despite only going out together for just over two months....possibly an unbeknown factor in his recent sudden lust for life.

Just as Latif was getting into his car; three miles away Saleem was alighting from the taxi, again telling the driver to keep the change from a proffered five pound note. Before returning to the vehicle he saw that it was now gone eleven o'clock and many of the High Street shops were open. He made his way to a Sports & Leisure shop, selected a track suit similar to that still in the bag in his car boot, together with a new pair of trainers. At the counter he was about to pay by credit card when, mindful of how the police were able to backtrack on many things these days, he elected to pay cash, asking the assistant for some silver coin change as he intended to telephone Mohammad from a public box.

Finding one in working order was, this time, not difficult although he was not too happy that it was of the open canopy type, affording less privacy than he would have wished.

Mohammad answered before the second ring. Saleem pressed the coins home.

Without introduction he whispered,‘ We need to meet. Are you working today ?’

‘No, and I have nothing planned that I can’t defer,’ came the response.‘ I can meet you at the usual place; just give me an hour.’

Saleem ended the brief exchange with, ‘Make it three o’clock, I have a few things to attend to my friend.’

Driving out of the car park he remembered the items in his boot and took the road out to the local rubbish depot where he joined a queue of cars depositing just about everything - including the kitchen sink.

His little package hardly seemed worth the wait . But ,the importance of disposing of the clothing he was wearing at the time of his 'killing' last night was, he concluded ,more important than anything at present. Ten minutes later with the tracksuit consigned to the clothing bin and trainers deposited in with a bin full of shoes and boots, he drove away with the happy thought that now there was nothing to incriminate him in any way should he for any reason come under suspicion.

On his return home he donned the new tracksuit while he scuffed up the trainers before putting them on and scraping his feet for ten minutes on the back step. Satisfied they no longer looked new he placed them in the bottom of a wardrobe and put the track suit into the washing machine with his underwear from the previous evening. Glancing at the kitchen clock he went to the fridge and got himself a ready meal that he quickly heated up in the microwave oven; certainly not a gourmet banquet but sufficient to appease his appetite and leave him ample time to reach the rendezvous with his second in command.

When he reached the Leigh-on-Sea station car park twenty minutes later he was expecting to have a wait for Mohammad but, as he parked his car a train was leaving the station and he spotted his fellow conspirator already descending the steps to meet him.

Sporting his usual grin, the six foot tall, swarthy, Palestinian greeted Saleem with a hug that threatened to crush his ribs. 'How good it is to see you again,'he exclaimed . 'I have been eagerly awaiting your call for days now - what's happened ?'

'Jump in,' Saleem gasped. 'We shouldn't hang around here it's too open. I'll drive around while we talk.'

While driving out of the car park the couple indulged in only small talk, Mohammad, although hardly able to contain his curiosity , awaiting his leader's introduction to the subject of the proposed attack.

'Asif thought you had been arrested,' Saleem suddenly said as he turned right towards the boat slipway on two-tree island, adding, 'He stupidly telephoned me at home last night,' and going on to explain everything to his friend.

Mohammad patiently listened without comment until Saleem finished speaking, by which time they had driven to the slipway and parked. 'I had to confide in you, it is a burden that needed to be shared. Have I messed up Mohammad ?'

'Certainly not !' exclaimed the big Palestinian. 'Do not dwell on it any more. The boy is a casualty of our war and, as you have said yourself, Asif's thoughtlessness has not given us any cause for concern. Your own cleverness in destroying any thing to connect you to the car, which will eventually be discovered, gives you nothing to fear.'

'I am glad to hear you say that my friend. Now I want to have a look at some boats around here and then I will tell you of the plan.'

They climbed out of the car and walked to the water's edge. Surveying the craft moored in the creek in both directions, Saleem shook his head murmuring, 'There's nothing suitable here.' and stalked off back to the car.

Perplexed , Mohammad dwelt breathing in the fresh sea air before reseating himself and asking, 'Do we need a boat for the plan ?'

'We do,' replied Saleem, 'A very fast one. Come, we will go somewhere less isolated and conspicuous.'

Ten minutes later they were seated in the, surprisingly busy, outside gardens of a Leigh public house enjoying a drink - among a babbling throng of young men and women but far enough apart to allow secretive conversation.

Saleem revealed the details of his overseas trip to acquire the required funds and munitions for his audacious plan; and the success of the meeting with the Al Quadea representative. For the most part the Palestinian remained tight-lipped, just occasionally interposing to query a minor point and, all the time, waiting for his friend to inform him of the target and expected results of their attack.

Finally Saleem beckoned him closer, leaning over to whisper the names of the places their bombings were to destroy.

Mohammad was breathless and shocked dumbstruck at the audacious scheme. There was so much he wanted to ask but did not even have time to recover his composure before Saleem added, 'I will go over the details of how we are going to carry out these attacks on Friday when we all meet up, I should have confirmation of approval by then . It is in everyone's interests my friend that I keep certain things to myself for now while the police are detaining and questioning so many of our Muslim brothers. I have not even told the others of the targets yet. Have patience for a few more days and you can be certain we will shock the world with our attacks if Allah blesses our cause.'

Although he considered Saleem a friend, Mohammad knew there was no sense in questioning the cell leader, simply saying in response, ' I have waited two years or more since I returned from my *holiday* to Pakistan. Have no fear I can wait for however long it takes.'

'Good, let's get you back for your train. Be careful and I will see you on Friday.'

The conspirators finished their drinks and motored back to the railway station, both deliberately joking and making general conversation to lighten the sombre atmosphere of the previous hour. Dropping Mohammad off near to, but not actually at the entrance, Saleem drove off without delay, leaving his *right hand man* to walk into the station concourse alone, thereby avoiding any CCTV cameras recording his car registration.

'You can never be too careful,' he uttered.

A train was in the station as Mohammad descended the steps. He sped onto the platform and jumped aboard the last carriage just as the doors closed. At that time on a Sunday afternoon the carriage was almost empty, the only other occupants being three noisy youngsters messing about at the far end. Dismissing thoughts of walking past them into a forward carriage, he plumped down where he was to digest the information he had just been given.

So engrossed was he in thinking of how Saleem was going to overcome problems he could see affecting the plans, he hardly noticed that the young teenage girl, encouraged by two spotty faced *toughboys* , had come and seated herself opposite him, her ultra short miniskirt hitched up to display her brief knickers.

'What you doing ogling my girl's crotch you dirty pervert ?'sneered the taller lad, obviously intent in provoking trouble and showing off in front of the others.

'Oh dear,' thought Mohammad, mindful that the last thing he wanted was to draw any sort of attention to himself . Trained in unarmed combat while involved with Hamas terrorists and, later, in the Afghanistan mountain camp gave him every confidence that he could easily have incapacitated all three troublemakers without the slightest effort - but where would that solution lead ?

Instead of leaping to his feet and smashing one of his powerful fists into the smirking face, as his instinct told him to do, he futilely tried diplomacy. ' I'm sorry, I was daydreaming and hadn't even realised the young lady had decided to sit there. I can assure you I am not in the habit of looking up girl's dresses,' he exclaimed.

'Liar, your eyes were popping out of your head,' screamed the girl.

'No yo……,' he started to say , interrupted by a wild swinging fist of the *showoff*.

The blow never landed. In a lightning movement Mohammad's own hand wrapped itself around the lad's clenched fist and twisted it away from his face. A sharp snapping sound told him he had inadvertently broken the boy's wrist - confirmed by a scream of pain.

The girl and smaller lad launched themselves at him as he rose to his feet, their pitifully weak blows hurting themselves more than him. But, the girl's screams concerned him more. Fearing her verbal outburst would attract unwanted attention, Mohammad back-handed her across the side of her head and she slumped back into her seat.

The whimpering bully boy on the floor looked up at him wide eyed as the powerful terrorist held the other youngster at arms length and lifted him bodily on to the carriage seat ….to look him directly in the eyes.

'Sit down and don't move !' he ordered in a voice that invited no resistance. 'Where do you boys live?' he demanded in order to discover where they would normally be getting off.

The now frightened lad blurted out the full address of a block of flats in Upminster, two stations before his own West Ham stop. 'And he's my brother.'

The girl groaned and sat up. Mohammad placed a finger on her lips and indicated silence with a 'shush.'

Nothing is going right he thought. First Saleem finds himself in a predicament and, now I too have an unfortunate situation to resolve. Surely Allah would show him how ?

The next stop was Basildon. That's it !. 'I'm getting off in a minute. Say nothing to anyone about your stupid actions and myself. Just take your brother to hospital and say he had an accident,' he threatened. 'Say anything about me and I will come after you and kill you. I know where you live !'

As the train drew to a halt in the station the subdued trio nodded assent in unison.

Mohammad alighted as the doors slid open and was grateful to see nobody at the rear end of the platform waiting to board the train. In fact he saw only four people step aboard further up the carriages. He quickly trotted forward and re-entered the train two compartments up as the doors hissed closed, hastily pacing through the next two carriages away from the rear of the train. He seated himself facing the rear and kept a watchful eye on the interconnecting door until the train pulled into Upminster station. He stepped into the carriage interconnection , out of sight but still able to view part of the platform, and was relieved to see the three young hooligans - the elder lad nursing his injured arm - stride towards the exit.

He dropped back into his seat with a sigh of relief, confident his ruse of deceiving his tormentors as to where he had alighted, should they ignore his threat, had succeeded. 'Of all the times,' he cursed to himself, 'why now? Surely nothing else can go wrong ,'he thought, mentally deciding not to tell Saleem of the incident.

Recognition of what he had become penetrated other thoughts as he drove home.' I could easily have killed them all, and many more like them if they jeopardised the plan,' he realised. 'Saleem and I will remain strong and resolute. Nothing will stop this opportunity to strike a blow for the Islamic cause.'

With his wife away visiting her ailing, sick, father, the house was silent on his return but this suited his wishes; giving him the opportunity to sit down at his computer and look up internet information on the targets Saleem had revealed to him. Only after spending an hour investigating the discovered facts did he realise he was making just the sort of mistake that would enrage his leader and lead to the downfall of the attack should he come under any sort of suspicion before it's implementation. Again, he thought, 'I will not tell Saleem of my indiscretion.'

Lying in bed later, awaiting sleep, he pondered on what he had been told about his not being required to commit the ultimate sacrifice for this attack. Ever since his boyhood in Palestine he had been inculcated into a suicide attack philosophy being the way a young man could best benefit the Islamic faith, and guarantee a place in paradise with seventy two dark haired *Maidens of Paradise*.

For the Palestinian youngsters the enemy were the Jews of Israel . But for others , Mohammad included, the indoctrination turned them against the West in general, having been taught that True Justice and Peace was only possible once Islamic Law was implemented. Any country, therefore, embracing Western culture and politics was a legitimate target for the terrorist bomber.

Saleem's reasoning as to why both he and Mohammad should not join the Amin brothers in martyrdom, made much sense in that the terrorist cells throughout Britain were not as numerous the speculative press would have the public believe. And, as Saleem had put it, 'It is considered our duty is to live and fight another day.'

Mohammad was still contemplating whether this was a contravention of his Islamic teachings and a betrayal of the faith as he drifted into sleep thinking ,'Perhaps I should disobey any such order?'

Saleem was still wide awake, unaware of his friend's misgivings , or Lasif's *change of heart.* As far as he was concerned, his only problem disposed of, it was now a question of finalising the details and obtaining a suitable craft - an essential item for the plan that could not be provided by his masters. He was , unsuccessfully, scanning the classified columns of his local papers and a 'Boatowner's magazine he had purchased on his way home. 'Damn!' he swore. 'Nothing here and the next set of *neap* tides less than two weeks away. I will have to make a determined effort during the week.'

The following morning he made his way to his Agency , the Monday visit being one of the few occasions that he actually spent time in the office usually going over ongoing matters with his very competent manager and making any arrangements requiring his direct intervention. It was doubly important he be around this day as he was expecting the special 'customer'to call and collect his coded itinerary and shopping list.

Bidding the two girl staff a cheerful ,'Good morning', he strode into his office followed by his manager. 'Anything I should know about this week Peter, any problems ?' he enquired.

'Not at all. We enjoyed a good week of bookings last week and have had no adverse feed back from any of the tour operators or airlines. Is there anything special you require this week ?'

'No, nothing. Just tell the girls to keep it up and we'll all be getting a bonus. I won't actually be around much myself this week but you can get me on my mobile if anything comes up you think I should know about. I've got a few things to sort out for a forthcoming trip to keep me occupied for the rest of the morning but then it's all down to you,' he lied to explain his presence in the office while awaiting his caller.

Just after eleven o'clock he called for a cup of coffee and walked out to join Peter and the girls for a break , re-entering his own office ten minutes later wondering if he was going to have to hang around much longer for his 'contact'.

He needn't have worried. A few moments later, Peter popped his head round the door to say, 'There's a chap outside asking to see you. Apparently he's starting up a new window cleaning round in the area and wants to know if we're interested. Doesn't seem to want to take no for an answer so I thought you might wish to see him , especially as that current chap is pretty unreliable.'

'Tell him I'm just about to go out but I'll give him a few minutes.'

Sally, Peter's protégé with the apt surname of Travell, ushered a pale, anaemic looking youth - probably no more than seventeen - into the office with raised eyebrows to signal her opinion.

Chapter 1

As the door closed , *paleface* as the others later called him, sat himself down opposite Saleem , held out his hand and said in quite a cultured voice, 'I'm no window cleaner. I'm told you have a message for me to deliver. It'll cost you thirty pounds. And, I have a telephone number for you to remember - do not write it down. Tomorrow you may use it from a public box without fear. Ask for *Cobra.*'

Somewhat taken aback by the youth's demand for money, which was almost certainly a, self claimed bonus in addition to a promised payment, Saleem was tempted to resist the extortion but decided in the circumstances on diplomacy, simply handing over a blank envelope containing his requirements.

Slipping the envelope into a pocket, the youth's hand returned outstretched while Saleem withdrew his wallet , fished out three ten pound notes and handed them over without comment.

The youth grinned , cheekily saluted and uttered, 'Nice to do business with you,' before backing out of the office, leering at Sally and leaving the shop door open behind him as he stepped into the street.

A laughing Saleem followed and joked to his staff, ' I don't think he's got the strength to lift the bucket. I think we'll stick to the usual chap Peter. I'm off now , see you on Friday.'

On leaving his shop, he walked through to the High Street and along to the W.H.Smith outlet where he enquired where he could find a chart of the Thames Estuary.

'Sorry Sir, that would have to be ordered. We could get one for you for Wednesday if you like.'

'Yes please. The name is Western,' he said using his manager's surname instead of his own. 'I can't leave you a phone number as I'm away for a few days and my mobile's playing up,' he lied. ' I'll call in personally on Thursday morning.'

With little else planned for the day he collected his car, drove to the seafront for an alfresco lunch and then continued his search for a suitable boat, visiting Leigh-on-Sea old town where craft were often seen on sale.

Unable to find anything that seemed remotely suitable for his plan, he managed to get into conversation with some local fishermen enjoying a late lunch in the sunshine. Their answers to his enquiries dismayed him. Even if he were able to obtain the *right* boat he discovered that his lack of boating expertise would probably be an insurmountable obstacle, the tidal vagaries and heavy river traffic certain to be a greater danger to his plans than any anti-terrorist body. 'You want a trip up the river mate, you'd better hire yourself a licensed boatman or you could be swimming home,' was the consensus of opinion from the watermen.

With an uncertain mind he returned home dispirited and downhearted; his mood further blackened when he saw a police car pulled up outside his house, tempting him to drive straight by. But, recognising such an action would not be that of an innocent person and certain that he had nothing to fear, he drew up onto his forecourt. As he got out of the car he was approached by a uniformed officer and policewoman.

'Would you be Mr. Hunter Sir ?' queried the tall, blotchy faced policeman, adding without waiting for confirmation, 'Nearly missed you; my colleague was about to leave you a note to contact us.'

Having nodded assent, Saleem - heart still racing - enquired, 'Is there something I can help you with Officer ?'

'We're making enquiries relating to what appears to be a fatal hit and run incident that occurred in Shoebury on Saturday night. The young man involved worked as a delivery boy for an Indian Take-away restaurant. We are just contacting all those he delivered to during Saturday evening as there are some aspects of the accident that suggest it may not have been a straightforward hit and run. Did you notice anything out of the ordinary when he delivered your meal Sir ?'

'No. How dreadful, such a pleasant chap as I recall. I cheerfully gave him a tip for his services. I'm afraid there's little else I can tell you. I didn't even notice what he was driving.'

'Thank you for your time Sir, I don't think we will be troubling you again. I assume this is your only vehicle ?'

'Yes, except for my trusty old push bike in the garage,' replied Saleem watching the Policewoman making a careful inspection of his car - especially the front end.

As he watched the law officers drive away his mood lightened , 'They obviously have not yet discovered the whereabouts of the dumped car. Even when they do there is no reason why I should be reinterveiwed,' he told himself.

Chapter 1

Alone in the house that evening he perused the local newspaper, the young mans death being given some prominence but as far as the report was concerned, simply a hit and run. His thoughts returned to the problem of the boat, considering a change of his original plans to one of getting at the targets by road; a consideration instantly dismissed as completely impractical and unlikely to accomplish equal devastation; plus the increased likelihood of being apprehended.

'There's only one solution,' he thought. 'We will hijack a suitable craft and crew, there is sure to be a fast boat over at Wallasea Marina we can take over. I will visit the Marina during the next couple of days , before Friday's meeting.'

The following day he waited until nearly noon before making the telephone call to *Cobra*. At first there was no answer and he thought he had not remembered the number correctly. But, just as he was about to hang up, a voice at the other end of the line enquired, ' Who is it,' without identifying themselves.

'Is that *Cobra*?' I am enquiring about the *Canadian* itinerary and supplies, responded Saleem without giving his name.

'There are a few matters to further discuss. I will meet you at the end of Southend pier at three o'clock. Carry a folded up newspaper in your left hand so I can identify you,' ordered the dismissive voice as the connection was severed.

As ordered, Saleem met with his go-between and, in an hour's question and answer session at the pier head and strolling back along the stem to shore, obviously satisfying the stranger when, on parting at the entrance, he was told, 'Your targets have been given full approval and, as discussed, the items you need will be provided at the time and place I have just told you. There can be no alterations to this schedule. You must meet the rendezvous at all costs or cancel the operation ! Allah be with you.'

Saleem had no intention of entirely relying on Allah to provide the answer to his remaining problem and spent nearly the entire next day sitting on the banks of the River Crouch acting like an avid ornithologist with his binoculars, camera and notebook. His camera shots and binocular viewings were, however, far more often trained on the motor craft to and froing along the river and in and out of the Marina moorings .Nothing he saw particularly pleased him until a sleek, sixty foot, powerful launch excited his interest as it slowly cruised by, the throbbing engine belying the hidden power the sedate cruise disguised. He snapped off a quick couple of photographs and watched the craft through binoculars until it's seaward journey deviated with a turn to starboard into the River Roach. 'I'll have to see what I can find out about that vessel ?' he voiced to the river mouth. 'But not today.'

After collecting his ordered chart the following morning, he returned home and spent the rest of the day thoroughly studying the Thames course and location of his targets, together with printing up enlargements of his River Crouch boat photos.

He awoke on Friday morning in a cheerful mood, the earlier week doom and gloom dispelled by the results of his meeting and progress towards finding the right craft for the attacks. To further his identification of the mystery craft he had seen he visited the local Library and spent some time perusing boat books. After an hour's fruitless endeavour, finding nothing like the picture in his pocket, he reluctantly approached the enquiry desk and , showing the studious looking librarian the photo, enquired, 'Could you show me where I can find anything about this type of boat ?'

Despite his age - Saleem guessed to be thirty five or thereabouts - his knowledge of boats appeared to be extensive. 'Yes Sir, you'll find that's a motor boat of the type used in the second world war. There's bound to be plenty of information in the World War 2 section just over there. Or, of course, you can use one of the computers to investigate.'

The idea of using the computer appealed to him far more than ploughing through more books; but not his own computer. Thanking his knowledgeable informant, he left the Library and visited a nearby Internet Café mainly occupied by students to await his turn and *ask Jeeves* to show him what he wished to know. Half an hour later, having successfully identified the craft as a former Air Sea Rescue launch of World War 2, and clutching a sheaf of printouts, he returned home for some refreshment before setting off to meet his co-conspirators.

He arrived at the East Essex Mosque's Committee room, some half a mile away from the Mosque itself in a quiet country road, twenty minutes before the agreed meeting time and pinned the Thames chart on the wall . Hidden in his briefcase were computer generated prints of the intended targets but these he kept concealed until the doors were locked behind Mohammad and the Amin brothers.

Nobody was late, all three terrorists walking in together a few minutes to the hour and striding straight up to the wall chart.

Saleem locked the door and indicated they should all sit down before opening his document case and withdrawing the literature.

'Gentlemen,' he began. 'I'm happy to report my plan has got the full approval of our Al Qaeda leadership. Mohammad is already aware of the targets but not of how we will be striking our blow for the Islamic cause. You have all had the necessary training in weaponry and explosives to enable us successfully complete this mission so I'm sure you are all eager to hear of the full plan. I do not need to remind you that everything you hear now is to remain the within these four walls and your minds only. Not a whisper of anything is to be revealed to wives, girlfriends, workmates or anyone; no matter how trustworthy you consider them to be!'

Having read the riot act he continued telling them of the weapons and munitions they would be using, explaining to the Amin brothers their

particular targets required the ultimate sacrifice as they had purported to wish. 'Mohammad and I have different targets,
hence the rocket launcher and large quantity of explosives,'he continued. 'Come, gather round this chart and I will point out our respective targets while my video camera is turned on. After our attacks, the whole world will see who is responsible for striking such a blow at our enemies.'

Using a pencil light torch he shone the beam successively on three points. 'We are going to disrupt the economy and commerce of the Country for many years to come. And, cause a large loss of life at the same time,' he declared. 'We will be destroying these three major targets on Thursday night,' he announced, allowing a pause for the astonishing news to sink in before adding, 'and, to provide a required distraction we will BLOW UP THE MONTGOMERY WRECK off the mouth of the river Medway .'

His stunned audience stared, open mouthed, at the chart as if expecting the points indicated to burst into flames. The silent response to his announcement lasted all of a minute before everyone sought to ask questions all at once. Saleem quietened them with a wave of his hand that appeared from behind his back clutching three envelopes.

'All your questions are answered here,' he declared. 'Each of you has an envelope containing your instructions concerning the collection of our supplies together with the whole plan of attack and your individual part in it. Mohammad and I have one more task to perform, the acquisition of a boat, and then you will be contacted with the message, *The trip is on*, meaning meeting up at the spot indicated in your instructions the next day.

Commit your instructions to memory and burn the originals. Our day draws nearer my brothers. Go now and may Allah be with you.'

Saleem removed his chart, locked up the building and the four conspirators dispersed into the night.

2

‘Fancy a cup of coffee boss ?’ came a disembodied voice from the forward hatch.‘Don’t know about you but it’s thirsty work down here.’

Bradley Murray plonked his paintbrush in a jar of thinners and replied, while putting the lid back on his tin of varnish and viewing the results of his endeavours,‘That’s the best idea you’ve had all morning,’ adding, as much to himself as his below deck crewman, ‘nearly there.’

For the past three days he had been scraping the dull grey paintwork off the deck of the sixty three year old ex Royal Air Force Air Sea Rescue launch that had been a family possession for nearly forty years, repairing boards where necessary and varnishing over his handiwork . Pleased with his own efforts, he shouted in the cabin, ‘How’s it coming along down there?’

‘There’s no need to shout,’ replied a voice from behind two steaming cups of coffee in oil smeared hands as a greasy ,overalled, figure emerged onto deck. 'Just about finished the fine tuning on both engines. We can run on either, port or starboard, or both together if you want to take off and have a petrol tanker follow behind to refuel before we get out of the river.'

The cups parted to reveal a grinning oil streaked face....property of one Trevor Swift, mechanic extraordinaire, ladykiller (his own description) and comedian. He was, in fact, Bradley's long-time friend from his boyhood days, since which time they had been almost inseparable except for brief spells apart while serving in the Armed forces.

'Ha ha, very funny. You'll laugh on the other side of your face when we run out of fuel and you have to row us home,' joked Brad. 'Don't know what else you had to do to the motors, they sounded perfectly alright to me when we had a trial run out to Wallasea the other day.'

'Yes, well that's the difference between a highly skilled genius with engines and a painter and decorator,'laughed Swifty, as he was affectionately known among the local fraternity of fishing boat skippers and anglers.

Handing over one of the cups as they sat down on the disarrayed cabin seat cushions, he continued his joking. 'Watch you don't get any of that varnish in your coffee, it'll probably kill you. Still you'll go out with a nice finish,' he jested, dodging Brad's playful punch.

'Nice cuppa Swifty.....if I scrape the film of oil off the top,' retorted Brad continuing the jovial repartee.'There's more oil in here than was in the Torrey Canyon before it got wrecked.'

'Joking aside boss, are you going to give the old girl a name ?'said the crewman, adding in reference to Murray's other craft, 'It will certainly show the old *Sprinter* a clean pair of heels so you could call it *Sprinter 2.'*

Brad hesitated; thoughtfully staring into his coffee before looking up, grinning and stating, 'We'll call her *Whaleback Swift*. This boat design was originally known as the "Whaleback" because of this distinctive curved humpbacked cabin and it's thanks to your, self-acclaimed, engineering genius it's old engines have been given the kiss of life. It's almost as good as new. I bet she's the only one of it's kind still afloat. I can't wait until we're motoring up and down the Thames on it.'

'Cor !, a boat named after me. I'd better get a bottle of bubbly to smash over the bows. You can hold a glass underneath for me - can't waste it. The river pilots will be surprised when we turn up with this; makes the old *taxi* obsolete don't it?'

Swifty's reference to his skipper's business contract of ferrying the Trinity House licensed Pilots to and from the larger ships entering or exiting the Thames Estuary using the thirty six foot *Sprinter*, reminded Brad that he would have to inform the appropriate authorities of his proposed replacement boat which would undoubtedly be subjected to inspection.

'Yes, there won't be much sense hanging on to the old faithful. She's given me good service and we've certainly had our fair share of fish aboard over the years,'he replied referring to his other source of income, charter boat fishing parties. 'But she'll have to go. I'll stick a notice up down at Old Leigh. That should bring a few enquiries.'

Reflecting on the River Pilots situation he wondered if he should seek to renegotiate his contract. After all, he thought, their trips would be much more comfortable in the larger, sixty three foot length, boat. And ,with a top speed approaching thirty seven knots if need be, compared to the old *Sprinter's* ten to twelve knots, journey times could easily be halved. Not that his existing contract was not already generous,

but, high speeds would eat up the fuel, an additional cost to be avoided unless recovered by an improved contract.
Knowing he was popular with the Pilots and having never failed to provide a good service he was hopeful an application for an added contribution towards his costs would be favourably met.

Swifty interrupted his train of thought. 'We could always bring her round here into the Roach while you're waiting for a buyer. That way you could use the existing berth for this beauty. Could even stick a "For Sale" sign on her, there's plenty of keen boating bods always around here. And, living just up the road at Paglesham makes it easier for you to keep an eye on her.'

'A good thought Trev but let's see if an Advertisement in Leigh Old Town brings any response first. It's more populated and busy any time of the year. I still think it's the best bet. Meanwhile let's finish up here, get the final painting completed and she's ready to go. Then we can get off down to the "Plough & Sail".'

The mention of a visit to the local watering hole was all the crewman needed to spur him back into action. Coffee in one hand, paint brush in the other and he was varnishing the remaining, sanded off, decking before Brad had time to empty his cup and join him.

Seeing his long time pal on his hands and knees reminded him of the time he found himself similarly positioned, but, in his case as a result of a severe beating at the hands of a gang of Iraqi guardsmen.

His *Special Boat Service* patrol, on a clandestine operation in Kuwait during the first Gulf war, had the misfortune to have been misled by faulty intelligence, resulting in an unexpected encounter with some Iraqi guardsmen. The ensuing melee saw the group split up and he suddenly found himself alone. While making his way back to the beach rendezvous he blundered into five of the invaders, the face-to-face meeting catching everyone unawares.

Brad was the first to recover , snapping off a couple of quick shots as he dived into a side passageway - noting with satisfaction one of his adversaries crumpling to the ground.
His gratification, however, quickly died as he realised he had cornered himself in a blind alley
.

The Iraqi fighters poured a withering fire into the passage, bullets whining off the metal waste bin providing Brad with his only cover. Fortunately for the SBS commando his assailants had only rifles and hand guns as no grenades were tossed at him - something for which he would have had no defence.

As it was he was dangerously low on ammunition, returning fire sparingly but more accurately, his selective response picking off another guardsman before an ominous click signalled the end of his bullets to leave him with just his lethal knife for defence. With still only silence from his intercom system he realised he could expect no assistance from his colleagues.

'This could be your lot Bradley,' he heard himself saying. 'If I can get near enough to them without getting shot I could, perhaps, grab one of them as a shield and snatch his weapon. It's my only chance.' So saying, he shouted out during a lull in the Iraqi assault, 'I give up, I'm coming out !'

'Throw out your weapon,' came the reply in near perfect English, at least one of his attackers obviously being an able interpreter.

He stepped out from behind his cover, hands raised above his head and almost expecting to be met with a fusillade of bullets in revenge for his shooting of their compatriots. Although ex-

cited and obviously hostile, the group levelled their guns at him
but held their fire, the English speaking officer beckoning him forward. 'Come, you will not be shot. You are now a prisoner of war.'

Unfortunately the angered troop's discipline melted away as Brad stepped up to them, a rifle butt immediately toppling him to his knees as they set upon him with their weapons, fists and feet.

Winded and breathless he struggled to regain his feet and put up a resistance to the blows being rained down on him. But, close to unconsciousness and with blood streaming down his head into his eyes, he managed only to get up on to his knees as the Officer raised his pistol and took careful aim at his prisoner's head, hissing, contrary to the earlier statement, 'Time to die Infidel !'

The tightening trigger finger never quite reached the critical pressure, a loud staccato of gunfire stitching a row of blood spurts across his back and propelling him forward over the crouched SBS man as the unrelenting rapid firing weapon continued it's sweep across the remaining two guardsmen.

Through a misty haze of weakness and gun smoke, Brad was conscious of being lifted to his feet by the strong arms of his rescuer before his vision cleared sufficiently for him to recognise his messmate.

'You came back Trev. You know that is strictly against orders....but I'm glad you did. I owe you one, that's for certain. Now let's get out of here before the whole of the Iraqi army comes to investigate.'

'Never was much good at taking orders, except for a round of drinks,' quipped his pal. 'Mine's a pint of best bitter when we get back, that's the sort of order I won't argue against.'

A scraping sound from behind them alerted them to danger. Spinning around Brad witnessed one of the *downed* Iraqi troopers lifting his weapon and aiming in their direction. The deafening report right next to his ear as he dived on the wounded soldier

showed the man had managed to discharge his weapon but was unable to counter the SBS crewman's instant reaction. It was a fatal mistake for the Guardsman to make; he should have feigned unconsciousness or death rather than be a hero.

Chapter 2

Brad's flashing blade severed the man's carotid artery to complete the job his rescuer's bullets had failed to do, an act distasteful but necessary in the circumstances. Climbing to his feet he quickly checked the other Guard, satisfying himself that there was no danger from that source before realising his compatriot was seated on the roadway attempting to stem a gush of blood from his thigh.

'Thought I'd got the bugger. Teach me to check in future,' groaned Trevor. 'Trust me to get in the way, I don't think I'll be playing football for a while. Give me a hand to strap this useless leg up and let's get back to the boat.'

Convalescing later in hospital Swifty confided in his friend. 'Looks like the end of the partnership me old 'oppo'. The doctors tell me that my left leg is now shorter than the right and I'm likely to be given a medical discharge from the Service. Still I could always walk in the gutter,' he joked, even his dismay at his plight failing to stem his irrevocable sense of humour.

'Swifty, pack that in now.,' said Brad snapping out of his reverie. ' Let's take her for a run up the Thames to show her off. By the time we get out of the River Crouch we'll have enough water over the Maplin Sands to cut across with no danger of running aground and be off Southend in no time at all. I might even moor up at the pier head and get you that pint of bitter that I never did buy you all those years ago. The *Jolly Fisherman* will be open by the time we get there. We can give the old *Plough* the pleasure of our company this evening.'

Keen to try out his retuned engines and fuel line modifications, Trevor needed no second bidding, especially with the promise of a pint in prospect.

'What a good idea boss,' responded the mechanic. 'Watch the paintwork, it's not quite dry yet. I'll release the old girl .'

Brad entered the wheelhouse and turned the ignition key. The engines did not even turn over and try to start. He repeated the procedure and met the same response…..nothing.

'I thought you called yourself a mechanic. Did you connect any batteries to this thing ?' he jokingly enquired.

'Try moving your left foot over a little and press down. It's a little security device I've incorporated. Don't want anyone stealing this beauty do we?'

When he did as suggested and the motors started but instantly died. He glared at his shipmate and growled, ‘ I suppose you’re now going to tell me these engines are so *thirsty* we’ve run out of the fifty gallons of fuel we put in a couple of days ago.’

Hardly able to contain his glee Swifty barged his skipper aside and discretely reached beneath a small shelf on the cabin wall to turn on another of his security innovations, a fuel cut out tap. Turning the ignition key resulted in the engines roaring into life, this time continuing to purr quietly on to the sounds of a bubbling exhaust.

‘You’ve got to have the magic touch skipper,’ he laughed before informing him of the secret fuel isolator. ‘ I’ve got an idea about a couple of other things when we next go on to the *Sprinter*. That photo of your old grandad and crew on their ASR 271 would look good on the bulkhead there and remind us of the days he took us out fishing as kids. I bet he’d be over the moon to see what we’ve done to his old boat. It’s a great pity he never got the chance to run her himself but he always said that he was certain you would put it back in good order and make it seaworthy again. And, I’ll pick up those two old shell casings of his in the chart drawer. They’ll look good polished up and glued next to the wheel here. Make great hooks to hang the keys on.’

Mention of his late Grandfather set Brad reminiscing again. 'Yes, I'll never forget him, or some of the stories he told us of his wartime experiences both flying and then on the Rescue launches. I don't know about you but it was him who taught me to love the sea, just as he did when discharged from the Air Force.'

Both men fell silent , each with his own thoughts of their childhood and ex Flight Sergeant Charles Murray's story of how he had come to purchase the boat they were now aboard.

When he had recovered from his wounds in a military hospital at Chatham, Kent, after a skirmish with a U-Boat, he told them one day on a fishing outing aboard his eighteen foot cutter, the war in Europe was over. He remained in the RAF for a short while but with virtually no Sea Rescue requirements became frustrated at being land bound and decided to give up a military career and return to *Civvy Street*.

On his release and return home to Suffolk he found, like many others returning from war, his five year old son looked upon him as a stranger and Jenny, his wife, was *distant*, the former happy household atmosphere quickly replaced by one of suspicion and secrecy. He told the young pals, ' You're too young to understand Brad, but your Grandmother - don't think bad of her - decided she wanted to move back to Yorkshire with an old *friend* she had recently met again and take my son Tom, your father, with her.'

Charles realised the love was gone and with no job and a hankering to return to the sea he put up little resistance other than to say he wished to visit his son whenever he had the opportunity, a condition readily agreed.

Finding a sea going job proved to be difficult. The Merchant Navy were 'fully crewed mate unless you got a Master's ticket.' And ,even finding a berth with an East coast fishing boat was not easy although he finally got work as a deckhand on the trawler Halcyon, out of Felix-stowe.

'Weren't much of a job boys,' he confided. 'Hard work and a slow chug out to sea and back. I wanted something smaller and faster....feel the wind in your hair and the swell beneath your feet. You pair already know what I mean, I can see it every time you come out with me.'

'So how did you get this boat Grandad ?' que-ried young Brad. 'And, what about that big boat you showed us ?'

'Well, young man, it's a long story but it was your Dad's idea that started it. Let's get the anchor up; it's time to go back home. I'll tell you all about it on the way back in.'

By the time they reached shore the boys had learnt that, true to his word, Charles had made regular trips to see his son who was not at all happy with his new *Uncle,* and the relationship between them soon blossomed. It was, therefore, no surprise when, on reaching his sixteenth birthday, Tom announced he was leaving the Yorkshire home to return south and be with his father.

Charles had, by this time, long left his trawler job and moved to Burnham-on-Crouch at the mouth of the River Crouch in Essex where he found work as an Assistant Harbour Master, a job that gave him the satisfaction he craved for - messing about with small boats.

With the job he was able to rent a comfortable, small, cottage , less than a quarter of a mile away from the harbour where he often accommodated his son on visits from Yorkshire. It was, therefore, a natural step for Tom, on deciding to leave the northern home, to join his father and seek work in the area.

Chapter 2

'I wanted him to continue his education - he was a bright boy as all his school reports indicated - and perhaps even go on to a University. But, it seemed from the few times I had taken him out with me on his visits, he had already inherited my love of the sea and wanted nothing more than to spend all his time on the water,'explained Charles.

'Your father, Brad, soon became popular with the local boatmen; often giving his time freely crewing for them and assisting with maintenance. In between helping myself, and anyone on the water with a boat, he spent many hours studying Admiralty and Fishery Charts and enrolled himself on a navigational course run by the local Yacht Club. He also made a point of noting everything down that he thought could be helpful at sea including; weather conditions, cloud formations, wind direction and tidal strengths etc.'

Opening a thwart seat cupboard he withdrew a dog-eared foolscap size book with a water-stained cover and showed the lads pages of neat handwritten information categorized and dated against fish catches. 'This is why Tom was recognised as the top charter-boat skipper for angling parties. And, why he could find fish when others struggled,' he proudly boasted.

He went on to explain to his grandson and friend Trevor how his son came to get a boat of his own and commence a charter fishing business. On his return South, Tom made a particular friend of an elderly, knowledgeable, skipper, Harry Evers, who operated an old converted Lifeboat, *Rescuer,* from out of the River Roach, raking up a fine, fern-like, weed from the seabed that was very profitably sold to the floristry industry in particular for dyeing and artistic use.

Harry, despite his advancing years, lived aboard his boat for most of the time; just occasionally staying ashore in a little terraced cottage he owned in the nearby village of Paglesham. He was, seemingly, never ill and was a regular tippler at the *Plough and Sail.* When he missed his usual daily visit it was not surprising that Tom was asked by the Publican if he knew where Harry had got to? Knowing how his elderly friend enjoyed his pint Tom was alarmed and promptly went off to investigate.

A check aboard the *Rescuer*, which he found to be locked up, did nothing to allay his concerns and caused him to visit the old man's home which was also locked. As he was about to leave, the adjoining cottage door opened and a wizened little old lady croaked, 'If you're looking for Harry, he's gone.'.

'Gone where ?' queried Tom. 'He never goes anywhere. I'm sure he would have told me he was going away.'

'Not gone way…'e's dead,' she cackled.

Dumbstruck and saddened at the news, it was minutes before he recovered to enquire further and discover poor old Harry had knocked on her door the previous evening to say he felt quite ill and, having no telephone himself, could she phone for a Doctor, before creeping back indoors. When the Doctor arrived an hour later he discovered Harry slumped lifeless on floor of his kitchen with an empty glass in his hand.

A week later a letter, from a Colchester based Solicitor, addressed to Tom arrived at Charlie's home informing him that the old Captain had made a 'Will' over a year previously, leaving his young protégé assistant his boat, boathouse and cottage. He was further advised that he was the sole beneficiary, Harry having no living relations, and that a modestly handsome sum of money was also included in the inheritance.

For Tom it was a dream come true. Saddened as he was at Harry's demise, he vowed to keep the memory of the old man alive, renaming the inherited rescue craft, *Old Harry*, and continuing to accommodate the usual charters - not wishing to disappoint any of the regular angling parties.

'The *Old Harry* quickly gained the reputation among anglers as being the most successful boat, bookings usually exceeding availability,' Charles told them. 'But, Tom was never a greedy person and always kept a couple of days free each week to spend in my company and do other things. That is how I came to purchase this boat Brad, and how I ,well Tom really, discovered the old Air Sea Rescue launch that I've now got up by the boathouse.'

It was strange, considering Charle's occupation and interests, that he had never actually owned his own boat until his son suddenly mentioned it would be a pleasurable pastime for the two of them to go sailing occasionally rather than motoring about the rivers.

In his position of Harbour Master it was not long before he soon learnt of the sale of a sturdy little eighteen footer, ideally suited for both sailing and motoring, being offered at a bargain price by the widow of a deceased Yacht Club member.

During one of the subsequent sailings the father and son enjoyed, the subject of the elder Murray's war exploits was discussed; initiated by the sighting of a sleek passing boat named *Spitfire* after the famous World War 2 aircraft.

'You'd love to own a fast launch like that, wouldn't you?' queried Tom on listening to his father's relating of a successful rescue in the southern part of the North Sea. 'I wonder if there are any still floating, that would be a good use for the money old Harry left me?'

It may have been the sort of conversation that was quickly forgotten but for a chance remark Tom made at the bar of one of Leigh Old Town's crowded Public Houses. He had gone to visit an attractive young lady restaurant assistant who he had recently managed to isolate from a bunch of admirers long enough to ask for a date. With the sort of figure men admire, and visually decidedly beautiful, Tom expected to hear she was already "spoken for". To his surprise - and great delight - she accepted his advance.

Waiting for her shift to finish he was soon in conversation with some of the local boatmen, many of whom he knew from visits to the popular fishing grounds at the mouth of the Thames Estuary. Telling one particular Dunkirk veteran and, *Leighite* skipper as many of the long established Leigh fishermen families were locally known, of his father's wartime experiences he was astounded when he was interrupted by his listener stating, 'Yes, I know the type of craft your Dad was on, there's one beached in a creek over the River up the Medway. Or, at least, there was a few months ago when I took the family over to Queenborough for an outing on the Bank Holiday.'

Tom was so excited and anxious to discover if the boat was still there he almost forgot his date, rushing out to the nearest telephone box to call his father with the news.

'It's a good thing he remembered to go back and collect his date,' said Charles. 'She and Tom got married two years later. She was your mother Brad!'

'So was the boat still there? Is that the big boat you showed us Grandad ?'asked the curious youngster.

'Well, it certainly was but we're at the harbour now. It's time we dropped Trevor off before his mother gets worried, and got home ourselves for tea. I'll tell you about that next time we go out. I'm sure your young mate wants to hear all about it as well.'

Brad's pleas to his grandfather throughout the week to continue telling him about the large craft lying dormant by the riverside boathouse were met with,'Just you get on with your homework. We'll go out fishing again at the weekend, just be patient until then.'

Charles wasn't quite certain in his own mind as to whether now was the time to tell the youngster about the loss of his parents that resulted in his bringing up the boy, eventually deciding that perhaps it was an opportunity to do so with the companionship of his likeable, genuine, friend of his own age to give him support. He certainly had no wish to alienate himself from his grandson, a danger by revealing the truth of his father and mother's deaths.

The boy's cheerful, happy carefree mood the following Saturday morning as they climbed aboard the cutter, almost caused him to lose his resolve to tell the truth of the ill-fated quest for the wartime boat. It would not be long, he felt sure, before the young anglers' curiosity again brought up the subject of the Air Sea Rescue launch.

'Are we going to catch Bass today uncle Charlie ?' questioned cheeky Trevor as the "adopted relation" tied on the boys' lifejackets.

'No Trevor, it's too rough outside the River today. You might be lucky but where we're going we'll probably get eels and flatfish but, it will be pretty calm. If the fishing's not up to much I will take you up river to the Big Boat and let you have a good look around.'

'Great,' piped up Brad. 'Is it the boat you were on in the war Grandad ? You said you would tell us.'

'And so I will Brad. Let's get fishing first, see if we can catch our supper.' So saying he opened the throttle and turned the lively little boat into the seaway, motoring across the choppy wide river into the calmer waters of the narrow River Roach and dropping anchor.

The fishing was good as the tide ebbed and the youngsters excitedly chattered between themselves about their catches throughout the morning, seemingly uninterested in pursuing their earlier inquisitiveness. When the sport died off around lunchtime, Charles opened a lunchbox , handed the happy lads sandwiches and drinks and, pre-empting the inevitable, returned to his story of the Rescue Launch.

Chapter 2

'You asked me if the boat the fisherman told your Dad about was still there. It was but it took a while to find it. And no, it wasn't the same boat I served on during the war. I thought it was when I first saw it but it was painted a different colour and had no number 271 on it. And there was no Air Force Bullseye roundel .You know , like the photograph on the sideboard at home.'

The boys remained quiet and attentive as he went on to tell them that Tom was as keen as himself to go over to Kent to see if they could locate the craft, making arrangements to take the *Old Harry* across the Thames Estuary to the River Medway at the earliest opportunity.

Checking his diary of bookings, Tom found he was unable to take a couple of days off until late the following week, regrettably just as a period of low neap tides occurred .

'We'll have to take the long way round right out past the East Swinn and down through the West Barrow. There won't be enough water over the Maplin Sands to cut off the corner,' he told his father. 'It will add quite a bit of time to the trip. The *Old Harry* is not the fastest of craft but it can't be helped and at least we won't be reliant on good weather; the old girl will take anything thrown at her.'

As it happened the day of the cross Estuary journey dawned fair and ,despite the enforced additional mileage, the *Old Harry* had entered the mouth of the River Medway by noon.

Cruising slowly upriver past the Isle of Sheppey, the pair were in high spirits, hopeful of soon spotting the wartime boat. But, related Charles, 'We got to Queenborough without a sighting so Tom anchored up, launched the small, deck-borne, tender and went ashore to make enquiries while I made some lunch.'

Spotting a Yacht Chandlers shop, Tom questioned the proprietor and discovered the boat they were looking for was well known to the man. 'But, don't ask me who owns it,'said the shop owner. 'It's been laid up there for about twenty years and I've never seen anyone aboard her.'

On his return to his own craft he revealed his findings to his father, up anchored and motored a few hundred yards further up the river into Stangate Creek....and there she was! Rust streaked with flaking paintwork and barely afloat in the shallows close to the bank, the vessel was a sorry sight: even the mooring ropes, stretching into the long grass ashore, mildewed and frayed.

Chapter 2

'It didn't matter to me boys. It was like meeting up again with a long-lost friend,' the old man told them. 'Even Tom had a big happy grin on his face and wanted to get on board it. But the water was too shallow for us to take *Old Harry* alongside.'

Undeterred, the young Murray again launched the tender and , within minutes, clambered up on to the deck where he had hoped to find some clue as to who now owned the craft.

'There's only a faded notice saying KEEP OFF - PRIVATE,' he shouted across to his father. 'There was something printed underneath but it's so faded it's no longer readable.
The cabin and hatches are locked with some old padlocks so I can't look below but the woodwork is still very sound. You know Dad, we could soon get this tidied up and ship-shape again for you,' he added excitedly.

Their elation was, however, short-lived when numerous enquiries ashore on the Isle of Sheppey and at Queenborough failed to find anyone able to assist in their quest to identify the owner. Leaving a contact telephone number with a few of the more helpful persons that he spoke to, together with a request he be notified if any information came to hand, was the best Tom could do.

'When we left the Medway late in the afternoon, catching the last hour of the ebb tide to help the trip home, I pointed out to Tom the masts of the wreck where I was rescued, sticking out of the sea just as they were on that day,' said Charles continuing the tale.

'Could you take us to see it Grandad ?' interceded Brad.

'Perhaps one day young man ,when you're older, but nobody is allowed to go very near it. It's dangerous.'

Brad's young friend suddenly seemed to realise, 'You didn't get the big boat then ?'

'No Trevor, we returned home empty-handed, as they say. It was two years later that I finally brought her back to Burnham, nearly a year after young Brad here was born.'

Charles clearly recalled the day Tom came bursting through the door into the Harbourmaster's office grinning ear to ear and excitably exclaiming,'You're going to be a Grandfather !'

'Just around the time you were born Brad, your father had a response to the request he had left over in Kent about the boat. Our interest had been mentioned when an elderly ex dockyard worker was overheard chatting in the local Public House about a gruesome discovery he had made on board a, shot-up, Rescue Launch towed into Chatham for repairs,' continued Charles

Realising he had committed himself to revealing the old man's find to the boys he added, 'You lads are old enough now to know about some of the horrible things that happen in wars. I've told you before that I was injured myself in battle. Lots of men, women and children were killed, often in terrible ways. The dockyard worker was telling his friends that, on moving away some mangled ironwork and decking, he suddenly saw a human eyeball seemingly looking up at him, the repulsion causing him to be sick over the side.'

The boys' mouth's gaped open in awe. But neither seemed able to speak, aghast it seemed but agog at the same time.

Not wishing to dwell on the macabre details and giving the inquisitive youngsters no time to pursue the subject of body parts, he hurriedly explained that the man told the Publican that he was, during the war, a civilian dockyard foreman working for the Admiralty. Towards the end of the war a damaged naval Motor Torpedo Boat arrived towing a couple of smaller Rescue launches belonging to the Air Force. Strangely, these craft were considered a priority for repair so were quickly patched up, repainted and made ready for sea. But the war in Europe ended and the craft remained perched up on blocks on the quayside for some weeks before some Navy and Air Force High Ranking Officers arrived together to look over the vessels.

Before the week was over, orders came through to repaint the launches yet again; this time an overall naval Battleship grey with pale blue/grey topsides. Just as this task was completed the war in the Far East was also ended.

'The boats were taking up valuable dockside space according to the foreman, so were lowered back into the water , towed out of the docks and moored in a creek up near Upchurch,' Charles related. ' He suggested the Public House Landlord tell Tom to contact the Air Ministry who were certainly the owners at the time.'

A stammering click of a reel ratchet interrupted Charle's narrative as the tip of young Trevor's rod arced dramatically.

'That's no flatfish or eel young man. I think you may have hooked your Bass. Keep the pressure on and take it easy. Let it run until you feel it slacken before you attempt to reel it in,' advised the adult. ' It's your fish, let's see you land it without my help.'

For his age, and despite his short height - a good eight inches less than the same age Bradley - Trevor was a strong well-built boy. But, it was a good ten minutes or more before he curtailed the large fish's struggles and drew the subdued specimen alongside the boat for Charles to net.

'That's got to be a good five or six pounds of prime Bass young Trev. Well done, your mother will be pleased when you walk through the door with this beauty.'

A sudden gust of strong wind accompanied by a downpour of heavy rain sent the three anglers scurrying inside the small cabin for comfort. Already seasoned sailors the boys were unaffected by the increased motion of the boat, their seasickness days long past, but Charles was concerned that the wind was blowing up to a fully fledged gale and had moved round to the North East.

'I think we had better go back now boys. It's going to get pretty rough on the way back now the wind's turned. I know you're not frightened of getting wet but we will be broadside on to the waves so we will be rolling about a bit,' he said motioning the youngsters back inside while stepping out of the cabin himself.

'Start the engine,' he shouted , knowing both boys were perfectly capable of doing so. 'I'll get the anchor up.'

A puff of smoke erupted from the exhaust indicating his command had been heard and acted upon, as he struggled to dislodge the heavy hook. To his surprise the craft then edged slowly forwards assisting his efforts in *breaking out the anchor.* Now how did they know how to do that he wondered as whichever of them was at the wheel cleverly nosed the bow of the boat into the wind, steadying the deck while he scrambled back to the cabin?

'Well done you two, that's excellent seamanship. I'll leave it to you to take us back home shall I ? You seem to know what you're doing.'

'Oh, can we ?' voiced the happy youngsters in unison. ' You can carry on telling us about the other boat Grandad,' added Bradley.

The usual fifteen minute journey back across the river took them over twice as long due to the turbulent waters necessitating a zig-zag tack to avoid a direct , more uncomfortable and perhaps dangerous, broadside approach to harbour - a manoeuvre very adeptly handled by both boys.

Chapter 2

During the extended excursion Charles continued telling them of the successful acquisition of the launch. Tom had, in fact ,already contacted the Air Ministry; attempting to glean further information about the boat but was disappointed when nobody had been able to assist in any manner. But, the old Dockworker's information pointed him in a direction not previously tried, that of the Admiralty; the assumption being that the craft, being R.A.F, what would the Navy know ?

It was however, as it turned out, completely the wrong assumption to make. Following a number of calls, Tom was eventually connected to a most co-operative liaison Officer who promised to see what he could do to assist. True to his word he returned the call within the week, informing him that his investigations had unearthed the history of the boat in question.

It seemed the Royal Navy had seconded the two launches, after cessation of hostilities in Europe, with the intention of shipping them out to the Japanese theatre of war. Before transport was arranged Japan surrendered and the launches remained at Chatham until their weaponry and batteries were removed before they were towed away to a backwater whilst their future use was decided.

A few years elapsed until a post war disposal committee decided they were no longer required for Britain's Armed Forces and would be scrapped or sold. The liaison Officer was unclear as to how they exactly came to be sold but was able to inform Tom that both craft had been purchased, at a knock down price, by the **Whitstable Ferry Company Limited** of Swaleview Road, Kent.

Unable to make any contact by telephone and having no response to a letter, Tom made enquiries at Company House in London, discovering the business no longer existed but being informed the registered Managing Director was a Mr. Harvey Daneman . Following further investigations he traced an elderly Mr. H. Daneman to an address at Herne Bay, his subsequent correspondence confirming it was the same gentleman who, remarkably, had forgotten the existence of the Rescue Launch.

'You must forgive an old man's memory Mr. Murray; the **Whitstable Ferry Company** was a long time ago, never really got off the ground. Myself and a business colleague formed the company just after the war when there was talk of a new Airport being built on the Maplin Sands at the mouth of the Thames Estuary. Had it gone ahead there would have been many workers residing in Kent wishing to take advantage of a fast ferry service across river. We stood to make a good deal of money.'

When the opportunity came along to purchase the two launches ,at a good price, the business partners didn't hesitate with the Airport scheme still the subject of Government debate. 'They were, after all, in pretty good condition and the ideal craft with a little modification for what was planned.'

'So when the Airport scheme never materialised, you were left with the boats and no alternative use ?' queried Tom.

'Exactly. But, it wasn't a complete disaster and had no affect on neither my nor D.B's - Dennis Batchelor my fellow Ferry Company Director that is - other businesses.
We elected to dissolve **Whitstable Ferries** and go our separate ways. The only assets really were the two launches so we decided to have one each.'

Tom learnt from the continuing conversation that Dennis took his vessel round to Folkestone a short while after where he had a hotel business. The craft was apparently , used by him for some years as a guests' TOUR BUS for sea trips along the Kent coast resorts before suffering substantial damage in a fire accident and condemning it to the scrap yard.

'I was never a seafaring man myself,' declared Harvey. ' I made a few half-hearted attempts to sell the boat but most wanted something smaller and more economical to run.
It just got left where it still is. I had thought I might be more inclined to get some use out of it when I retired, but old age and illness have confined me to a wheelchair and I'm quite content with home comforts. Don't get old young man.'

'So you would be willing to sell me the boat ?' queried Tom. 'I'll give you a fair price.'

'Keep your money. My time on Earth is coming to an end and I've got more than enough myself and nobody to leave it to. Martha died nearly five years ago and we never did have a family - too busy making money in those days. Come and see me anytime at the Care Home and I will arrange the paperwork.'

Tom was astounded at the old man's generosity and before replacing the telephone handset, promised to visit him the following weekend.

Chapter 2

'He couldn't wait to tell me the good news,' Charles told the boys. 'So we both went to see Harvey at Herne Bay on the Saturday. He was a charming old chap and had already drawn up a sales document selling Tom the boat for just one penny ! He was adamant he did not want any more, suggesting that if we felt so inclined we could make a fifty pounds donation to his local Church for their Organ Restoration Fund , he himself having been the organist there in his younger days. And, that's how we were able to purchase the old warship but, ever since that day, I wish we had never ever found her !'

Charles dreaded the thought of continuing the subject that would, he felt sure, estrange Bradley, and possibly also his young friend. Temporarily reprieved by their arrival alongside the quay, he finished cleaning their catches as the lads clambered up the steps and expertly made the boat fast.

'What's the matter Grandad ?' yelled an alarmed Bradley on seeing his Grandfather fall over backwards clutching his chest as he was about to hand up the fish bags, the gutted catch spilling out all over the deck.

Struggling to sit up, the pale-faced elder gasped, 'Give me a hand up Brad, not feeling too good.'

The nine year olds both leapt back aboard the rocking craft and attempted to assist the fallen Harbourmaster , their combined efforts finally settling him back against the engine hatch cover where the elderly seaman summoned up enough breath to gasp, ' You'll need to get help, Doctor Simmonds should be in the Clubhouse.'

Bradley stayed with his sick Grandfather while Trevor ran over to get assistance, returning quickly with the Doctor and a couple of Club members who, after a brief examination, collectively hoisted the ailing man on to the quayside.

The arrival of an ambulance coincided with that of young Trevor's mother who led both boys away back to an old open-backed truck.

'Get in boys,' she ordered. 'Bradley, you can come home with Trevor until your *Mum or Dad* gets home,' referring to the young Murray's adopted parents, Charle's sister and brother-in-law who lived next door.

Unable to have children of their own, the couple had taken on the responsibility of Bradley on the tragic deaths of his real parents and had brought him up as their own since the age of one, loving him as their own son.

Bradley had no recollection of either his real mother or father but , as soon as they felt he was old enough, had been sat down by his Grandfather, together with his surrogate parents, and told the truth, only the details of the *accident* being withheld at that time.

'Will Grandfather be alright Aunty Harriet ?' asked Bradley, the concern showing on his face as he questioned his friend's mother in the manner she had always insisted; despite being no true relation.

'I'm sure he will. Just you don't worry now. I'll get you boys some tea - you must be hungry - and then I'll telephone the hospital.'

All Bradley could remember after that was his *parents* calling to collect him and going off with his nominated Aunt into another room, returning shortly after downcast and tearful. He cried himself to sleep that night when, on return home, his *mother* informed him that his Grandfather had suffered a severe heart-attack from which he never recovered.

'Ahoy there you two ! Got the old lady up and running then,? came the shout from a passing family launch - awakening Brad and Swifty from their reveries.

Waving a friendly greeting in reply as he gunned the engine drowning out any meaningful voiced response, Bradley edged the craft forward into the main channel while his crewman stowed away their mooring ropes and clung to the short fore mast as his skipper steadied the boat on course.

To comply with the River's bye-laws, they crept slowly out past the *Bed of Shells* off Foulness point before notching up the throttles to speed past other craft making their way out of the River mouth.

Less than ten minutes later, with a watchful eye on the depth gauge, Brad swung the wheel to take them over the outer reaches of the Maplin Sands into the East Swinn, through to the West Barrow and into the mouth of the Thames Estuary.

As Southend pier came into view so did Swifty, appearing from below to state, 'As good as new Skip. Running sweet as a dream and the bilges are dry as a bone. Crikey ! Is that Southend just up ahead already ?'

'Sure is. Get ready to hitch us up. We'll pop up to see the Coastguard and then into the pub for that pint I promised you before taking an excursion up river to the *Sprinter* mooring. I need to snap off a couple of photographs to advertise it.'

Fifty minutes later they nudged alongside Brad's other boat and the crewman jumped aboard, returning within minutes clutching a framed photograph, a folder of charts and the two 20mm shell cases. 'Got them boss. I assume we'll be using *Whaleback* straight away - save another journey. I'll put this lot in the chart cabinet for now.'

Noticing the admiring looks the sleek launch received, both at the pier head and when close to shore off Canvey Island and along the northern banks up to the congested area around Tilbury, Brad decided to motor back at speed along the southern reaches as a timed test run.

Approaching the Isle of Grain just twenty minutes later , he slowed the vessel and picked up his binoculars peering out towards Southend pier head and swinging slowly along towards Shoeburyness. 'There you are,' he quietly whispered, as much to himself as his perplexed crewman standing alongside. 'You've never seen the old wreck where my Grandfather finished up after that U-Boat encounter in a boat like this that he told us about as boys, have you?'

Not giving his friend time to reply he went on, 'Well, it's just over there. I'll cut back across the shipping lane now, you'll get a good view. It's just about low tide so the masts will certainly be sticking out of the water and with this calm sea we might even see some of the upper works.'

'No, never been very near to it. Don't bump into it though. Do that and from what I've heard about the cargo we could be meeting your Grandad again,' joked his pal. 'I've always said I want my ashes scattered at sea, but I did mean ashes and not bits of body.'

'Not much chance of that Trev. Nobody is permitted anywhere near it these days. Remind me to show you Charles's newspaper cuttings about it later.' They motored by slowly, viewing the stricken vessel through their field glasses before again opening the throttles for a fast return to Burnham. Testimony to the powerful crafts' seaworthiness and Swifty's expertise with the engines, the journey was accomplished in only forty minutes despite a brief moment at idle, just off the Maplin Sands, while Brad paid homage to his dead parents in a personal ceremony of casting a small model boat -

a replica of one his father had made him as a baby long ago - afloat in the approximate area of their accident.

Ever since his Grandfather died and the *Whaleback* became part of his inheritance, Brad had vowed to, one day, honour his father and mother in such a manner once he had the old Rescue Launch back in operation - the launch an important component in view of it's part in his parents's accident. Charles had cursed the boat that day, the day his heart had gone out of the proposed restoration and saw the tatty ASR beached at the family's boathouse on the banks of the River Roach where it remained untended for many years until Bradley became interested.

He eventually learnt the details of his real parents deaths not from his adopted parents -who would always avoid the subject completely or brush it aside with , 'We don't really know too much ourselves. Now your Grandfather's gone the only witness to what happened is old Alfie Underwood and he's blind drunk for most of the time so you'll be lucky to get any sense out of him. We only know that your Grandfather blamed himself for the tragedy. He would never discuss it.' - but from diaries discovered among

Charles' effects in the Paglesham cottage left to him in his inheritance.

It was, in fact, nearly three years after Charles' demise that the diaries first came to be discovered, the cottage being locked up following a 'Will' dispute when a *long lost* cousin appeared out of nowhere to claim he was a beneficiary . The claim had no validity whatsoever but with the wheels of justice grinding interminably slowly the false claim delayed probate until Bradley was just short of his thirteenth birthday. Even then most of his inheritance was held in Trust until his sixteenth birthday, a few days after which he joined the Royal Navy.

Accompanied by his adopted parents, and Charles's Executor/Solicitor, Bradley stepped into the cottage almost expecting to see his Grandfather seated in his usual comfortable armchair in front of a roaring fire , just as he had many times in the past. In fact, it was just as he remembered it, everything neat and in it's place - albeit now covered in a fine dust, their entrance disturbing the powdery film to produce a myriad of floating particles highlighted in the sun's rays streaming through the curtains.

'Grandfather once showed me a book with photographs of himself and my other father with some of the big fish they had caught and with all the details of where and when they were caught. He said , when I was older, he would give it to me so I would know the best places to fish,' enthused Bradley.

'You must be talking about these,' exclaimed his stepfather reaching up to the top of a tall oak bookshelf , removing three quite large scrapbook size tomes and creating another shower of dust. ' These are just like rather large diaries, lots of details here Bradley and certainly will make interesting reading.'

'If there's nothing else you want at this time, I suggest we return to my office and you can decide what you wish to do about the cottage until Bradley becomes sixteen,' suggested the Solicitor.

It was Bradley himself who responded, adamantly stating, ' I just want it locked up. I have what I came for and I don't want anyone else living in it. One day I'm going to live here myself.'

Recognising the determination on the boys' face, none of the three adults attempted to argue the point at that time although the Solicitor, feeling he should proffer professional advice, whispered, as Bradley paced ahead, 'It would make economical sense to sell the property or, at least, rent it out. I know the boy has a tidy sum of money put aside for him from the sale of his father's cottage that he inherited but perhaps you can persuade him the property will still require maintenance even if left empty.'

On the return journey home Bradley started thumbing through the journals but put them to one side when his stepfather asked if he would like to visit the High Speed Rescue Launch. Receiving an enthusiastic, 'Yes please,' he turned the car about and sped past the cottage down to the riverside car park where they left the motor and walked the quarter of a mile to the boathouse. Unlike his adopted son, he had no seafaring instinct and in some ways hoped they would find the boat vandalised and wrecked to quench young Bradley's enthusiasm . It was a hope not fulfilled, Bradley's happy countenance as they approached, testimony to his continuing zeal.

The well oiled lock opened easily and the trio walked through to the gangplank leading on to the vessel's deck, the first time Bradley had actually been aboard. At first glance, apart from the paintwork having suffered a little more deterioration from the ravages of the elements, the sleek craft had avoided the attentions of delinquent youngsters and curious mariners, there being no apparent damage.

Unlocking the cabin door so the boy could see inside and also view the powerful engines, the parent shivered with a feeling of revulsion ; having been told of the boat's history by his brother-in-law, fully expecting to find an eyeball staring up at him. It was the first time he had been aboard the launch himself, being purely custodian of the keys after Charles's death.

Having no wish to enter himself, he awaited the youth's return, calling to his wife who had remained on the river bank, 'We won't be a minute. Just letting Bradley have a good look around to stop his continual asking.'

Bradley poked his head out of the wheelhouse, emerging with a rusting Mauser pistol in one hand and two shell cases in the other. 'Look what I found in the bilges,' he gleefully shouted waving the gun in the air.

His stepfather gasped in horror. ' Put the gun down on the deck and come over here. That could be very dangerous. Let me see those shells you have there.'

Content the brass, verdigris covered ,casings were harmless he handed them back to the teenager and cautiously picked up the gun . On close examination it was evident the weapon was severely corroded and beyond danger. 'I think we should get rid of this, don't you?' he asked not awaiting a reply and throwing the German pistol into the middle of the river. Seeing disappointment on his son's face he added, ' Ask your mother for some metal polish when we get home. You can keep those shell cases and polish them up. Your Grandfather must have kept them for some reason, perhaps there will be some mention in those journals you have.'

Back in the car returning home, Bradley had little opportunity to study any of the three books as his step-parents discussed with him what he wished to do with the old war launch. ' It's now over forty years old Brad. Don't you think you should consider selling it while it is still afloat ?' suggested his stepfather.

'No. I want to keep it for when I'm older.' Brad stubbornly replied. ' I want it dragged back up the ramp into the boathouse so me and Trevor can clean it and paint it .Look,' he said opening one of the books at a photograph of the old Flight Sergeant's launch , 'I'm going to make it like this.'

Chapter 2

That evening, straight after dinner, Brad and his stepfather sat down together to explore Charles's records which they found to be both comprehensive and fascinating in their content.

Charles had chronicled his life history from his wartime service until a few days before his death. As they viewed writings, pictures, drawings and photographs they became so engrossed they lost all track of time.

There were a number of photographs of the High Speed Launch, with and without the crew members, most identified with captions beneath and interspaced with explanations and brief narratives - some of the exploits having previously related to Brad. Nevertheless, the couple spent a good deal of time perusing the first of the journals and the folded boat plan they found enclosed.

The chiming of the mantelpiece clock at nine o'clock brought Brad's stepmother back from the kitchen with two steaming mugs of cocoa. 'I've never known you pair so quiet.
But it's time you were in bed Master Murray. Do you know what time it is?'

'I 'm not tired yet and I must find out what Grandfather wrote about my other parents accident. I won't be able to go to sleep until I know.'

complained Brad. 'Please, we've just got to where they are going to tow it back.'

Although they were aware of brief details concerning the boating accident, the step parents looked at one another - almost resignedly - before agreeing to his request, to some extent intrigued themselves as to exactly what had been penned by Charles.

'Just another half an hour then, no longer,' his stepmother said sternly.

Bradley opened the second book and began to read the continuing narrative out loud, only very occasionally pausing to ask, or be asked, a pertinent question.

Following Tom's successful purchase for his father, they were then faced with the task of fetching the warship back to the family boathouse to carry out the necessary repairs and refurbishment, the main amount of work being overhaul of the engines.

Tom decided to drive down to the Isle of Sheppey to investigate the possibility of getting the boat's own engines started , returning enthusiastic about his trip through the Dartford Tunnel beneath the river shortening the journey into Kent, but with no good news on the purpose of his visit.

Chapter 2

' The motors need stripping down, cleaning and re-assembling I would say,' he told his father. ' They have been unused for so long I think , even with new batteries, any attempt to start them would result in serious damage until re-.oiled. Everything else seems okay though. The steering is free enough and the electric winch is still well greased and should function once we have power to operate it again.'

It was, therefore ,decided that at the weekend the two men would travel across in the *Old Harry* to tow the launch back, making use of a flooding tide for the trip to Kent and catching the ebb to assist the return.

With fine weather forecast Tom suddenly had the idea of making it a family outing. 'We'll have a few hours to spare waiting for the tide to turn. Mary would love to come
with us, you know how she enjoys sailing and cruising. Since the baby came along she's not been able to get out much.'

' What about little Bradley ?' said Charles. ' He's a bit young, better see what Mary thinks.'

Following a family discussion the collective decision was that Bradley's mother would benefit from a break and that little Bradley could safely be left with Charles's sister for the day - assuming she was willing.

The childless couple were, 'absolutely delighted ,' at the suggestion of being parents for the day, eagerly absorbing Mary's instructions for feeding the child and carefully listening to Charles's orders regarding radio contact with the *Old Harry* via the radio transmitter/receiver he would bring in from his cottage next door. ' If you need to speak to any of us at any time just turn on the power, depress the transmit switch and speak. It is all set up on the right frequency,' he informed his Sister.

Leaving young Bradley with his Aunt and Uncle just after nine in the morning ,the family trio of seafarers boarded Tom's lifeboat just as the autumn sunlight pierced the morning mist, heralding a fine day ahead.

Slightly behind schedule they left Burnham just as the tide started to flood into the River, pushing against the current for thirty or forty minutes until clear of the Maplin Sandbanks.

Tom handed the wheel to Mary as they turned into the Thames and their speed increased with the tidal flow now assisting them. He and Charles turned their attention to the heavy tow rope, lashing on a lighter cord for the purpose of hauling the thick hawser across to the Rescue Launch.

Traffic in the Estuary was heavy with a variety of ships from Barges to large Oil Tankers on both inward and outward journeys, making crossing the main shipping lanes a hazardous exercise. Mary was untroubled, competently judging distances and their course to avoid any hint of danger: bringing the old lifeboat safely into Stangate Creek in time for lunch.

Dropping anchor as close as they could to the Launch, Mary descended into the cabin to prepare some lunch while the two men , with the aid of the *Old Harry's* rubber dinghy, transported the lighter leader rope across to the larger vessel and hauled the tow rope over the bulwarks to make fast to a foredeck bollard.

After an enjoyable lunch in the now hazy sunshine, Mary made up a pack of sandwiches and thermos flask of hot coffee for Charles to take aboard the Launch for the journey back which Tom explained, ‘ Probably take us four or five hours to get back. We'll have the tide with us if we leave about four o'clock but what sort of speed I can get the *Old Harry* up to with a bloody great warship dragging behind remains to be seen. Better give Betty a call on the radio

Mary, let her know what time to expect us home. .Ensuring everything was safely stowed away and that Charles was happy to cast off, Tom nudged the lifeboat's motor ahead, slowly taking up the slack tow and watching for his father's signal that all was well. Given a thumbs up he increased the engine revs and was happy to see the ASR boat start to swing into the centre of the creek.

Once clear of the bank he reversed the lifeboat back alongside the larger Launch, positioned a number of rubber fenders between the two craft and lashed the boats together for the journey out of the Creek and River Medway, a method considered more suitable for the confines of the narrow waterways.

Almost straight away Tom recognised that he had underestimated the weight of the large Launch, finding it necessary to push the *Old Harry's* engine to three quarters ahead to proceed at a modest two or three knots, although he had no wish - in view of the number of small craft in the Medway - to make any greater speed.

As they cleared the Isle of Sheppey headland into the Thames, after a tortuous fifty minute passage along the Medway, they immediately felt the effects of the increasing current and a strengthening North Easterly wind.

Despite assistance of the ebbing tide, progress was slow, the almost head on wind counteracting their advance across the Estuary and, at times, catching the bulk of the larger craft to drag them well off course.

‘ We might be better trying a direct tow under a short rein,’ shouted Charles from the deck of the Launch. ‘ Heave to for a bit before we get too far into the shipping lanes. We’ll unhitch and see if we can maintain a steadier course.’

‘We’re not going to get in by nine o’clock at this rate are we?’ queried Mary. ‘Should I let Betty know . Any idea how long it’s going to take us Tom ?’

But for the fact they were leaving little Bradley for longer than they had thought, Tom would have been perfectly happy for the journey to take two or three days, loving the thrill of the spray in his face and challenge of the conditions.

‘ It depends on how strong this wind gets and how long it’s expected to last. It wasn’t forecast so it will probably blow itself out soon. Just explain to Betty and apologise. I’m sure she will be happy to keep Bradley overnight if necessary.

Oh !, while you're on the radio, see what the latest forecast is will you ?'

Unfettered, the Rescue Launch drifted astern as Tom turned *Old Harry* back on course into the wind and carefully matched his speed to maintain a taut haul of the towed craft.

Although this manoeuvre improved their ability to remain on course, the general conditions and heavyweight drag caused them some concern about the crossing of the shipping lane; both Tom and Charles agreeing that they should make a direct northerly course, the shortest route available to them at their slow speed.

Assessing the Estuary's marine traffic accurately the coupled craft transversed the large ships' highway keeping well clear of any danger but, due to the sluggish journey ,found themselves only just off Shoeburyness as darkness descended.

' The latest forecast is for this wind to increase to force six for a short while before decreasing to three in the early hours of the morning,' said Tom to Charles as he allowed the two craft to drift together for a brief discussion.

It was decided they should continue along the edge of the Maplin Sands as far as they could towards the East Swinn while they had the tide in their favour, hoping to reach the mouth of the River Crouch as the tide turned , again in favour for the run back into Burnham.

Unfortunately they only they had only reached the western end of the West Barrow channel by the time the tide started to turn and the wind gathered force to nearly a full gale. Although the wind and tide together smoothed the troubled choppy surface to heavy swells, even at ' Full ahead' the coupled vessels were barely making any headway and Tom became concerned at the rate his fuel was diminishing.

Ensuring he did not allow the tow rope to foul his propeller, he backed up to the ASR and yelled to Charles, ' We'll have to anchor up for an hour or two until this wind drops.
I'll cast you off as soon as you get the hook down and make sure you're not drifting and then lay off a little so we don't collide if the wind changes. Signal me with the torch if you need to talk but we should all try to get a few hours sleep. Should be safe enough here close to the Sands' edge.'

Without it's own power the Launch was showing no navigation lights so Tom anchored the *Old Harry* thirty yards off to starboard and turned on his mast head light, illuminating the old lifeboat to any passing vessels and protecting the unlit craft.

Charles confessed, in his journal, that he still felt uneasy and was determined to remain awake on lookout despite a weariness felt from the long day's strength-sapping time at the helm.

Staring into the darkness of an open sea is unlike any other visual experience. On land there are usually discernible contours and a certain amount of background lighting to keep the eyes alert but at sea the blackness is complete and any rocking motion, other than a violent turbulence, lulls the watcher into an unconscious sleep. And so it was with Charles.

Something awoke him with a start, imposing on his unplanned slumber. The darkness was still intense; or so it seemed as he fumbled for his torch and shone it's beam on his watch face to reveal he had only dropped off for a little over an hour and dawn still some time off.

Rising to his feet he peered through the windscreen ahead and noted a single green light off to the north east as a ship appeared to be crossing the East Swinn. Glancing to the rear he was surprised to see the navigation lights of a small craft half a mile away but; unmoving.

Chapter 2

Then it suddenly hit him ! Where were the lights of his son's boat ? Certainly not just off to starboard where they were when he last looked. The lights he could see to the south west of him must be the *Old Harry* , the lifeboat having dragged anchor during his slumber. But why only navigation lights showing, the powerful masthead lamp extinguished? It could only be a bulb failure and conditions too rough for Tom to do anything about it, or the couple were asleep and unaware.

' If only I had thought to bring a signal pistol and cartridges aboard with me,' he murmured when his attempts at making contact with the flashlight brought no response.

Some sixth sense, an unexpected foreboding, and a distant thudding sound carried on the wind made him turn round towards the bow ....and shriek, ' No!' as he noted the single green navigation light he had spotted earlier had turned to a widely spaced red and green of a large ship thundering directly towards him.

Powerless, and with a sense of helplessness, he froze awaiting the inevitable collision:
remaining motionless as the dark iron sides of a medium sized coaster steamed past fifteen feet from his frail craft . Tumbling over in a twisting

mass of arms and legs as the wash of the large ship threw his Launch into a violent maelstrom of turbulence, he scrambled to his feet in time to see the lights of his son's boat disappear as the errant merchantman intersected his view.

Watching the vaguely discernible outline of the large ship against the lighter backdrop of the Kent coastline, Charles awaited a resighting of the *Old Harry*, not willing to accept the terrifying thought that the incident was anything other than a near miss.

When no lights reappeared after what seemed to Charles an interminable few minutes, the dreadful truth dawned......his son's boat had been run down.

The feeling of utter despair at his own inability to attempt any rescue operation of his son and daughter-in-law numbed his normally adept brain; until the sound of a familiar chug chug restored his power of thought to look round and sight the navigation lights of old Alfie Underwood's diesel driven trawler coming up from the direction of the River Crouch.

Clawing in the scuppers for his torch, he was relieved to find it still working and urgently flashed an S.O.S. in Alfie's direction. Whether the old man actually ever understood the mes-

sage Charles never did discover. Nor ,for that matter, what he was doing out on such a night. But it had the desired result , his battered fishing boat nestling gently alongside the ancient Launch - a remarkable achievement given the conditions and
the less than sober skipper clutching a half empty bottle of rum.

Jumping aboard, Charles barged the hapless owner aside , grabbed the wheel and screamed, ' My son and daughter-in-law are in the water, a bloody blind merchantman has just sunk their boat .Get on your radio and inform the Coast-guard !'

On reaching the approximate spot they found little evidence of the collision, a few splinters of shattered wood and a single lifebuoy the only flotsam visible in the slowly lightening dawn.

Despite a lengthy search, during which they were joined by the Southend and Sheerness Lifeboats, it was two days before Tom and Mary were found when a major section of the *Old Harry* washed up on the beach of the Man made Island just east of the Shoebury Boom, a wartime structure jutting out into the Thames Estuary. The subsequent Inquest determined that Tom and Mary were unlawfully killed by persons unknown. No identification of the ship responsible was ever established beyond doubt and the popular consensus of opinion was that the merchant boat had been 'cutting the corner' close to the Maplin Sands edge and the crew were, probably, not even aware they had run down the smaller craft. It was concluded that Bradley's parents had been trapped in the cabin at the time of impact and that the bulk of the stricken vessel had sunk in deep water, retaining ,as an ex lifeboat, a degree of buoyancy that tidal flow eventually carried to the Island.

A tearful Bradley closed the journal and ,bidding 'Good night' to his adopted parents added, ' I don't blame Grandfather. It wasn't his fault and he tried to save them. It was just a bad accident. One day I will take Grandfather's boat back to the spot and have my own small farewell ceremony for them.'

That one day turned out to be a long way off, over twenty years elapsing until Bradley fulfilled the childhood dream and re-launched the renovated wartime vessel - twenty years that saw an ungainly, underweight, skinny teenager transformed by Her Majesty's Royal Navy and Special Boat Service into a battle-hardened, tough, weather-beaten respected seaman.

Chapter 2

3

Bradley Murray eased the *Whaleback Swift* alongside Bell Wharf in Leigh Creek as crewman Trevor Swift stepped down from the deck to ensure the suspended fenders were providing adequate cushioning before securing the Launch
.

The happy, laughing, band of anglers disembarked loaded with both tackle and heavy fish bags, cheerfully waving to Brad in the wheelhouse and remarking, ' Thanks Skipper, great days fishing. See you next month,' before trudging off to the nearby car park.

Swifty started to unhitch the vessel, shouting to his employer friend , 'Better get a skate on , excuse the pun. Don't forget we've got to collect Captain Gifford and get her back to Sheerness .She won't be too happy if we keep her waiting.'

'Excuse me,' a softly spoken voice interrupted from behind. ' Are you the owner of this boat ?'

Chapter 3

Turning around Trevor found himself facing a casual, but smartly dressed, man sporting a lightweight jacket, open neck shirt and colourful cravat. His pale complexion highlighted dark bushy eyebrows above a pair of finely framed spectacles shielding azure blue eyes.

' Can I help you ? I'm the owner.' enquired Brad on emerging from the wheelhouse.

' I'd like to speak with you about chartering this boat. I understand from the publican up the road that you hire it out from time to time,' the stranger replied.

'Not exactly my friend,' laughed Brad. 'It's not a drive yourself vessel for any Tom Dick and Harry to swan off in for an afternoon cruise. This boat comes complete with crew'.......... 'and we're not cheap,' interrupted Swifty. ' Takes a bit of handling, a boat of this size, don't it Skip ?'

Brad withdrew a business card from his pocket and handed it down to the man. ' I'm afraid I can't spare the time to talk at the moment. We've got a date with a lady and we're already running late. If you are still interested give me a call before ten tomorrow morning.'

The *Whaleback* backed away from the wharf and slowly proceeded out of the creek, carefully and expertly maintaining position and almost scraping the marker buoys defining the narrow twisting waterway. On reaching the deeper water of the Ray at the Leigh Buoy the handsome craft literally 'took off ' as Brad pushed the throttle Full Ahead and headed East .

Only when the Launch disappeared from view, obscured by Southend Pierhead, did the would be hirer turn away and return to his car, stopping en route to make a telephone call to his London - based Al Qaeda controller.

'A problem has arisen that I need to talk to you about. Did you receive the ticket I sent and can you make use of it? he softly enquired.

'Affirmative,' came the single word response as the connection was severed.

Ensuring he was unobserved, he then removed his spectacles, false eyebrows, tinted contact lens and cravat before returning to his vehicle where he deposited his reversible jacket in the boot before driving home.

As the speeding ASR launch reached the outer reaches of the Thames Estuary, Swifty, lowered his binoculars and tapped his Skipper on the shoulder. 'Just off to starboard up ahead. He's seen us and is already slowing down. I wonder how "Her Majesty" will like the new boat ?' he questioned referring to their, soon-to-be, passenger; one of the few female River Pilots.

'Don't worry about Sandy, she's not that snooty you know. Bet she wants to take the controls herself; she'll handle it O.K.,' said Brad as he nosed the Taxi vessel in towards the ladder hanging down the container ship's side.

'Won't be able to reverse it into any tight space though,' joked the crewman. 'And anyway, we all know she fancies you. I bet she'll not be in any hurry to get back once she's on board.'

In truth, Brad was never short of female admirers, his, model like, rugged good looks and friendly disposition attracting a host of would-be girlfriends when in any social gathering. But, perhaps surprisingly, he had never married and, despite the current trend of living together, remained unattached in any manner, the single status suiting his lifestyle.

He had, in fact, an adopted family. Trevor's wife Nancy and four year old daughter Naomi enjoyed his company so much they would telephone him if more than three or four days elapsed without his returning with his friend for dinner. He had known Nancy as long as his crewman, having met her, with a friend Janet, whilst on a touring holiday with Trevor eight years previously. Whilst Brad and Janet enjoyed the brief holiday liaison before parting to return home, Trevor and Nancy's flirtations developed further; culminating in their marriage two years later.

Sandy Gifford adeptly descended the ships' ladder and dropped onto the *Whaleback*, accepting Swifty's assisting outstretched hand. 'Hello boys. You finally got her up and running then ?' she greeted admiringly looking around before creeping up on Brad and encircling her arms around his waist. 'Move over, let's see what she can do then,' she added as the Skipper dropped astern of the mammoth vessel now increasing speed in a froth of huge propeller wash.

'Well I must say Brad, that's the most exciting ride I've had in years,' grinned the Pilot as they neared Sheerness ; adding to the innuendo, ' I won't mention how quick it was though, might damage your reputation.'

As they set sail for the return to Leigh, Trevor voiced the question that Brad was himself already contemplating. 'I wonder what that chap wanted the boat for? He didn't look the usual angler type and looked to be almost angry when you told him he couldn't hire the boat on it's own . Probably won't hear from him again.'

But, he did; at five to nine the following morning to be exact, when the shrill tone of the telephone disturbed his leisurely breakfast.

'Is that Mr. Murray ?' enquired the caller as Brad lifted the receiver to his ear while sipping his coffee and mumbling, 'Speaking.'

'My name is Hunter Stevens. You may remember we briefly met yesterday down at Leigh. I was enquiring about chartering your boat and I think I may have given you the wrong impression. It was also your expertise that I require.....and, of course, am willing to pay for.'

Brad gulped down the remaining beverage in order to respond but, before he could do so, the dulcet voice continued, 'I am a film producer and have a number of scenes to shoot along the Thames Estuary in the near future. You have been recommended to me
and your boat is ideal for the purpose.' The lies slipped easily off Saleem's tongue.

'Perhaps something could be arranged but I have contractual commitments that may make accommodating your own requirements an impossibility. I would need to have full details of when, where and how long your filming is scheduled to take before I could accept the contract and negotiate a fee,' replied Brad.

'I'm sure our timetable can be very flexible Mr. Murray. I have to go away for a few days but I would happily meet you on my return to discuss the matter further. You can be assured your fee will not be a problem.'

Replacing the receiver, Saleem turned towards Mohammad. 'Main problem resolved my friend. How long have you got the keys to this house ? Can we be connected to it in any way ?'

'Do not be concerned Saleem. The Estate Agent tells me the owners are away for at least another two months and , this late in the season, they have no further holiday lettings booked. If I need to extend it beyond the two weeks already paid for there will be no problem. And, most importantly, there is no way the false name and address I used for the booking can be traced. They were more than happy to obtain the unexpected two week extension fully paid.'

'Good,' said the Terrorist leader. 'This telephone can be safely used then. When I have gone, tell the Amin brothers to come here after dark tomorrow. I have some minor changes of plan to discuss after my meeting with our Commander tonight and this quiet location makes an ideal meeting place away from prying eyes.'

Saleem satisfied the big Palestinian's curiosity about the needed changes, explaining that he had spent some time over the past few days going over the plan in his own mind to foresee any possible problem areas.

'Just two points gave me some concern,' he told his co- conspirator. 'Talking to local boatmen in the area, it soon became apparent that none of us has sufficient sea experience to guarantee we would be able to navigate the Estuary - especially in the dark - and successfully reach our selected targets without mishap. We must, therefore, not only obtain a suitable craft for our purpose but, also, a competent skipper who we can either bribe or ,more likely, force into carrying out our plan. The man I have just spoken to is that person: you will meet him soon. We should, however, leave nothing to chance. We must have Mr. Murray and his crewman followed . I have an idea that will ensure they are compliant to our needs.'

Saleem's right-hand man simply nodded his assent, remaining silent while his leader went on to express his second anxiety.

'I had originally intended to place a timer controlled explosive charge on the first of our targets but, I have since discovered that the timing devices being supplied are capable of being set for a maximum of only twelve hours in advance. This would mean the diversion created would take place some six hours before we can take advantage of the confusion and mayhem to avoid detection approaching our other targets. My meeting tonight should overcome this problem....we simply need a couple of radio signal command detonators.'

Having enlightened Mohammad , Saleem bid him farewell and drove away to change before going to meet his Controller on his fact-finding Estuary trip aboard the Paddle Steamer *Waverley.*

Brad jiggled the telephone handset on it's seating, listening to ensure the caller had disconnected before dialling up his crewman. 'Guess who I've just been speaking to ? No, I'll tell you,' he said before Swifty had the opportunity to reply. 'That chap you said wouldn't contact me again. Apparently he's a film producer and needs to shoot some background scenes out in the Estuary. At least, I assume he meant only background as there was no mention of actors.'

'I've always said I could be the next James Bond with my rugged good looks, suave personality and attra'...... 'Yeah, yeah, Trev,' interrupted Brad. ' The only acting you can do is acting the fool. I just can't see either of us as film stars: anyhow, I haven't accepted the charter yet. Oh !, by the way, I've dug out all those newspaper cuttings and info Charles accumulated on that Montgomery wreck we passed the other day. If I'm still invited to dinner this evening I'll bring them along.'

Threatened with the wrath of four year old Naomi if he didn't take up the invitation, Brad laughed and rang off with a final, ' Tell her I'll be there but I'm still not going to marry her.'

With no scheduled charters for the day, he poured himself a second cup of coffee and opened up Charles's journal, soon becoming engrossed in the story of the wreck himself.

Not only had his Grandfather collected a number of old "Southend Standard" and "Kent Messenger" newspaper cuttings but had obtained, from somewhere, actual close up photographs of the wreck at low water.

The story made interesting reading and, the more he read the more chilling the tale became. 'I wonder if there is anymore up-to-date information on the Internet ?' he asked himself .

He spent the next couple of hours on his computer discovering a number of little publicised facts about the wreck and some alarming prophesies that, until now, he had not even considered despite spending much of his time in close proximity to the foundered vessel.

'Certainly makes for an interesting discussion this evening,' he murmured aloud and glancing at his watch to find computer forays had eaten away the time he had intended devoting on stripping down a spare outboard engine for the *Whaleback's* tender. Nevertheless, he had no regrets about the time spent increasing his knowledge of his Grandfather's "Saviour vessel" and inserted the printed off additional information in the journal before readying himself to go out to purchase, top-up, groceries for the boat.

Having no wish to make unnecessary journeys, he changed his work attire for a pair of smart Chinos and crisp pale brown shirt - immaculately pressed, the lack of a female in the cottage being no hindrance to his personal pride in his appearance.

Chapter 3

Grinning to himself at his reflection in the mirror, he realised he was dressing up not for a 'hot date' but for a little girl for whom he had great affection. Neither Trevor nor Nancy would have considered themselves great beauties but, between them, they had produced an extremely pretty, long blonde-haired, child who had stolen his heart from the time of her birth.

It seemed little Naomi recognised she had made her first conquest and , as usual, ran to meet him as he drew up outside the Swift's bungalow and planted a big wet kiss on his cheek. ' Hello Uncle Brad. Come and see what Daddy has made me,' she said dragging him off towards the house and into her bedroom.

In the corner of the room stood a magnificent Dolls House, as tall as the little girl herself. 'Look,' she laughed, pulling the hinged front open to reveal individual rooms detailed with miniature furniture and furnishings.

Taken aback at the manufacturing skill shown by his crewman friend, he jokingly shouted through the open door, ' Now I know what you were up to whittling away at those bits of wood with that little knife of yours whenever we anchored up anywhere.

I always said you'd be better off in the building game with that "builders bum" of yours.'

Before Swifty could retort, Nancy called out, ' Dinner's on the table, and it's your favourite pan-fried Skate Brad. Better get in here quick before that greedy husband of mine scoffs his and yours. Naomi has had hers. Let her play while we eat; soon be her bedtime.'

After the superbly cooked dinner, Trevor and Brad cleared the table things away while Nancy saw her daughter to bed, returning just as the pals were reseating themselves with Charles's journal.

Brad spread the loose photographs on the table top and pointed out one that was not of the wreck. ' I don't know where Granddad got that one but it's how the S.S.Richard Montgomery was before it sank. I don't suppose it is actually the Montgomery but one of the two thousand seven hundred and ten purpose-built vessels constructed by "Uncle Sam" to aid the Allied War in the Atlantic. Their sole purpose was for transporting heavy cargo: they weren't exactly glamorous being plain welded square-hulled craft.'

'I don't think I'd have been too happy on one of those in a big sea,' piped in Trevor. 'Likely to break it's back if it's only welded. Give me good old rivets and nuts and bolts anytime.'

'Well that's what happened to the Montgomery really,' continued Bradley. 'It loaded up with about 7,000 tonnes of ammunition and bombs at Hog Island, Philadelphia, in August 1944 and sailed in convoy across the Atlantic. Such was the volume of explosives aboard, the crew made a nervous joke about the lifejackets on board, suggesting they would be better off with parachutes if they got hit. Fortunately that particular convoy escaped the detection of U-Boats and made it across without loss. The Montgomery 's luck, however, ran out when it reached the Thames Estuary where it was supposed to join another convoy to France. There were so many ships in the River at that time, both at anchor and in transit, that the poor old Liberty boat was ordered to anchor up quite close to the sands in the Great Nore anchorage just off Sheerness. Although it never came out in the subsequent Board of Enquiry, that order was a big mistake. Allegedly, The King's Harbour Master of the Thames Naval Control - the authority responsible for ship control at the time - made a serious error in ordering the vessel to a berth just north of the Middle Sand where, at low water, there

was only five fathoms of water. It wasn't too long before the Harbour Master's error became evident when around dawn a force eight gale blew up . A combination of a flooding tide and the gale force wind was sufficient, in the shallow water, to swing the ship towards the submerged sandbank as it dragged anchor. Other nearby vessels, spotting the danger, sounded their sirens to alert the Montgomery's watch Officer. It is doubtful, even then, whether he was aware of the perilous situation as he failed to wake his, peacefully sleeping, Captain while the ship was pushed onto the crest of the shoal.'
'Get Brad a drink Trevor. The poor man must be gasping,' interceded Nancy.

'No, no. A cup of coffee will be fine Nancy. I've got to drive back along twisting lanes in the dark later. I 've seen too many accidents on those roads where people have just left the pub.'

Nodding acquiescence, she retired to the kitchen while Brad and Trevor turned the Journal's pages and sorted through various cuttings, many of which were later "duplicates" of the original facts.

'That Harbour Master could be said to have caused the disaster then. Mind you, in fairness, who would have thought a large ship like that would be troubled by a force eight in the relatively sheltered waters off Sheerness?' questioned Swifty as his wife returned with steaming cups of coffee.

'If it had not been anchored it probably wouldn't have been . It was dragging up on to the sandbank that sealed it's fate. And, even then, it might have got away with it if the
tide had been flooding in for much longer . It would probably have "unstuck" itself quite easily if the tide hadn't started to ebb. Initially the ship remained sound and attempts were made to refloat it by calling out *lighters* - barges from the River Medway to unload some of the explosive cargo. Unfortunately, with the gale still raging, the Kent Port stevedores made slow progress and as the tide receded further the Montgomery started to heel over to starboard. That was all the excuse the stevedores needed to abandon the dangerous task of craning the munitions aboard the barges and quickly return to shore.'

'They would have had a hard job keeping up with me, and I would have been swimming,' joked Trev, relieving the tense solemnity of the related saga.

'I don't know about that. In those conditions, and bearing in mind the cargo, they demanded, and got danger money - up to as much as £82 per week. That was a small fortune in 1944 that created quite an official protest. But, they wanted the explosives removed so they had to pay. Looking back now I expect those same officials wished they could have emptied the ship whatever the cost.'

'I take my life in my hands every time I get in the *Whaleback's* tender with you,' burst in Trevor humorously. 'It's a good job they don't have speed camera traps on the water the way you motor out to the boat at top speed. One of these days I can see us smashing headlong into the side. Danger money. Yeah , that's what I deserve.'

Nancy took the opportunity of her husband's interjection to slip out to the kitchen and return with a steaming coffee percolater ; topping up the cups without consultation.

Brad continued between sips of his beverage. 'The stricken vessel settled firmly in the sandbank to cracking - gunshot - noises and groans as the plates began buckling causing the alarmed crew to pre-empt any Abandon Ship order and take to the lifeboats for the safety of the nearby Kent coast. Surprisingly, initially there was little too drastic about the situation as the plates held firm and the Authorities immediately assembled an emergency operation in preparation for refloating the ship. While the Montgomery had grounded on a neap tide and the next set of "springs" were a fortnight away, preparations for the necessary cargo removal were recommenced later in the morning with the return of the barges alongside and use of the ship's own , undamaged, lifting equipment. Less than twenty four hours later however, with little floatation or support both fore and aft, the welded hull succumbed to the intolerable strain and cracked just forward of midships at the front of number three hold. Such was the influx of water, the pumps were unable to make any impression and number one and two holds were also quickly engulfed. The Captain gave the order to Abandon Ship. As most of the crew had already left previously there were actually only a handful of volunteers and two signalmen remaining on board. With the ship heeling over to starboard they were grateful to receive the order, convinced they were destined to depart the world in a huge explosion as the cargo shifted and detonated.'

'I know you two had your own scary moments in the Navy but you were part of the Armed

Forces. Those men were just Merchant Seamen weren't they? Isn't it sad that many of today's younger generation have no idea of how much we all owe to the bravery of those men, especially sailing on floating bombs?' questioned Nancy sombrely.

'I know what you mean,' responded her husband. ' Just imagine what it must have been like knowing you were sitting on tons of explosives and possibly sailing into the sights of some U-Boat Captain's periscope. The crew of the Montgomery must have considered themselves doubly lucky , surviving both the trip across from America and a shipwreck !'

Brad slid some photographs of the submerged wreck across the table to his companions, pointing out some showing just the uppermost tips of the ship's masts protruding and others depicting much more of the vessel's upper works.

'See how little of it now shows at high water. I've been close enough myself to see how easy it would be for a large ship, only marginally off course, to plough into it. What would happen if that occurred is open to conjecture; acknowledged experts seem to have different opinions and solutions? Apparently there have been twenty four "near misses" recorded by The

Maritime and Coastguard Agency, the State's controlling body for wrecks. They have the benefit of radar and, now, closed-circuit Television, so are confident there is no danger to the public but there are plenty of others who disagree.'

'That little six foot square notice on it, *Unexploded ammunition*, that I saw through the binoculars doesn't seem to be much of a barrier. What distance is the exclusion zone around it ?' asked the crewman.

'It's actually only two hundred square yards but to be fair to the MCA it is very well monitored. When I was looking up current information I came across an example of the time half a dozen men from Peckham, South London, attempted to fish the wreck; hopeful of netting a large catch to sell on to their local Chinese Restaurants. How on earth they thought they would avoid snagging their net on the wreck the article didn't say. We know, Trev, don't we, that there is some great fishing to be had around wrecks but these
guys must have clueless if they thought they could drop a net amongst the rigging and successfully retrieve it? Although it was night and they were using inflatable dinghies, they were

detected and reported to the Harbour Master who promptly went out and escorted them back to harbour where their boats were seized.'

'Did they get much of the munitions off ? ' enquired Nancy. 'I've lived around here all my life and wasn't aware we've got a massive bomb right on our doorstep.'

'Well, apparently number four and five holds remained above water for some time so, although the refloating attempt was abandoned, the salvage operation continued until they were emptied.....which still leaves three holds full of shells, bombs and explosives, estimated at more than one thousand four hundred tons,' he replied ominously.

The trio continued discussing the time Brad, as a young boy, was taken to see the wreck by his Grandfather, a time when the surveillance procedures were obviously less vigorous as they were able to approach to within a few feet of the projecting masts. Charles had told his young grandson that it was almost certain there were some large Conger eels inhabiting the wreck but refused to accede to pleas from Brad to try fishing for them. 'It's far too dangerous a spot. I should not have even brought you near here. I just wanted to see it again for myself, ' he confessed.

'I wonder if it really is much danger now after all this time?' said Trevor quietly.

That really is the question my friend. It's considered by many to be like a huge time-bomb ticking away; some saying the clock has stopped and others that it could strike at any time.' Brad sagely replied.

At that precise moment the clock did strike.........the chimes of the mantelpiece timepiece intruding on the conversation to announce it was ten o'clock.

'Time for a bite of supper,' announced Nancy. 'Hold on a minute Brad while I go and rustle us up a snack. You've got me most interested now and I don't want to miss anything else you to have to say. Trev, you pop in and check on Naomi . I won't be a few minutes.'

Left alone briefly, Brad 's thoughts for some unknown reason switched to the film producer. What sort of sea shots did he want? What sort of film was he making ? Why was he seemingly so keen to use the *Whaleback* ? And, why was he prepared to pay whatever Brad asked ? ; all questions , he mused, that would soon be undoubtedly answered. But, he realised , it was an intuitive nagging suspicion that he was not what he claimed to be that was intruding on his thoughts. Who are you really and where are you now my friend he thought ?

Hunter Stevens, alias Steven Hunter, alias Saleem Hakimi, was, in fact, at that very moment stepping down the gangplank of the *Waverley* in the Pool of London, having travelled up stream from Southend-on-Sea on the pleasure trip's "Evening Showboat" cruise.

In his Hunter Stevens guise he had boarded the Paddle Steamer at Southend pier head to the syncopated rhythm of a jazz band and immediately found himself a seat in the lee of one of the funnels. Protected from the slight, but chilly, wind and away from the main throng surrounding the musicians on the after deck towards the rear of the vessel, he patiently awaited his London controller who, he hoped, was also aboard.
Having never met his Al Qaeda go-between, and with no description of him, he was relying on the notified description of himself being sufficient for contact to be made.
When he had still not been approached as the steamer passed Canvey Island, he began to fear the rendezvous was, for some unknown reason,

not going to be kept . Withdrawing a pair of small binoculars from his pocket he descended to the main deck and strolled over to the guard-rail, well forward of the musical extravaganza and ,deserted.
Intent on viewing the shoreline and huge Liquefied Petroleum Gas tanks, well illuminated in the darkening approach of night, he was making a mental note of jetty and wharf positions when he sensed, rather than heard, someone approach. The slightest hint of a Jasmin perfume as he turned towards the now audible footsteps confused his expectations of the arrival of his "contact".

'Don't you like the music ?' questioned the petite, dark-skinned, pretty young woman. ' It's much warmer amongst the crowd and everyone is very friendly.'

Bewildered by the unexpected encounter, Saleem stuttered, 'Er !, yes but I was expecting to meet someone. I would feel out of place on my own.'

'Not a young lady I hope. I too am alone and **I'm mad about jazz,'** stressed the newcomer.

'Traditional or Modern ?' gasped the Terrorist on hearing the previously agreed contact code but not expecting the words from a glamorous young girl. Would she now correctly answer to confirm her identity ?.

'Traditional only,' she smiled knowing it to be the right response. 'I am Shauna Khan,' she lied concealing her true identity. ' Come, let us mingle and enjoy the music for a while. We have plenty of time to discuss matters alone later and I really do like Traditional jazz.'

'Just wait a few moments please Shauna. I want to view the Coryton Oil Refinery that's just coming up on our right,' he politely requested while again raising his binoculars and scanning the shoreline.

Satisfied at what he saw, he succumbed to the pleasurable company of his new acquaintance and, stopping en route to purchase some soft drinks, joined the gyrating masses on the aft deck.

The happy, carefree, partying crowds reminded Saleem of his earlier Travel Agents trip to Bali where he, himself, nearly became a victim of a Terrorist nightclub bombing. Barely five hundred metres away at the time of the explosions ,he witnessed, first hand, the horrendous results but was unmoved by the torn and dismembered bodies of the happy-go-lucky partygoers who had passed by his alfresco table earlier. Allah would never let a true believer like myself be harmed…..only the Imperialists and Infidels he later declared on relating the gory details he had seen to the Amin brothers. In his mind's eye he could see young Asif , eagerly anxious to meet his waiting virgins, easily joining such a crowd in a copy-cat suicide ; imagining the resulting carnage as the explosion swept the confines of the deck .But no Asif, he reminded himself, no such 'soft target' for you . If Allah is good your destiny lies in a lonely death , the following outcome being far more deadly and long-lasting than any ,so-called, "major incident" slaying.

As the *Waverley* approached the awesome four hundred and fifty metre wide, sixty five metre high , brightly lit-up Queen Elizabeth 2nd Bridge , he took Shauna by the hand and walked her away from the dancing crowd back to the seclusion of the foredeck.

'We must act as young lovers,' he whispered. ' I was expecting the Controller himself or Yassin who I met before. How much have you been told of this operation ?'

'Have no fear Saleem. I know only your name and that I am to memorize your additional requirements. I know nothing of what is planned;

unless you wish to tell me. I want only revenge for my husband's death and have been informed that what you are doing will be a major victory for the Jihad .'

Her revelation and obvious distress convinced the Terrorist that the reservations he was feeling about the use of an unexpected "go-between" were unfounded. Observing they were still almost alone, the nearest other passengers being a middle aged couple leaning over the paddle wheel some twenty feet away, he quietly listed the "extras" needed before enquiring what had happened to her husband.

'Nearly two years ago, Sajid went to visit relatives in Pakistan who had been arrested on suspicion of aiding a fundamentalist organisation. As a qualified lawyer he thought he would be able to help them. Within a few hours of making enquiries about them he, himself , was arrested and subjected to humiliating torture before being put on a plane back to England.'

'Why was he arrested and then immediately deported ? Did he have any connections or anything in common with them ?' queried Saleem.

'I cannot say for certain, he was a very pious and impetuous man. But, he was also very reticent and I, sometimes, used to think he was hiding things from me; especially when I discovered by chance that he was the defending lawyer for that young Iranian, Ramzan Ahmad .You may remember, three years ago he was arrested trying to blow himself up during that protest demonstration outside the Royal Courts of Justice.'

'Yes, I do recall it. As I remember, the demonstration was nothing to do with the cause of Islam but something about "Fathers for Justice". If the newspapers are to be believed Ramzan was acting alone as a one-man Crusader who sought to use the gathering as a way to maximise casualties but was unsuccessful when the home-made device failed to detonate.'

'It was after that I found he became progressively uncommunicative, often hearing him in whispered conversations on the phone, but never being told who he was speaking to. He would also spend more and more time reading the Koran. But, I never saw him with any strangers and the only time there was any thought in my mind that he was anything other than a hard-working attorney was when he suffered a period of paranoia claiming he was being followed everywhere.'

Saleem waited for the girl to go on but she remained silent as a group of four drunken revellers suddenly encroached their secluded position. Fortunately the excess drink had made them no more than passive merrymakers, the usual loud-mouth, looking-for-trouble, leader of such groups being absent on this occasion. He smiled to himself however when his sharp hearing caught a passing comment of, 'Cor, did you see that. I'd give her one any day ?'as the foursome turned back towards the music.

Shauna gave no indication that she had overheard the coarse remark, continuing, ' He telephoned me from Heathrow shortly after his plane landed to say he expected to be home in around an hours' time. We were living at Bethnal Green at that time so when he hadn't arrived after two hours, and I had no further telephone call, I began to become concerned so called his mobile phone. There was no response; no ring tone or anything at all. I waited a further half an hour and was just about to telephone the police when the intercom buzzed and a voice enquired, "Is that Mrs. Khan ? It's the police, may we come in ?" I admitted a plain clothed man and uniformed policewoman who asked me to sit

down before telling me that Sajid had been killed in an accident on the Underground.
I was, of course, terribly shocked and upset . When they left I realised I had not even questioned the circumstances of his death.'

Choking back tears she informed Saleem that it was only when she was later interrogated by two other visitors , who announced themselves as 'Special Branch', that she discovered her husband had, *accidentally fallen in front of a tube train at Piccadilly Circus station.* They were quite callous and suggested that Sajid was known to them as a radical Muslim zealot and did I have any knowledge of his friends? ' I was vigorously questioned for over an hour before they left,' she sobbed. ' It was then that I started attending prayers again where I met Hass………,' she stopped herself 'Our mutual friend.'
Recognising the distress caused by the recollections, Saleem drew his new found companion close, embraced her slim frame and whispered, 'Do not upset yourself. Sajid and many others will soon be avenged. You suspect his death was not an accident ?'

'To get home to Bethnal Green from Heathrow Airport he would have been on the Piccadilly

Line, changing at Holborn for the Central Line. There was no reason for him to be on Piccadilly station at any time unless he got off the train early to avoid someone who was following him,' she replied making no attempts to extract herself from his clasp.' I now think that his claims of being followed was not imagination at all.'

'I truly wish I could speak to you more but I see we will be docking soon. Are you catching the coach back to Southend ?'

'No Saleem, I still live in London but perhaps I will see you again in the future.'

'Not as you see me now,' he said wistfully. ' With all the CCTV cameras around these days you will not be surprised that I am disguised. Tell me; as our friend sent you in his place, did he indicate at all that I can continue to expect full co-operation?'

Still snuggled up close, Shauna answered in the affirmative: seductively adding, 'and mine too. Can you tell me of your plans . Will I really ever see you again ?'

'It is better for everyone concerned that you do not know but, yes, I am not yet going to meet my maker. Do you have a telephone number I can contact you at ?'

Chapter 3

Eagerly responding with the number which Saleem entered into his mobile phone, she enquired whether he would tell her of his ?

'For now you must use only the telephone number I have given to you to pass on to our contact. That is safe until our operation is carried out. Now, are you sure you can remember the list of additional items I require ?

'I have an excellent memory Saleem.'

Noticing the Paddle Steamer was passing under Tower Bridge and the music had stopped, Saleem reluctantly released his embrace and gently escorted Shauna towards the disembarking point and the jostling trippers. During the short walk to the awaiting coaches he discovered his consort was a remarkably young looking thirty one year old who lived alone in Central London. His enquiry as to what work she did brought a response of Civil Servant at some obscure Government department he had never heard of.

Bidding her farewell with a light kiss on the cheek as he boarded the coach, making sure he was just about the last to do so in order to claim the last remaining double seat to himself, he settled back to contemplate his viewings of the targets but found himself continually thinking of the beautiful girl who had just entered his life.

'Here you are then. Some nice cheese and biscuits with your favourite Cocoa nightcap,' said Nancy re-entering the lounge and breaking into Brad's meanderings.

'The little angel's tucked up and sound asleep,' reported Trevor returning from his check on his daughter and promptly picking up a plate and cup before seating himself down. ' I was thinking ,while tucking Naomi back in, I know it's now sixty one years that ship's been laying there so I suppose everyone thinks it's perfectly safe but it's a wonder they never tried to get the rest of the cargo out of it.'

'Well, three years after the war's end and again in nineteen sixty seven, the Americans offered to do just that but our Government took the attitude that the explosives were probably safer left untouched submerged in water and declined the offer. To be fair to successive Governments over the years, regular surveys that have been carried out have always resulted in a similar conclusion,' said Brad pensively.

Chapter 3

'Ah!, but are we being told the full truth. We all know how Government departments can be economical with the truth ?' questioned Nancy.

With a mouthful of cheese and biscuits and unable to answer immediately, Brad slid over some literature printed from his computer depicting a recent sonar image of the wreck. Hastily swallowing his snack he proceeded to explain.

'I don't think that is the problem. The surveys are certainly carried out. Up until 1984 the Ministry of Defence's own salvage divers kept a check on the state of the vessel. Following a question in the House of Commons in 1980, the then Undersecretary of State for Trade, Norman Tebbitt, replied that removing the bombs was always likely to be an unacceptable risk. But, in 1981 Royal Navy divers spent nearly a month thoroughly surveying the munitions as well as the ship's hull, swimming right into the cargo areas holding the bombs and came to the conclusion that it would be safe to salvage them, albeit that they were still considered capable of detonation.'

'It's a wonder, with our diving experience in the Navy, we were never involved in a survey dive ourselves . Certainly would have been interesting,' Trevor chimed in.

'I don't think they would have let you loose around anything explosive after that *minimal* charge you were supposed to have used on that obsolete target ship during the NATO exercise in the Mediterranean. You weren't even supposed to sink it , let alone blow it in half !'

Nancy burst out laughing. ' You never told me about that,' she chortled. ' Sounds like you could have had the part in that Michael Caine film, "The Italian Job", where he says, *I only told you to blow the bloody doors off.*'

'It's the sort of mistake anyone could make. They definitely said two kilograms of explosive, not two grams. How was I to know it was only supposed to signify a successful attack? And, I don't know why the Eyeties kicked up such a fuss. It was only an old tin can that was going to be sunk anyway.'

When the trio stopped laughing, Brad continued recounting the wreck's history. 'I'll tell you one thing,' he said. 'Anyone diving on that ship needs pretty good eyesight. The merging of the Medway and Thames rivers creates quite a disturbance of the sandbank and the waters around the wreck are normally murky tosay the least. In fact, a team of divers conducting a survey for the Maritime and Coastguard Agency back in 2003 reported they could see little more than six inches in front of them. That was, I think, the latest survey carried out although it is said there is another scheduled for this year.'

'Well, we're out in the Estuary most days and we've not yet seen anyone. I would have thought that's the sort of thing to do during summertime when the days are longer.' interrupted his crewman. ' There's not that much of the year left and it's dark by seven o'clock now. I bet they don't do it......another bloomin Government cut back.'

'Is that when these sonar images were done then ?' queried Nancy looking at the pictures clearly showing the severed hull.

Nodding affirmative while reaching for another cheese biscuit, Brad explained that the MCA were the owners of the wreck, the Governments' designated body responsible for shipwrecks among other things and, as such, with so many conflicting opinions as to what should be done, if anything, about the potential hazard, had the 2003 survey carried out to possibly formulate an acceptable plan.

'They moored a diving platform above the wreck but had to wait for the passiveness of neap tides before attempting descent as, even with the sonar scan cables attached ,the diver was in danger of being swept away in any stronger flow. The rusting hull is now razor sharp in places so the divers have to take great care. And with fishing nets also caught up around the wreck, anyone who dives needs to make sure they carry a sharp knife. The leading diver this time did an excellent job with the state-of-the-art sonar gear, resulting in those clear pictures. It is pretty obvious that the decks are beginning to collapse which means that soon the fragmentation bombs just below them are going to be released from their confinement. It seems it is only a question of time before bombs begin to get fished up. Who's to say one won't explode and trigger others ?'

'Strange isn't it ?' commented Swifty. 'I seem to remember as a boy the pleasure boats used to take tourists out around the wreck sightseeing. And most of the local fishermen have fished around it from time to time. There didn't seem to be any worries then or, perhaps, we were all ignorant of the danger.'

Chapter 3

'We still are to some extent. The Government commissioned independent consultants some five years ago to carry out a risk assessment. They concluded the safest course would be to remove the remaining munitions. This was followed by a meeting, in 2001, at Southampton to discuss what should be done. But to date, some five years later, this assessment has still not been published so we are unaware of just how much danger we are in.'

'It would seem they are certain no natural detonation is likely after all this time so what's so wrong in just leaving well alone ?' asked Nancy.' You know what they say, *Let sleeping dogs lie*.'

'Well there is always the danger of a German mine drifting into the wreckage and triggering an explosion. They dropped hundreds in the Estuary during the war and, as we know, they still continue to be caught at times in fishermans' nets to this day. Admitted it's not a likely scenario, but, it could happen. Far more of a worry though is the possibility of the wreck being hit by one of the many large freighters, container ships or passenger liners that pass close to the site daily. The seaways are not the wide open spaces that they are thought to be. Look at the examples of the accidents in the expanse of the English Channel that nobody would have expected. Way back in 1971 a Peruvian freighter sank after colliding with a Panamanian tanker and was promptly hit by not one, but two ships. And, much more recently in 2002, you may remember seeing on the television news a Norwegian car-carrier and Bahamian container ship collided; sinking the car-carrier. Within two days, despite being marked and notified to ship owners, it was hit by a Dutch ship and then again by a Turkish vessel!'

'Strewth, put like that it's worse than the M25,' exclaimed Trevor. ' But you did say that the Montgomery is closely monitored by radar so, surely, any ship getting too near could be warned off in time.'

'That's true but remember, some of those large carriers can't just sharply change course or stop like we can on the *Whaleback*. Obviously the River Pilots we often take out to put on board at the Estuary mouth are well aware of the danger so there should be little chance of a ship steering into it. But, breakdowns occur in large ships as well as small. Remember that "gin palace" luxury yacht that we managed to get a line on and tow away from the Maplins a few month's back when their steering mechanism developed a fault. And, it's by no means certain the passage of time has rendered the munitions harmless. A New Scientist Magazine investigation revealed that some Government experts themselves believe it is possible some of the fuses could be unstable and capable of detonation:while others put forward the view that by now any fuses would have deteriorated to a harmless state.'

'I wonder if the politicians really think it's safer to leave it untouched or whether it's a question of money ? queried Swifty. 'What are the alternatives I wonder ?'

Brad finished his cocoa before answering that particular enquiry , giving his crewman the opportunity to fetch out a bottle of rum and a couple of glasses. The skipper shook his head to decline the fiery liqueur but Trevor , knowing his friend's strict no drink if driving principle, pre-empted the refusal. ' No arguments, it's getting late. Make him up a bed Nancy, he's staying the night.'

When his wife left the room Trevor poured their nightcaps as Brad explained what various explosive experts had suggested. It was true, he said, that most favoured the 'status quo' but others had suggested careful removal of the bombs by divers. Others supported the idea of entirely covering the wreck in concrete and at least one eminent specialist wanted the authorities to surround the ship with a watertight - cofferdam - construction that could be drained to permit removal of the munitions in the open air.

'That sounds a bit of a dangerous avenue. Surely out of water any instability would be increased by the rise in temperature that is bound to occur and there is always the question of what to do with the bombs cleared from the ship's holds,' argued Swifty.

'I'm no expert on the types of ordnance we're talking about here. Our training was, as you know, with more recent explosives but I suspect the idea would have been to keep the shells and bombs wet throughout the operation. The obvious solution as to disposal would be to load them on to another ship and transport them well out to sea and dump them in deep water where, even if they did detonate, collateral damage would be limited to the seabed itself, suggested Brad. 'Certainly some Politicians are concerned. Both Sittingbourne and Sheppey; and Southend East Members of Parliament have voiced concerns on behalf of their constituents……and so they should bearing in mind that the nearby coastal areas that are in the front line of any calamitous explosion are home to some 130,000 people. The potential for a huge loss of life shouldn't be underestimated; Sheerness alone, the nearest town at a little over a mile away, has some 11,000 inhabitants.'

Catching the last of the Skipper's words as she returned from her domestic chore, Nancy interjected, ' And, isn't there an Oil Refinery about the same distance away on the Isle of Grain ? You can see tanks from the end of Southend Pier quite clearly. Is it possible that could explode as a result of the Montgomery going up and cause more devastation ?'

'It's a frightening prospect isn't it ?' said Brad answering her question with another of his own. 'The potential for a widespread chain reaction, if all the remaining munitions detonated simultaneously , is pretty alarming. There was a Liberty ship explosion after the war that ,while not exactly comparable, has some relevance to what we are talking about here.'

Trevor decided this was the moment he just had to 'pay a visit to the little room', having delayed an urgent need engrossed in Brad's informative narrative.

Coincidentally Hunter Stevens was also urgently seeking a toilet, his dallying with Shauna before boarding the vehicle on the London Embankment, rather than utilising the nearby Public Convenience while he had the opportunity, causing him much discomfort throughout the return coach journey.

The urgency, however, was not sufficient for him to overcome the revulsion of using the unlit, vandalised and smelly car park facility before jumping in his car and speeding off towards his home.

Unfortunately, his racing exit attracted the attention of two police patrol officers parked up in an adjacent street enjoying a McDonald's and coffee. 'There's a chap in something of a hurry at this time of night Dave. Let's see what's put a rocket up his backside shall we ?' said the driver accelerating after the disappearing tail-lights to the chagrin of his blotchy-faced passenger who found himself suddenly coffee less and lap-soaked.

Single-minded and unaware of being followed, Saleem screeched to a halt outside a Public toilet block on Southend seafront and ran inside to relieve his aching bladder, sighing with satisfaction as the dull pain subsided.

Chapter 3

I should take this opportunity to transform Hunter Stevens back to Steven Hunter before returning home, he thought. But, just as he started the metamorphosis, footsteps and voices announced the arrival of his pursuers.

'Would you be the owner of the vehicle outside Sir ?' enquired a voice from behind as he hastily pushed his false eyebrow back into place.

Turning around Saleem found himself facing the same police officer who had visited him with enquiries about the delivery boy's killing. He just stopped himself from saying hello again, realising he was, he hoped, unrecognisable as Steven Hunter.

'Yes officer, is there something wrong ?'

'Did you know you were touching speeds of fifty miles an hour when you left the car park . What's your hurry ?'

' It was just that I was bursting for a pee and needed to find a toilet quickly. That stinking dark hole jokingly called a *Convenience* in the car park should be locked up or demolished. It's a health hazard if you ask me. I wouldn't use it if you paid me to.'

'That's as may be Sir,' said blotchy face sympathetically. ' But you were breaking the law and exceeding the speed limit by a considerable degree. I shall have to report the matter and have to advise you that you could be facing prosecution. Can I see your driving licence and insurance please?'

'I'm afraid I don't have them with me Officer.'

'Then you will have to present them into the station tomorrow Sir. What's your name and address for now ?'

Saleem's brain was racing. His licence and documents were in the name of Steven Hunter, the name blotchy face would have known on his visit to his home. And he couldn't fail to recognise the address. Could he give a false name and address ? No, they were bound to check his details against the car registration.

Fate intervened in the form of a drunken yob reeling into the toilet and stumbling into blotchy face, temporarily becoming a priority over the Terrorist. Dragging the protesting youth out to the Panda car, Dave called out to his driver, 'Get his details and let's get this scum bag back to the station.'

The fortunate interruption gave Saleem time to assess his options and elect to state his name as Hunter Stevens with his correct address in the hope that blotchy face, having the drunkard to deal with, did not enquire further of his colleague. When I produce my documents, he reasoned, I can easily say I thought I had to give my surname first. If only I had managed to get out of my disguise before that bloody nuisance of a policeman came in, he thought, I wouldn't have anything to worry about .

He watched the patrol car disappear towards the town before removing his false appendages. 'Of all the bad luck,' he mumbled to himself. ' If anything else develops from this cursed incident I'll simply have to say I had been attending a fancy dress evening with friends. I do look a bit like the older Roger Moore; even if I say so myself.'

'Get that bloke's name Pete ?' queried Dave turning round to look at his prisoner in the back seat. 'I got the feeling I've seen him before.'

'Yeah, Stevens and you probably have seen him, spitting image of James Bond 007', laughed the driver.

'That's better. Got to keep the Thames topped up,' joked Trevor on his return. 'What was that you were saying about a Liberty boat blowing up Brad ?'

'It was pretty horrendous really .It was loaded up with ammonium nitrate fertiliser
which, you would know Trev, can be mixed with certain other matter to make a powerful explosive. In fact it's used by armies all over the world; and terrorist organisations. The Bali bombers were one group who used it for their cruel attack. But, as I said, it's not a particularly good comparison as a ship load of that would probably be two or three times more powerful than the ammo on the Montgomery.'

'But, what was the result of it *going up*?' queried Nancy as keen as her husband to discover what Brad's research had revealed.

The clock struck midnight but neither listener showed any signs of fatigue , eagerly awaiting further information.

Swifty leant over and poured another generous measure of rum in Brad's glass as his skipper continued.

'The vessel was the SS Grandcamp and it was docked at the time in Texas City, pretty shallow water like the Montgomery. What caused it to blow up was, of course, never discovered; there was no evidence to examine. Even now it is still considered America's worst industrial disaster. Being in dock it was inevitable that the casualties and damage were severe, much greater than if the ship had been out to sea. When it exploded it created a fireball that soared some 4000 feet high and a tidal wave that swept one barge nearly 200 feet inland. People living 150 miles away heard the explosion.'

'Good grief, there must have been some terrible injuries ' exclaimed Nancy.

'The death toll wasn't far short of 600 and, of course, there were at least the same number injured to varying degrees. Such was the power of the initial fireball, two small light aircraft were literally knocked out of the sky.'

Nobody spoke for a good few minutes as imaginations temporarily struck the Swift's speechless and Brad took advantage of the silence to down the remainder of his drink.

Trevor finally broke the tense atmosphere, gasping, 'And, we've still got a potential disaster like that right on our doorstep….and the Government does nothing about it. I bet they'd bloody well do something pronto if it was just outside the Houses of Parliament.'

Anxious to play down the enormity of the facts he had revealed to his friends, Brad quickly sought to allay their anxieties. 'Yes, but let's all remember, even though the experts can't agree on the best solution to it's removal or otherwise, one thing they are all agreed on is that it would take a series of mistakes, poor navigation or accidents for there to be any danger from a shipping collision. And it would now take a hell of a detonation to promote a wholesale explosion. Short of an old mine drifting into it, a pretty unlikely happening, I think we can feel pretty safe in our beds tonight. Which is where we should all be now don't you think ?'

Rising to his feet after a thoughtful few minutes, Swifty, following the others out of the room prophetically uttered, ' There is another way the Montgomery could go up. I can't think why they would want to do it but, WHAT IF TERRORISTS DECIDED TO BLOW IT UP ?'

4

The shrill beep, beep, of the grey telephone on his old-fashioned desk startled Commander James Beaman in his top-floor , equally out-of-date, office in Thames House. He had arrived at the M.I.5 offices particularly early to revue what information the department had managed to ascertain on a new Terrorist threat that undercover operatives had discovered was being planned.

Thoughtfully staring out of the window with a cup of coffee to his lips, the unexpected interruption at such an early hour caused him to spill some of the hot liquid as he swung about to snatch the handset.

'Damn !' he swore: not at the additional stain on the carpet but at the loss of his early morning caffeine stimulant.

'No, not you,' he laughed recognising his caller. 'Just spilt my habitual *fix*. What with that and having given up smoking I can see myself being in rehab by the end of the day.'

'You are going to need another cup of coffee, and a whole pack of cigarettes I'm afraid,' said his caller solemnly. ' I'm sure that Hassam does not know he is under close observation and suspects nothing but he is being overly cautious. He is acting very nervously and hasn't left the house in days except for a brief stroll to the post box very late last night.'

'Which post box?' broke in the Commander . 'Hold on a moment,' he continued punching in a short number on an internal phone. ' Peter, get someone down to the post box at.......... Where ?' he screamed into the grey phone.

The agent revealed the location and waited patiently while the information was passed on.

'Go yourself Peter. There's a letter in the box we need to look at . Don't accept any nonsense from the collector. If need be use your powers of arrest under the "Anti-terrorism Act".'

Satisfied his instructions were clearly understood and being acted on, he returned to his caller. ' What else can you tell me ? Have you found out what is being planned ? I am getting nothing from any other source and, at the moment, we have very little to go on.'

Chapter 4

'I regret I have discovered little more than anyone else. Hassam has mentioned no targets by name, hinting only at the fact there is more than one attack taking place and that there will be widespread economic consequences in addition to hundreds, if not thousands, of casualties.'

'The M.I.5 Chief swore. 'Christ, we're getting nowhere fast. Have you been able to uncover any dates or any names we can follow up on ?'pleaded the desperate Commander.

'The only things I have managed to learn in addition to Hassam definitely being an Al Qaeda go-between is that he is not controlling the actual attacks; simply providing the armaments and explosives being requested which, I can confirm, have just been added to. Also, the leader of the team is a man that I know only as Saleem - no surname - and I think he lives in the Southend-on-Sea area,' confided the informant.

The puzzled M.I.5 man questioned the caller further gleaning every last bit of information before ordering, 'Come in undetected and view some photographs to see if we can make some identification possible ? We have a poor quality photograph of the man you call Saleem but from a partially obscured viewpoint. It may be of more use if you can describe him to our artist.

We would probably have had him under observation but for a piece of bad luck. Charlie Walsh followed the coach back to Southend intending to keep him in sight all the way back to his home but, just as they approached the seaside town itself, he was forced to pull in to a petrol station having run so low on fuel. He put in just a couple of gallons to quickly get back on the trail of the coach but, being unfamiliar with the area ,suddenly found himself having taken the wrong turning off a roundabout . He actually saw the coach again but by the time he was able to re-track it had disappeared from view. Enquiries resulted in his eventually catching up with the vehicle at its dropping off point but by then all passengers had dispersed and there was no sign of Saleem. In hindsight, given the fact it looks like we are going to have to involve outside forces at some time, I should, perhaps, have got the local Southend lads to follow him once the coach returned. At least we would then have had him under constant observation. I have to report our progress to the Director General this afternoon. Thank goodness it was on her instructions the "Operation" has been kept in house until now. She is not going to be very pleased.'

Chapter 4

'I did think of joining him on the coach back Sir but , as I had already said I live in London , it would have been suspicious and, of course, I had no transport in Southend. I will, however, be in within the hour to see if he is on our files anywhere and at least the telephone number should be a help: shouldn't it Sir ?'

'Hopefully , hopefully, ' replied the dejected, unhappy, M.I.5 Commander.

Saleem Hakimi was a happy man that morning. He had presented his documents at the police station and met no difficulties.

Mohammad Sadat was a happy man that morning. He had just had his application for British citizenship ratified.

Latif Amin was a happy man that morning. He had been accepted by Saisha's family as a worthy suitor.

Asif Amin was a happy man that morning. He had just lost his virginity.

Having successfully cleared the previous evening's debacle, Saleem made his way to the *safe house* to make a number of telephone calls, first ringing Bradley Murray. 'Good morning Mr. Murray, it's Hunter Stevens. Can we discuss the charter now I have a time schedule?' continuing before Brad could speak; ' We would like to hire you and your boat for two days and NIGHTS, commencing in three days time.'

'Do you mean from the Wednesday ?' queried Brad. 'And you wish to stay out overnight ?'

'That's correct Sir. Most of the filming we wish to do is during darkness and I should, perhaps, point out that we will be requiring to travel at least as far as the Knock John Tower, and possibly the Black Deep. I mention that as we wouldn't wish to run out of fuel or provisions. I trust your crewman will be able to keep us "fed and watered".'

Brad was taken aback, mentally assessing the costs involved in both time and fuel before answering. ' We have no Pilotage requirements currently in the diary, my contract with the Authorities being only "As and when required" for those times when their own launches and crew are unable to meet ships' needs. But I do have angling party charters for Sunday and Wednesday. We won't be dropping Wednesday's lot off at Burnham on Crouch until early evening. They are regulars so I would not wish to cancel their booking.'

'No. no. That would not be expected of you. As long as we can be aboard by about 9 p.m. and it would be convenient and beneficial to our schedule if we could embark from Wallasea Island.'

'Mmm ,' said Brad thoughtfully. ' Providing my assistant can leave his wife and young daughter for that period of time - which may not be an option - I will happily take your money, strange as your requirements may be ?'

'I'm sure the right incentive will overcome any reservations. I am willing to pay you THREE THOUSAND POUNDS CASH for the inconveniences incurred accommodating the unusual request.'

Brad gasped at the generous fee offered before recovering his composure to acquiesce as though the sum was not at all unusually high. ' I should tell you that the weather forecast for the latter part of next week is for wet and windy conditions that may make for an uncomfortable time afloat : certainly not ideal for filming. If you cancel the booking there will obviously be a cancellation charge. By the way, what's the film about ?'

'Excuse me one moment,' said Saleem knocking on the desk. 'There's someone at the door,' he added playing for time to think up an answer.

Rustling a few papers he picked up the handset and light-heartedly joked, ‘ Don’t worry Mr. Murray, we’re not afraid of getting a little wet. There will be no cancellation, our tight schedule will not permit it. Whatever the weather throws at us we will have to accept and you can be assured your fee will be paid in full when we arrive on Wednesday evening.’ He was hoping his promissory response would be sufficient to dismiss the film subject question for which he had no pre-determined answer. But when only silence exuded from the earpiece he quickly continued, as his brain raced to provide a viable scenario, ‘ It’s not a film as such. We need a series of background shots of ships , the old wartime forts and various landmarks up to the Queen Elizabeth bridge for a customer of ours. We are an Advertising Agency working for a determined group against expansion of the LPG terminal on Canvey Island, but that’s all I can tell you without compromising Customer confidentiality. Perhaps I may be at liberty to tell you more when we meet up on Wednesday. Let’s hope Al…..a, all will be well with the weather.’

Replacing the receiver he breathed a sigh of relief and thumped the desk top in frustration. ‘ You crass idiot,’ he screamed at the empty room in realisation that he had, unthinkingly, almost blurted out ‘Allah will be kind.’

Recognising he had almost made a serious mistake, his earlier sense of euphoria disappeared to be replaced by a feeling of apprehension and doom. It took the sound of someone entering the front door to snap him out of his gloom. ‘I am most happy to see you this morning Mohammad,’ he said in greeting his second-in-command before going on to relate the previous night’s happenings and morning’s subsequent events. ‘ I am fearful that my recent stupidity will jeopardise all we have planned. Tell me you have good news.’

‘I have indeed Saleem. Be cheered, your minor misfortunes should be forgotten; no harm has befallen any of us as a result of the unfortunate incidents. Allah HAS been kind. I have the uniforms and a gun ! Nothing can now stop us.’

‘Tell me my friend. How did you obtain them ?’

Mohammad laughed. ‘I simply hired the uniforms from a Theatrical hire shop using the same false name and this address. The security company employed by both establishments should have considered how easy it is to copy their guards’ tunics. With a few minor additions and alterations we now have two *Thamesguard Security* uniforms that are virtually indistinguishable from real ones, especially in the dark.'

The uniform problem resolved by Mohammad's resourcefulness lightened Saleem's despondency. ' What about the gun ?' he eagerly enquired.

'I thought about a replica - they're easy to purchase - but decided our whole plan would fail if the gun were to be recognised as not real. The boat skipper must be in no doubt about it if it is necessary for us to force his co-operation. It is unlikely the offer of a large sum of money would suffice once he becomes aware of our intentions and begins to suspect he and his friend will be unfortunate casualties once their usefulness is over. Once we have the other weapons and explosives on board we will all have guns .But, as you yourself explained, they must be forced to take us to the rendezvous or there will be no attack on anything.'

'Yes Mohammad,' agreed Saleem. 'Now I have a radio-control detonator I have another idea that will ensure Mr. Bradley Murray and his mate do not give us any trouble and comply with my orders. So: did you get a genuine weapon ?'

Chapter 4

The big Palestinian laughed again. 'I certainly did. Remarkably simple really, I just visited a certain street in West Ham and let it be known that I wished to purchase some packets of cocaine and would pay top price. Within half an hour I had bought four packets, no questions asked. I then went down by the docks to a seedy transport café that is reputed to be the favourite haunt of drug addicts.' Mohammad paused amused at the perplexed look on his leader's face.

'Ha !, I can see you asking yourself. What have drugs got to do with a gun ? The answer is, with drugs you can get hold of anything you want. It was simple to pick out who were pushers and who were seeking to beg, buy or steal to satisfy their cravings. I approached a group of obvious addicts and simply asked who wanted the cocaine: the price being a handgun in exchange for the drugs. When I returned the following evening I was waylaid ,before entering the café, by a crazy, wide-eyed, specimen of humanity who claimed he had a gun hidden not too far away that he would exchange for the cocaine.'

'Were you not afraid of being attacked and cheated ?' interceded Saleem.

'Naturally. The type of character I was dealing with could never be trusted. I told the addict I had the drugs hidden nearby but would have to see the weapon first to satisfy myself it actually existed and was genuine. He asked me '.....the phone rang interrupting the conversation.

Snatching up the handset the Terrorist leader put the earpiece to his ear but said nothing, listening to the soft female voice enquiring whether he had enjoyed his river trip the previous evening and was it beneficial to his plans ?

He smiled to himself, thinking I must have made a favourable impression: not expecting to hear from Shauna again so soon. Too embarrassed to show the excitement he was feeling in front of Mohammad, he brusquely replied, 'Most certainly,' before falling silent again.

'Have you got someone with you Saleem ? I am reporting your additional requirements have been sanctioned and will be included in your delivery. That is all I have been told to communicate to you but I wondered if we could meet up again next week.? I have a day off on Wednesday,' said Shauna seductively.

Exultant with the good news and apparent personal conquest he, unthoughtfully, replied, ' That is excellent news but no ,Wednesday is an important day I have had ringed on the calendar for some time. I will telephone you back shortly when Mohammad has left,' inadvertently revealing to the *go-between* the name of one of his cell members and that Wednesday was almost certainly the day of his planned attack.

Surprisingly, or possibly thinking Saleem was speaking directly to their Al Qaeda Controller , Mohammad failed to realise his leader had revealed far more than was advisable to his caller.

'That was confirmation the radio controlled detonators and extra armaments will be delivered with our other supplies. Now what was that you were saying before we were so rudely interrupted ?' Saleem light-heartedly enquired : still on a *high* from the call.

'Well, the addict requested I follow him to where he had the gun hidden. It was not far but very dark at the end of a deserted wharf where a derelict broken container served as a shelter. He told me to wait while he disappeared inside and quickly reappeared with a semi-automatic pointed at me.

"Don't fink you can try any tricks mate," he snarled at me " Just get the stuff and get back here quick."

I actually had the packets of drugs in my pocket so produced them and told him I was perfectly willing to honour the deal, drugs for the weapon. Unfortunately, with gun in hand, he thought he could just take the drugs and keep the weapon, hissing at me: " Hand them over here mate and then bugger off before you get hurt."
The gun obviously gave him a sense of bravado as he was a weedy , pasty faced ,character about twenty five years old,' continued the sturdily built Palestinian producing the pistol from his pocket and placing it on the table. 'He thought he was invincible with this.'
'So what happened. How did you persuade him to hand over the weapon ?'
'I told him that I would kill him if he didn't,' explained Mohammad.
If Saleem was shocked at his friends' casual threat he didn't show it, remarking: 'Would you have killed him if he hadn't ?'
'He didn't, so I DID !'
The Terrorist leader was the first to break the ensuing silence. ' Just like that ?' he queried in wonderment. Not at the Hamas's man's ability and willingness to kill for the cause but at the bland statement of fact as though it were an everyday occurrence.

Chapter 4

Mohammad slipped his coat from his shoulders to reveal a bloodstained shirt sleeve, the upper arm material visibly torn displaying a blood-soaked bandage. Seeing the alarm on Saleem's face he quickly explained he was not badly hurt and not harbouring a bullet. The wound was, he made clear, minor ; resulting from his initial lunge at the scruffy individual when he pretended to toss over the drugs.

'I really should have foreseen the possibility of a double-cross seeing the nature of the character I was dealing with,' he said. ' I think he was surprised when the gun went off and I didn't notice my wound until the adrenalin rush subsided as the *vermin* lay at my feet stunned by my attack. I checked the gun and found it empty but there were three more bullets in his anorak pocket.'

'That's good, we only need one for now to prove our seriousness. Are you sure you are still able to carry out our plans ? You know, of course, that you cannot go to hospital.

We have experienced too many unfortunate incidents that could have jeopardised our operation already. A gunshot wound would invite some very awkward questions.'

The Palestinian terrorist assured his leader the wound was not troubling him, a lie he hoped would appease any concern. In fact gone was his earlier euphoria on receiving news of his citizenship, the increasing pain and discomfort of his arm ausing him to question whether, without expert attention, he would be up to the tasks ahead in a few days time.

Saleem appeared to not notice his second-in-command's painful grimace as he embraced him with a relieved smile. 'All is well then my friend. Our day of glory will soon be with us. But what of your drug addict.? Was the gunshot heard ? What did you do with him ? Will his body be discovered ?', the questions bombarded Mohammad.

Careful to mask his wound concerns, he replied off handily to encourage the sense of well-being. 'We have nothing to fear on any matter. I doubt very much that his type will be missed by any of the low-life he hung around with. And, no, the gunshot attracted no attention. I hid in the shadows for ten minutes before returning to the scum who proved to be so untrustworthy. He was still in a comatose condition and put up no resistance when I rolled his body to the edge of the dock and pushed him over. There was barely a splash but his clothing snagged up on a broken timber. I was forced to lower myself into the freezing water, unhook him and push him out into the river. He soon disappeared as the current caught him and dragged him off. Even a conscious swimmer would find it difficult to survive the strong tidal flow. I have no doubt his body will eventually be washed up somewhere but , most likely, his death will be considered an accident or, at worst, death by misadventure.'

'Good. Now I have to telephone the Amin brothers with some final instructions. My Irishman contact left a small package at my Box number address yesterday,' confided Saleem. ' We have the capacity to manufacture a small, radio signal controlled explosive device suitable for the *insurance* needed to ensure Messrs Murray and Swift do not give us any trouble. I will telephone Latif on his mobile and instruct him to carry out the installation before meeting us on Wednesday. We should have no further need for this house after today Mohammad. Start checking we have left nothing to incriminate ourselves while I make the calls. We can then lock up and leave.'

Grateful of the opportunity to leave the room and check on his wound, the Palestinian made

his way to the bathroom and undid the soiled bandage. The inflamed gash suppurated a yellow discharge tinged with blood. Cleaning the skin tissue as best he could with a wetted handkerchief, he then wrapped half a roll of toilet paper around the festering cut to replace the discarded bandage until he could better attend to the wound.
Realising the deeply torn skin had become infected, probably through his immersion in the oily scum topped filthy water around the desolate dock, he vowed to visit his cousin Abu - a qualified Pharmacist - at his Chemist shop in Ilford on his way back home.

While Mohammad was tending to his troubles, Saleem eventually managed to awaken the young Asif from his birthday night's celebrations and instruct him to liaise with his brother for a final task before the main operation itself. Fortunately the instructions were simple, Asif's drink befuddled brain, still happily dwelling on the loss of his virginity, being incapable of thinking of anything else than the previous evening's pleasures. Although Westernised to some degree, his father's strict Islamic teachings had deprived him of the liberal attitudes of his similar aged friends.........until now. Having reached the age of eighteen and got his father to reluctantly agree to his having a party with friends, Asif was soon corrupted by those companions ensuring his glass remained constantly full of the Demon drink throughout the evening. Unused to strong alcohol he quickly became intoxicated: a state his unscrupulous friends soon exploited by approaching a rather brazen plain girl - well known locally as the area's *bicycle* - who used her undoubted shapely body rather than looks to attract a never ending stream of short-lived boyfriends.

The young Birthday Boy suddenly found the girl seated next to him amongst the group, snuggling up closer than any member of the opposite sex had done in the past. Before long she had taken his hand and placed it on an ample breast, whispering in his ear, ' I've got a birthday surprise for you upstairs. Come with me.'

In a drunken stupor the youngster allowed himself to be led to a top floor bedroom where the girl lost no time in undressing him. 'Tut tut, just look at that,' she murmured disapprovingly. 'That's no good to either of us. Let's see what I can do about it then,' she grinned.

Her seductive striptease would undoubtedly have produced the desired effect on any hot-bloodied male but was lost on the inebriated Pakistani teenager who sat on the edge of the bed entranced by the sight of emerging mammaries and dark shadowy inner thighs, as the girl slipped out of her undergarments, but unmoved in his own nether region.

' Oh , you poor dear. You are in a bad way,' she said sympathetically, moving over to the bed and dropping to her knees in front of him. 'I know just what you need.'

Such was the girl's sexual expertise she soon managed to get Asif to a state of semi sobriety and realisation of awakening feelings of indescribable pleasure. For the next hour she patiently instructed and coaxed the inexperienced young man in the techniques of carnal desire and pleasure, satisfying her own needs as the rapidly sobering novice sought to enact the *studs* featured in the top-shelf magazines in the family shop.

The incessant buzzing of the telephone on his bedside table, when Saleem's persistence awoke him, appeared to be continuing in Asif's thumping head as he swung his feet to the floor and staggered into the bathroom. Standing in front of the wash basin he viewed the sorry looking reflection returned by the room's mirror and muttered to himself, 'No *Maiden of Paradise* is going entertain you looking like that Asif. Better make yourself presentable as soon you will have seventy two of them to satisfy your every desire.'

'Are you coming down to see to the shop while I go to the Cash'n Carry ?' shouted his father from the bottom of the stairs. 'Your mother can't see to everything herself.'

The angry interruption to his lecherous thoughts snapped him out of his reverie and focussed his mind on how he was going to *escape* from his parents and shop work on Wednesday. His father, for certain, would want him around until the shop closed at seven o'clock in the evening. And then his mother would not let him go out without his evening meal, leaving just enough time to reach the rendezvous with the rest of the 'Cell'. But, Saleem had just instructed him to help Latif on Wednesday and, what would they do when they found he had not slept in his bed and was missing on Thursday morning ?

'Coming right down !' he called out while splashing cold water into his face and smoothing back his hair. The icy cold wash lessened the thunder of the drummer playing in his head as he descended to the shop to be met with his scowling father demanding, 'Who was that on the telephone. I didn't recognise the voice ?'

That's the answer thought Asif, replying, ' It was a Television Producer I met at the Mosque. He wants me to play a part in a documentary film he is making about the events in Birmingham a few months ago but it means going up to London for a couple of days.'

'You must go of course. What part are you playing ?' said his mother excited at the thought of HER son appearing on Television.

Having started the lie he elaborated; inventing a character of, "Jamil". He bravely fought off three thugs when they tried to set fire to his car during the street violence. He doesn't wish to take part in the film himself as he lives near to the scene of the disturbance and doesn't want to be recognised. I may even have to say a few words.'

The delight on his mother's face and softening of his father's scowl encouraged the young would-be terrorist to quickly add, ' I would be away Wednesday and Thursday: how can I accept the part ?'

'We can manage for a few days .I assume you will be well paid of course ?' snapped his father.

Chapter 4

'Now help your mother top up the shelves and watch out for those thieving youngsters while I'm away.'

Grateful to see his father drive off and thereby avoid further questioning, Asif busied himself around the shop for a while until he excused himself on the pretext of visiting the kitchen to take a couple of Aspirin for his headache.

Away from his mother's vision he telephoned his brother as ordered. ' Latif, it is Asif.

Saleem said I should contact you in case you need my assistance on Wednesday. What have you to do ?'

'Do not concern yourself my brother. I need no help other than for you to collect a package from Saleem and deliver it to me before Wednesday afternoon. You will find the parcel hidden beneath an upturned dinghy chained to the sea wall next to the Yacht club slipway at Thorpe Bay. Saleem has just phoned to say he will ensure it is there tomorrow evening after dark.'

'I know the place. I will collect it and bring it to you straight away,' said Asif eagerly.

'That will not be possible. I will not be here,' stated his elder brother. ' The recent gales have brought down many telephone lines. We are all on emergency repairs for the next forty eight hours which is why I need you to collect the package for me.'

The young terrorist interceded with the inevitable questions. ' What is in the parcel Latif ? And when should I deliver it then ?'

' You must be very careful Asif. The package contains explosive material and you must hide it until Wednesday when I will meet with you at Waterside Farm car park on Canvey Island; two o'clock. I have a job to do for Saleem on the Island.'

'I will be there without fail.'

'Make sure you are not seen and tell no one of our meeting,' ordered the elder terrorist on severing the connection.

Mohammad pulled the door closed, checked it's security and, satisfied, left the *safe house* shortly after his leader had departed, confident that the premises were *clean*. The pain in his arm had dulled to a modest ache but he noticed a stain appearing through the sleeve material, indicating continuing blood seepage. A glance at his watch alarmed him as he realised that, by the time he had dropped off the house keys to the agent, there would be hardly sufficient time to get to his pharmacist cousin's shop before he closed. He suddenly realised if he found the shop locked up he had no idea of exactly where his cousin lived….and he really did need some professional medical assistance if he was to be fully fit for the challenges to be faced in a couple of days time.

Saleem had driven off in high spirits, having finalised plans and seemingly still *invisible* to the Authorities despite the mistakes they had all made. Mohammad's mood was less cheerful, the earlier euphoria of his good news having evaporated with the realisation that his injured arm would prove to be a personal handicap and an operational disadvantage; recognised when he unthinkingly used his right hand to open his car door. A sharp pain shot through his upper arm muscle causing a feeling of nausea . He gratefully slumped down into the driver's seat. It's almost as though Allah is teasing me, he thought pensively. I become a full British citizen just as I plan to strike against the Country's commerce and infrastructure. And, having obtained - or at least will shortly have obtained - the necessary means, I am most likely unable to play my full part in the attacks.

The following morning agent Jefferies was also in pain: his ultra full bladder threatening to explode if forced to endure containment for much longer.

' Where the bloody hell's that postie got to ?' he asked himself fidgeting uncomfortably in the less than generous seat of his small sports car parked a few yards from the post box. ' I've got to go before I wet myself,' he gasped emerging from the vehicle and dashing into the garden and around the side of the nearest house.

His relief was two fold as he strode back out to the pavement and spotted an approaching mail van, the alleviation tempered by the sight of a Traffic Warden standing by his car eyeing the number plate and writing on a pad.

'Hang on there mate I'm on Government business,' he called out as the postal vehicle drew up and the driver jumped out.

'That's a new one,' sneered the Warden. 'Usually when someone's on double yellows it's................' He never finished the excuse, stumbling over the bonnet as the Agent pushed him aside to grasp the postal worker on the shoulder as he opened the box.

'I need that mail, friend,' he said forcefully as the alarmed mailman turned to face his assumed attacker.

The heavy set postman appeared to be about to launch his own attack on the smaller built Agent but stemmed his advance when Jefferies shouted out, ‘ Hold it. I’m M.I.5.’

‘Yeah, and I’m James Bond,’ said a scornful voice from behind as the Warden scrambled to his feet. ‘ And you are in serious trouble friend. Molesting a Council Official is an offence to add to your illegal parking.’

‘Don’t be a bloody fool man. I’m sorry I pushed you out of the way but this is National Security business. I really am who I say,’ responded Jefferies. ‘ Here’s my Identification. Now be a good fellow and clear off before I have you arrested.’

The Warden slunk off in a huff, mumbling under his breath something about ‘We’ll see who gets arrested.’

‘Let’s see that I.D. How do I know that’s genuine ?’ enquired the confused mailman.

Empathizing with the man’s predicament, the Agent took his mobile telephone out of his pocket and punched in a short number. The response was immediate, a voice snapping, ‘Beaman: you got it Peter?’

'Well not exactly Sir. The postman would like some confirmation of my identity before handing over any of the Queen's Mail. Can you assist Sir ?'

'Give me five minutes but whatever you do don't let those letters out of your sight.'

In less than the requested time, Jefferies' phone buzzed. ' Stay where you are ,someone will be with you shortly,' ordered the Commander.

'Oh no !' groaned the Agent as the Traffic Warden reappeared accompanied by a police constable. Adding, in an irreverent comment about his superior, ' Jimmy boy will be livid if this idiot creates a problem.'

There was to be no problem. A scream of tortured tyres heralded the arrival from around rthe corner of a black, unmarked, Ford Mondeo sporting a flashing blue lamp on it's roof. Screeching to a halt two inches from the rear bumper of Jefferies sports car, the passenger door flew open to disgorge a high ranking Police Officer who was soon joined by the grinning driver.

'The cavalry's arrived Pete. You've met Superintendent Kimpton from the Met,' said driver, fellow M.I. 5 agent Charlie Walsh, as the Chief

Police Officer strode past him to confront the Traffic Warden and constable.

Within the space of a few minutes the Warden was ushered into the Mondeo, the constable continued on his beat and the mailman got back into his van and followed Jefferies car to Trafalgar House. Five minutes after reaching Commander Beaman's office the matter was resolved: the post office worker being sworn to secrecy under threat of imprisonment if he discussed the early morning's events with anyone other than his Superior who had already been made aware of the importance of avoiding any chance of the post box fracas getting back to the London Al Qaeda leader.

'I'm afraid we are going to have to detain the Traffic Warden for a few days. Superintendent Kimpton is not at all happy with the man's belligerent attitude,' the Commander told Jefferies. ' We cannot take any chances. Something big is being planned and time is not on our side. Fortunately, the woman in the house you visited is quite deaf and neither heard nor saw anything. And, luckily, the few passers by appear to have dismissed the incident, no reports having been notified. Have you managed to sort anything out from the letters ?'

' There were twenty three letters in the box Sir. Fourteen of them are Company mail, easily identified by the name on the envelopes. Three are utility bills and two are obvious Birthday , or similar, cards, leaving just four possible. The back room boys have them already and promise to report soon.'

'None to a foreign address then ?'

''Fraid not Sir. Shall I return the other letters ?'

'As soon as the boffins have identified Hassam's one,' responded Commander Beaman. 'Check whether Sam's in the building will you ? We should have a conference after I've seen the Director General . And you had better chase up the letter, it could be our best lead yet.'

Jefferies found himself very busy for the next hour, first visiting the general office where he found Sam scanning computer photographs of suspected Terrorists. 'Any joy with the mug shots ?'he enquired receiving a shake of the head in reply. 'Charlie Walsh's long range effort not much help then ?'

'It's been enhanced but we know he's in disguise. There doesn't seem to be anyone in our files to match; even without the spectacles and a different hair style,' said Sam. 'I'll have to call the artist in, see if he can do anything from my description. Has the Commander discovered anything from the telephone number I passed on ?'

'Yes, it's the number of a house next to the River Crouch at Hullbridge in Essex, belonging to .....wait for it: Dean Bright, lead singer of *The Sparklers*. They're on tour promoting their new release " Try it sometime", so it's obvious someone else is in there. The boss has sent a couple of the lads to take a peek and make some discreet enquiries. It's the best lead we have at the moment.'

'I'm not as useless as you all think then am I ?' grinned Sam.

'You know me. I've always said you're good for one thing,' retorted Jefferies cryptically as he exited the office to see if the downstairs back-room staff had identified Hassam's letter.

Mohammad was struggling to write a letter to his mother and sister, both manually due to his painfully inflamed arm and, verbally as it was what amounted to a suicide note.

Having found his cousin's pharmacy closed the previous afternoon, he stopped on the way back to his house at a twenty four hour opening Su-

permarket and purchased some bandages, antiseptic and painkillers. Fearful of trusting any of his near neighbours, he sought no assistance in redressing his wound, wincing at the removal of the firmly adhered toilet paper wrapping. By the time he finished bandaging his arm he was sweating profusely and staggered as he got to his feet to get some water to wash down the strong pills; taking four in one swallow before slumping back onto his settee.
He was uncertain, when he awoke, as to whether he had passed out or simply fallen asleep. What was certain was that it was daylight: he was cold , hungry with a mouth like the bottom of a parrot's cage, and his arm throbbed. He was surprised to see it was close to eleven o'clock; no wonder he was famished. A few slices of toast and a strong coffee improved his well-being sufficiently enough to focus his mind on the dilemma he now
faced. There was no way he could swim with his arm the way it was and he would be of little use lifting heavy boxes, two of the tasks he was to have carried out once their attack had been started.
'I should inform Saleem. I can take Lasif's place and he mine,' he said disconsolately and

risking his leader's wrath by disobeying his orders not to be contacted at Getaway Travel. ' But first I must say goodbye to my family. They must know that I am going to a better place and that my sacrifice is for the good of all Islamic people.'
By the time he finished compiling the letter, amounting to a three page plea for forgiveness, it was well after one o'clock.

'Is that clock right ?,' queried Jefferies , not expecting an answer and not getting one. 'No wonder I'm hungry; bloody lunchtime. See if you can come up with any answers for the old man while I pop out for a sandwich will you Prof ? Got to see him at two thirty.'
The scientist looked up with disdain as the Agent raced out of the room. 'Supercilious bastard,' he muttered to his female assistant, unaware of how incorrect he was and of the high esteem with which Jefferies was held amongst his fellow spies.
'Sir.' said the girl. 'None of these four letters are the one you are looking for. I have prints from three of them and none match those that Sam obtained for us. But, I tried the two with cards inside and this is almost definitely the

one,' she added placing a pale blue envelope on the desk. ' There are NO prints on this one. Somebody wore gloves when handling it !'

'Well done girl,' exclaimed the Professor. ' That'll wipe the smile off that young whipper-snapper's face. Let's see what's inside shall we ?'

Carefully slitting open the envelope ,the scientist withdrew the card, avoiding as much finger contact as possible. Lifting it open with the edge of the paper knife his brow creased with confusion at the message inside.

Good luck with your Canadian sea voyage. The buoys will be glad to see you on schedule.

Turning the card over on to it's front revealed a drawing of a ship with a large **Bon Voyage** title.

'Someone can't spell correctly,' said the young assistant. ' Look at the way they've spelt boys ?'

'Hmm, where was this addressed to ?' he queried, at much to himself as the girl.

'That's a peculiar thing,' she replied. ' It's to a Mr. S. Hunter in Hullbridge, Essex.'

Mohammad propped the finished letter up against his wife's photograph on the sideboard together with the brief note addressed to her, confident that she would forward the correspondence on to his mother. Staring at the photograph he had an overwhelming desire to pick up the telephone and call her, nostalgia for his family and homeland bestirring thoughts of happier, care-free, days from childhood through to courtship and marriage. It was ordained that Alena and himself spend their lives together; the marriage being arranged between their families before the young Palestinian girl even became a teenager. It was a strange, thought Mohammad, in comparison to Western practices. He barely knew Alena before their marriage but courted the shy youngster subsequently until a sincere love blossomed between them. If there was one thing, he mused, that he regretted about his soon to be departure from this world, it was that Alena had not borne him an heir.

Although he already knew she would be with her father until the end of the week, he picked up the phone and dialled a Manchester number, anxious to hear her voice once more before his ultimate sacrifice.

Careful that neither his tone of voice, nor anything said, betrayed what he was about to do, he; nevertheless, unwittingly created a sense of unease in Alena.

'You sound very unhappy Mohammad. Are you alright ?'
'I'm missing you my wife. I will not be here when you return as I am going away with Saleem. I just wanted to tell you I love you.'
Alena knew better than to pursue the matter, responding only to reciprocate her love before Mohammad severed the connection.

Startled as the telephone on his desk buzzed loudly: just as he finished wrapping up the small explosive device boxed in an empty butter tub, Saleem dropped the package in alarm, mistaking the sound for that of his door buzzer.
Sighing with relief on realisation it was his telephone, he snatched the handset from it's cradle and barked, ' Sally, I told you I would be busy for fifteen minutes.'
'I'm sorry Mr. Hunter,' said his assistant apologetically. 'It's just that I have a gentleman on the line who won't give his name but says it is urgent he speak to you personally.'
His curiosity aroused, he told the girl to put the call through, receiving a second shock on instantly recognising the whispered voice of his second in command.

Chapter 4

'I'm so sorry for contacting you at work. Is it alright to speak ?'

Recovering his composure, Saleem quietly replied, ' Yes my friend. What is it that is so urgent it couldn't wait until we meet up on Wednesday ? For you to risk contacting me here it must be important.'

'I have let you down Saleem. My wound is not so minor and has become infected. I feel so weak I know I will not be able to make the swim or help very much with any heavy lifting.'

The Terrorist leader's mind was in a turmoil. Could anything else go wrong ? Why had he not considered the possibility of losing a member of the team before their attacks were launched. Could they just collect the arms and explosives for now and delay the actual operation until Mohammad was fit again ?

Assuming the lack of a response to his revelation was due entirely to the surprise of the news, the big Palestinian continued; ' Latif is a good swimmer. If I look after our captive crew - I can still handle a gun - he could replace me for that part of the plan. We are about the same size so the wetsuit should be okay and yourself or Asif could crew the dinghy.'

'Can you be certain you will be well enough to take any part in our attacks ?' queried a concerned Saleem. ' There is far too much explosive to consider hiding it. Once we have it on board the boat we cannot delay matters. You are aware of how important our timing is to achieve maximum destruction and casualties.'

'I am going to see my Cousin shortly to have the wound properly dressed and collect some antibiotics. I am sure I will be able to manage my other tasks successfully.'

'We have come so far together Mohammad. May Allah give you the strength you need to finish what we have started and take your rightful place in our fight for Islam. Now go and visit your Cousin, our day will soon be with us.'

On replacing the receiver Mohammad sat staring at the telephone, briefly contemplating recalling his leader to tell him that he had lied and such was the pain and stiffness of his arm there was no way he would be able to handle a sniper's rifle or rocket launcher. I should have said that I will show Latif how to fire the rockets and that I will take his place for the suicide bombing. But, no, he thought: better that Saleem thinks all will be well and not consider any scaling down of the operation due to the incapacity of his *right hand man.*

Staring out of his window at the darkening clouds quickly scudding over the towering blocks on the other side of the river while awaiting the arrival of his Agents, Commander James Beaman's mood matched the gathering storm.

Normally staid but tinged with a touch of humour, the M.I.5 chief was as sombre as any of his staff could remember for a long time when they filed into the room, the usual quips of " be late for your own funeral,"or " sorry to have interrupted your afternoon nap," being silenced by the presence of the Director General herself.

' Close the door will you Davison ?, said the Commander soberly. ' You all know the Director so we'll waste no time in getting to the nitty gritty of why we're here this afternoon. I need an update from everyone on this Terrorist threat you are all working on. You may have noticed Richard Meade is missing. We've got an address for that telephone number Sam came up with, Meade's on his way there now to check it out. In fact, he's probably arrived so I should hear from him soon.'

Looking round at his Agents, the Commander continued. ' I've brought the Director up to date on how we know, thanks in part to our German counterparts, that a Terrorist Cell operating in the Home Counties and London is preparing to launch a major strike in the very near future. Unfortunately, despite our best efforts, we still have very little intelligence to identify any of the targets or the persons involved.'

'Do you have any idea when the Terrorists intend to strike Commander ?' asked the Director General calmly.

'We know it's pretty imminent ,' replied the Chief. 'But, unless anyone has any further information for us this afternoon we are as much in the dark about the day as we are about the targets. We do know the name of the leader of the Cell, and have a description of the man known as Saleem, but he only came to our attention late in the day and we were, unfortunately, unable to arrange for him to be tracked. The name Mohammad has also been mentioned but in neither case do we have a surname unless any of you can tell me otherwise.'

As the Commander's immediate deputy, Jefferies elected to speak out first. ' We know Saleem comes from the Southend-on-Sea area and that he has plans for Wednesday. But that's about all on that line of enquiry. The Prof.... oh , sorry Maam, Professor Woodhouse and his assistant Kate eventually managed to identify the letter posted by Hassam.......',

'Hassam being the London Al Qaeda Commander we've had under observation for some time ?' interjected the Director General.

'Yes Maam,' continued the Agent unfazed by the interruption. ' It wasn't actually a letter at all, simply a **Bon Voyage** card. But, ' he grinned like the cat who got the cream,

'it was addressed to the house where the Commander has just sent Richard !'

'What !' snapped Beaman. 'Why wasn't I informed immediately ?'

'I only found out myself on the way up here Sir. It was only when they were unable to link any of the letters to Hassam that Kate tested the cards and discovered one devoid of any fingerprints; a real giveaway of someone being extremely cautious.'

'So now we know Saleem's surname then ?'

The Commander's grey telephone beeped shrilly before Jefferies could respond.

'That you, Meade, what's the situation ?'

The *hmmms* , *too bad, how long* and *stay there Andy Davison will join you* comments of the Commander to the unheard voice on the end of the telephone gave the listening Agents few clues as to the results of Agent Meade's investigations at the suspect house.

Replacing the receiver, Beaman stood silent for a few moments thinking before informing his hushed audience. ' It seems we may have just missed Saleem and friends. The birds appear to have flown the nest according to Meade.'

'Is that certain Commander ?' queried the D G seated uncomfortably on the corner of Agent Kathy Doyle's desk watching the buildings across the river light up successively as darkness descended: promoted by thunderous black storm clouds.

'We won't know conclusively until we get people in there but according to Meade the place is in darkness and securely locked. There is, apparently, no sign of any activity and the only person he has seen in the vicinity is an old chap walking his dog.'

'I'm to go down there myself am I Sir ?' enquired Davison looking less than enthusiastic as the first heavy raindrops peppered the window.

Chapter 4

The Commander thought for a moment and walked over to the Director General, whispering something quietly to her before answering the Agent's question. ' Yes, but don't go yet until we've finished here.'

A *Crazy Frog* mobile phone ring tone suddenly cut through the tense atmosphere in the room, causing a ripple of subdued laughter as an embarrassed Charlie Walsh feverishly searched his pockets for the offending instrument.

With a slight smile on her face the D G took advantage of the interruption to whisper something back to the Commander before standing and apologising to the gathering.

'I'm sorry but I have to leave. I have a prior arrangement with The Minister. I'm sure our Country's security could not be in better hands. I wish you good luck in your hunt and pray you are successful. You have my unqualified backing for any actions Commander Beaman deems necessary to thwart this threat.'

So saying she strode out of the room to a round of applause from the Agents.

'Come in,' said Saleem pleasantly in answer to the door buzzer.

Sally Travell entered his office with a tray of tea and biscuits. ' Thought you might like a cup of tea if you're staying on Mr.Hunter. Is that package to be posted ? I'm off in a minute with the rest of the post.'

'Thank you Sally but no, it's a present for my young nephew, ' he replied; adding, on noticing her gaze fall on the small transmitter sitting on his desk, 'One of those clever robotic cars. Should have wrapped the control unit up with it.'

'Would you like me to do it for you ? Won't take me a few minutes.'Rather than invite curiosity by refusing, Saleem conceded to the suggestion, thinking, 'it won't make any difference I can soon unwrap it once on board the *Whaleback Swift.*'

Back in the outer office Sally started to parcel up the transmitter, noticing the abnormal design of the unit. Unlike any of the ones she had previously seen with their small joystick control or directional push buttons, this model was much heavier with a simple lever switch and single push button.

'What have you got there Sally ?' enquired the Agency Manager.

Chapter 4

'It's a control box for a toy car Mr. Hunter has got for his nephew on his desk. I'm just parcelling it up for him. Very unusual it is.'

Peter Western walked over and picked the transmitter up, curiously moving the switch to the on position. The push button immediately illuminated . ' I wonder what will happen if I push this ?' he said with an impish grin on his face and finger hovering over the button.

'The car is already packaged up. Push that and you'll probably **kill him** !' joked Sally making a grab for the unit. ' When the parcel suddenly shoots across his desk it will give him a heart attack .'

'Put that down NOW Peter !' ordered Saleem sternly from his office doorway. ' Press that button and we'll all be dead.'

The Manager immediately deposited the transmitter back on the desk top and stepped back with a look of horror on his face.

'Ha ha,' laughed Saleem nervously. ' You should see your face Peter. I only meant my nephew will kill us all if we break his toy. He's been after it for ages and wrapped as it is I would think any attempt to operate it would certainly damage the internal circuits.'

'Sorry Mr. Hunter ,' apologised Sally. 'It was my fault I sh.......' 'No, no,' interrupted her employer. 'I could just as easily have wrapped it up at home. Serves me right for keeping you from getting away. I've probably caused you to miss your bus. Leave it now. Just you get off.'

Recovered from his fright, Peter volunteered, ' I'll take her home boss. It's the least I can do; my stupid playing about.'

'No harm done Peter. Don't worry about it,' said the relieved Terrorist. ' I'll lock up. See you in the morning. I'll be in tomorrow but then I'm away for a couple of days.'

As the door closed behind his departing staff, Saleem slumped in the nearest chair and mopped his brow while staring at the venomous, blinking, green eye of the transmitter.

He cursed himself. 'Why did I leave the battery in ? If Peter had pressed that button it would have been disastrous.' Not, he realised, that there would have been any chance of the *mini bomb* on his desk exploding but, it would have set off the detonator still in his briefcase, the resulting minor explosion inviting unanswerable questions and, possibly, a visit from the police and fire department. Snapping out of his self incrimination he rose, switched off the offending unit, picked up the explosive package, and locked up. Running to his car as the first heavy spots of rain began to fall, heralding a miserable night ahead, he set off to deposit the bomb at the rendezvous arranged with Latif.

Forty miles away, Commander Beaman was arranging a rendezvous of his own - for four o'clock in the morning! Following the Director General's exit from the conference meeting he uncovered the room's large "Operations Board" and directed the Agents to contribute all they had discovered about the Terrorist plot to the facts already written on the illuminated display.

'I'll run through what we've got so far and then we'll see what we can add,' he said with his back to his staff as he penned up the latest information.' We know a Terrorist Cell is about to carry out a strike but we have no idea how many persons are involved. We know the leader only as Saleem: unless Jefferies has a surname for us from the letter.

We think another member of the Cell is Mohammad whatever; again no surname.

We know, or certainly suspect, Saleem resides in the Southend-on-Sea area.

We know he has recently taken a boat trip up to London; reason unknown. We know he is expecting a delivery of armaments. He recently requested extra via his London based Al Qaeda chief who we have had under observation ever since our tip-off. We have no positive identification of him, an artist's impression being the best we can offer at present. We now have an address in Essex that the cell are using: at this time uncertain as to whether it is the base for their operations. We do not know how, where or when their requested bomb-making equipment is to be delivered, or collected. We have no idea of their target or targets. In other words we have almost **Bugger All** to go on unless any of you have got something useful to add Peter, you were about to tell us the surname of Saleem . Let's start by putting that up.'

'Well Sir, we still don't know. The card in question was addressed to a Mr. S. Hunter, not Saleem anybody .'

'Great,' sighed the exasperated Commander. ' Now we have another complication. Who the hell is he ?'

'The best answer we can come up with is that it's either another member of the Cell or, more likely- given the very English name- an alias for whoever is renting the house in Hullbridge. Which, in case anyone doesn't know, belongs to Dean Bright.'

'We should be able to find out who is renting the property tomorrow morning, it's bound to be through a local Estate Agent,' piped up Agent Doyle.

Commander Beaman added the name of S. Hunter to the board, turning round to utter, 'If Meade confirms the house is still occupied we won't wait for tomorrow morning we'll mount a raid later tonight.'

'Excuse me Sir I've been thinking,' said Sam. 'It's obvious we are running out of time and, apart from Sabaa,….sorry, most of you know him as Hassam, we have no idea where any of the Terrorists are. Would now not be a good time to arrest and question him? He surely knows the target even if he doesn't know all the Cell members. If we can get him to reveal the target we may be able to stop the operation and save lives.'

'We already have the Director General's approval to bring Hassam in if necessary but we will wait until we've had a chance to have a good look at Bright's house. There may well be information to be had once we're inside. Until we know what the target is we don't want to alarm the Terrorists and let them know we're on to them.'

'The other thing I was contemplating,' continued Sam, 'Is Southend seems an unlikely place to attack. There's not much there to attract suicide bombers. The town's only claim to fame seems to be its pier and even that keeps catching on fire. I can't imagine anyone wasting themselves, or explosives, on it. The usual plan is to maximise the number of casualties and even blowing a big hole in it is not likely to kill more than a few people. We know the Cell leader lives in the area but that's the only thing we have to connect us to Southend : other than he took a boat trip from there up river to the Pool of London on an obvious scouting expedition past such prime targets as Canary Wharf. Perhaps we're allowing ourselves to be misled.'

The M.I.5 Commander walked over to the coffee machine and poured himself a cup before replying. 'Are you saying you think the attack, when it comes, is not going to be by individual suicide bombers but an attack by an explosive laden boat ?'

'Well Sir,' interjected Jefferies. ' If the obscure wording in the Bon Voyage card is a coded message there does appear to be some sort of nautical basis to this operation and it does mention *Can*adian sea voyage. I can't help wondering about the word Canadian. Why not just Good Luck on your voyage? And why send a card at all if, as Richard Meade seems to think, the occupants of the Hullbridge house have already departed ?'

The high pitched ring tone of the Commander's telephone again stilled the Agent's murmurings as he seized the handset. 'What's the latest ?' he prompted.

Quiet as the room was, the listening Agents were unable to glean anything from the brief exchange. Even when their Chief replaced the receiver he quietly paced back and forth for a few moments before enlightening them. ' Meade reports the house has definitely been deserted. When it was fully dark he reconnoitred the premises and found a rear window slightly ajar so was able to make an unforced entry. The place had been thoroughly cleaned. So, in the idiom of Jefferies thoughts, *We're up the creek without a paddle.*

Take a ten minute break ladies and gentlemen. I want to think.'

'Just taking a short break father. I promised Jamil down the road a loan of a couple of DVD's,' lied Asif.

'Don't you be too long you hear. It will be closing time soon. You will have to check the shelves while your mother gets a meal,' grumbled the elder shop owner.

Asif pulled his tracksuit hood over his head against the wind and now heavy rain before trotting the few hundred yards from shop to seafront. It was, as he expected, deserted of pedestrians and although the occasional car sped past he was confident nobody took any particular notice of his jog along to Thorpe Bay.

'Bloody nutter,' called one belligerent youth from a car load of youngsters speeding past towards an evening out in Southend as he was about to cross the road. With the next nearest vehicle well in the distance, he raced across the road, over the sea wall and dropped down on the stones next to an upturned dinghy. Lifting one side, his hand immediately fell on a small package which he withdrew and carefully slid into his tracksuit pocket. Ten minutes later he was back in the shop.

'You're soaked,' said his Mother. ' Go and get changed before you catch a pneumonia. Your cousin caught it and developed complications. Three days later he was dead !'

In three days time I too will be dead thought Asif….but not through pneumonia.

'This is what we will do,' Commander Beaman began on his return. 'Davison, you get off and relieve Meade. We need to keep an eye on the house all night in case anyone returns. If nobody does we'll go in tomorrow morning with the forensic experts. Sam, I want you to go to Southend tomorrow. Take the artist's drawing of Saleem with you and see if you can find anyone who can identify him. I hear Leigh-on-Sea is the centre of the boating community in the area. I suggest a few enquiries there might be worthwhile. The rest of you can go home and get a few hours sleep. We will be raiding Hassam's house early in the morning at four o'clock. Get back here for three thirty to collect your weapons. Hold on a minute Sam before you go. I want you to liaise with Peter on your movements tomorrow. Have a quick chat.'

A few moments later the Commander and Agent Jefferies looked wistfully at the attractive departing figure of Agent Samirah Ahmad.

5

Brad switched on the VHS transmitter receiver and twiddled the controls to tune in to the shipping forecast before securing the *Whaleback* and motoring ashore in the tender.
Despite the film Director's assurances of putting to sea come what may, he was concerned that, if earlier forecasts were correct, Wednesday and Thursday were going to be very uncomfortable conditions afloat. His angling party were all seasoned sailors and he could always find them some fish within the comparatively sheltered waters of the River Crouch. But, a force six to eight south westerly gale would undoubtedly prove to be a gut-wrenching, sickening experience for *landlubbers*. It was unlikely, he thought, that all the film crew would be able to stomach such conditions. If the forecast turned out to be correct he would, he decided, do his best to convince Hunter Stevens it would be

folly not to postpone their intended filming sequences. It surely couldn't be that important that a few days delay would make any difference?

" ....Humber and Thames: Southerly force four, veering South Westerly occasional force five: later force six."

'Mmm,' murmured the skipper thoughtfully before retuning the VHS set to the Port of London Authority's Vessel Traffic Service at Gravesend; from which any request for Pilot transfer assistance would originate should the usual excellent Estuary Service require an additional craft. Not that skipper Murray needed the occasional supplement to his income from fishing parties and other charters; being self-sufficient with both his parents and grandfather's inheritances. In fact, some wise investments in property produced a steady annual return more than adequate for his needs - without his marine activities fees.

Swifty met his skipper as he roped the small dinghy to the Wallasea pontoon; having taken him out to the launch at their Hole Haven mooring earlier in the morning for Brad to take the vessel round into the River Crouch for the next day's angling party. Returning ashore, the crewman had walked the few hundred yards to his home past the Calor Liquefied Petroleum Gas Terminal to where Brad's year old Mercedes S class sport was parked; without giving a thought to the dangers of living on top of a potential *firebomb.*

He was, however, reminded of the risks when reading the previous evening's newspaper as he enjoyed a cup of tea before taking Nancy shopping : then going out to pick up his ex naval employer.

' Did you read that bit about Calor's proposed increase in the number of storage tanks?' enquired his wife. ' The eight they've already got could incinerate the whole of the Island if they went up. This is a nice property but I sometimes wish we could move well away from here, especially for Naomi's benefit.'

'So do I sweetheart but we'd need to win the lottery or pools for that to happen .'

'Not much chance of our doing that then,' responded Nancy.

'Why do you say that ? What's wrong with our money ; someone has got to win ?'

'Yes,' Nancy burst out laughing. 'But, don't we have to buy a ticket ? You gave up two weeks after the Lottery started when you didn't win . Come on, take me up to the shops in that nice car of Brad's.'

The Mercedes drew up in the Marina car park just as Brad tied up the *Whaleback's* dinghy to the pontoon walkway and stepped ashore.

'How's that for timing?' called out Swifty. ' I'd have been here sooner if I hadn't had to drive past Snooty Henderson's place three times before he saw me in this flash motor.'

' In that case you'd better get back in the driving seat in case we pass him on the way back. Take me home James,' said Brad matching his crewman's light hearted banter.

During the journey back to Canvey Island the pair discussed the weather forecast for the rest of the week; and the Film Director's insistence that there be no postponement of their charter.

'There's something nagging at the back of my mind about this job,' said Swifty with a solemnity that his Skipper would not normally associate with his comedian friend. ' What sort of filming are they doing in pitch blackness ? And, I don't buy the excuse of "client confidentiality". Why can't we know exactly where we are taking them ?'

The same questions had been going through Brad's mind for the past couple of days.' I toyed with the idea of cancelling the charter,' remarked the Skipper. ' But, as I told you before; any additional bookings we get over and above our normal work will, after expenses, be equally split between us. I reckon you're in for a bonus of nearly fourteen hundred pounds: I didn't feel you would like to forego that,' he grinned.

'Put like that, I'd take them all the way to Rotterdam if they want,' responded the crewman already thinking of what a handsome addition to his new house fund the extra money would make.

'Three thousand !' said Saleem counting out aloud the notes taken from the hidden safe at the back of a wardrobe in his bedroom. He had , at one time, thought of not paying over the agreed fee; or even of bundling up paper cut to size with just a few twenty pound notes on the outside, but had decided enough had gone wrong already. 'Can't risk any sort of confrontation with Messrs Murray and Swift before we even get off,' he had said to Mohammad. ' We don't want to produce your gun until we have to; and certainly not until we're well under way. After all, it's not as though they will be keeping it for where they're going,' he laughed ominously. Putting the bundled notes into a briefcase with the small transmitter that had almost been catastrophically used, he locked the clasps and took the case down to his car which he had earlier driven out of the garage onto the forecourt. He went back inside the house and returned with a large holdall. As expected, his next door neighbour appeared on cue.

'Off on your travels again Steve ? Not going anywhere near the Middle East I hope? There's hardly a day goes by now without somewhere out there being bombed by those
brain-washed suicide fanatics.'

'Just off to Canada for a few days. I expect to be back on Friday,' he replied jumping into the car and driving off with a wave. *Fanatics: brain-washed* ,what do such middle-class crass idiots, safe in their own cosy world, know of the ambitions of his oppressed people, he thought as he drove towards his Travel Agency. Doesn't he realise this is a war? Still now, if the police or anyone else enquire about his absence, Mr. Nosey Parker neighbour will undoubtedly falsely enlighten them.

Thinking about the money in the case on the seat next to him, he hoped Hassam had included a " refund" in the armaments delivery in case it was not recovered from his intended victims. I could ask him when he confirms the delivery is on time. I should have had confirmation by now, he thought apprehensively. I will have to phone from the Motel shortly before going into the office.

Ten minutes later he booked a room for the night under a false name and using a fictitious northern address plucked from a Bed and Breakfast Handbook before leaving home. The Motel ,just north of Southend, was barely twenty minutes by car from his house. However, mindful of the mistakes he had made and concerned in case his deceit at the Police station was discovered, he had decided to not return to his home that evening; avoiding any possibility of further problems before commencement of the operation.

Still no contact from Hassam, unless, he suddenly realised, he had been trying to get in touch at the rented Hullbridge house. He gave a few minutes serious thought about any potential danger in using the Motel phone and decided there was none.

I must have misdialled, he thought when his attempt to ring the London controller was met with a number unattainable continuous tone. When second and third redials produced the same result he was tempted to try for a connection via the operator but, somewhat concerned by a feeling of trepidation, decided instead to try later; possibly even via Shauna. He picked up the phone again and dialled his Agency office. 'I'll be a little later than I thought,' he told Sally when she answered his call. 'I have to pop over to a friend at Rayleigh,' he lied; the true intention being to return to the Hullbridge house and check Mohammad left no traces of their recent habitation......a visit prompted by the sense of unease he was feeling and the discovery of a spare key he still had in his pocket.

Commander Beaman , having returned from hospital following a minor operation involving the removal of a few shards of glass and dressing the wound, stood in the wreckage of Hassam's house. All but destroyed by an explosion a few hours earlier during the dawn raid, the smouldering precarious remaining structure resembled that of a second world war blitz bombing.

'You shouldn't be here Sir. This lot could come down any minute,' said Agent Jefferies in genuine concern. 'The forensic boys will be in there as soon as the Fire Brigade lads say it's safe. There's nothing you can do here; best go and get a few hours shut-eye. If we're right about tomorrow being the day of their attack we're all going to get very little sleep tonight.'

'What went wrong Peter ? How could he have known we were coming for him ?'

'Perhaps he didn't Sir, but was prepared for the eventuality. I'll have a word with the boys in blue to keep everyone away until our lads have finished. The next door neighbour is already complaining that he needs to get back into his house but the Fire Chief certainly won't allow that ; even if we did.'

'I'll see you back at headquarters Peter. I fear this fiasco may have scuppered our chances of getting this lot before they can do any damage.'

'Are you sure you are alright Sir ? That's quite a limp you've got there.'

'Don't worry about me. Take a look in the mirror when you can: you look like a refugee from the Black and White Minstrels,' said the Commander light-heartedly in an attempt to dispel his second-in-command's concern.

On the drive back to Thames House, the M.I.5 Chief murmured to himself, 'Was I right to try for Hassam? He's not going to lead us anywhere now.'

It had all started so well. Pete Jefferies, Charlie Walsh, Callum O'Toole and Kathy Doyle had all returned to the Agency's Headquarters on time to be kitted out with bullet proof vests and their favourite weapons. At ten to four the two unmarked cars coasted quietly into the end of the short avenue where the head Terrorist resided and pulled up behind a black van with darkened windows. Four balaclava hooded Special, armed response, police officers emerged and quietly joined the M.I.5 agents. Once they had all been issued with mini intercoms the Commander issued instructions for half the force to cover the rear of the house but not force an entry until Callum, the Secret Service unit's lock-picking expert, had first tried to gain a silent entry through the front door.

'You'll have to give me five minutes boys,' came a whispered comment through the earpieces for the benefit of the waiting assault team. ' To be sure he doesn't want uninvited guests; there's a Yale and two Chubb locks on this door, and that's solid oak.'

'But, can you get in ?' enquired the anxious Chief.

Chapter 5

'I can Sir but I'm just checking for any alarms. It seems clear: just one more to go and we're in,' responded the Irishman.

A few moments later Callum, Jefferies, the Commander and two of the police marksmen were standing, seemingly undetected, in the spacious hall of the large detached house.

'Let the others in,' ordered the Commander to nobody in particular but satisfied his command had been acted on when the other four joined them. ' We know Hassam is definitely at home; we've had the house under constant observation but it is ominously silent. We'll leave one of us at both the back door and front to cover any *breakout*. Now, quiet as you can, let's split up and search each room in turn. Four of you upstairs, remember there's two levels, and two of you with me.'

'Top floor all clear,' reported one of the police Specials. 'But there's wired explosives all over the place. We'll need the bomb squad in here.'

'Same here. All first floor rooms clear Sir. Quite a bit of bomb making material in one though,' stated Agent Jefferies. 'Coming down.'

Having himself entered and searched all the ground floor rooms - and found them empty - the perplexed Chief 's first thought was: someone has fouled up. I bet one of the watchers fell asleep. When I find out who it was I'll have him drummed out of the Service !

' Where's Kathy ?' questioned Charlie, interrupting the Commander's reasoning as they all gathered back in the hallway and switched on the main lights. ' I thought she was down here with you Sir.'

'She was. I left her in the kitchen examining the contents of some of the cupboards. Better go and get her; we're best off out of here until the bomb squad make the place safe.'

Two minutes later the Agent was back, beckoning the others with one hand while placing a finger across his lips.

As they filed into the kitchen behind Walsh they quickly saw the reason for his indicated silence. A tall larder unit at the end of a run of base units was swung back away from the tiled wall revealing a narrow opening and descending stairs.

One of the police marksmen crawled over to the opening and carefully pointed his torch over the stair lip; illuminating a short flight of wooden steps into a dank smelling cellar.

When no burst of gunfire or sound of any description emanated from the void, he slowly rose to his feet and, with automatic carbine raised in front of him, plummeted sharply down the stairway to land crouched on his feet ready to return fire. The cellar was empty.

The Commander and Jefferies made their way down into the vault when the Anti Terrorist Squad officer called out, ' You'd better have a look at this Sir.'

In the far corner of the cellar the officer pointed out a second set of steps leading to a wooden door in the ceiling. Jefferies rushed up the stairs and pushed open the hatch. The fresh chilly night air rushed in as the Agent stepped out onto a small concrete patio at the rear of the house adjacent to the open back door. There was no sign of either Hassam or Kathy Doyle.

'Get out, get out !' There's a timer device with less than ninety seconds ticking away !' screamed a voice in their earpieces.

A front downstairs window shattered as two of the team hurled themselves through what was their nearest exit and ran for the road followed by Walsh, O'Toole and another armed response officer making a more dignified, but still speedy, exit from the front door.

Commander Beaman was physically ejected out of the cellar by the combined efforts of Jefferies pulling and a police Special pushing; stumbling on top of the M.I.5 Agent as the final team member crashed into him from behind.

The three of them never quite made the safety of the parked cars ,the night sky suddenly lightening - as an instant dawn - a fraction of a second before their eardrums were bombarded by a horrendous explosion behind them; the force of which catapulted them into the roadway.

Their body armour and helmets saved the trio from serious injury as debris, bricks and glass showered them; ricocheting off walls and vehicles to pepper their inert bodies.

Jefferies was the first to clamber to his feet as the other operatives emerged from behind the missile-dented van to assist their team-mates. He could see Charlie Walsh mouthing, ‘ Are you all O.K.?’ but heard nothing, his ears still ringing from the aural battering.

The Anti-Terrorist Special sat up and nodded an affirmative but was noticeably bleeding from a deep cut on his chin, and, seemingly unknown to him, carried a unique gun capable of shooting only around corners; the short barrel having been twisted almost at right angles.

Chapter 5

Commander Beaman was the last to respond having had part of a garden wall collapse on him. 'I'm fine: just get this stuff off me.' Willing hands soon removed the rubble and helped him to stand and brush off the coating of brick dust.

'You look like you've copped a nasty cut or two Sir,' commented O'Toole. 'Your trouser leg is ripped apart and I can see at least two embedded shards of glass protruding.

No Sir! Don't remove them until the medics take a look. It may be better to leave them where they are for the present, there doesn't appear to be too much bleeding.'

Already his men were ensuring the road's residents , raised from their beds by the explosion - and some still wearing nightclothes and dressing gowns - were shepherded away from the smoking ruins.

A cacophony of sirens and bells heralded the arrival of additional police, an ambulance and two fire engines; one negotiating the chicane of rubble and an upturned car to mount the pavement directly in front of the demolished property.

'Keep everyone well back and see if you can get the gas turned off,' Commander Beaman heard the Fire Chief shout as he approached the official. ‘ Get a hose on that next door house, those flames are dangerously close.’

Swiftly identifying himself the Commander explained the need to get his forensic team into the ruins as quickly as possible ,the Fireman promising to urgently investigate the safety aspect and report to Agent Jefferies.

‘I’ve got the Met boys setting up road blocks Sir. We’ll get him; he can’t have got far without transport but I’m worried about Kathy. There’s no sign of her here, she must be with him. He must have been in the cellar, caught her unawares and taken her hostage.’

‘I don’t know what to think Peter. Somehow, it seems Hassam knew we were coming. As you said yourself, his bed was still warm. But, if he’s got her, as seems likely, where has he gone and why has he taken her ? Oh drat! It looks as though I’m going to be dragged off to hospital any minute now,’ said his boss eyeing the approaching ambulance paramedics. You’re in charge until I get back. We’ve not had much so far but; Good Luck.’

The, now fully recovered, senior Agent watched the Ambulance disappear into the early morning dawn, realising, now the house fire was almost doused and throwing out less heat, that the awakening day was both decidedly cold and beginning to get increasingly wet as the fine drizzle turned to a heavier downpour.

His earpiece suddenly crackled and he recognised the voice of Agent Greg (Scooter) Scott manning the H.Q communications.

'Got a location for you. Kath……ponder…….ing okay…..barge down at….'

'You're breaking up. Is that you Scooter ? Say again.'

A continuous series of crackles and silences was the only response. ' Damn !' swore the deputy Chief thinking it was Greg's intercom at fault, realising it was, in fact, his own that had been damaged only when Charlie Walsh rushed up to enquire, ' Did you hear that ? We should get down there straight away. If he's got Kathy he's trapped himself.'

'Not all of it, my intercom is playing up. It was Scooter though, wasn't it ?'

'Yes; he's tracked Kathy with those new helmet transponders . They're down at one of the Waste Transfer Station jetties near Victoria Railway Bridge. If we're quick we can block off any way out for him other than the river.'

Jefferies pondered on the situation. ' Get two of the police marksmen. We'll leave Callum in charge here with the other two and get down there; but let's proceed cautiously, he's bound to look if he was followed .'

As Jefferies was leading his party on a sprint through the Battersea streets towards the river, Samirah, having risen early, was already preparing herself for the journey to Southend; packing an overnight bag with the usual clothing and toiletries. Before zipping the valise shut she ensured she also included her mobile telephone charger, ammunition and her favourite handgun; the Kel-Tec P32 Automatic, wafer thin and weighing less than seven ounces.

Perhaps I should contact the Commander before I set off. Hassam should be in custody by now, she thought sitting down to a light continental breakfast and reaching for her phone. She was about to disconnect the unanswered call when the Chief responded to the dialling tone.

'Commander Beaman, Samirah here. Just checking on any updates before getting off down to Southend. Have Meade and Davison found anything at the Hullbridge address and has Hassam said anything ?'

Chapter 5

'Sorry about the delay in answering Sam. I'm in the hospital and I'm getting told off for using my mobile phone. I haven't heard from Meade this morning yet and things didn't go entirely to plan on our ……'

' You're not hurt Sir, are you ? ' burst in the Agent.

' No, no, minor flesh wound that's all,' replied the Commander. ' Hassam's got away unless the others have tracked him down while I've been in here. Let me ask you Sam:
how well do you know Kathy ? She's missing and we think that either Hassam has her, although we can't think why he would want a hostage , or she's following him but her radio's packed up.'

' As you know Sir, she is our newest recruit; only been with us just over a year but I've always found her competent and useful. I'm sure she'll be alright. If Hassam has her he'd better watch his back. Given the slightest opportunity she won't let the team down. He could have made a big mistake if he's taken her. If not she's sure to find a way to get a message back in.'

'Hmmm, better get off as soon as you can. See what you can discover about this S. Hunter. Phone me later,' ordered the M.I.5 Chief. 'Now there's a thought , ' he muttered to himself as he put the phone back in his dishevelled, dust-streaked ,jacket. Sam was an accepted confidant of Hassam's: could she be a traitor ? After all she hadn't asked what had gone wrong or what had happened. He brushed the intruding thought aside. ' What's the matter with me?' he asked himself. 'Sam's been with us nearly five years, there's no way she would betray her Country. No,' he mused, 'her father may have been of Middle East descent but Sam was born in England: this is HER Country. But, it does seem that Hassam was forewarned of our raid ?'

The subject of the Commander's speculations finished dressing ; buckling on an armoured vest and flattening her already small pert breasts before deciding against wearing the cumbersome protection and donning a tight fitting black jumper , figure flattering trousers and a pair of knee-high boots. ' You never know you might need to use some feminine wile,' she said to the reflection in the mirror. ' Even I can see my bum doesn't look big in this.'

Leaving her Chelsea flat and turning on to the Embankment, she looked across the River and pondered on her Chief's words. Just what had happened over there ? She thought she had earlier heard a sound like an explosion and there was a plume of smoke rising above the buildings at Battersea. Will anything ever go right on this investigation? Where is Kathy ? Where is Hassam ?

If her eyesight had the magnification of binoculars, her look across the Thames would have given her the answers, the sweeping glance in the dawn light travelling across the very barge Hassam was, at that moment , searching in the cargo holds.

The four man assault team, led by Agent Jefferies, crouched down behind the embankment wall while Charlie whispered into his intercom microphone.

'Kathy, can you hear me. Where are you ?' Only silence met his request. ' It's no good Pete, she's not answering. The trouble is we don't know if she's on that barge or what we're facing if we try to get on board. Half an hour ago it was dark enough to have attempted creeping along the pier but now, that would be suicide.'

' Excuse me Sir,' said one of the Police Specials who had found himself a well concealed vantage point that gave him a good view of the moored vessel; ' there's someone on board carrying a gun. Looks like the same as the one you're carrying. He appears to be searching for someone or something. I've got a good target. Should I take him out ?'

'No, hold your fire. We need to take him alive if at all possible. Charlie, get me that rope off the rescue lifebelt over there. I'm going for a swim but the current is strong here. We'll slip down behind the pier stanchions while Hassam is busy. I should be able to float out and get on board without being spotted.'

The icy cold water took his breath away as he slid into the River with a rope secured about his waist. With a few powerful strokes and taking advantage of the sweeping tidal flow, he quickly made his way, undetected, to the end of the pier ; gratefully, grasping one of the rubber tyre fenders hanging over the side of the barge.

With the numbing cold sapping his strength, he lost no time in hauling himself out of the water and carefully peeking over the barge's bulwark. Hassam was twenty feet away with his back towards him, busily lifting a tarpaulin hatch cover on one corner and peering into the gloomy cargo hold.

The Agent rolled himself over the barge side and slithered across the open deck to the nearest hatch side before creeping back towards the small rear wheelhouse. Luck was with him, the Terrorist suddenly disappearing into depths of a hold. He stood, signalled his presence to the team ashore and stepped into the tiny steering cabin.

Kathy lay crumpled in the corner, blood oozing from a savage head wound and lesser neck injury. Jefferies felt for a pulse and was relieved when the female Agent groaned and attempted to sit up before collapsing back against the cabin wall.

Surprised at stumbling across his colleague straight away, when he had assumed Hassam was searching for her, his normal quick thinking brain was momentarily inert . Without his helmet, which he had left on the embankment before his swim, he had no way of informing those ashore of the situation. Where was Kathy's headgear, he wondered ? And what, or who, is Hassam seeking if not the Agent ? One thing was certain, he realised, the injured woman had to be removed from danger before attempting to apprehend the violent Terrorist who had to be surprised if they were to capture him unharmed.

The delay in his thinking almost proved fatal. Hoisting the casualty over his shoulder, he stepped out of the wheelhouse and, peering forward to ensure Hassam was still within the cargo space, stepped up onto the sloping gang-plank to the pier.

He had almost made it to the top when the Terrorist reappeared and immediately spotted the fleeing couple.

Heedless of any noise or the increasing river traffic as London awakened, the irascible Hassam raised his weapon and prepared to scythe down his tormentors. An evil grin crossed his face as his finger tightened on the trigger; dissolving to surprise and pain as two sharp cracks rang out.

Beneath his flimsy frock coat length tunic, the Al Qaeda go-between concealed a belt of powerful explosives. The two Police marksmen's bullets impacted into Hassam's body fractionally separated by milliseconds, both intended as disarming shots to save the lives of the M.I.5 Agents.

The first caught the Terrorist high up on the right shoulder, propelling him backwards and upwards: the second, slightly lower, clipping the top of the explosive girdle.

Jefferies, for the second time that morning, found himself flat on his face as behind him Hassam exploded in an incandescent flash.

Chapter 5

He was barely aware of a weight being lifted off him as his team rushed to his and Kathy's aid ,but soon revived sufficiently to enquire about the female Agent's welfare.

'She's not good I'm afraid,' said Charlie. ' Saved you in a way by taking the worst of the blast. I don't think her injuries are life threatening but she'll be out of action for a while. We've already got an ambulance on the way.'

Turning back to the barge; behind and slightly below him, Agent Jefferies, hardened as he was to grim sights, almost puked at the spectacle that met his eyes. There was literally nothing left of the Terrorist; any resemblance of a human being lost in a smoking shapeless bloody torso and shredded clothing.

Alerted by one of the Police marksmen, a River Police launch drew up alongside the barge, the first Officer leaping aboard promptly turning back to retch over the side while his colleague stepped on board and covered the bulk of the remains with a plastic sheet.

Such was the force of the explosion however; blood gore and body parts were wide spread, the disintegration dismembering and decapitating Hassam.

Remarkably the Terrorist's head, apart from being separated from the body, was completely unscathed; cleanly severed and slowly rolling along the scuppers in tandem with the vessel's gentle motion. Even more bizarrely an arm and hand - still holding Kathy's automatic carbine - had smashed through the wheelhouse window and lodged itself pointing directly at Jefferies, just as it had a few minutes earlier.

'I'll leave you to sort this mess out Charlie. I'll check on the Commander and Hassam's house. There's quite a crowd gathering on the embankment now. Get the local constabulary to keep them away.'

Striding back through the streets towards the demolished house, the Agent was aware of all the curious stares he was attracting as the roads got busier; from both motorists and pedestrians. Soaking wet ,dishevelled , still with a blackened face and carrying his weapon, it was not surprising, he realised , that people heading towards him suddenly dispersed to the other side of the road. Amused, he laughed to himself, recognising the funny side of the situation. 'Here I am, risking life and limb to keep them safe in their beds at night and all I get in return is being shunned.'

Chapter 5

'You look even worse than when you left earlier,' said Callum as he saw Jefferies approaching. ' How'd it go down the river? Did you get the bastard ?'

'No; our bad luck seems to continue. The Police lads had to fire at him to protect me and Kathy. There was no way he was going to allow himself to be taken alive: he was wearing a suicide belt: he just BLEW UP !'

'Bloody Hell! First his house and then himself,' swore the confused Irishman. ' So we're still up the creek without a paddle. I can't see the boss being too pleased.'

'We're about to find out Callum old lad. I phoned him at the Hospital to pass on the bad news and said I'd meet him here. If I'm not mistaken that's him coming over now.'

'Who's that coming down the lane now ?' enquired Andy Davison munching a McDonald's Big Breakfast Egg and Baconburger.

'That's the car that went up ten minutes ago while you were up the road getting our breakfast,' replied a bleary eyed Richard Meade. 'I was taking a leak in the bushes at the time so didn't get much of a look at the driver.'

Wiping the steamed up windscreen with his sleeve, Davison raised a pair of binoculars to his eyes . ' Just one person , driving pretty slow but not turning in the entrance. Seems to be looking at the house though. You got the registration number ?

'Yeah. I'll phone it through and see how much longer we've got to sit here before the forensic mob arrive.'

'Don't bother: here they are. Just get in touch with the Commander and find out what he wants us to do next. Oh !; and don't forget to remind him we've had hardly any sleep.'

The two M.I.5 Agents edged their car out of the carport next to the house, surprising their scientific colleagues . Winding the window down , Richard related the Commanders instructions to the Scientists' leader. ' If you find anything, even the slightest clue, let him know immediately. We're off for some well earned zed time.'

'Watch yourselves then. Some maniac driver nearly caused an accident as we drove in,' commented the Technician.

Rewinding the window to shut out the cold morning air, he drove Davison to the car park at the end of the lane where the other Agent had left his car.

Chapter 5

'The Commander said he wants us to stay in the area but to get some sleep in a local Hotel. He'll let us know later where we're off to next. Follow me, I know where we can get our heads down for a few hours.'

Saleem's back roads journey to Hullbridge took him longer than expected due to an unexpected mobile telephone call which, under other circumstances, he would have answered while driving. Anxious, however, to ensure nothing he did brought him to the attention of any authority, he pulled off the road on to the grass verge to respond .

It could be Hassam and confirmation of the delivery, he thought before the monotone voice of his caller echoed in his ear. ' Congratulations! Our computer has selected you for a Free Holiday to Hong Kong. Simply…' The Cell leader cursed and cut the call off.

While I'm parked I'll take a chance and try Hassam again on my mobile. There's no reason my calls should be monitored, he reasoned. The result was the same, a disconnected signal; leaving him with a sense of unease.

The rear wheels of his nondescript Rover car spun futilely as he attempted to drive back on the road off the soft verge. 'Oh no !' he groaned trying reverse and a quick slam into first gear. The car shot forward back onto the road, directly into the path of an oncoming van which, in testimony to the driver's alertness and skill, avoided collision by millimetres and ran off the road only to come to a halt in the exact spot just vacated by the Rover.

Saleem pressed his foot to the floor and, with a screech of burning rubber , disappeared around the bend of the deserted road before the van driver had even emerged from his vehicle. Mindless of whether or not the man was injured, he continued at high speed into Hullbridge, slowing only when he realised he was exceeding the speed limit and the turn off into the formerly rented safe house was just ahead.

He drove up the tree and hedge lined lane and, was about to turn into the driveway entrance when he thought : There's something unusual . It's not as we left it.

Continuing on up to the *dead end* of the lane, he turned the car and drove back past the house entrance very slowly, realising suddenly what it was that he felt was different.

'There's a vehicle in the carport. And it looks as though someone doesn't want it seen,' he muttered to himself. ‘ Why would anyone want to do that ?’

It hit him with alarm. No call from Hassam: no connection to his telephone, and now, someone at the safe house. It could only mean something had happened to his Al Qaeda contact. Nobody, other than the Cell members, had any knowledge of their using the property. The only other possibility was one of their own Cell had, unlikely though it seemed, somehow been identified and revealed the location under interrogation.

Whatever the explanation, he realised: OUR OPERATION HAS BEEN COMPROMISED.

He increased speed, anxious to get away from the house before his own actions invited suspicion and pursuit, resulting in his almost again colliding with a second van as it turned slowly into the narrow lane.

Samirah pulled up behind the van and strode into the house.

‘Hello Sam; what can we do for you ? You’ve just missed Meade and Davison,’ said Technician Harry Smith appreciatively eyeing the glamorous female Agent up and down.

‘It’s you I’ve popped in to see actually. Have you discovered anything yet about who’s been using the place ? Anything about a S. Hunter at all ?'

'Sorry Sam; got nothing for you at the moment. The place has been thoroughly cleaned although they always leave something behind. Don't worry,we'll find it . Leave us your mobile number and I'll ring if we come across anything ; after letting your boss know first of course.'

'Thanks Harry,' said the Agent disappointedly. 'I was really hoping you had something. We've got very little of help at all at the moment unless the boys have managed to get anything out of Hassam. I should think they've got him in custody now but I can't imagine him being an easy nut to crack.'

'You obviously haven't heard. Richard Meade just told us , after speaking to Commander Beaman, that the *snatch* went wrong. Hassam is not going to be talking to anyone, apparently he's spread all over a barge on the Embankment.'

Samirah was dumbstruck. What on earth could have gone wrong she wondered as she drove off ; heading towards Southend-on-Sea. ?

Twenty minutes later, following the instructions of her car's satellite navigation system, she drove along Victoria Avenue towards the Town Centre, seeking the main Police Station.

Chapter 5

'Drat,' she exclaimed as she suddenly realised she had just passed it on her left and missed the turn off into the car park.' That's lucky for once,' she murmured as a roundabout immediately loomed up in front of her; permitting a quick about turn. Two minutes later she was parked and talking to the duty Sergeant who promptly ushered her through to an interior office. There she was met by a Senior Officer who informed her he had already been told by M.I.5 of her mission in Southend.

'We have nobody on record by the name of S. Hunter,' he said looking at the Identifit drawing Sam presented. 'And, there is only one in the local phone book: at a Leigh address.'

The Agent's eyes lit up at the mention of Leigh. 'At last,' she said joyfully,' a breakthrough.'

'Sorry to disappoint you Ms Ahmad but we've already checked. This S. Hunter is a widow, Sheila Hunter, and is seventy two years old. There's not much else we can do to assist you at present other than to get some photostats of that drawing distributed to see if anyone recognises him; but that's something of a long shot I'm afraid.'

Leaving her mobile number Sam thanked the Chief Inspector and, somewhat deflated, left to locate a convenient hotel for the night before motoring into Leigh-on-Sea.

On her way back to her car her mobile rang. ' Any leads ?' enquired the voice of Commander Beaman.

Explaining her worthless visits to both the Hullbridge address and Police Station, she continued disconsolately, ' Harry told me about Hassam. Are there any clues about this attack in his house I can follow up ?'

' I'm afraid you haven't heard the full story. Hassam's house is a smouldering wreck. He blew it up before fleeing with Kathy as a hostage. If there's anything of use in the ruins it's likely to be days before we find out.'

'It just gets worse doesn't it Sir. Is Kathy o.k. ?'

'She's in hospital, caught the full blast of the explosion and has had a nasty knock on the head. I've just heard from the Doctor, she's recovering consciousness and will be able to tell us what happened in an hour or so. But, unless Hassam let anything worthwhile slip while he had her captive, we're still, using Jefferies nautical metaphor, *dead in the water.*'

Chapter 5

Booking into a comfortable looking small hotel guest house half a mile from Leigh Broadway fifteen minutes later, she felt the pangs of hunger, having not eaten since her early morning departure from London.

Deciding to kill two bird's with one stone, she donned a thick warm anorak and elected to walk into the main thoroughfare before following the guest house proprietor's directions to a recommended eatery utilised by the local fishermen. Passing a number of fashionable boutiques she had to resist the temptation to follow her young woman's instincts to stop and inspect the displayed merchandise . Before long she found herself overlooking the Thames Estuary at the top of Leigh Hill .'What can be worth attacking out there ?' she asked herself staring at the choppy water and lifting her coat hood against the cold wind . Descending the Hill past some sad looking empty shops and impressive looking, but derelict, old Hotel , she crossed the railway line into Leigh Old Town. Walking along the old cobbled street she passed an exclusive, glass-fronted restaurant that, although busy, was, she noted , the habitat of suited businessmen rather than the fishermen she sought. She dwelt briefly in front of a Boat Chandlers that displayed some advertisements for the sale of boats but hurried on when a sudden squall of heavy rain emptied the street of other visitors.

A smart Mercedes car swung into the car park of the recommended Public House just as she walked into the warm comfort of the friendly bar. The driver leapt out and, head down, followed her in out of the rain ; his impetus propelling him into Sam's shapely rear.

'I'm terribly sorry,' exclaimed the stranger. ' It was clumsy of me. In my haste to get inside out of the rain I just didn't see you.'

'No harm done. I'm not that fragile,' said Sam smilingly as she noticed how handsome her unintentional assailant was.

'Leave her alone Brad. You can't go molesting every young lady coming in here you know', joked the barman who, she noted, obviously knew the good-looking regular.

Before Brad had time to respond the barkeeper addressed Sam directly as she lowered the anorak hood revealing, as far as all the male occupants of the bar were concerned, a stunning beauty they would normally associate with models or film stars. 'Sorry about that Miss; he's normally quite tame, just have to keep him on a lead,' he said with a wink.

Chapter 5

'Take no notice of Vernon, he's the local comedian . We all say he should be in the theatre......an operating one to have a brain fitted,' quipped Brad. ' We've not seen you in here before. Let me buy you a drink, it's the least I can do to rectify my clumsiness.'

'Thank you but I came in to make some enquiries about boats for sale and for a spot of lunch rathe......'

'Then I must buy you lunch,' interrupted Brad. 'I don't like eating alone ;we can dine together and you can ask me anything you like.'

' How can I refuse your kind offer,' responded Sam enthusiastically in realisation that here was an opportunity to conduct her investigations at the same time as enjoying the company of a very handsome companion.

The barman handed Brad a menu with a envious shake of his head and whispered, ' I don't know how you do it.' And raising his voice added, ' Today's Specials are on the blackboard.'

Showing Sam to a vacant table by the window overlooking Leigh creek with it's moored fishing vessels, the boat captain introduced himself with a smile . 'Bradley Murray, Skipper of the Motor vessel, *Whaleback Swift*, at your service.

Who is the beautiful young lady I'm taking to lunch ?'

The M.I.5 Agent hesitated for a second before replying, quickly assessing which name to give before deciding to play safe and use her alias. ' I'm Shauna: Shauna Khan and I'm a mere Civil Servant,' she said without giving further details.

'I can recommend the Sea Bass with the Sea-food tomatoes and new potatoes if you like fish dishes. Or if yo…….'

'The Bass sounds delicious,' cut in Samirah.

Neither of them ordered a starter but Brad went to the bar to order their meal and for drinks , giving the Agent the chance to telephone her Chief and enquire about Kathy.

' She's been stitched up and had the flash burns on her legs treated ; but she'll be kept in hospital for a few days to ensure there's no after effects from the blow on the head. She's still groggy and can't tell us much at present. The doctor has promised to let me know when she's fit enough for Jefferies to question her. I don't expect you have anything further yet yourself but Harry Smith was going to phone you to say they've recovered the charred remains of what appears to be a Business Card. He thinks they may be able to do something with it when they get back to the lab later this afternoon. Keep me up to date on any developments.'

'Anyone I should be jealous of? ' said Brad mischievously returning with their drinks.

' Just my boss. Believe it or not I'm actually still at work' replied Sam replacing her phone in her pocket.

'Only a Shandy for me, I'm driving,' explained Brad depositing Sam's glass of La Fleur Chambeau wine on the table. ' Now what is it your work entails and how can I help ?'

Before she could answer her consort's question a James Bond theme ring tone from her pocket signalled an incoming call on her mobile phone.

The waiter sat the plate of Thai Lamb Curry and tray of various chutneys on Saleem's table in the Motel's Restaurant just as the Terrorist finished dialling Shauna's number.

Curtly dismissing the attendant's ,'*Anything to drink Sir ?*'enquiry as the recognisable dulcet voice of the remembered go-between responded to his call, he enquired, 'Is that you Shauna ?' awaiting confirmation before continuing. ' I have not heard from Hassam and there is no connection to his telephone. Are you in contact with him? Can you get a message to him for me. It is urgent I know if my delivery schedule is on time? '

The pause before answering and , clipped, ' Can I phone you back ?', indicated to him that the girl was not alone .

'That will not be possible Shauna. You do not have my number and it is not safe for me to divulge it to you. Make an excuse to get away in ten minutes time and I will phone again.'

Putting the phone down he picked at his meal with one hand while dialling Mohammad's number with the other. After an interminable wait, he was about to hang up when the call was answered. Enquiring after his deputy's health, he was relieved to be told that the injury, although still painful, was less inflamed and that the cousin had provided an antibiotics course that had been started. 'You WILL be alright for tomorrow evening then ?'

'I was sleeping when you phoned Saleem. My Cousin says I must get as much rest as possible and that I should start to improve in a couple of days. It is obvious I will not be fully fit until then. Is there no chance we can delay the attack ?

'I cannot contact Hassam, my friend. We must assume everything about the delivery is on schedule in which case there can be no postponement. Unless you hear from me before tomorrow morning, please phone the Amin brothers with the message, *The trip is on.*'

Wishing his friend well he pushed his plate aside and, looking around to ensure no other diners had entered since he last looked - and that he was still well clear of any tables in use - he redialled Shauna.

Brad laughed as Shauna finished her call. 'Now I know what you do. You're a *Spook;* but not a very good one. That was James himself calling was it ?'

Alarmed that somehow her dinner companion had correctly ascertained her occupation, and even knew her Commander's name, she suddenly realised the grin on his face was an indication of nothing more than a tease.

'Oh heck, you've guessed. My real name is Pussy Galore,' she said poking fun back.

'That's a work colleague's idea of a joke; altering the ring tone on my mobile in retaliation to my altering his to the annoying Crazy Frog.'

'So what is it you really do and why do you want to buy a boat?' said Brad returning to a more serious conversation.

'Well I do actually work for the Government: in Customs and Excise,' she lied. ' I'm not looking to purchase a boat though, just seeking information on any recent boat sales in conjunction with an investigation we are carrying out in relation to a tip off about a drugs shipment. You may be able to help me with your local knowledge but, first, I must pop out to the ladies room before our lunch arrives.'

She had timed her departure from the table to perfection, her phone again ringing just as she entered the Ladies Toilet vestibule. Thankfully the area was empty.

'Can you now speak freely ?' enquired Saleem; continuing when given an affirmative, 'I need to know if you have an alternative contact number for Hassam ,or if there is any way of getting in touch with him. Tomorrow we have a rendezvous to keep but have had no final confirmation of the time.'

In the knowledge of Hassam's demise, Samirah realised that, perhaps, Saleem's concern could be used to M.I.5's advantage. ' I may be able to get him to call you. Does he know how to contact you ? If not, I will need to know.'

'He does not have my number. See if you can contact him and I will phone again in an hour's time. It is not safe for anyone involved to reveal this number.'

As soon as the connection was severed, Sam immediately tried , last number caller, but received only , *the caller withheld their number.* She was about to call Commander Beaman when two other women came through the door. Realising any further delay in returning to her table would be inviting curiosity from Brad, she elected to postpone the call until after her lunch.

' I was beginning to think you had deserted me for being so nosey,' said Brad acting very gentlemanly in standing to usher her into her seat. 'Just in time though. Here comes our lunch.'

The whole small sea bass and accompaniments set in front of them reminded Sam of how hungry she was; having had only a light continental breakfast in the last eight hours.

Cooked to perfection in an undisclosed sauce, the tender fish melted in her mouth. ' This is absolutely superb Mr. Murray. I'm not surprised you recommended it. And what is the delightful stuffing in these tomatoes ?'

' Enough of the Mr. Murray young lady. It's Brad to you or I won't answer any of your questions, ' said Brad with a smile.' Don't ask me the quantities but it's a mixture of: white crabmeat: cooked mussels: soured cream: dry vermouth: black pepper and salt. The topping in this case is, if I'm not mistaken, a little lumpfish roe.'

'Another question then Brad. Do you always treat new acquaintances to such a sumptuous meal or do I look so undernourished you decided I needed fattening up ?'

Laughing in response to the question, the boat skipper retorted, ' If I answered yes to that enquiry I would have to visit the optician. When you leave here after our lunch, every one of those fishing buddies of mine over at the bar will come up and ask me, in their usual banal parlance, ' Who was that *drop dead gorgeous* girl you were with ?'

It was Sam's turn to laugh at the, previously unheard of, simile which she correctly assumed was a compliment.

By the end of their main course it was obvious to any onlooker that the couple were completely at ease with one another, enjoying a mutual repartee in their conversation which was interspersed with both seriousness and humour. 'As you were powdering your nose at the time, I took the liberty of ordering you a Fruity Tiramisu for dessert. I'm sure you will enjoy it ,' said Brad seeing the waitress approaching to clear to clear the table.

'I'm sure I will if it is not too long in coming. I really do have to go shortly,' said Sam somewhat wistfully. ' Thank you for both the meal and information you have given me. I will have to inform my section head it appears our informant was mistaken about the drugs....at least in this area if you are positive there have been no new boats on the scene or boat sales in Southend and Leigh recently. If the River Thames is involved in any shipment I had better try over the Kent side.'

' Before you go, where are you staying ? Can I give you a lift ; it may start raining again any minute? And, most important of all, when can I see you again? I have had the most enjoyable afternoon,' Brad suddenly blurted out , fearful that this beautiful girl was about to walk out of his life as quickly as she had entered it.

'Don't be concerned. I'm booked in at a local hotel just up the road for tonight. It's only a short walk and it will give me a chance to think what I'm going to put in my report before returning to London tomorrow. I too have had a lovely time but, as I told you, I live in Chelsea and am only here for a couple of days. You say you have a party of anglers from the Essex Police Social Club to take out tomorrow so we will not be able to meet up again before I leave. If you ever come up to Town I would love to see you again; I'll give you my mobile phone number.'

Emotionally disappointed, Brad realised that in the short while he had known her he had developed strong feelings towards her and would make every effort to see her again at the earliest opportunity. 'I'm staying in Leigh myself this evening. I have a flat that I use when required for early morning starts in this area. If you find yourself with any spare time later you are welcome to pop in or phone me and I will come and collect you. Take my card, I'll write the Leigh address on the back.'

Looking at her watch Sam saw she only had ten minutes in which to get in touch with the M.I.5 Chief before Saleem again phoned. 'Thank you again Brad. I really must go now and I don't think I'll have much free time tonight but, I'll certainly keep this card,' she said with a light peck of a kiss on Brad's cheek.

As she ventured outside in the rapidly dropping temperature, she pulled up her hood and set off back towards the Town at a sprint: both to keep warm and find somewhere to privately telephone Commander Beaman. She had only gone fifty yards when she noted a little café with only one occupant or customer. Fearful of not being able to speak to her boss before Saleem called back, she pushed the door and entered.

The lone occupant was, in fact, the proprietor; a pleasant faced middle-aged woman who immediately left the newspaper she was reading and returned to the counter. ' That's right dear, come on in out of the cold. What can I get you ?'

Within the next two minutes Sam learnt that it was: 'late season,' 'late in the day', and 'trade not so good at this time of year', from the talkative owner: ' except around lunchtime and if a few of the cockle boat crews come in.'

Placing an order for just a cup of tea, she retreated to a table at the rear of the establishment where, providing she kept her voice low, she would not be overheard by the woman.

'Please answer,' she whispered pleadingly as she dialled her Headquarters. Agent Jefferies answered the phone and her prayer.

'Get me Commander Beaman quick as you can Pete. I'm expecting a call from Saleem any minute and need to speak to the Chief first.'

The Chief's deputy put up no resistance . 'Hold a second, he's on the other line.'

Sam quickly explained the situation when the Commander responded within twenty seconds.

Immediately grasping the dilemma his female Agent was facing, he directed Sam to hold on while he spoke to Jefferies. ' When he phones back, if you can't get him to divulge his number, tell him you have managed to get in touch with Hassam and he has confirmed everything is according to plan. There has been a development that could mean we have thwarted the planned attack but, if we have, we still need to locate and capture the Cell members. Saleem is our only lead; let's not scare him off. You should go now before he rings. Phone me from your Hotel later.'

In his Hotel room Saleem put the handset back in it's holder, stood up from the bed, and walked over to the wardrobe to drag out a bulky holdall. If she's on the telephone it is probably to Hassam, he thought. I'll try again in a moment. Opening the bag he withdrew a large Video Camera and tripod which he set up facing a blank wall. Ensuring the battery was showing a full charge he locked the camera to the on position and walked round to stand in front of it. Looking straight into the lens he began to speak: 'Infidels, Unbelievers and Islamic Traitors of England, by the time you see this you will know that the true believers have struck a mortal blow against Britain for it's support of acts of Terrorism against our peoples. Our attacks yesterday have crippled the economic structure of the South East England and will have far-reaching effects. Some of our brothers, seen on this film, have willingly sacrificed themselves to prove to the British Government and the World that Islam will prevail. Nowhere will be safe from attack in our war until the decadent Western society ceases to interfere with our lands and peoples. Now is the time to tell your Governments only they can stop the needless slaughter of innocents. Al Qaeda is strong. More attacks will follow until our destiny is fulfilled.'

Switching off the camera he removed his false beard, hairpiece and turban, stuffing the items into a plastic bag weighted with a brick for later disposal at sea. He redialled Shauna's number.

Brad left the comfort of the restaurant after a second cup of coffee, during which he made certain he had entered Shauna's number into his mobile phone directory, turning up the Old Leigh High Street to take his boat advertisement into the Chandlers shop for display. After a short discussion with the owner about the inclement weather and next few day's forecast, he started to walk back to his car; stopping in amazement when he thought he heard the same James Bond Theme he had heard earlier on Shauna's phone. Looking back down the deserted thoroughfare he decided it must have been his imagination. She should almost be back to her hotel by now, he thought. I'll phone her from my car.

Sam was standing at the Café counter paying her bill when she spotted Brad, head down against the wind, pace past the window, putting himself between herself and the footbridge back over the railway line. I can't let him see me now. Saleem will be ringing any minute, she thought, remembering that he had told her about the advertisement he had drawn up to place in the Chandler's shop window. Slipping quickly out of the Café she stepped across the road and crouched down under a trailer supported boat out of sight of the pathway but able to witness Brad's return. A few moments later she saw the boat skipper briskly walking back towards the

restaurant car park. She froze as her phone rang with it's distinctive call sign.
'Miss Ahmad ?' enquired an unrecognised voice that sent a shiver of apprehension through her body. Who was calling using her real name but not addressing her as Sam ?
'Speaking,' she replied.
'Sorry to disturb you Miss. Sergeant Oliver here, the Chief Super told me to give you a call about the drawing you left for copying. Our own copying machine has been broken for the past week so we've had to send it out to one of the local print shops. D.C. Simpson usually mends it for us, he's a dab hand with that sort of thing, but he's off on sick leave at present. It does mean, I'm afraid, that we won't have copies for our patrol boys until tomorrow.'
Sam's brain was screaming 'Get off the line,' but she calmly said, ' Thank you for the information Sergeant, goodbye.'
'Oh, before you go, the good news is we have faxed a copy through to other Essex Police Stations along with the car registration you provided. Have a nice evening Miss.'
Thank goodness for that ,thought Sam as the call was ended. Should I see if Saleem has called? James Bond immediately announced

himself again, to Sam at an overly loud volume in the quiet cobbled ,almost deserted ,street. Stabbing a finger at the answer button she heaved a sigh of relief as Saleem's voice pleaded in her ear, 'Did you speak to Hassam ? Was that him you were just on the phone to ?'

Mindful of the Commander's instructions, she replied, 'Yes. He did say he would speak to you direct if he had your contact number.'

A train roared by a few yards away, drowning out Saleem's next words. ' Did you hear what I said?' queried the Terrorist. ' Did he confirm the delivery is on time ?'

Sam was in a quandary. Commander Beaman had emphasised the importance of Saleem thinking all was going as planned, even at the expense of not getting him to reveal his phone number. If she told him she didn't know which was why she wanted his contact number, would he still refuse to reveal it and, perhaps, bring forward the time of his proposed attack? She decided she could not take that chance, the team of Agents requiring all the time they could get.

'Yes Saleem. Nothing has changed about the delivery, there are no delays.'

'That, at least, is good news. But, what about my other question. Why wasn't I able to get through to him on his normal line? What number did you contact him on? , Give it to me, I might still need to get in touch with him,' ordered Saleem.

Sam was prepared for any such request, snapping back, ' I cannot do that ! I have strict instructions not to pass the number on to ANYONE, including you. You must realise there is no difference in your own secrecy. We all know how previous bombers have been traced through phones and records.

'You are right of course. It is nerves affecting my every thought now we are so near to launching our attacks.'

'So by this time tomorrow we will all be rejoicing in another victory against the hated Western decadents . Let us hope many unbelievers are destroyed.'

Saleem fell for the trap. ' Not tomorrow Shauna, but soon. The world will know by Friday that Al Qaeda is not a spent force just because our leader Osama Bin Laden has been forced into hiding by the Imperialist Americans.'

His next words made her blood run cold. She could not believe what she was being told about the expected number of casualties. He rang off as her body trembled with a combination of the chill late afternoon air and abhorrence at what she had just heard.

Returning to the warmth of his car, Brad put a call through to Swifty before trying Shauna, requesting, when his crewman answered, that he be picked up in the morning from his Leigh flat as he had decided to stay there overnight rather than go back out to Paglesham. ' There's no sense in taking two cars to Wallasea; we can both go together and leave one here. I'm about to give Detective Sergeant Astley a call to let him know the forecast. I know they won't want to cancel but they may want to bring along lighter gear in case we're confined to the River for comfort.'

'Let's see if you're safely back at your Hotel my lovely,' he murmured to himself as he completed his call and rang Shauna.

The Agent answered out of breath through her exertions of running back to the Hotel after her call from Saleem, anxious to tell the Commander of what she had just learnt.

She was, in fact, just entering the lobby as the call from Brad embarrassed her, the amused grin on the face of the desk clerk testimony to childishness of the ring tone.

Chapter 5

'Just checking you got back okay. Shows what an effect you had on me. Ten minutes after you left I was walking back to my car from the Chandlers and thought I heard your phone ringing. You sound puffed, are you alright ?'

'You caught me just about to have a shower,' she said, an almost truth as that was her intention as soon as she got to her room. ' Had to rush back to the phone. It's nice to hear from you after all this time,' she joked to deflect any further questions. 'Then I'm going to get on with my report, have a light supper and an early night. Which is what you should do if you have to go to sea tomorrow. I'll try to ring you sometime during the day.'

Feeling like a lovestruck teenager, she reprimanded herself . Now is not the time to dwell on romance: you have an important job to do. The welfare of the country comes before any personal feelings or involvement.

Throwing her coat off on to the bed, she immediately rang the Commander's private line. When her call went unanswered, she redialled the general office number and was rewarded with the strong Irish brogue of Agent O'Toole breathing, ' That you Sam: the old man said he was expecting you to call? Unfortunately he's not here at he moment, he and Pete are in with the Director General. Left me minding the shop.'

' Thanks Callum, any messages ?'

' I'll let him tell you himself but it looks as though we have stopped the attack before it got started. I've no idea of how long they will be in with the DG but I'll let them know you called immediately they come back.'

It was, in fact, over two hours later before her call was returned; two hours during which she showered, wrote a brief report and slipped down to the dining room only to find it closed. 'We don't usually serve evening meals Miss unless we have advance orders. But there's a few Café Bars no more than a few hundred yards up the road if you want something hot. Or, the Co-op will still be open : they sell sandwiches and there is tea-making facilities in your room,' said the helpful concierge.

Deciding sandwiches would suffice for the evening she returned to her room and grabbed her coat and mobile phone sitting on the bedside unit.

The road from the Hotel to the well lit main road was ominously quiet and very dark; the cloudless night; overhanging trees; and sparsely spaced lamp posts all contributing to a worrying stroll for any lone young female. Not that Sam was easily frightened, knowing her Agent's training had well prepared her for any eventuality, including unwanted attention or unprovoked attack.

Just as she left the shop, the inevitable happened....her phone rang. Snatching the instrument from her pocket ,she decided to leave the call unanswered until she returned to her room and put the phone back in her coat. Unaware that her actions had been witnessed by a sloppily dressed , thin-faced, tall teenager, she walked unhurriedly back towards her Hotel. Soon after leaving the main thoroughfare she heard soft running footfalls behind her and was on the point of turning round when she was savagely pushed to the ground. Releasing her grip on the carrier bag containing her sandwiches as she felt a hand reaching into her pocket, she attempted to twist round and grasp her attacker's wrist. For her endeavours the only reward was a sharp kick to the stomach, winding her, and a ripped coat pocket .

'Bastard,' she screamed scrambling to her feet as her assailant fled with her mobile phone. 'You've picked the wrong victim this time; I need that phone.'

Confident that his victim, a slimly built petite girl, offered no threat, the youth slowed to a walk after a few moments; his poor physical condition attested to by his wheezing after the exertion.

Even when Sam came running after him, such was his contempt for her, he made no effort to escape, holding up her phone and sneering: 'Come to beg for this back have you little girl ?'

Although certain any plea would fall on deaf ears she quietly said, ' It would be better if you returned it voluntarily, I don't want to hurt you.'

The teenager let out a loud guffaw, snorting, ' Go home if you know what's good for you. There's only one person likely to get hurt around here….you if you don't clear off.'

Sam looked up and down the deserted street, to the amusement of the youth who assumed she was looking for assistance. With nobody in sight she turned as though to walk away. The assailant never really knew what happened next, his only recollection , on recovering consciousness ten minutes later draped over the hedge of some-one's front garden, being a blur of arms and legs flying at him; seemingly from all directions as he sought to defend his body from a barrage of chops and blows.

Chapter 5

During the youth's ten minute open-air slumber, two happenings occurred that were to have subsequent consequences on the M.I.5 investigation.

The first when patrolmen, Police Constables Dave Sharp and Peter Anderson booked in at the Police Station for their night shift. ' Anything we need to know before we get off ?' queried Anderson . ' Dave's just gone out back to get the car round.'

'You were supposed to have a photo fit drawing of someone the Met boys are anxious to find but we don't have any spare copies at present. And keep a lookout for a Rover 200, black car, registration WH 53 AGW. They want to trace that too but, under no circumstances - if you happen to spot it - are you to stop it ! Just radio in the info and follow it discreetly.'

'Me and Dave pulled one of those up last Friday night but it wasn't that registration. You should have a record of it because the driver was supposed to bring his documents in the next day.'

'Yeah, he did. Still you know what one looks like then don't you ?' laughed the duty Sergeant. 'Here's to a quiet night.'

Anderson climbed into the passenger seat and grinned at Dave. 'Let's go and get our fish and chips and find a nice quiet lay by, we could be in for a boring night.'

The desk Sergeant put his cup of tea down and picked up the drawing of Saleem. ' I suppose I could have at least showed them this,' he uttered. ' Wouldn't have been much use though, asking a bit much for anyone to remember an unfamiliar face without a photo.'

The second was that of Skipper Brad Murray suddenly remembering that he hadn't let
D.C Astley know of Wednesday's forecast. His call went unanswered but he was invited to leave a message which he did. To make doubly certain the message was picked up he decided to also text the communication, receiving a confirmed SENT to set his mind at rest.

Back in her Hotel, following her, already forgotten, brush with the mugger, Sam rang her Chief and apologised for not answering earlier, making the excuse of having popped out of her room for a few moments. She quickly related the details of her conversation with Saleem, excitedly pointing out that she had, at least, managed to establish the attack was obviously planned for

Thursday; giving them another day to pursue their quarry.

The Commander interrupted to state that examination of the barge where Hassam had met his end, revealed the vessel was a huge floating bomb. 'The holds were filled with Ammonium Nitrate and drums of Diesel Oil. All that was missing to turn that lot into an explosive nightmare was some sort of propellant, like Nitro Glycerine,' said Beaman

'We think that was all Hassam was waiting for and he, himself, was involved with the operation which was to be an attack on Canary Wharf which we have now stopped.'

'I hope you are right,' said Sam hesitantly, 'According to Saleem the numbers of dead and injured was likely to be MORE THAN THIRTY THOUSAND.

6

'It's not too bad at present, force four I'd guess with the odd gust to five,' said skipper Brad to Detective Constable Astley. ' But it is scheduled to increase later this afternoon. Do your lads want to stick it out here for a while longer or get back into the River ?'

The Essex Police Angling party spokesman staggered along the deck, competently bracing himself to combat the *Whaleback*'s motion, and had a brief word with some of his colleagues before returning to the wheelhouse.

'They all say the fishing's good here; getting plenty of whiting and a few decent codling so unless it starts to kick up really rough they're comfortable enough here.'

'Well it's near enough lunch time. I'll get Swifty to make us all another cup of tea, I expect your boys will all be tucking into their sandwiches soon,' said Brad, adding as an afterthought, 'unless anyone wants soup.'

Latif opened up his lunchbox and sat in the rear of his B.T. van, with the doors open, eating a sandwich while awaiting the arrival of his younger brother at the arranged car park rendezvous. On arrival at the Sports Centre car park himself, he was surprised to find it half full: until he remembered it was half-term, the numbers of four x fours testimony to many young mothers having brought their children along to swimming and other activities. He drove to the far end of the car park before letting his office know he was taking his lunch break, hoping that Asif would not be delayed as his, "unscheduled", secret additional job would have to be carried out during the break.

He had just poured himself a hot drink when a Mitsubishi Pajero 4 x 4 approached and slid to a halt a few feet away. Now where would Asif have got such a motor ?, he thought.

A smartly dressed woman, wearing an expensive looking suede coat and boots got out, left the engine running and walked over to him. ' You are on the way to my place then? About time too, I've been waiting in all morning, we've been without the phone for two days now. It's a good thing I've got a mobile,' she snapped at the bewildered telephone engineer.

'I'm afraid not Madam,' said Latif politely. 'I have only one more scheduled call at Benfleet before my shift ends. Another engineer must be calling on you.'

The woman went berserk, almost physically attacking him. 'I've waited long enough. You're sitting here doing nothing,' she roared. 'I'll be reporting this.'

The last thing the Terrorist wanted was his presence on the Island known to his bosses; he didn't officially have any reason to be there. He stood up just as the woman stepped closer and hissed, 'You bloody Pakis come here , take our men's jobs and then don't want to work. Why don't you get back to your own country ?'

Unfortunately her aggressive behaviour alarmed Latif as he rose and, thinking she was about to strike him, made to protect himself, accidentally catapulting the contents of his cup down the front of the woman's coat.

'You cretin! You're in trouble now! I'll see you're fired for this,' she screamed jumping back into her vehicle and, without looking, reversed……..straight into Asif as he drove up on his motor scooter.

The young Amin brother was, fortunately, thrown clear of the spinning wheels that rolled over his motorcycle before the shaken woman brought the vehicle to a standstill.

White-faced ,she emerged from the 4 x 4 no longer arrogant or ranting. The horror etched on her face relaxed a little when she saw Asif struggling to his feet assisted by his elder brother.

'I think it is you who will find themselves in trouble now,' said Latif venomously, stung by the woman's previous racist comments.

'I'm okay. A few bruises that's all. But look at my bike ?' cried Asif . ' How will I get to the rendezvous tonight ?' he added unthinkingly.

The woman had recovered some of her composure and , with the accident victim's disclosure of being uninjured, sought to assert her previous dominance. ' It's your own fault coming up behind me like that. You're lucky I'm not claiming for any damage to my vehicle.'

Certain that his brother was uninjured, Latif saw the opportunity to escape from the dilemma he had, only a few minutes earlier, been in. ' In that case Madam, I think we had better call the police don't you ? Let's see what they have to say about who's fault it is.'

As expected, the female driver had no wish to involve any authority in the situation, especially as Asif chose that moment to let out a groan and clutch his side. 'Well perhaps we should forget about it being anyone's fault and make our own solution, don't you think ?'

Given the opening he was looking for, Latif replied, 'I was going to suggest, especially as my brother and I are now in a hurry, that we just forget the incident which appears to have been unwitnessed by anyone else. We can claim on his insurance for the scooter and your vehicle damage is superficial. But, of course, I can hardly do that when you report to my company . Obviously, I shall have to relate what happened and they will no doubt say the matter must be reported to the police.'

'I think, under the circumstances your idea is better. You can rest assured I will not be complaining and here's twenty pound for your brother to take a taxi for the journey he mentioned tonight,' said the woman fishing in her handbag, grateful to escape the situation so lightly.

Chapter 6

'That's got to be twenty pound,' said Swifty as he gaffed the huge cod one of the angling party had just reeled in alongside the boat. ' It's definitely the best we've had on board this season so far.'

As the big fish flopped onto the deck a large rogue wave hit the *Whaleback* broadside on, catching the standing captor unawares and propelling him across the deck to crash into the starboard guard rail; and very nearly over into the turbulent waters.

Quick reactions by a colleague averted what could have become a tragedy, an outstretched hand grabbing the hapless angler's flailing arm as he released rod and reel over the side while seeking a handhold.

'Thanks Ted, thought I was going for a bath just then,' said the grateful angler. 'Haven't lost my fish have I ?'

'No, but your gear has gone in the drink.'

Swifty hoisted the flapping fish off the deck into a basket, and, turning to the fortunate angler added, with a grin, ' Here you are, still hooked to your line. If you pull the line in you should retrieve your equipment. Make history that will, the only time a *fish has caught a rod and reel*.'

'We had better all reel in and pack up. We've had a good day's sport and the wind is definitely getting worse,' said D.C. Astley. 'It 's going to be a bumpy ride back in and some of us are on duty later. Got to keep an eye out for this Terrorist character they say could be in the area. Shouldn't be too hard for any of you lot to spot if that photo fit faxed through last night is any good.....a definite resemblance to Roger Moore, 007.'

The mention of James Bond immediately reminded Brad of twenty four hours ago when he had just left his new found lady friend. Perhaps she had not yet returned to London and, if , as he expected, their later charter was called off, he would telephone her in the hope of a late evening date.

'It's a bit breezy and wet up forward ,' chirped Swifty returning to the warmth of the wheelhouse after stowing the anchor. ' Must be at least force six now and, unfortunately, we've also wind against tide for the trip back. It's going to be a roller coaster even if it doesn't get any worse.'

'This will be a fully fledged gale by tonight,' said the Skipper thoughtfully. 'And we are supposed to have another charter. I somehow think we'll have an unavoidable, but sensible, cancellation.'

At the top of the telegraph pole, the strong wind tore at Latif's clothing as he disconnected the telephone wire leading to Mr and Mrs Swift's bungalow. Descending the ladder to where his brother was waiting in the van, he signalled a thumbs up, picked up his toolbox and walked up the pathway to knock on the door.

'Good afternoon Madam,' said the Terrorist, flashing his identity card. ' I understand you may be experiencing difficulties with your telephone. May I come in ? '

'It was working this morning, my sister called,' said Nancy cautiously . ' Who said it isn't working ? Can I see your identity properly please ?'

'A sensible precaution Madam if I may say so. You can never be too careful these days,' responded Latif stepping slightly aside in order that his British Telecom van became visible, and representing his I.D. ' It was a lady down the road who actually complained of a fault. It's just that you are connected to the same cable so I suspect you will also be in the same situation.'

Nancy retreated to the telephone on the hall table and lifted the receiver as the engineer followed her in. ' No, there's nothing on here at all now.'

'Is this an extension phone or main one ?' queried Latif examining the socket.

'It's the only phone in the house other than my husband's mobile; which he's left behind again.'

'Yes, I thought so. I suspect the problem might be with the phone itself. I'll just nip out and get the test phone or, could you pop down the path to my van and ask my lazy assistant for it while I check this box .'

With Naomi due out of nursery school any minute, Nancy was preparing to walk the short distance up the road to collect her. ' Will you be long. I have to fetch my child from school very shortly ?'

'I shouldn't be more than a few minutes once I have the test phone.'

'I'll get it. You carry on with what you're doing,' said Nancy disappearing up the path to the gate.

Latif leapt up from the floor, opened his tool box and removed a giant matchbox size package bound with black tape, from which a small switch protruded. He pushed the switch and a small green lamp on the end illuminated. Peering through the doorway he saw Nancy had nearly reached the van. Throwing open the nearest door off the hallway, he found himself in a child's playroom, dominated by a splendid doll's house. He was about to quickly retreat when he recollected seeing something similar in a toy shop: the front hinged open to display miniature furniture inside. Frantically scrabbling about he found that, not only did the front come open but, the roof hinged back to reveal a battery housing and switch to operate mini lamp bulbs within the house rooms. Marvelling at the workmanship of the model he; nevertheless realised he had only a few more minutes to hide his bomb and had, in fact, stumbled across the ideal place….inside the roof of the doll's house.

Five minutes later, he rang the Swift's number from the top of the telephone pole. 'It should be alright now Madam,' he said when Nancy answered. 'It wasn't your phone, the fault was in the line.' He waved to the housewife hurrying up the road as he climbed down from the mast and returned , profusely sweating, to the van.

'Is it done and is it working ?' enquired Asif anxiously. ' When it was thrown out of my scooter's carrier it must have been damaged.'

'Don't worry my brother. The lamp came on just as we were told it would. It is armed and awaiting just a radio signal from Saleem. He will know it is now *live*.'

Saleem sat on the edge of the bed in his motel room staring at the small radio transmitter sitting on the bedside cabinet and occasionally shifting his gaze to the hands of his wristwatch. Surely nothing else has gone wrong he thought? A green lamp flashed on the transmitter, flickered and went out before lighting up again with a steady glow.

The Terrorist leader sighed with relief, picked up the unit and checked the push button security cover was firmly in place before carefully placing the lethal device in a pocket of the camera bag.

Feeling less apprehensive than he had earlier, he lay back on the bed and let his mind run through the remainder of his plans for the day. I will have an early dinner in the restaurant, settle my bill and get dressed in warm clothing before Mohammad comes to collect me. Should I leave my car here? How much of the events of the last few days was his own paranoia: fearing discovery and, how concerned should he be about the secretive *visitors* to the safe house? Would it be possible to continue as Steven Hunter, Managing Director of *Getaway Travel,* after the attacks ?

He answered his own questions. Yes, leave the car. It had been stopped with correct number plates and, probably - if he was correct about the safe house being watched - also reported with the false number now adorning the vehicle. The anti-terrorist agencies could possibly tie the two together and he had no further false registration, nor any further use for the car. He was right to be concerned, but not unduly. After all, in a few more hours the operation would be commenced and if, at that stage, they were still unknown to the authorities it was highly unlikely they could be stopped.

The third question gave him more of a dilemma however . In the aftermath of the attack, there was little doubt the occurrences of the past few days would eventually be cross referenced resulting in the discovery of Steven Hunter's association. The house in Thorpe Bay was only rented and he was sure nothing incriminating remained, the charts and plans required being in his second bag at the end of the bed. His visit to the rented premises of his Company, Getaway Travel ,earlier in the day had enabled him to raid the safe of all the cash and contact the Bank to

arrange transfer of other funds to an offshore account, leaving only a minimal sum..
That, he now realised ,was a mistake. The anti-terrorist Agencies would trace the transaction and realise that no "suicide bomber" would require money for where they were going. Too late now to return it, but, if a body were to be found later, identifiable only by documents rather than facial features, Steven Hunter could be dead while Saleem lived on to plan and carry out further attacks against the sworn enemies of Islam. Such an idea would be relatively easily accomplished; after all there will be plenty of corpses around that could be readily mutilated and given the false identity.
There was only one other thing that remained a concern, he wanted to make sure his filmed message was broadcast to the world immediately following the attacks. 'I must post it to the BBC tonight before I board the boat. There will be no chance once we have left the Marina,' he quietly uttered to himself while removing the cassette from the camera and replacing it with an unused one. 'Yes, they will definitely screen it in the public interest. There will be no bigger news.' Placing the film in a ready-stamped *Jiffy bag*, he sealed the package, threw it on the bed, left his

room and made his way down to the dining room for an early dinner.

Samirah threw herself on the bed after a tiring three hour journey , stuck in the late afternoon traffic of the A13, on her way back from her meeting with her M.I.5 Chief.
'I accept what you say Sam. We could be congratulating ourselves prematurely. Nothing is certain,' he had conceded. 'But, the contents of that barge were not a legitimate cargo and were certainly not intended for agricultural use. That lot going up anywhere would cause tremendous damage and casualties. If we're right and it was intended for Canary Wharf, Saleem would have had his thousands of deaths.'
'It does seem you are right Sir but all the while we haven't got Saleem makes me nervous, and there's that rented house at Hullbridge. Why so far away if it's a London operation? Remember, as far as we are aware, Hassam did not know he was under observation. Why not use his house, it was pretty secluded ?'
'I wish I had the answers. We have two operatives on the barge and a "spotter" in place if anyone approaches. I'm nervous too with all that potential huge bomb sitting in the heart of Lon-

don but we can't move the barge or unload it in case anyone is watching.'

A sudden knock curtailed their conversation, causing the Commander to immediately bark, ' Enter.'

The sombre face of Technician Harry Smith peeked round the frame and, seeing Sam, apologised on bursting into the room, ' Sorry Sam, didn't mean to interrupt but I did promise an immediate report on our visit to that Pop star guy's house this morning. Whoever cleaned up did a real thorough job. The only prints we got were obviously the owners, except one which we got off the ceramic pull handle of the old Victorian style toilet. That, unfortunately belongs to someone unknown, there's no match in the data bank. It may even be that of a past visitor and not one of the Terrorists.'

'So nothing of any use to us then Harry ?' queried the Chief.

'Well I wouldn't quite say that . We have a plaster cast of some tyre treads which we're working on to identify. That may help identify the type of vehicles they are fitted to.'

'Bet it's a Rover 2000. That's what nearly hit you according to Richard Meade,' said Sam.

'And we've already got the whole of the Essex constabulary looking for that.'

'Ah Sam, I didn't say one set of treads. We've got four in all and one is from a motorcycle of some description.'

'Well done Harry, that seems to tell us there are four people we are looking for. You know how urgent the identification of those vehicles is; let us know the minute you have anything further.' ordered the Commander. 'Nothing else ?'

The Technician frowned and hesitated before saying, 'Well, it hardly seems worth mentioning. As I said, the place was as clean as a whistle but we did find the remains of a business card that someone had burnt in the fireplace. A small part of it had slipped down the side of the hearth and we even managed to get the burnt part to hold together long enough to read a bit of it.'

'Does it help us man?' screamed the Chief.

'I shouldn't think so, at least not much as all we were able to discover was that it appeared to be advertising a charter boat service.'

'Go on, what else ?'

'The whole piece had, in small print, the words **Angling parti** in the top left hand corner, we took that to read Angling parties. Beneath that, in the same small letters was **Private Chart** , obviously Private Charters. And, in the bottom left hand corner we were able to read, **Telephone B** and that's all, presumably either a name or place.'

'What about the name of the craft itself ?' questioned Sam.

'Just about as much use as the rest I'm afraid. In the middle of the card on the only unburnt piece it reads **M.V. SPRI** ; that's it.'

'What's your best guess at the rest Harry ?' queried the Commander.

'The lads came up with a host of possibilities, the consensus being **SPRITE** the most probable.'

'Thanks Harry. Let us know about those vehicles as soon as you can.'

When the Technician departed the Commander called Agent Jefferies in to join them, murmuring to Sam, 'I think you are going to have to return to Southend, see if there's anything you can find out , ' adding, with a twinkle in his eye, ' Perhaps your new found boat skipper friend you mentioned so enthusiastically knows of a boat named Sprite.'

Jefferies came in beaming like a Cheshire cat and slapped a small diary down on the Commander's desk. 'Got them, the whole bloody bunch.'

'What's this ?' asked the Chief.

'Found on the remains of our late Terrorist ; scorched around the edges but otherwise undamaged. No names but three telephone numbers we've already been able to trace to the Southall area. The anti-terrorist squad boys are on the way over there, we should have them in custody soon.'

Samirah sat thinking about the unexpected news while the Commander and Jefferies enthused about the surprising piece of luck, suddenly quietening the pair with the announcement, 'I don't think it's the same Cell.'

'What makes you say that Sam ?' queried the M.I.5 Chief. ' We'll know soon enough if one of them turns out to be Saleem and one Mohammad.'

'I think we've had an extraordinary piece of luck and stumbled across a second group that were controlled by Hassam. We have to ask ourselves why Terrorists from Southall travel all the way into east Essex to meet ? It doesn't make sense. And we know Saleem lives in the Southend-on-Sea area. Don't forget, I had to go to the resort and take a boat trip on the *Waverley* in order to meet Saleem. He definitely caught the coach back to Southend, Charlie Walsh can confirm that.'

The Commander nodded his head in semi agreement before answering. 'Possibly so Sam but there could be a simple explanation. We don't know if the house in Hullbridge was a regular meeting place or was only used once or twice to finalise plans to transport some highly explosive propellant from Essex up to the barge, probably by boat. That would explain Saleem's presence in the area if he was chartering a vessel. There's no evidence to suggest he actually lives in the area; could be staying at a hotel or lodging house. He may have even been staying at the house for a while although the neighbours have already been questioned and say they only ever saw a British Telecom van in the driveway.'

Both Samirah and Pete Jefferies remained silent, awaiting the Commander's orders. He turned to them and was about to speak again when the telephone rang. The call was brief, the M.I.5 Chief listening without comment until replacing the handset with, 'Thanks Harry.'

The interruption gave the two Agents the opportunity to flick through the pages of the diary where Jefferies pointed out the telephone numbers and the few other notations on an occasional page. It was obvious the small journal had been used as a simple notebook.

'What if those numbers are innocent enough and not of Terrorists ?' whispered Sam.

'They almost certainly are. The Met tells me they are all located near to a Mosque they have infiltrated, a certain militant sheikh using it to indoctrinate some of the local youth.
What's the betting when these three are brought in they're all under twenty five.'

'That was Harry,' said the Commander. ' The tyre treads have almost positively been identified as belonging to a van of some description, two quite heavy saloon cars and an old scooter, possibly a Vespa. I wonder if any of your Southall suspects can be tied in with any of those Pete ?'

'It may be a few hours yet before we find out the answer to that question. I was thinking Sir; now we've withdrawn Meade and Davison we've no one back down in Essex. Perhaps Sam has a point and we should still be looking for a link now we've a little more to go on. Someone must know of a boat named Sprite and, the local coppers may have even come up with something on the identikit picture.'

'I was thinking the same before you came in Pete. Book yourself back in to your hotel Sam and get off ; the roads will be hell this time of day and in this diabolical weather.'

Kicking her boots off, Sam tucked her feet up on the bed, glanced at her watch, and reached for her coat. Seven thirty five; just time to try Brad before going back out for a meal. Her call went unanswered. 'Strange,' she uttered. 'Just my luck, he may have known of the *Sprite* and saved me a lot of time.'

Vowing to try again later, she tidied herself up in the bathroom and, mindful of the previous evening's experience , picked up her car keys and went out to find a suitable eating place.

Seven thirty, nice timing to go and get a meal round at the "Plough & Sail", thought Brad, stepping down from the deck of the *Whaleback* onto the pontoon at Wallasea Island after dropping off the angling party and his crewman at Bradwell.

Chapter 6

He stepped up on to the sea wall and the full force of the wind hit him as he peered into the darkness seeking the headlights of Trevor's car on it's way round from Bradwell.

At that precise moment his mobile phone, which he had forgotten and left aboard the launch in it's usual chart drawer out of any wet, rang. Unfortunately, such was the sound of the wind in the rigging of the many yachts at the Marina, he failed to hear the incessant Nokia "Dom Jolly" ring tone which ,on a quieter evening ,would have still been audible from his viewing point. Spotting two sets of vehicle headlights in the distance, one almost certain to be that of his crewman, he strode down the steps into the car park and went to meet the approaching car. Ten minutes later the seafaring couple were seated in the restaurant area of the Public House ordering a welcome hot meal after their cold, rough, day afloat.

'Lend me your mobile Skip. Better let Nancy know where we are; she'll only worry if I don't phone and like the idiot I am I left mine at home.'

Feeling in his coat pocket Brad embarrassingly admitted, 'Who's the idiot. I've left mine on the boat, looks like we'll both have to use the public phone outside. I've got a call to make as well.'

With a grin Trevor left the table to make his call, 'Order me the Steak and Ale pie Brad. Should I tell Nancy we'll be back tonight after all ?'

'I haven't heard from our film producer, unless he's phoned in the last twenty minutes. I can't imagine they'll still want to go out on a night like this but I suppose you had better say you'll phone back later after nine o'clock.'

Agent Samirah set her knife and fork down on the side of her empty plate and fished in her coat pocket for her mobile phone while awaiting an after dinner coffee. She first tried Brad's number again with the same result as her earlier attempt and was just thinking of contacting her M.I.5 Chief when her phone rang.

'Thank goodness I changed that awful 007 ring tone,' she whispered to herself. To her surprise it was Brad who she, incorrectly, assumed was out of range of her mobile service provider.

After listening to her previous day's consort's explanation she joked, 'I thought you had gone off me already, and me a lonely girl back in town. So you don't yet know whether you are coming back into town tonight ?'

'I should think there will be a very good chance that I will but it will be pretty late. More importantly if this weather doesn't improve I should imagine I'll be spending tomorrow ashore. What brings you back to Southend, are you still working ? We may well be able to meet tomorrow if you are not busy.'

Sam hesitated before replying, pondering how much time her enquiries would take in the morning. ' That would be nice, perhaps we can meet up for lunch. I do have some work to complete in the morning but will, hopefully, be free around midday. You could possibly help me find out what my company has sent me here for. With your knowledge of the local area do you know where I can find a boat named *Sprite* ?'

'What sort of craft is it ?' enquired Brad.

'As far as we know it's a motor vessel like your own, not a yacht or anything.'

'Then I can tell you young lady you are wasting your time looking around this part of the world. I would certainly know of it unless it's just turned up in the past couple of days: is it important ? I could make some enquiries for you but I fear you won't find it anywhere along the north side of the Thames Estuary.'

'In that case I may have to go across to Kent tomorrow. I don't know for sure how important it could be but I will speak to you in the morning. I've just got to pop along to the Police Station now so…..'

'Not in any sort of trouble are you ?' interrupted Brad, the concern showing in his voice.

'No, no,' laughed the Agent. ' Just got to see if they have been able to trace someone my department is looking for. Tell you all about it later. Bye for now lover boy .'

Brad replaced the receiver with a perplexed look on his face. What sort of job was it that sent a lovely looking young lady all over the country, chasing boats and missing people ?

One thing was certain. If he could trace the *Sprite* for her he'd earn himself a few "brownie points."

Had Sam been a little more explicit he would have earnt those points straight away. A description of the business card's colouring and wording, albeit burnt, would have resulted in the Skipper recognising it as one of his own old cards for the *SPRINTER*. And, had she mentioned the name of S. Hunter, Brad would almost certainly have associated it with his film producer's alias of Hunter Stevens.

'You coming Brad ?' enquired Trevor donning his anorak. ' We'd better get back in case that film mob turn up; it's gone eight thirty. You've probably got a message on your phone cancelling but I'd hate to think of them sitting there waiting for us with all that lovely lolly they're bringing.'

Driving back along the dark, unlit, country roads towards Wallasea Island, Swifty suddenly braked to a halt. ' You see what I see Skip ?'

Where the road in front of them dipped, the marshes on either side were showing only a few tufts of grass and heather above a sea of water which was just beginning to lap across the road itself.

'It is a 5.7 metre tide tonight but this blinking gale has pushed it up a bit, the road's going to be flooded shortly until the tide drops.'

'There's not much we can do about that Trev,' said Brad unconcerned. 'If they don't get here soon they'll just have to wait, that is if they are still determined to go out tonight.

I should think the road will be impassable in another ten minutes time until around ten thirty tonight. Let's get on into the warm and a nice cup of coffee. We'll worry about them later.'

The clock above the reception desk read seven forty as Saleem settled his bill and tipped the concierge who had struggled with his heavy holdall case. ' Will it be alright if I leave my car in your car park this evening. I am going with a friend shortly and will probably not be fit to drive later?' he lied. 'I'll collect it in the morning.'

'Certainly Sir. I hope you enjoyed your stay . Not a good night to be going out, it's blowing a real gale now and there's rain in the air. You may be getting wet later.'

'If you think I'm getting out in that lot you can go and drown yourself,' commented P.C. Anderson slamming the patrol car door back shut. 'Anyway it's not the one they're on the lookout for; wrong registration and I don't even think it's black.'

'I think you're right, looks to be more of a dark green in this light,' responded his partner P.C. Dave Sharp loud enough to make himself heard above the drumming rain on the roof. 'Did you pick up that photo fit the Serg mentioned last night ?'

'No, I thought you'd got it, no sign of it on the desk as I came out.'

'Must have blown on the floor when that pompous D.I. Davies couldn't even be bothered to close the door; blowing a right gale through the office it was.' said driver Dave seemingly unconcerned.

'We'll be for it in the morning if the Serg finds out we haven't even looked at it yet. Still, only a duck would want to be out on a night like this.'

The irascible *duck* in question not only wanted to be out, but was out in the torrential rain standing in front of the flooded roadway beside Mohammad's van fuming at the driver of a stranded Peugeot. ' You imbecile,' he snarled at the unfortunate motorist wading out of the near waist high water. 'We have an urgent appointment and you are stopping us getting by. Get that motor out of the way.'

The hapless motorist, soaked by his immersion and the heavy rain, was in an equally belligerent mood. Well-built and in his early twenties he was not intimidated by the aggressive Terrorist. 'Who do you think you're talking to mate? You don't think I wanted to stall in the middle of that do you?' he barked indicating the torrent behind him. ' I've got an appointment too with my girlfriend. You'll just have to wait until the tide drops: just like me.'

Saleem, mindful of his rendezvous time that allowed for little delay, lost any remaining self-control and launched himself at his drenched tormentor, screaming , ' Mohammad, Latif, come and help.'

The big Palestinian and both Amin brothers spilled out of the van.

Faced with the unequal odds, the motorist re-treated back into the flood water towards his vehicle, stumbling as Saleem's charge propelled him backwards with a splash. Before he could get back to his feet the head Terrorist's foot forced him back down, his head disappearing into the black rushing stream.

Fear lent the man strength. He twisted Saleeem's foot aside and raised his head and shoulders above the surface. Shaking his head, he was trying to regain his standing when, through blurred eyes he saw - seemingly almost in slow motion - a gun butt descending towards his temple. His futile attempt at deflecting the blow with his arm was far too slow,

Mohammad's brutal swing easily brushing aside his flailing limb to smash the heavy pistol into his head.

The motorist's body slid back beneath the water. 'Keep his head under,' ordered Saleem in a more controlled voice. 'He must not be allowed to report our presence here tonight. We will hide his body back down the road in the ditch where he'll not be found for days,' he added calmly as though murdering the luckless man was given no more thought than swatting a fly.

'No,' he suddenly said with a change of mind. 'Let's drag his vehicle out of the way and push it off the road into the saltings. I have a better idea.'

The elder Amin brother fetched a rope from the rear of their van and waded into the stream. Opening both front windows he passed the rope through the car and back to the van where he attached it in a similar manner. Two minutes later the Peugeot emerged up the slope clear of the flood as Latif slowly backed the van.

On the flat road the brothers found the vehicle easy to push and, following Saleem's instructions, steered the car off the hard road onto the soft edge of the grass saltings where it toppled down the slight incline onto it's side.

'Now, put that corpse head down in that water filled ditch alongside the car,' he ordered. ' When he's discovered, it will look as though he ran off the road and banged his head before collapsing into the water and drowning.'

'I don't reckon they're coming Brad. Look at the time, nearly ten fifteen. You sure there was no message on your phone ?' said Swifty pouring himself another cup of coffee.
'Must have seen sense and decided tonight was not the sort of night to spend at sea. Or, perhaps, they turned back when they saw the road was flooded. Your turn to poke your head up over the wall just to check. If there's no sign of them you can take your car back home and I'll sleep aboard tonight. In the morning the forecast is for a bit of a lull so I will probably bring the boat back round to Hole Haven creek.'
The crewman donned his oilskin coat and disappeared out of the cabin's warmth up to the wheelhouse, peering through the rain streaked side window before venturing out into the night. A few moments later he burst back in. 'Forget your beauty sleep Skip, a white van's just pulled up in the car park; I reckon it's our film crew. Nobody else would want to come out here to-

night unless they had to. I'll go and see if they want a hand.'
'Hold it Trev. I'd better go and see them. I'm sure they will want to postpone when I tell them what the conditions are like outside the river.'
The cabin door flew open before he had even grabbed his oilskins. Saleem - in his Hunter Stevens guise - entered, followed by the tall Mohammad who had to duck his head beneath the frame. Both men were soaked through, a pool of water instantly forming around their feet where they stood.
Saleem reached into his coat pocket and withdrew a large bundle of £20 pound notes, the outside ones slightly damp where the heavy rain had succeeded in penetrating the clothing.
'Here's your money. Let's get going straight away. I have a chart and will give you instructions as soon as the rest of my crew are here with some equipment that they are bringing on board now.' ordered the Terrorist chief in a tone that invited no argument.
Both Brad and Swifty were flabbergasted at the obvious irritation and aggressive attitude emanating from the drenched bedraggled figure in front of them.

Unruffled, Brad motioned the pair to sit on the bench seat beneath the ship to shore radio. ' Mr. Stevens, you should be aware that we have gale force conditions out at sea tonight. This boat is solidly built to withstand all weathers but it will be foolhardy to leave the river until this gale diminishes. Even then, the sea will remain an uncomfortable place to be for some hours afterwards. It is my recommendation, in the interests of your own and your film crew's safety, you postpone tonight for the next favourable set of conditions.'

Saleem jumped back up, screaming in fury at Brad, ' I will not abort this mission!' menacingly adding, ' This boat is going , with or without you. We are already late. '

'It's late. There's nothing more you can do tonight Sam, get to bed ,' suggested Commander Beaman returning the Agent's call to report a complete lack of developments on attempts at tracing the *Sprite*.

'Shall I try over the Kent side tomorrow Sir ?' questioned Sam before hanging up.

'No, we've had no indication of anything over there. We must be missing something. The Southall trio have been arrested and are now being interrogated but, it seems you may be right and they are not anything to do with Saleem. You must pursue your own line of enquiries but it might be an idea to try down at Old Leigh again in the morning, your Brad may be out of touch and, the local plod could always come up with something.'

Inwardly pleased at her Chief's suggestion to remain in the area, where she might be able to meet up with Brad again, she looked at the phone in her hand and was tempted to ring the handsome skipper. But, deciding she was letting personal feelings interfere with
the priority of her mission, she put the instrument aside and turned on the television news channel.

" …..the South East taking the brunt of the fierce gales," said the newscaster. " Our reporter ,Malcolm Weeks is at Margate where the full force of the wind has caused flooding and some structural damage. What can you tell us Malcolm?"

The picture changed from the newscaster in a comfortable studio to the windswept seafront of the Kent resort with the reporter, head bent against the wind and knee deep in water. " As you can see; tonight's high tide backed by this

afternoon's gale has caused some flooding along the seafront and, behind me here, you can see one tree virtually uprooted. The whole parade resembles a ghost town: the usual groups of revellers, drinkers and youngsters finding home comforts or in town establishments more to their liking tonight. It is hoped that the worst of the flooding is over, high tide scheduled in just over ten minutes time. But, by that time, much of the beach will have been deposited where I am standing, leaving the authorities with a massive clear up operation."
"Are there any reports of injuries Malcolm; and is it expected that any improvement will be seen soon ?"
"There have been reports of a few minor injuries caused by flying debris but no news of any serious casualties. Two or three boats have already broken away from their moorings and are now little more than matchwood on the beach . The local coastguard spokesman tells me he expects others will meet the same fate as there is no likelihood of the gales dying out for a few hours yet . The weather centre at Bracknell suggests the worst of the gale will be over by early morning although there is the probability of in-

creasing winds again tomorrow evening, with the possibility of a localised thunderstorm."

"Thank you Malcolm," said the Newscaster as the picture switched back to the studio. " We have in the studio with us, to discuss the violent weather we are currently experiencing, Professor..". The screen went blank as Samirah turned the set off and prepared for a shower and bed.

'Well Brad,' she murmured as she spotted the skipper's business card lying next to her phone, ' nobody but a complete idiot would deliberately set out to sea on a night like this; and I know you're no idiot. I look forward to seeing you tomorrow after all.'

'You are an idiot if you still want to go out in these conditions,' intervened Swifty.

'And what do you mean by MISSION and being LATE ? What sort of film crew are you lot ?'

The Terrorist looked at the crewman with hate-filled eyes as he withdrew the semi-automatic pistol from his pocket and pointed it directly between Swifty's eyes.

'What the hel...,' Brad started to say before the muzzle of the gun swung in his direction and Saleem interrupted, 'Quiet both of you, if you

know what's good for you. I have no wish to kill you but be quite certain, if I have to I will ! ' Noting a key in the lock of the below deck cabin; pointing with a sweep of the weapon, he ordered, 'Now get down there while my men bring some equipment aboard. Hold it a minute. Mohammad, check their pockets: make sure they have nothing they can use as a weapon or any mobile phones.'
As soon as the duo descended into the sleeping and galley area, Mohammad slammed the door shut behind them and turned the key.

Leaving the big Palestinian in the wheelhouse, Saleem returned to the van where the Amin brothers were anxiously waiting by the open back doors with two large holdalls and a leather case. 'Get that lot on board at once,' he snapped . 'Then go and park the van up behind that large yacht on the cradle support next to that boat-house over there. Hurry, we must not miss our appointment; our mission has begun.'

'What do you think is going on skip ?' asked Trevor as the lock clicked behind them. ' I said there was something fishy about that bloke the minute I set eyes on him.'

Chapter 6

Brad looked thoughtful for a minute before replying. 'One thing is certain, he's no film producer and there's something about that big , quiet, foreigner with him that I don't like. Reminds me very much of that Iraqi officer, when we were out in the Gulf, who was anxious to put a bullet into my head before you intervened. This character looks as though he would be happy to do the same.'

Swifty, with one ear to the door, interrupted; 'Sounds like there's two more of them and they've dumped something heavy in the wheelhouse.'

'That's not so good, makes the odds somewhat worse. We may have been able to take the two of them when they let us out of here, which they will have to do if they want to move from here. Even if they managed to find out how to start her up, there's no way they could handle a boat of this size without good seamanship experience.'

'You mentioning our Naval experiences has set me thinking,' said Trevor in a perplexed tone. 'Stevens, or whatever his name is, said the words *Abort* and *Mission*. They're normally associated with military actions. You don't think this mob are anything to do with the Army people on Foulness , do you ? '

'I shouldn't think so Trev, unless there's some secret gear or explosives they're after. But four of them wouldn't be much of a force against the numbers of army personnel on the Island. And, where would they go to get away? The sea's the only escape route. No, old friend, I think it is more likely they are drug smugglers intending to meet up with a ship somewhere off our coastline. Remember he said he had a chart and that they are late. I bet that we're supposed to take them out, at all costs, to rendezvous with their shipment.'

'We could get out and leave them to it boss. They think we're confined in here but I can soon unscrew those bulkhead screws , remove this panel and crawl through into the engine room. From there I can get back aft and back up on deck through the engine room hatch.'

'True but if they spot us before we get back to your car, remember they have a gun and will undoubtedly use it. I don't think Nancy would be too happy to become a widow. Better play their game for now and see if we get a better opportunity to turn the tables on them later.'

Chapter 6

Brad suddenly bent down to the lifebelt stowage locker and, grinning, retrieved and held up a screwdriver. 'Now at least we have a weapon. Pity we haven't got a mobile but mine's still in the chart drawer in the wheelhouse; if I get a chance to get it.'

Saleem pulled off his soaked outer coat and hung it up inside the wheelhouse door, retrieving both the tiny transmitter and mobile phone from the pockets. The transmitter he placed on the bench seating against the bulkhead and, deciding he had no further use for the phone put it back in the sodden coat.

The Amin brothers entered the wheelhouse, each with a large holdall which they unceremoniously dumped on the deck.

'Be careful with that equipment you oaf,' snarled Saleem at the younger man. ' That is our tracking unit: without that our mission is over before we start. We will never find the rendezvous with the transit ship and our explosives. Take the receiving unit out of that case and put it up on the bench, the power unit is in the other bag. Hurry, they won't wait for long and invite awkward enquiries if they are spotted on radar.'

'What about us Saleem ? Won't we be picked up on radar and tracked ?' enquired Mohammad.

'I have investigated the situation my friend. Don't worry, I chose this craft for that very reason. Without a radar reflector wooden boats return a very poor signal and this vessel is made entirely of wood. Give me the gun and go and remove the reflector mounted on top of this cabin. It is highly unlikely, especially in this weather, that we will be noticed where we are going and we will display those large canvas PILOT signs around the outside of the cabin when we come back into the Estuary; just like the time I first saw this boat at Leigh-on-Sea. That should avoid any inquisitiveness if we are spotted.'

Mohammad ducked out of the wheelhouse, returning within a few minutes with the metal deflector. The Terrorist chief ordered him to dispose of it over the side and beckoned to Latif to release their prisoners.

"Control to 224; come in 224; where are you over? " the tinny voice implored through the speaker, interrupting P.C. Sharp's reading of the newspaper in the dim light of the patrol car's interior.

'No peace for the wicked. Better get that Barry ; could be something more exciting than sitting here bored out of our minds.'

'Two two four to Control, we're taking our break in Rochford square, what's up ,over?'

" We have just got a report of a car off the road at Wallasea near Paglesham . No further details, the young lady who reported it was too frightened to stop in the dark. You appear to be the nearest, please investigate and report.....out."

P.C. Barry Anderson screwed up his fish'n chips wrapping, slid down the window and accurately lobbed the paper ball into an adjacent waste bin. ' Drive on my man. Probably just a courting couple pulled into a layby. It will be pitch black out there with no lights. Who knows, if we approach quietly we might catch them at it; make the night more interesting eh ?'

'Well should be easy enough to spot, there's only a single road into Wallasea once we get past the Paglesham turn off.' responded the driver. 'Let's hope you're right and it's nothing. Don't fancy being stuck out in the wilds for the rest of the shift awaiting ambulances and the like.'

Less than ten minutes later their headlights brushed over the overturned Peugeot as they rounded a shallow bend, the vehicle still half immersed in the soft mud of the marshland and tidal flood.

P.C. Sharp stood on the brakes and the police car skidded to a halt a few yards short of the road dip which still had a foot deep stream of ebb tide water covering the surface.

Grabbing a flashlight from the glove compartment, P.C. Anderson leapt out and shone the beam in front of him, carefully avoiding stepping off the roadway as he approached the small French , forlorn looking, car. The clear cut beam penetrated the coal black surroundings to pick out a motionless front wheel before sweeping over the windscreen and illuminating an empty interior.

'Empty Dave,' he called back, turning to return to the patrol vehicle. The haphazardly swinging beam caught a leg and foot protruding above the edge of a salting's mud hole before swinging back to focus on the macabre sight.

'Better get on the radio for an ambulance and the accident investigation boys. Looks like we've got a drunk gone off the road; there's no sign of a collision or damage to the vehicle.

Chapter 6

And, from the position of our friend here, he's not going to wake up with a sore head; he's not going to wake at all.'

Better wake the Captain,' said the Russian Second Officer of the **Prince Sviatoslavl** wallowing in deep troughs ten miles north of North Foreland near to the Kentish Knock, on a northerly course en route for the German port of Bremerhaven.

'We must increase speed . Tell the Captain there is no sign of the launch: they must have abandoned the rendezvous in this storm.'

'I am already here Aleksei. You are correct, we cannot delay any longer. Prepare the flotation collars and sea anchor. Have someone lash those crates together.'

'Are we adopting the alternative plan Captain ?'

'We will give them a further ten minutes. If there is no sign of them after that we will have no choice but to cast the crates adrift; the signal transmitter will continue to send it's call for some hours yet. If they are coming and delayed by the storm they will be able to locate the cases long after we are gone on our way. We have been well paid but we certainly cannot dock in Bremerhaven with those crates aboard.'

The Officer left the bridge to supervise the preparation of disposal of the unwanted illicit cargo, returning a short while later to report all was ready for the deliberate jettisoning ; a minor problem with the cargo hoist crane being fixed within the next few minutes.

Turning to the port side lookout, the Captain enquired, ' Still nothing Dmitrii ?'

' Not a pinprick of light Captain, black as Hades out there.'

'That's it Aleksei; get rid of those crates even if you have to have them manhandled overboard.'

Peering over the port bridge wing, Captain Georgii Borisova saw the brightly coloured orange flotation bags slip by in the relative calm of the lee provided by the ship's side before ordering the helmsman to bring the ship back on course and increase speed to leave the cargo tossing in their wake. The brilliance of the diminutive flashing LED light of the transmitting device remarkably, despite the heaving sea and spindrift, remained intermittently visible astern of the Russian vessel for more than ten minutes before disappearing to leave a pitch black void.

Chapter 6

A flash of light suddenly lit up the cabin interior as the door opened and Latif shone a powerful torch beam in to reveal Brad and Trevor casually lounging on their bunks, seemingly unperturbed by their incarceration.

'Come ,' he ordered stepping back into the wheelhouse where Asif was rummaging through the bench locker; hauling out the heavy canvas notices.

The duo emerged to find themselves facing the lethal looking automatic in Mohammad's firm grip and Saleem nursing a small metal case from which there protruded a small aerial and illuminated green button.

'Right Mr.Murray, we should get underway immediately now. There is a chart on the bench, the red cross on it denoting where you are to take us at the best speed.'

'What makes you think we are going to take you anywhere, gun or no gun ?' replied Brad.

'Because if you don't do exactly as I say I will press this green button,' said the Terrorist leader threateningly. ' In so doing ,your friend Mr. Swift becomes a widower. It will set off a bomb we have placed in his daughter's doll's house at his home on Canvey Island.'

'You murdering bastard,' screamed the crewman, unthinkingly launching himself across the wheelhouse towards Saleem. Fast as he was, Mohammad appeared to have been expecting the attack; quickly stepping in front of his leader; blocking the attempted assault ,and swinging the pistol at Trevor's head.

Instinctive reaction, or his Special Boat Service training, saved him from serious injury as, at the last second, he twisted himself under the descending weapon and caught just a glancing blow on his shoulder as he crashed into Saleem.

The unexpected collision propelled the leading Terrorist back through the open door, his feet catching on the sill ;sending him sprawling on his back and the bomb transmitter scudding across the open deck into the gunwales.

Darting through the doorway, the crewman threw himself across the deck and had just got his hand on the lethal signal device when a heavy foot crushed his wrist to the boat's flooring.

'Move another inch and I will blow your brains out,' growled Mohammad bending down to retrieve the transmitter.

'Give me that !' hissed the hate-filled voice of the Terrorist leader. ' That was your first and last mistake Mr. Swift. I warned you of the consequences of disobeying my orders. Now your wife and daughter must die.'

His poised thumb descended towards the lit button, halting when Brad, held in the doorway by the Amin brothers, shouted, 'STOP! We will do as you say.'

Such was the malevolence of Saleem, even then he appeared to be intent on carrying out the murderous act; stopped only by his second in command's strong grasp of his wrist and whispered, 'No Saleem, now is not the time. We need them to get us to our rendezvous and targets.'

Mention of the rendezvous brought Saleem back from his adrenaline fired provocation that threatened the whole mission.

'Get inside all of you,' he snapped. 'Latif, you and Asif tie those PILOT banners along the cabin sides. Mr. Swift, you go and release us; no more funny tricks! Mr. Murray, take us to the meeting point.'

Brad gunned the engines as Swifty hauled their mooring ropes back aboard, nudging the wheel to take them into midstream before glancing back at the chart Saleem had spread on the bench. One glance was enough to cause him to immediately throttle back.

'You must be mad. There's a fully fledged gale blowing and you are asking to be taken to a dangerous spot for boats of our size in such conditions. The confluence of the outer reaches of the Thames Estuary, the North Sea and English Channel is often an area where sea states can be extremely turbulent, the three way tidal battle for supremacy - dependent upon wind force and direction - creating a transversing nightmare for any small boat sailor. In gale force conditions even a large ship losing power would find itself battered off course and in danger of grounding.'

'I am not asking you Mr. Murray, I'm ordering you to take us there!' commanded Saleem. 'We do not have the luxury of delaying our trip. No more arguments or I press this button.'

A hissing emitted from the ship to shore radio set mounted on the wheelhouse bulkhead, reminding the Terrorist leader of it's presence. ' Two more things Mr. Murray. You will make no attempt to use the radio, I could easily destroy it if necessary, and; once we are out of the river turn off your navigation lights and the main lights in here.'

Chapter 6

'The radar deflector's missing Skip,' exclaimed Swifty as he re-entered the wheelhouse. ' Should I rig up a temporary one, we'll be difficult to pick up in this weather as it is ?'

Before Brad could respond Saleem snapped, 'You will not! That is the idea, we do not wish to be observed.'

The leading Terrorist beckoned to the Amin brothers to follow him down into the main cabin, leaving Mohammad guarding Brad and his crewman.

Trevor stripped off his wet weather clothing before joining Brad at the wheel, whispering, ' Can't we do something Skip? I've got to get that transmitter off that Stevens guy: he's a nut-case. I can't even warn Nancy.'

Mohammad, seated at the rear of the cabin, made no attempt to stop them conversing despite their hushed tones being drowned out by a combination of engine noise, wind and sea. Not once, however, did the small gun in his large fist waver from their direction.

'The others don't appear to be armed. If we could take that off him we could handle them even though outnumbered,' said Brad quietly. 'But all the while Saleem - that's Mr. Stevens's real name if I heard our bearded friend back there correctly - has that little box of his we daren't make a move. As you say, he's so tense he'll snap at the slightest provocation; we can't put Nancy and Naomi in danger.'

'Maybe we'll get a chance later on. Have you noticed *Blackbeard* is holding the gun in his left hand and hardly using his right arm? I think he's really right handed but for some unknown reason seems reluctant to use that side at all,' responded Swifty.

'You could be right. He definitely winced when you knocked past him after Saleem. Might be to our advantage to remember that later.'

The cabin door slammed open interrupting further conversation ; the younger Amin brother with a hand over his mouth scrambling for the outer deck rail. Unfortunately, he chose the wrong side of the boat, the ejaculating spume of vomit promptly returning in the face of the gale force wind to splatter the youngster with a second serving of his earlier dinner.

Brad grinned at his crewman. 'And we're not out of the river yet. Let's see what sort of sailors we have on board, shall we ?' he said opening the throttles of the twin engines to propel the *Whaleback*'s sleek hull towards the open sea.

Chapter 6

'It's enough to make you sick. Why us ?' complained P.C. Dave Sharp as the car radio blared out another order for the duo to check out the whole area after the ambulance and Doctor had left with the corpse of the Peugeot driver. 'See if there are any other vehicles around. There's a pub down at Wallasea Island. They should be closed by now but you know what these country places are like: there could be a few locals still drinking up who may have seen something earlier,' said the duty Sergeant's gruff voice from the speaker.

'There's our early return to the bright lights of town gone. I know this area, there's only two places to look; the boatyard up by the Marina and the Pub car park.'

'Let's get on with it then, I'm bloody starving. It's alright for you, I could eat that fish'n chips you had earlier..... should have joined you then I guess.'

The car parks at both the public house and Marina were devoid of vehicles. It was only when the patrol vehicle's headlights swept past a large yacht on turning back that P.C. Anderson suddenly uttered, ' Hold it Dave ! There's a van parked over there: let's investigate.'

'Strange. Empty and unlocked. Someone doesn't appear to be concerned if it gets stolen. Nothing else here though. Better radio it in Dave. Let's go and find you some supper somewhere.'

'Fancy a bit of supper Skip, a nice greasy bacon sandwich,' said Swifty in a voice loud enough to be heard by their captors. 'Or, I've got some of that thick pea soup.'

Asif, seated on the deck: looking decidedly green, groaned and promptly retched into the bucket held between his legs. His brother, Latif, looked unconcerned by both the mention of food or the bucking, rolling motion of the vessel. But, Saleem made a quick exit out on to the rear deck and even the impassive Mohammad stood back from the tracking instrument he was studying on the bench to gulp in some fresh air at the doorway.

Clear of the River mouth, the full force of the gale was hitting the craft from the forward port beam and attempting to force the vessel off it's north easterly course. The wind against an ebbing tide created the most uncomfortable of situations; the heavy swells lifting and dropping the boat while, at the same time, the windswept waves caused a twisting roll.

'Let's hope he goes overboard, or at least drops that confounded signal device over,' whispered Trevor.' Where are we now ?'

'Just passing the Whitaker beacon. In these conditions I reckon on at least another half an hour before we get to that spot on Saleem's chart. They obviously expect to pick up a signal on that equipment they have before then: probably some sort of guidance unit.'

The crewman peered through the forward screen "Clearview" wiper, seeing nothing but blackness: murmuring to his skipper, 'There's nothing out there yet that I can see; certainly no large ship which I would have expected. Another thing I've been thinking about is your idea of them being drug smugglers. Would drug smugglers go to all the trouble of installing a bomb in my house ? And, three of them are definitely Middle Eastern ; all four probably, Saleem is no English name.'

'One thing Trev,' said Brad in a hushed tone. 'Three of them are also certainly finding things not to their liking. If they get any more sick it may be our chance to take back control.'

The terrorists' electronic equipment suddenly uttered a bleep, causing Mohammad to step back inside and scan the small illuminated screen. 'Latif, inform Saleem we have a contact.'

So now we know thought Brad. They don't seem to care that we know their names and can obviously describe them. That can mean only one thing. Whatever the kidnappers were planning, he and Swifty were not going to survive indefinitely.

'Mr Murray, come here!' ordered a sorry looking, pasty -faced, Saleem on re-entering the cabin. ' We are here,' he said, stabbing a finger at a white blob on the outer rim of the screen. ' Steer a course to arrive here,' he added pointing to a flashing red pinprick of light in the centre of the visual display. 'A ship awaits us.'

'That's about ten to fifteen miles away. Even in these conditions we should be able to spot their running lights from here if the ship is of any size. I 'll get my binoculars from the chart drawer.'

Hoping he would also be able to sneak his mobile phone out of the drawer, he raised a hand and smoothed an eyebrow, a signal to his crewman from their Special Boat Service days that some sort of diversion would be useful.

Chapter 6

An imperceptible nod from Swifty , manning the wheel, showed his cryptic message was understood.

Just as he approached the drawer, the *Whaleback's* engines spluttered and coughed as the crewman's concealed hand manipulated the fuel cut-out tap beneath the cabin wall shelf.

The eyes of all four Terrorists turned towards Swifty - seated in front of the engine control console - alarm showing on their faces.

Brad quickly opened the drawer, reached in and fumbled among the rolled up charts for his phone.

'Looking for this Mr. Murray ?' said the amused voice of the terrorist leader in his ear, his seasickness temporarily forgotten as he smilingly displayed Brad's mobile phone. ' I took the precaution of searching the drawers while you were incarcerated below when we first came aboard. At first I thought I had put my own phone in there and forgotten as it is the same model . And, don't take me for a fool Mr. Swift,' he roared. 'I don't know what you did but I suggest you sort the engine out immediately .'

The crestfallen Skipper picked up his binoculars without answering and stepped back to the windscreen, noting Saleem hand the phone and bomb transmitter to his Lieutenant before rushing back outside. Handicapped by his injured arm, Mohammad commanded Latif to put Brad's phone in the pocket of Saleem's coat hanging on the wheelhouse door.

'There's nothing to be seen , there must be something wrong with your equipment,' said Brad putting down the field glasses and striding over to the Terrorists' guidance unit.

The red light blinked strongly and their own position had moved considerably closer. Perplexed, the skipper stepped out on to the undulating deck, tightly clasping a mast stay to remain on his feet while he stared out into the coal black night.

A groan from the prone figure of Saleem , slumped against the aft cabin with a pool of vomit between his legs, temporarily distracted the boat captain's gaze at what appeared to be an intermittently flashing blue light a few miles ahead.

'Port five degrees Trev,' he shouted back through the doorway. ' See it. There's a flashing blue light just up ahead. No sign of a ship's lights though. Better slow in case there's something there.

Chapter 6

The news of the contact roused Saleem sufficiently to raise himself up and stagger back into the wheelhouse. 'What is it Mohammad ?' he croaked. Where is the ship ?'

Swifty, guided by Brad's signalled directions through the windscreen from the foredeck, carefully edged the powerful launch alongside the flashing light. The skipper, holding the guard rail with one hand, leant over with a long boat hook and hauled in the signal device attached to a stout rope which he walked back along the deck towards the stern where he securely fastened it to a deck cleat.

'There's your drugs or whatever Gentlemen; three crates ,' said Brad scornfully on stepping back into the cabin. 'Your ship appears to have chucked them overboard.'

'We must bring them on board immediately,' said Saleem struggling to overcome his nausea .

'That will not be possible in these seas,' exclaimed the Skipper.' You have only one fully able person and either myself or my crewman will have to stay at the wheel. Two persons will not be able to get those crates on board unless we find some calmer waters.'

'We need to head towards Southend. We do not have time to go back into the River Crouch. I don't care how you do it but I must have those packages on board…..or else,' said Saleem viciously.

'Then we will tow them behind us until it is safe to get them on board without losing someone over the side. We should get a bit of shelter close in to the "Man-made Island" off Foulness, especially with the tide ebbing and the sands becoming dry. If the forecast is correct the wind should also decrease soon for a few hours before returning later in the day.'

The Terrorist leader conceded to Brad's sensible suggestion and an hour later the *Whaleback* dropped anchor in sheltered waters; with less than four feet under the keel.

Saleem, already feeling less nauseous, ordered Brad and Swifty to lift the crates aboard with the assistance of Latif, the younger brother still in a semi comatose condition being of no help.

In the cabin with Mohammad and Asif, their leader looked at his watch, grinned, and uttered the fateful words:' It is Thursday, the day the whole world will remember.'

Chapter 6

7

'Nice to know someone remembered,' said the Desk Sergeant in a jokingly sarcastic manner. 'Gone midnight and it's the first cuppa anyone's brought out. I could die of thirst out here. Got any biscuits, it's another couple of hours before my canteen break ?'
'Getting a bit lonely out here are you ?' replied policewoman Thomas; discourteously known amongst her colleagues as "Mae West" on account of her ample bosom. 'Nothing much happening anywhere it seems, a couple of call - ins that's all,' she added placing a few sheets of paper on the desk.

The Sergeant sipped his tea and picked up the messages. *Shop door unlocked at bottom of High Street, owner contacted. No further action required.* Putting the note aside he started to read the second , as radioed in by P.C.s Sharp and Anderson. *Creeksea Ferry Inn and Essex Ma-*

rina car parks checked as requested following fatal accident on Wallasea road. Pub car park ,only dark blue locked Mondeo, registration DAA 35W . White Ford Transit van, registration TGS 66L , unlocked and empty in Marina car park, engine still warm. Marina checked, no obvious occupants on any boat.

'Didn't that pretty young Government Agent, who popped in just after I came on duty, say something about a white van?' he said to the empty office.' I wonder if the boss has been told ?' He picked up an internal phone: punched in a short number and spoke briefly to the person on the other end. 'Typical; had to be D.I. Davies didn't it ? If it is something to do with that suspected Terrorist character they're after, no guessing who will take the credit.'

D.I. Davies, although not the most popular man in the Force, was a competent Officer.

Within minutes he had the results of a vehicle registration check in front of him. 'What do you make of this?' he called over to a colleague lounging back with his feet up on the desk. 'Got a white van left abandoned that is registered to a Mohammad Sadat at a Leytonstone address.'

The lazing detective suggested, 'The Guvnor's gone home long ago, it might be a good idea to let that London Anti-Terrorist squad know; they're looking for a white van thought to be in this area.'

Commander Beaman, unlike the Southend police chief, had not gone home and was still in his office discussing the day's events with Pete Jefferies and Richard Meade.

'If Samirah's information is correct, today could be our worst nightmare. The more I think about it the more convinced I become that she is right and the barge is the least of our worries. What did Saleem say to her ? By Friday : that leaves us less than twenty four hours ,' commented Jefferies. 'If only we could get a breakthrough someh….', the harsh ringing of the outside phone on the Commander's desk curtailed the conversation.

Meade, being nearest, lifted the handset to his ear and listened silently before beckoning for a notepad and covering the mouthpiece with his other hand. ' It's Southend C.I.D. for you Sir. Shall I take a message ?'

The Chief signalled an assent.

'We may have got Pete's wish. The Southend boys have located an, apparently abandoned, white Ford Transit van at a place ten miles north of Southend in a Marina car park. The registered owner is a Palestinian refugee, a Mohammad Sadat' said Meade in a gleeful voice.

'Phone Southend back and tell them to get someone out there to keep an eye on that van until we get a crew there to examine it,' ordered the Commander. ' We know that one of the Terrorists is named Mohammad; Samirah discovered that when Saleem inadvertently disclosed it to her. It's too much of a coincidence that we have a white Ford transit and an owner by the name of Mohammad for there to be no connection with this threat. I'm sorry Pete, I know you didn't get much sleep last night, but I think you had better get a gang together and get down there. It could be our best result to date.'

'There was another incident in the area that may be associated,' interceded Meade. 'The van was discovered by a patrol who were investigating an apparent accident on the lonely road leading to the Marina, a young chap having gone off the road into some marshland. It was thought he had hit his head on the windscreen, stumbled out of his car into a water-filled dyke, and drowned. The Doctor who attended voiced an immediate opinion that the injury to the youngster's head could not have been caused by the accident; promising to produce a definitive report in the morning.'

'In that case Peter, make sure you are armed. We don't know who we are dealing with here. They could still be in the area.'

'Don't forget Sir,' Samirah is already in Leigh-on-Sea. Should I wake her and advise her of the discovery ? She could ensure the local constabulary don't go sending their own people to mess things up until I get there with our experts.'

'You get off straight away Pete; Richard or myself will put Sam in the picture after I've had a chance to think of our best plan of action. I really do have to put in an appearance at home ,for a few hours at least, but I will be back in very early. Let me know what you find when you get a chance.'

The Senior Agent gathered his coat off his chair back and, stopping only to make a telephone call, accompanied the Commander down the corridor, leaving Agent Richard in charge of the office for the rest of the night.

'If this is a lead, I can't help wondering if we are looking in the wrong area Sir,' he said on catching up with his Chief. 'I know the area concerned a little: spent a week's sailing holiday with a mate at Burnham a few years ago. The

River Crouch is only a few miles south of the River Blackwater which is where the Bradwell Nuclear Power Station is.'

'Not much use blowing that up these days Peter,' commented the Commander. ' It was decommissioned in 2002 when it's licence expired.'

'But didn't I read somewhere that the spent fuel rods had still not been shipped off to Sellafield for reprocessing. If they were blown up, wouldn't that release atomic particles into the atmosphere and contaminate a wide surrounding area like that Chernobyl accident did in Russia ?'

The Commander stopped. 'You go on Pete. I'll pop back and tell Meade to see if he can find out whether you are right. We've got to consider every possibility I suppose; no sense in taking any chances.'

'We can't take a chance Trev. It's a good idea but what if the weather gets worse again and you are not spotted in the morning,' Brad whispered to his crewman on hearing of his plan to *accidently* fall overboard while hauling in the crates and swim the short distance to the Man-made Island in the darkness.

At first, the plan had seemed a way out of their dilemma, Trevor hiding out until the boat moved off and then using the small torch to signal any passing vessel - or wait for morning light and hope to be spotted. Once ashore he could alert the authorities of their kidnapping; get Nancy and Naomi out of the bungalow and the bomb squad in to remove the explosive.

'And, I wouldn't trust that maniac leader. He is mad enough to press the button out of sheer frustration if either of us disappear. Even if you got away with it that water is going to be cold at this time of the year, you'd freeze to death all night out on that Island soaking wet and with no shelter. No, we'll get a chance later I'm sure. That youngster, Asif - is that what they called him ? - is so sick he's no problem.'

'Nor is that big bloke really,' said the crewman recognising Brad's sensible assessment of the idea. 'One good hit on that right arm of his and we've only got a one-handed opponent.'

'If only we knew what they are planning; perhaps they'll let something slip when we get those crates on board.'

Under the watchful eye of the Terrorist leader and his deputy, Brad, Swifty and Latif dragged the first of the crates over the stern, gasping at the effort required. The second and third crates, less weighty, proved easier to handle and soon joined the first on the rear deck where Saleem ordered the ropes and flotation chambers cut away.

'Cover those two long boxes with a tarpaulin Latif while our *friends* here carry that heavy one through to the cabin.'

The stench of vomit inside the main cabin hit them as they opened the hatchway, but Asif had, in the relatively calm waters of the Island's lee shore, made something of a recovery and was now on his feet making some attempt to clean his soiled clothing.

'Go and help your brother, and while you're there, clean that disgusting mess off,' commanded the unsympathetic Terrorist leader. 'You,' he added addressing Swifty, 'Go and get something to open this crate. Keep an eye on him Mohammad.'

Trevor, followed by the big Palestinian, went back out on deck and opened the tool locker bolted to the deck in front of the wheelhouse. Withdrawing a two foot long crowbar he was tempted to use it on his gun-wielding captor, confident he could successfully disarm him without harm to himself. The thought, however, of Saleem with his detonating device made him hesitate long enough for Mohammad to grasp the tool and wrench it from his hands. Grinning maliciously, he motioned the exasperated boatman back to the others.

'Tie them together on that bench seat while we open this box, I want to put this transmitter down for a while,' said Saleem feeling less nauseous in the calmer waters..

The Amin brothers came back in just as the top of the crate was levered back to reveal a black rubber wetsuit and small oxygen tank. Latif lifted the suit out and held it against him. Satisfied, he examined the air cylinder and tapped the gauge before signalling a "thumbs up" to his chief.

Beneath the suit the remainder of the box was full of shoe-box sized packages wrapped in oiled parchment. Saleem signalled for them to be lifted out and stacked on the deck, ten in all, his smile widening with every parcel deposited at his feet. Peering in the now empty crate, the Terrorist Chief 's smiling visual expression changed to one of bewilderment quickly followed by dismay and finally a snarling anger. 'Where are the detonators, timers and transmitter

?' he fumed. 'The imbeciles have forgotten them.'

The Amin brothers backed away from their red-faced leader, fearful of his violent temperament; but Mohammad, imperturbable as ever, quietly calmed the atmosphere with a simple, 'Wait.' as he disappeared out onto the deck. Less than a minute later he was back cradling one of the other packing cases.

'They contain only rocket launchers and high explosive rockets my friend, useful only for the final part of our mission.'

'This one is longer and larger than the other Saleem. I think it contains more than you suspect.'

His composure recovered, Saleem grabbed the crowbar and eagerly prised the crate open. As with the first case opened, waterproof wrappings ensured the contents remained dry despite their recent, unscheduled ,immersion in the sea. The Terrorist lifted out the longest package and unwrapped it.

Swifty, forgotten ,along with Brad, in the excitement of the past five minutes, let out a long low whistle as the familiar form of a missile rocket launcher came into view. 'You're bloody

Terrorists aren't you ? Who do you intend murdering with that you spineless cowards ?'

Saleem stepped over to the bound captives , lifted the crowbar and swung it towards the crewman's defenceless head. Unable to twist himself out of the way of the descending iron bar ,Swifty sought to duck beneath it but, hampered by his attachment to the skipper, only succeeded in partially avoiding the intended blow which, had it struck him fully, would most certainly have killed him.

As it was, Brad's sideways jerk at the right moment pulled his threatened pal away from the wild swing, but not sufficiently far enough to avoid some contact, the crowbar catching the boatman a glancing blow high on the forehead .

Swifty , blood spurting from a nasty gash, slumped to the deck pulling his hapless companion with him. The explosion of stars in front of his eyes cleared to leave a blurred vision of a savage evil looking Saleem bending over him with the crowbar raised for a second strike; before unconsciousness overtook him and blackness descended.

The blackness of the deserted Marina car park was matched by P.C. Sharp's mood. 'How long

do they expect us to sit here twiddling our thumbs. Why couldn't someone else come and stand guard ? That crowd from London could be hours yet.'
'Could be worse Dave,' responded his mate. ' At least we're in the dry and there's nothing to stop us getting our heads down until they arrive. Got any of those sandwiches left ?'
'That's all you ever think about, your stomach and sleep. Me, I'm going to take a look inside that van at the back before anyone gets here.'
'They said don't touch it. Might be something to do with that Terrorist character we're supposed to be on the look out for….when we get the photo fit. Anyway, it seemed to be empty when I looked earlier.'
'Ah, but you didn't take more than a cursory look in the back. You couldn't have seen much through that back window. Why should the C.I.D. boys get all the glory? If there's any clues or anything in there it'll help my application for a transfer to Criminal Investigation. I've always fancied myself as Southend's answer to *Columbo.*'
'Yeah, you've got the sloppy raincoat alright but, with that broom head moustache of yours I'd suggest Inspector Frost ,' joked his partner.

The would-be Detective was disappointed to discover P.C. Anderson was correct in stating the back of the vehicle was empty, almost as though it had been swept clean.

Turning his attention to the driving compartment, he searched the door pockets and glove compartment which were also empty but, on stepping back out of the van door, he spotted a piece of paper wedged between the frame and seat cushion.

A blast of his patrol car's horn warned him of the impending arrival of the Anti-Terrorist Londoners. Snatching the paper from the seat ,he raced back to the car in time to see the approaching headlights of two vehicles and was safely ensconced in his seat when the cars pulled up alongside.

'We'll take it from here chaps,' said Agent Jefferies. ' Nobody been back to it I suppose?'

' Not since we've been watching; it's all yours mate,' replied P.C. Smart affably. 'We're off back to the station; it's past our break time.'

'Okay *Columbo,* you've solved the mystery of the "White Van case", have you ?' said Anderson sarcastically as the Agents moved off.

Chapter 7

'You drive Barry, I might have something here,' responded his partner waving the piece of paper at him.

Opening the paper out as they drove back towards town, it was evident it was a receipt from a costume hire company; but a combination of poor interior light and feeble printing from the machine that produced it, made the rest of it indecipherable. 'It's nothing, just a bill for a fancy dress outfit someone hired.'

'It could be important. Keep it until we get back to the canteen and have a proper look.'

'Let me have a proper look,' said Brad referring to Swifty's gashed head. 'There's a first aid kit in the cupboard down below that I'll need to patch him up.'

The crowbar had not reached it's target a second time, Brad's firm grasp on the bar, as it descended towards his crewman, stopping the intended blow at the same time as Mohammad had clasped his arms about the Terrorist leader and pulled him away.

'No, Saleem, we still need them if we are to be successful. Don't let them anger you; just remember what is at stake. As it is, you have hit him hard and it is likely he will be unconscious for some time.'

'Throw him in the forward cabin and lock him in; he's bleeding all over the deck,' said Saleem contemptuously. 'Untie Mr. Murray; he can see to him and then come and get us to our first target.'

While cleaning Swifty's wound and tightly bandaging his head, Brad thought about the armaments and explosives he had just witnessed being unwrapped. Although uncertain of the exact nature of the explosive material, it was evident that the power such quantities would produce would be massive. With timers and signalling transmitters it was apparent they were well trained in the use of such items. There was no doubt now what they were: all pretence of film makers completely dispelled and, his guess of drug smugglers also utterly incorrect.

Swifty groaned and his eyelids flickered ,disturbing his Skipper's train of thought but, the momentary return to semi consciousness quickly lapsed, leaving Brad contemplating what actions he could take against his captors. With all four now armed with handguns, and the bomb detonator still active in Saleem's possession, he recognised the dire situation he found himself in; especially with his crewman now incapacitated. Uncertain as he was about the immediate plans of the Terrorists, one thing he was certain about was that he and Swifty were not intended to have any future.

'Leave him now, we need to go,' ordered Saleem through the doorway.

Stepping back up into the wheelhouse, Brad noted that Latif had donned the wet suit and was testing the breathing apparatus, his brother assisting.

Mohammad was seated on the bench seat with a small dismantled electronic box on his lap. 'That's fixed,' he declared gleefully as a buzzing emitted from the device.

'Good work my friend. Connect the detonator wire and put the cover back on; we must be at our target in half an hour's time when the tide is at it's lowest,' enthused Saleem.

An unexpected larger swell, probably resulting from a large passing ship further out in the Estuary, suddenly caught the *Whaleback* beam on, violently rocking the craft and sending the three standing terrorists careering across the cabin to end up in a tangled heap on the deck.

As they struggled to their feet, Mohammad cursed and dropped to his knees. 'One of the small plate fixing screws has fallen on the deck somewhere: I'll never find it in this dim light.'

'Never mind, we cannot turn on any more lights. The flimsy blinds on the windows are next to useless. We do not want to make ourselves easily visible to any ships or shore watch stations. Three screws will be sufficient,' said the, seemingly, unconcerned leader. 'Mr. Murray, take us as near to the wreck of the S.S. Montgomery as you can; no arguments please if you know what is good for you and your mate. Asif, are you recovered sufficiently to go out on deck and check we have no lights showing, and make the dinghy ready?'

Feeling far from well, the youngster welcomed the opportunity to get out of the confines of the wheelhouse into the fresh air, especially as the launch moved out from the lee shore into deeper waters and started to dip its bow into the waves. 'I will see to it Saleem: should I load the explosives ?'

The Terrorists' intentions suddenly dawned on Brad. 'You cannot put a bomb on the wreck . The Government will not be held to ransom and give in to any of your demands; even if you can get near enough without being detected,' he yelled.

Chapter 7

Saleem laughed - an evil sneering chuckle. 'You are mistaken Mr. Murray, we need get no nearer than a few hundred yards in this boat which is unlikely to be detected by the radar surveillance. The final approach will be by your rubber dinghy.'

'You are mad. This storm has not blown itself out yet; the sea is still pretty rough and, seeing your man in his wet suit, I assume you intend doing more than just dumping an explosive charge over the side. Do you know how dangerous that would be? The sands will have been well stirred up; he won't be able to see more than a foot in front of his face even with a powerful lamp.'

'We are aware of the risks but it is essential that we place our bomb directly into one of the holds containing the old munitions. Latif is a powerful swimmer and I myself will be supporting him from the dinghy. As for the Government giving in to our demands: WE ARE NOT GOING TO MAKE ANY.'

'You don't mean to say you actually intend to blow the ship up ?' said the skipper incredulously. 'Why ? Some experts say it would result in one of the biggest non-nuclear explosions the world has ever seen, but the damage would probably be confined to buildings' windows at Sheerness and Southend. There could be some flooding of course: it is estimated that a two to three metre high wave would be created, causing problems for the low lying areas of the Kent coastline and, dependent upon the state of the tide at the time, possibly places as far up river as Canvey Island and beyond.'

'Yes, we know all that Mr. Murray; that's exactly what we want it to do.'

'But, you're not going to deny you are Terrorists. I thought your sort were only interested in causing as many deaths and casualties as possible. Unless there are any ships unfortunate enough to be nearby at the time of the explosion, however huge, the human death toll could be nil. It doesn't make sense, all this effort, discomfort and danger for a few hundred broken windows.'

Brad's efforts at getting Saleem to reveal more details of their intentions came to an abrupt halt before he was able to introduce into the conversation the subject of rocket launchers and a sniper's rifle; as noted when the crates were unloaded.

'Saleem , the charge is ready. The receiver and detonator are attached together with the signal wire,' interrupted the Palestinian. 'If you are accompanying Latif, I should explain what you should do.'

The Terrorist leader joined Mohammad on the bench, leaving Brad to ponder over the developments. Faced with the overwhelming odds and the ever-present threat to Nancy and Naomi, he conceded he had no option, at present, than to do as he was ordered.

'That light you see just up ahead and to the left is the marker for the "Montgomery",' he said as he throttled back the engines to a quiet purr , leaving the launch wallowing in the two foot high swells.

Latif picked up the double package assembled by Mohammad and followed Saleem out into the dark; the Palestinian quickly shutting the door behind them to maintain their blackout. Seating himself back down next to the shelf where Saleem had left the small transmitter, he spoke directly to Brad. 'Mr. Murray, I'm sorry about your friend, Saleem is sometimes overstressed. But, do not antagonise him; he is most determined....we all are. As you have just said, our blowing up the wreck is hardly likely to kill anyone. You could even say we are doing the nearby townspeople a favour, removing the threat once and for all. Just do as Saleem asks and both you and your friend will come to no harm,' he smoothly lied.

Brad was not fooled for a minute. With eight of the ten explosive parcels remaining; together with two missile launchers and rockets, it was evident more than just detonating explosives in the wreck was planned. He even thought of making an attack on the big Palestinian while Saleem and Latif were away and the young Asif outside on the deck. But, almost as though he had read his thoughts, Mohammad smiled, shook his head and emphasised his thumb resting on the transmitter button.

'Just keep this boat where it is Mr. Murray, my compatriots will not be long and we don't want to drift far in this darkness.'

'And what if they can't find their way back to us; it's pitch black out there? I doubt I could hardly see the dinghy, even with my night vision binoculars.'

'Asif is guiding them with an infra red beam: they will be back on board by three o'clock.

Saleem looked at the luminous dial of his watch as he looped a rope around a mast stay of the sunken wreck and watched to see if the dinghy was still at the mercy of any tidal flow. The craft drifted slowly back to take up the slack that the Terrorist had left. As expected, with a low tide forecast of 2.48 a.m., there was no significant influence to affect Latif's dive on the wreck.

On a thumbs up signal, the elder Amin brother back flipped over the side of the dinghy, surfacing seconds later to take the package handed to him by Saleem who played out a thin aerial wire as the swimmer descended into the depths of the hull. The chief Terrorist waited patiently, unmoved by the eerie, gurgling and slopping sounds emanating from the wreck; his adrenalin fired mind even telling his stomach to ignore the uncomfortable motion of the flimsy boat in the calmer, but far from smooth, waters.

Latif felt his shoulder brush against the Montgomery's submerged bridge and wheelhouse, lying at a thirty degree angle to the seabed. He had never imagined his vision would be so impaired, incorrectly assuming Brad's warning was exaggerated in an attempt to obstruct Saleem's plans.

The least zealous of the Terrorists, he contemplated just dropping the bomb to the seabed alongside the wreck . Would that not be sufficient to cause the old ordnance to explode ? Knowing he would be thoroughly questioned on resurfacing, and fearful of somehow betraying his failure to actually plant the explosives deep inside the ship, he decided to carry on as ordered in the certainty that Saleem's wrath would surely result in his being killed; something he still hoped to avoid.

A tug on the rope around his waist reminded him that his leader, having released hardly any of the safety line, would be aware that he had not yet dived to any depth. He slowly started feeling his way down the side of the ship.

Above his head Saleem checked his infra red vision goggles and viewed his return path, noting to his satisfaction that the *Whaleback* was just about where he expected it to be. Glancing again at his watch, he became a little uneasy when he noted Lasif had been over fifteen minutes in the wreck. He tugged on the safety rope and it suddenly went slack in his hand. Hauling the loose line back onto the dinghy he shielded the end inside his oilskin coat and projected the beam of a small torch on to it. The frayed, ragged, end told its own story of having become rubbed against a rusty jagged gash in the ship's rotting structure: the diver possibly not even aware of the perilous mishap.

Chapter 7

Latif was, in fact, aware of two problems he faced and was at that moment fighting to control his rising terror. Having placed the bomb actually in a hold full of slimy fused cluster bombs, he had backed his way out of the below deck opening only to find himself suddenly entangled in part of a fishing net. His struggles to free himself only seemed to entrap him more and, unbeknown to him, were the cause of his safety rope parting. The second problem he was well aware of concerned his air supply. His small tank's capacity of around thirty minutes had barely five minutes remaining.

As he reached down his leg for the knife strapped to his right calf, he gave the safety line around his waist a tug……..and met no resistance. Panic overtook any remaining control as he realised he had no wish to die for any cause, his new found love for Saisha having overtaken his former zealousness. He began slashing wildly at the netting surrounding his body when his fright turned to sheer terror as the huge head of an evil eyed, open mouthed , conger eel - disturbed from its lair - struck at his eye mask.

Attempting to defend himself from what was, in fact, merely curiosity by the large fish, he sought to bring the knife up and stab at the creature. It was a fatal mistake. Disorientated by his contortions in the net he lashed out and struck the unyielding metal side of the wreck, the unexpected resistance causing him to release his grip on the dagger; his only hope of escaping the clutches of the knotted meshwork encircling him.

He struggled for the surface as his breathing became laboured and any sense of rational thought about his predicament disappeared. A mist began to appear before his eyes as his lungs sought to extract life giving oxygen from his now empty tank. He snatched his mouthpiece away in a confused idea that it was stopping him breathing. Water and sand flooded into his lungs as he opened his mouth to gulp in the non existent air. A few frantic struggles later Latif's invasion of the wreck was revenged by an unforgiving sea.

Saleem attached the end of the signal wire to a small, tennis ball size, buoy with protruding aerial rod and gave it a light tug to ensure that, unlike Latif's safety rope, it was still firmly attached to the charge below. Satisfied it was, he gently dropped the float over the side. With another look at his watch he ,shrugged his shoulders , released the dinghy from the mast stay of the wreck and started the small outboard motor; lining up his return to the *Whaleback* without further thought of his obviously dead ,or adrift, fellow conspirator. He may have been more concerned had he known that the repaired detonator device attached to the charge had allowed a little water to seep into the casing: due to the missing screw!

'You've got a screw missing you have,' said P.C. Anderson to his driver as he got back in the patrol car.

'Couldn't miss an opportunity like that could I ?' replied P.C. Sharp with a cheeky grin. 'I've arrested her a few times for soliciting. It's surprising what these girls will do to avoid being taken in,' he added cryptically.

'Yeah ! Well you can take me in as soon as you like, it's past our break time sitting here waiting for you to satisfy your lust. And you can thank me that we're not on our way back out to that van now that the London boys have finished for the night. The Serg radioed to send us on guard duty again; until they get a truck out there to take it back to the compound. I told him we hadn't had a break from the time we came on duty and persuaded him to send someone else.'

Fifteen minutes later, sitting in the Station canteen, the temporarily off duty officers were approached by the duty Sergeant. 'Get a move on you two, we've had the anti-terrorist people from the Smoke on again. They've just faxed us a second picture of another suspect, found in the flat of that van's owner. As soon as you've finished that tea, come through to the office before you go out again; see if you recognise him at all.'

Sharpy, as he was known among his station colleagues, pulled the folded invoice from his pocket and opened it out on the table. 'What d'you make of this then Barry ? A weeks' hire of two Guards uniforms. Don't say what though: could be Army; Prison or even Security.'

' When is it dated ? You should pass it on to the C.I.D lads.'

'Just a couple of days ago. I'll say we found it blowing about in the boatyard. Don't want to let anyone know I had a snoop in the van. I suppose we had better go and take a look at this other suspect.'

'Looks like Father Christmas with that beard,' said *Sharpy* , glancing down at the photo. 'But his eyes look as though they'd scare the living

daylights out of little kids. Can't say I've seen him around here; have you Barry ?'
'No, I'd remember that cold look easy enough. Don't forget that invoice you found Dave, the Serg can pass it on.'
P.C. Sharp handed the document over with the contrived explanation. 'You should have given it straight to those investigators from London. That Agent in charge, Jefferies I think he was called, said that apart from a few prints the van was as clean as a whistle and should we come across anything that could be of any help we should get back in touch with him straight away. I got the feeling that something big is going on that they are not telling us about. Presumably you haven't seen the other guy either ?'
Sharp by name and sharp by nature, the P.C. did not divulge they had not even seen the photo fit; quickly asserting, before Barry Anderson dropped them in the proverbial;'Need to have another look. We thought we might have done but neither of us was certain. Got a copy here Serg ?'
The desk officer raked among his papers and produced the artist's impression of Saleem.
Both constables almost lost their composure as they viewed the print, the likeness to their speed-

ing toilet seeker of a few nights previous was unmistakeable.

Glancing at each other to ascertain each had recognised the man in question, Anderson broke the silence. 'The more I look at this Dave; the more I think it's very much like that chap we stopped for speeding on the seafront recently; don't you think ?'

Catching on to his pal's quick thinking, *Sharpy*, with a questioning look, replied, 'Can't be certain. It was pretty dark remember. Still you could be right.'

'What was his name ?, queried the Sergeant.

'Stevens wasn't it Barry? You took his particulars.'

Anderson withdrew his notebook and flipped it open. 'Yes, that's it, Stevens; Mr. Hunter Stevens.'

It was as though someone had just turned on a light bulb in the Sergeant's head. 'What did you say ? You sure it was not Steven Hunter ?'

'Is it important then Serg ?' questioned P.C. Sharp. 'I interviewed a Steven Hunter a week ago about that hit and run in Shoebury: he didn't look anything like this guy. You sure you're not confusing the two?'

Chapter 7

'Wait here! Don't go back on patrol unless I tell you to. I won't be a minute.'
He disappeared into an inner office and checked a journal to establish the details of the visitor for a documents check a couple of days back. There it was; no doubt about it, Mr. Steven Hunter with a home address in Thorpe Bay. 'If only I had looked in the book before. Why has nobody picked this up Smithy boy?' he murmured to himself while dialling the C.I.D. office upstairs.

'I think I might have something interesting for you lads,' he said when the phone was eventually answered. 'Or, more accurately, a couple of my boys have. They think they recognise that first photo fit and.......... didn't I see a memo saying the Anti-Terrorist squad in London had asked for help in tracing a S. Hunter ? Guess what ? This guy is a Steven Hunter !'

The sleepy, uninterested, voice on the other end suddenly snapped, 'Send them up straight away. I'll get on to London, they're bound to want to speak to them.'

Richard Meade was sitting at his desk studying the *Suicide notes* discovered in Mohammad's empty flat a earlier, when the Agents broke in. Tells us nothing, he thought, other than the obvious; this guy is about to commit homicide and suicide at the same time.

The phone shrilled loudly in the quiet of the nearly deserted office, Andy Davison the only other occupant intent upon trying to extract the sim card from Hassam's bomb-damaged mobile phone.

'Meade here. Who's that ?'he queried as it was the outside line.

Seconds later he flicked down the office speaker switch and signalled to Davison as he looked up at the interruption.

The Southend C.I.D. man's initial information was soon supplemented by astute questions to the P.C.s from the Agents. Snatching up a pile of impressions of Saleem in various guises, as imagined by the sketch artist, Meade requested a description from P.C. Sharp of the Steven Hunter he had interviewed. Leafing through the sketches as the P.C. spoke, Davison suddenly picked out one and uttered, ' Eureka.!'

'Thanks boys, well done. Don't do anything for now , we'll take it from here,' said Meade cheerfully as he rang off. 'Andy, get hold of the boss. It's nearly four o'clock, he's had a few hours sleep and he said he wanted to know the minute anything useful came in.

Chapter 7

I wonder where this Saleem, come Steven Hunter is right at this minute ?'

'Where are we now Mr. Murray ?' asked the Terrorist leader peering through the windscreen at the cluster of lights in the distance.

'We are steaming up the Ray gut off Leigh towards Two Tree Island. You said you wanted us to anchor up for the day in some quiet waters where we will attract no attention. I often moor the boat up here waiting for the tide if we have a night fishing party to pick up at Bell Wharf. We won't be disturbed once we are on our mooring buoy.'

'Good; you can get us all some breakfast and see to your crewman as soon as we are secured. I will make arrangements so we can all get some sleep during the day.'

'*Swifty* needs proper medical attention. I need him back on his feet if the weather turns nasty again, as is forecast, and you want us to take you back out.'

'Then you'll just have to do the best you can because we are certainly going to require you again tonight,' said Saleem maliciously.

Brad gently nosed the *Whaleback* up to the mooring, ordering Mohammad to take the wheel while he ran out and picked up the buoy with a boat hook to attach the craft. Clipped to the foredeck, adjacent to the anchor rope, the skipper had always kept a double edged axe for emergency severing of the line if ever in danger of being run down by a wayward steamer while they were anchored up fishing: as had happened in the past to a fellow skipper. It would have been a simple matter to unclip and arm himself with the weapon ,but he could, at that time, see no advantage in doing so.

Returning to the wheelhouse he was just in time to hear the Terrorist chief say, 'Asif, stop your grieving and go and make sure that other rocket launcher is completely covered. We don't want any passing yachtsman to spot it. Latif is now enjoying his rewards with the pleasures of his *Maidens of Paradise*.

The young Asif had been distraught when Saleem returned to the launch without his brother. 'Why is Latif not with you ?' he had cried out as the dinghy came alongside.

Disregarding the question, the Terrorist had clambered back on board and barked at Asif, 'Never mind that now. Help me get the dinghy back on deck.'

Chapter 7

Confused, alarmed ,and with a feeling of dread that he already knew the answer, the teenage sibling, still feeling seasick, collapsed to the deck; retching bile.

'Get back inside. You're no good to anyone in that state. Send Mohammad to give me assistance,' snarled Saleem aiming a kick at the curled up youth who was sobbing uncontrollably on his knees.

Barely audible, Asif passed on the leader's order as he staggered back into the cabin. Mohammad handed over the pistol with a degree of reluctance, knowing the boy would be no match for Brad; especially in his state of *Mal de Mer.*

'Mr. Murray, keep the boat as steady as you can while I assist Saleem for a few moments. I advise you not to consider harming Asif. Remember; I still have the detonator in my pocket. Your friend would not thank you if I were forced to use it,' he warned.

Alone in the wheelhouse with the uncomfortable youngster, Brad contemplated disarming Asif and then fully opening the throttles of all three engines: the result of which would most certainly be ,at least, the pair on deck sent sprawling or ,probably even better, causing them to tumble overboard. He dismissed the idea almost as soon as it came into his head......**that bloody transmitter!**

Asif groaned, slumped on the bench seat, and in a whispered croak asked the skipper for a drink of water.

Brad responded by saying he could not leave the wheel but he could get himself a cup, just inside the small galley kitchen two steps down at the back of the cabin.

Such was his need, the youngster neglected his prisoner for half a minute while he stepped down, picked up a paper cup, filled the utensil and gulped the refreshment down.

The brief respite from continued vigilance gave the skipper the chance he was waiting for. In seconds he had reached Saleem's coat hanging on the wheelhouse door, snatched his mobile phone from the pocket and returned to the wheel before Asif stepped back up. Unable to surreptitiously slip the phone into his pocket without the young Terrorist seeing, he dropped the instrument into the plastic chart holder attached to the cabin wall by his left hand.

The cabin door slammed open as the two senior Terrorists returned, Mohammad warily a couple of paces behind Saleem and with his thumb hovering on the transmitter button.

'I'm glad you have been sensible,' he said handing his leader a towel to dry himself with.

'Where is Latif, Saleem ?' asked the young Pakistani anxiously; a question Brad was also asking himself.

'Probably dead !' Saleem replied angrily. 'He did not resurface. I waited long after his air tank would have been empty and, the safety rope had chaffed through. He was either swept away or trapped. We cannot worry about him,' he added cruelly. 'We must consider how this affects our plans. We will discuss it further later on ,when Mr. Murray finds us a convenient mooring for the day.'

Asif looked stunned, again retched , excused himself, and went down to the main cabin area where he remained for the journey across the shipping lanes: up river into the mooring the skipper had selected, re-emerging only when the engines went silent.

As the launch swung round to face the incoming tide, the first traces of the dawn were defining the difference between sky and sea; silhouetting the outline of Southend Pier stretching a mile and a quarter out into the Thames Estuary.

'Early dawn is always the best time for a raid,' said Agent Jefferies to his two fellow officers. 'If he's at home we should surprise him unless, like Hassam, he has somehow got wind of us coming.'

'He'd better be there or we've wasted our time turning round and coming back. We could have been back in H.Q by now,' grumbled the seconded Met officer. 'Why couldn't your boss have got the locals to check it out first; or that female Agent you say is already in the area?'

Pete Jefferies patiently explained that one of the reasons was they were armed, the local police were not. And added, 'Commander Beaman is contacting Sam to meet us there. In fact she is possibly already ahead of us, but will know better than to go in on her own. Callum, you could ring her mobile to se……no wait ! If she's at the house at this time of the morning, any telephone ringing could alarm the occupants if they happen to be awake.'

He needn't have worried. When Sam's slumbers suffered a rude awakening from her boss, as soon as he had issued his orders she put the phone down on the bed , threw back the covers and sped into the bathroom to quickly wash and dress. Returning to the bedroom, she grabbed her coat from the back of a chair, checked she had her pistol in the pocket, picked up her car keys and rushed out in to the chill morning air; forgetting the almost hidden mobile phone.

A quick reference to the local area map in her car located the house road and her shortest route: from her lodging house straight onto the seafront road at Chalkwell and along the Esplanade to Thorpe Bay. Had her journey been a little later, in better light; and she looked out to sea; she could possibly have seen the *Whaleback Swift* making it's way into the mouth of the "Ray", enroute for the out of way mooring.

Driving slowly past the suspect house in the quiet residential street, she drew into the kerb twenty yards further on and switched off the engine: only then realising she had omitted to pick up her phone when she thought of calling Pete Jefferies.

'Damn!' she swore, 'I hope he's not trying to get in touch with me.'

With no knowledge of how long it would be before "reinforcements" arrived, she decided to reconnoitre the premises. Emerging from her vehicle, she quietly closed the door and slipped silently over the low garden wall and up to the house. Peering through the front windows where, she noted, no curtains were drawn, she saw no signs of life in the dim interior. She then examined the adjacent garage; the up and over metal door lifting to her touch. Raising it no more than a foot, she slipped underneath and found herself in a tidy, but empty, workshop. As her eyes became more accustomed to the gloom she noticed a door at the rear, leading, she assumed, to the back of the house.

Careful to avoid bumping into anything ,she made her way to the opening and tried the handle. To her surprise the door swung open. Just as she was about to step through she heard the distant sound of a police car siren and the throaty sound of a powerful car passing outside. Recognising the exhaust noise of Pete Jefferies' turbo-powered Subaru Impreza WRX Sti, she crawled back out of the garage in time to see him pull up in front of her own car.

Before she had reached the emerging Agents, a Police car, siren blaring and lights flashing, screamed up the road and pulled up obliquely across the front of the Subaru.

Chapter 7

The two occupants leapt out and approached the three Anti-Terrorist Officers, one turning back as their radio blared out their call sign.

Not waiting for his colleague, the first policeman roared at Jefferies. 'Southend seafront is not your personal Le Mans track. You were touching a hundred along there just now !
Show me your licence, you're...' He never got to complete the sentence, the second patrol officer rushing up to pull him aside and whisper in his ear, 'Leave it Mick. Orders from the Sergeant, they're M.I. 6 Anti Terrorist Agents on a raid which we appear to have fouled up. But grab that woman; there's also a report ,just phoned in by a neighbour, of a female prowler.'

The, pyjama clad, neighbour in question chose that moment to come out into the street and join a gathering throng of bystanders; most still in dressing gowns. 'That's her,' he cried out. 'Saw her with my own eyes, looking in the windows and forcing her way into the garage.'
Agent Jefferies was fuming. 'She's with us you idiots!' he bawled at the patrolmen. 'You have possibly warned a dangerous Terrorist of our presence.'

'We were not informed until a few moments ago who you were Sir. We were only doing our duty,' said the elder of the two police officers, unruffled and politely.

'There's no Terrorist in that house,' interrupted the nosey neighbour. 'Mr. Hunter lives there; been there a long while. He's a nice gentleman, runs a business in Southend.'

'Thank you Sir, perhaps you can give my colleague what you know about Mr. Hunter, and a description, while I and my other staff make our own conclusions.'

Beckoning to the nearest policeman, Jefferies requested he clear the crowd of inquisitive onlookers before departing and strolling, with his other Agents, up to the front door of the house where he banged loudly.

The hollow echo seemed to confirm what Samira had already thought, the place was deserted. The Senior Agent ordered a reconnaissance of the rear.

Hearing sounds inside, he pulled Sam back from the door and drew a heavy automatic pistol from a holster inside his coat . The door opened and Agent Callum O'Toole stepped out. 'They never learn: skylight window left open ,soon got in but it seems deserted. Greg's having a look around now.'

Chapter 7

'I hope he's being cautious, we don't want any repeat of the Hassam raid. You'd better get off Sam. Those two patrolmen who discovered the van are still waiting at the station for someone to interview them about the guy who lives here. Their shift finished half an hour ago so they won't be happy kept waiting. We'll give this place a good going over and then meet you for a late breakfast before informing the Chief of this latest disappointment.'

Sam waited a few moments to ensure her fellow Agents were okay before driving back into Southend; deep in thought for most of the way. 'We really are getting nowhere with this investigation. Something is going to happen today but WHAT, WHERE and WHEN ? I didn't have time to ask Pete if they have any new leads. I guess I'll find out over breakfast.'

'I don't want any breakfast,' lamented Asif when Mohammad proferred a plate of eggs and beans. 'Just a cup of tea.'

'You should at least eat some dry toast young man. I've heard it is good to put something in your stomach after being seasick,' piped up an uncharacteristically cheery Saleem. 'Tonight you will need to be strong.'

'But how can we carry out all the attacks. Latif is no longer with us?'

'Have no fear Asif. I have thought of a modified plan that will enable us to still destroy every target. When Mr. Murray is sleeping below I will tell you what we will do.'

Brad reappeared from the forward cabin with some soiled bandages in a bowl of bloody water; depositing the used cloth strip in the galley waste bag and emptying the water before turning towards the Terrorist leader and snarling, 'The bleeding has stopped and he's recovered consciousness, no thanks to you. You will regret your actions Mr. Hunter, you have my word on it !'

'I don't think you are in any position to be making threats Mr. Murray,' said Saleem with a smirk on his face. 'And, please, call me Saleem. Now, I suggest you have a little breakfast and then join your crewman for a sleep while you can. We will not require your services until this evening.'

Brad racked his brains to think of a way he could get hold of his phone before being incarcerated for the day but, with the Terrorists' presence in the wheelhouse, resigned himself to accepting it would not be possible. His train of thought turned to an alternative strategy that he decided to discuss with his crewman before implementing.

He made himself and Trevor breakfast and returned to his crewman lying on the single bunk in the forward cabin. The door slammed shut behind him and he heard the key turn in the lock.

Swifty struggled to sit up, his head swimming and sensitive to any movement, a condition quickly recognised by his employer friend who gently assisted him into an upright position. The refreshing cup of tea to swill down two painkilling pills, together with some marmalade toast, quickly improved the crewman's state of health, his pallid complexion soon giving way to a rosier hue: more like his old self.

'Sorry Skip, that wasn't too clever was it ?'said *Swifty* in little more than whisper . 'Me
and my big mouth; deserved to have my brains knocked out…if I had any.'

Relieved to see his long-time friend was obviously not going to suffer any long term effects from his beating, Brad immediately told him of their present location, explaining that the blow to his head had rendered him unconscious for a number of hours. He went on to explain that, as he was sure Trevor would realise, a short swim from their position would easily put him ashore where he could notify the authorities of the situation. And that, if he could persuade Saleem to put him into the main cabin, he could readily escape through the rear engine access hatch and slip over the stern.

'But, there is too much at stake. Saleem is undoubtedly a schizophrenic who will press that confounded button to murder Nancy and Naomi if he thinks he is in anyway in danger of being discovered. If either of us is discovered missing you can be sure he will delight in carrying out his threat.'

'I'm not much use for the physical stuff at the moment but I could; somehow, create a diversion Skip; if that would help.' offered *Swifty* realising, on trying to stand, that he was still feeble on his feet and prone to again passing out.

'No old friend, that would be foolhardy. It is daylight outside now so the chances of escape unseen are pretty remote anyway. And, even if I did get assistance, they could get nowhere near without being spotted. They intend taking turns to sleep throughout the day but there will always be one of them on guard. I have another idea that will, at least, interfere with whatever they have planned : could even result in my getting hold of that loathsome transmitter.'

He went on to explain his intentions before telling the crewman to take the opportunity to get some sleep, and more rest, before nightfall when Saleem had indicated they would be leaving their mooring. He hammered on the cabin door.

The door to Commander Beaman's office flew open as Richard Meade poked his head round the frame.'Got a few answers for you Chief. The fuel rods are still in situ at Bradwell Nuclear Power Station and there is only a skeleton staff on site at present to supervise the removal. The Essex Police Chief isn't being too co-operative: I asked if he could station a couple of his men there for the next couple of days. Said he hasn't any firearm trained officers to spare and was a bit sarcastic in suggesting truncheons and Mace sprays would hardly stop determined armed attackers.'

'We'll send our own people if necessary Richard. What else ? ' snapped the M.I.5 Chief.

'Pete Jefferies has reported in. Saleem is definitely Steven Hunter and has also used the name of Hunter Stevens to confuse matters. Sam was able to establish the firm link when she called in to the Southend Police HQ earlier. Unfortunately, he wasn't at the house in Thorpe Bay. Neighbours say he hasn't been seen since Tuesday morning. I've got one of the latest recruits looking into whatever we can rake up about his past but initial results are not promising.'

Probing questions by the Commander revealed that Jefferies and O'Toole had returned to Saleem's house ,after their breakfast meeting with Samirah, to continue a more thorough search in the hope of finding any clue as to the Terrorists' whereabouts or plans.

The only leads so far, the Agent explained, were a scrap of screwed up paper bearing the words *Prince Sviatoslavl* that Pete Jefferies picked up from behind an empty kitchen unit swing bin and; an Invoice from a Theatrical Costume Hire Company in Stratford - for two Guards uniforms - that Samirah had faxed through from her visit to the Police HQ.

'Have we got personnel chasing those ?' questioned the Chief.

'Well, no Sir, we haven't yet. The problem is we've got nobody to put onto it at present, until that Met chap we've been loaned gets back from Southend. I took the liberty of suggesting Pete put him on a train back if they had no further immediate use for him. He should be reporting in soon. I hope that's alright Sir ?'

'Yes, well done Richard. When he gets in send him over to the Hire place: see if they can tell us who rented the uniforms and what sort of Guards they were? Better see what you can find out about this Prince whatever yourself.'

'I was about to do that Sir. The consensus of opinion is that it sounds like the name of a ship. I'll get right on to it.'

'What about Kathy. Have we heard how she is ?'

'She's O.K. Sir. Says she can't remember much about how she got injured other than her legs being pulled from under her and tumbling down the steps into Hassam's cellar.
Says she's going to discharge herself this morning. I told her that if she does you would be certain to say she must go home and get a few days rest before returning. I hope I did right; didn't want to disturb your own rest Sir.'

'You've done well Richard. If we are short staffed this is what we will do. The two suspects we picked up in Southall claim they were only known to Hassam because he was their landlord. That part of their story is true, but we know they are involved with the barge as the forensic lads found traces of Ammonium Nitrate on their clothing. It could, however, be true that they don't, as they profess, know what Hassam intended to do with the vessel.'

'What about the third suspect, have we got him yet ?' interrupted Meade.

'No, but you may be wrong about a him. According to neighbours, a young woman lives at the address and the phone company say their billing goes to a, Ms. B. Duggan. She may rent the place but, apparently, seems to come and go at weird hours and is often missing for days at a time.'

The Commander went on to explain, with a lack of manpower, and given the circumstances, nobody had been left watching the flat but neighbours had promised to contact the unit immediately she returned. 'She is unlikely to be anything of a major threat without her two male counterparts,' he had concluded. 'Therefore; I am going to downgrade the threat of the barge and send the two operatives on board up to Bradwell: there seems to be more danger there.'

'What about the Met observer chappie Sir ? He's already complaining his position is difficult to maintain with any secrecy and he is getting no relief take overs during the day. He's had to leave his vehicle on a few occasions to take a leak and snatch a sandwich from the nearest snack bar.'

'Yes; well we can't leave the vessel completely unattended. Tell him he can go aboard and keep guard. That way he's got galley facilities and a toilet.'

'Trevor needs to use the toilet and I haven't finished in the galley,' snapped Brad stepping up back into the wheelhouse.

'Quickly then,' ordered Saleem. 'We all need to get some sleep. One of us will be on guard at all times ,so don't get up to any tricks Mr. Murray.'

'What can we do against armed men, especially if we are locked in the main cabin area with the stronger door,' suggested Brad craftily. 'That way, whoever is on guard has an easier job, and access to the galley.'

Saleem , surprisingly, agreed without argument; descending into the forward cabin and commanding young Asif to take the first watch while he and Mohammad slept.

When *Swifty* emerged from the tiny toilet, the teenage Terrorist shepherded them into the cabin and locked them in before seating himself on Brad's wheelhouse seat where he could see both out of the windscreen and side window; as well as the main cabin door.

Watching from the forward cabin doorway, Saleem, satisfied his young conspirator was carrying out his orders competently, beckoned Mohammad to join him before closing the door.

Inside the main cabin, Brad assisted his still feeble crewman onto a bunk before withdrawing the hidden screwdriver from his boot and start unscrewing the fixings attaching the rear wall panel.

Winking at his patient, he released all the screws and signalled to him to groan while he eased the panel free: covering the slight squeak as the partition opened. Warmth and a slight smell of engine fumes drifted into the cabin, quickly dispersing when the skipper eased a porthole open a notch.

With a quick listen at the door to ascertain all was quiet, he slipped through the opening, made his way between the engines and stood beneath the aft deck hatch in semi darkness before easing the cover up an inch or two. To his surprise, little daylight flooded in to the hold, the surprise giving way to glee with the realisation that Asif had draped the tarpaulin, covering the weaponry still on deck, completely over the hatch giving him complete concealment for his emergence, should, for any reason, the youth decide to look towards the stern.

Careful to avoid disturbing the cover too much, he peeked out before, on seeing a clear deck, creeping forward to the wheelhouse and raising himself up for a quick peep through the window.

The brief glance was sufficient for him to note Asif seated at the wheel reading, or at least appearing to read, one of the dog-eared novels he normally kept on board for relaxation if not fishing himself when he had larger parties; or if he was staying on the craft overnight.

A second quick look revealed what he was hoping to see, the threatening transmitter had been left by Asif on the edge of the chart table adjacent to the wheelhouse door, within easy reach. It would have been a simple matter for the skipper to open the door, grab the offending instrument and throw it overboard before the surprised Terrorist had any chance to stop him.

One thing deterred him from that course of action. Not a fear of being shot or killed, a sacrifice he was prepared to make if it was to save the lives of Nancy and Naomi, but a concern that he had no idea if immersion in water would cause an internal short circuit resulting in a signal being transmitted.

'Be patient,' he said silently to himself; confident that his well thought out plan of action would bring the desired result.

Keeping low, he scurried back to the stern and crawled beneath the tarpaulin, stopping as he dropped back into the hold when he found himself face to face with the long wooden crate secreted under the cover. A sudden thought occurred to him and he raised an edge to let in more light, revealing that the case had been opened, the lid only placed back in position.

Carefully avoiding too much movement, he eased the wooden slat aside to inspect the contents: a lethal looking missile rocket launcher. He immediately recognised the powerful weapon as a Soviet built model with a range of one thousand yards. The weaponry course of his time in the Special Boat Service also reminded him of another fact about the weapon, the firing mechanism being an electro magnetic type within the trigger grip......capable of easily being sabotaged.

He felt in his pockets for a suitable instrument but had only the screwdriver, a useful tool and

possible weapon but with a blade far too large to be of any use for his purpose.
Dropping fully into the rear compartment he felt for the waterproofed switch , clicked on a feeble light and lifted the lid of a toolbox strapped to a broad shelf screwed to the inner hull wall; *Swifty'* ,"Get us out of trouble," Jack of all trades assortment of tools and miscellaneous bits and pieces.

He fished out a piece of stiff wire, some spent matches and a smaller screwdriver. Within minutes he had disabled the Russian weapon by forcing the wire into the trigger mechanism until he heard a satisfying crackling of damage to the small circuit board. Although confident the launcher was now incapable of firing, he made certain by jamming a number of broken match pieces into the trigger opening. A squeeze of the trigger itself , before sliding the lid back in place, produced no movement, a solid resistance confirming complete disablement.

'Saleem's made his first mistake,' Brad whispered to his crewman on his return. 'I guarantee Asif will be asleep before much longer. Anyone as seasick as he was is left feeling weak and tired; without being up all night without a wink of sleep. I'll give it another thirty minutes and then see if I can get hold of that transmitter.'

'You're right, he won't be much use as a guard. We could probably get away and swim to shore with the transmitter before anyone realises we are gone. But, you're wrong about it being his first mistake, that was his clobbering ME.'

The Skipper looked at his friend sympathetically before replying in a hushed tone. 'That might be an option if it were low water and a short swim to the mudflats but, we're only an hour off high water: it's far too long a swim in the freezing water even if I could get my wetsuit from the other cabin We'd never make it and, in your condition ,I would think the last thing we should be considering is you going in the drink.'

'But I'm worried about Nancy and my daughter; just throw that gadget over the side, that will solve one problem.'

'I thought of that myself Trev. The trouble is we don't know whether that might be the last thing we want to do with it. If water penetrates the internals and causes a short, it could send the very signal we have to stop. At least we've now got access out on deck, there's just a chance that another boat will pass by close enough to speak to without awakening our captors.'

Chapter 7

'It's a good thing Saleem still needs us or I reckon we'd now be in Davy Jones' locker,' said *Swifty* thoughtfully. 'If you go and pinch that signal device I suspect he'll go beserk: could shoot us out of hand, you've seen him completely loose it.'

'Don't worry on that score Trev,' responded his Skipper with a grin, 'I'm not going to steal it, just borrow it.' He crawled back down into the engine compartment.

Less than ten minutes later he was back grim faced as he replaced the panel with a single screw to hold it in place.

'Kick me for being so stupid,' he said in a despondent tone to his perplexed looking crewman. 'Asif was asleep alright, as I suspected but, it was the wrong transmitter: Saleem must have taken the other one with him.'

'How can you be certain Brad, we only glimpsed the other one when he came back from putting the bombs on the wreck? I saw him put it down but took no notice of it after that.'

'It is similar but has no push button like the first one, just a switch,' said the disappointed Skipper. 'I've disabled it anyway,' he continued holding up a small circuit board. 'Took this out and reconnected the battery so the lamp is still on : makes it seem to still be "live". At least they can't blow the wreck up now, but I should have concentrated on trying to get hold of my phone. Trouble was, Asif was slumped with his head on the console shelf right up against the chart pocket. There was no way I could get to it without disturbing him.'

Mention of the phone reminded *Swifty* that he had said he would phone his wife in the morning. What we she do when she didn't hear from him , he wondered ?

It was as though Saleem had read his mind. The door swung back and the Chief Terrorist stood there holding out his mobile phone, which the crewman incorrectly assumed was Brad's.

'Something was worrying me while I was modifying my plans since the loss of Latif, I couldn't get to sleep. You didn't mention it Mr. Swift, but surely your lovely wife will be wondering why you haven't come home this morning, or contacted her at all. You will do so now. Tell her you will be away until late tonight ; but be careful what you say, we wouldn't like my thumb to slip, would we ?' he uttered maliciously.

Caught unawares, the crewman was unable to quickly think of any way he could warn Nancy of either her own danger or, his and Brad's predicament.

Satisfied with the content of the call, Saleem snatched the phone back. 'Now my concerns are nullified , perhaps I can get some sleep. I suggest the pair of you do likewise. We will be leaving here around six o'clock.'

'Tell him no later than six o'clock,' said Commander Beaman to Richard Meade, in answer to the seconded Met man's enquiry as to when he was likely to be relieved. 'I'll get on to Superintendent Kimpton and ask him to send a replacement mid afternoon if possible but, he's probably as short staffed as we are when on Terrorist Alert.'

The Agent relayed the message before putting down the phone and turning to his Chief. 'Pete Jefferies reported in Sir. He says they have found nothing else of any significance at Hunter's house. Wants you to phone him with new orders although he sounded dead beat to me: two nights without hardly any sleep. Samirah has apparently gone to Steven Hunter's Travel Agency to see if he's around, or if she can discover his whereabouts. Says she'll phone in lunchtime unless anything happens meanwhile. And, that accident victim out on the Wallasea road last night was, I'm told, definitely knocked on the head before he was drowned. Southend C.I.D. are dealing with that at the moment but I've told them we need to know if they come up with any tie in to our Terrorists.'

'Well done Richard. You'd better tell Jefferies to grab a few hours sleep and go off yourself. I'll get in touch immediately anything happens or we get any further leads.'

'Thank you Sir; just a couple of other things before I go. The Met Officer should be phoning in shortly about those uniforms, he's on his way to Stratford right now. And, Kathy's left hospital; says she's coming in here on her way home. I tried to dissuade her but she insisted on being brought up to date in case there is anything she can do from home.'

'Thank you Richard, now off you go.'

Left alone the M.I.5 Chief , sighed resignedly, 'What a mess, a tired out staff , still no definite sighting of Saleem and no idea of what the others look like. I just hope Charlie Walsh and Andy Davison get in shortly with some better news or Sam has some luck in Southend.'

The office door opened as Walsh and Davison entered accompanied by Agent Kathy Doyle.

Chapter 7

The female Agent looked pale and wore a stylish berry at a rakish angle - from which the edges of a bandage protruded - and had obviously obtained fresh clothing from somewhere: her blood-stained tunic and slacks being replaced by a smart sweater, new slacks and a long top coat. Shrugging off her companions supporting hands, she, uninvited, sat down in the nearest chair and said, 'Before you ask. I'm perfectly okay apart from a headache. I know you won't let me stay, and I must say I'm looking forward to getting home for some decent food and a good soak in the bath, but I had to come by to pick up my car so bring me up to date on what has happened; I might be able to help…I do my best thinking in the bath.'

'It's nice to see you back in the land of the living Kathy, but you really should be at home resting for a few days. What happened at Hassam's house ?'

'I'm not certain Commander; I just remember falling down some stairs and then I blacked out and must have remained unconscious until I awoke in hospital,' replied the most recently recruited Agent. 'I remember hearing a noise at the back of that unit in the kitchen and discovering it swung back. The only thing I recall after that was my feet being pulled away from under me and tumbling down into the cellar. I didn't even get the chance to call for back up.'

Charlie Walsh interrupted to state, 'Fortunately for you the new tracking chips installed in our helmets work efficiently. As soon as we discovered you missing, the Prof's assistant, Kate Sherwood, was able to guide us to the barge where you were being held. Pete Jefferies got on board and was bringing you out of danger when Hassam appeared. A couple of the Met's Anti-Terrorist marksmen had to shoot at him….we won't get much out of him: he's dead !'

Kathy appeared shocked at the news, the colour slowly returning to her cheeks draining with the revelation before she recovered her composure to enquire, 'Did he say anything before he died ?'

'He was wired up with explosives which the shots triggered. There wasn't much left of him to question…..more's the pity; might have managed to get him to talk.'

'Obviously Kathy,' said Commander Beaman, 'there's nothing you can tell us if you didn't even speak to Hassam. I've got to go and report to the D.G. so I'll let Charlie bring you up to date but, you're to get off home. If you feel better in the morning you can come in, but only for light duties.'

When the Chief had departed and Walsh acquainted her of the latest findings, the female Agent was making her way out of the office when she suddenly turned to the two male occupants and dropped a bombshell of a statement. 'One thing that probably is important: I came round for a few minutes when I was on the barge and heard Hassam on the phone to somebody. I caught part of the conversation: he was telling the listener that the barge was ready and safely moored and would be travelling up to Lambeth Pier opposite the Houses of Parliament next week when the explosives arrived. I should have remembered to tell Commander Beaman before he left but I'm still a bit confused and not my self at the moment.'

Agent Andy Davison shot out of his chair and raced after the Commander.

8

Agent Samirah Ahmad sat sipping a sweet coffee opposite a smiling Peter Western, seated at Steven Hunter's desk.

Not for such a beauty, the insipid hot tasteless liquid from the Travel Agency's customer Coffee Machine, thought the awestruck Manager when Sam introduced herself.

'Sally; make Ms Khan a real cup of coffee,' he ordered. 'We'll be in the office.'

'What did your last servant die of you arrogant twit ?' muttered the young assistant under her breath. 'Show you a nice pair of breasts and a tight little bum and you're putty in their hands.'

Typical of the, at times, smarmy Manager; Sam's entrance to the premises saw him leap to his feet uttering, 'I'll deal with this lady Sally. I'm the Manager, you can call me Peter Ms.......', he waited for Sam to speak, continu-

ing when she murmured, 'Shauna, Shauna Khan.'
'Well Shauna, I hope you don't mind me calling you that, sounds so much better than a formal Ms Khan, I am completely at your service. What can we offer you: a nice two weeks in the Mediterranean sun or, perhaps, further afield, Australia or New Zealand ? Popular destinations these days.'

Sam gave a little chuckle before answering. 'Sorry, I was amused at the notice on your door, " Anyone entering here will be advised to go away ." A friend of mine, Saleem, suggested I might find Canada interesting.'

The mention of Saleem and Canada produced no reaction from the Manager opposite, disappointing the Agent who had carefully watched for any sign of recognition. 'Actually,' she added, 'I thought Saleem was a Senior partner or Director of GETAWAY TRAVEL.' 'No, our sole Director is Mr.Hunter. You must be mistaken. If he was here I'm sure he would know of anyone by that name if they were associated with the Travel business. I certainly have no knowledge myself . If you care to leave me your phone number, I'll ask him when he returns in a few days time,' said the crafty Manager, reluctant to let Sam go without obtaining a future contact.

Recognising there was nothing to be gained by further questioning, and anxious to escape the attentions of the amorous Manager who had moved round the desk to lean over her with pen and paper poised, Sam abruptly stood up jogging his arm with her coffee cup and spilling the contents down the front of his trousers. Peter Western let out a yelp as the scalding liquid penetrated his clothing .

'Oh ! I'm so sorry; please forgive my clumsiness. I'm afraid that I am in rather a hurry this morning ,I'll pick up some brochures on the way out.

Winking at the young assistant as she opened the door and returned to the street, she called back, 'Something came up, a cool glass of water might be in order for your boss.'

The mention of bosses reminded her of the need to call in herself. Reaching in her pocket for the phone she remembered she had forgotten to pick it up before rushing out.

'Damn!' she swore, as she returned to her car. 'I could have tried Brad too and seen if he has had any joy locating the SPRITE.' Making a mental note to call in and collect it once she had made enquiries about the craft down at Old Leigh, she took a small notepad and pen from the glove box before driving off and listed herself a few questions to ask the Commander later. Returning the pad to the compartment she dislodged the Costume Hire Company Invoice, stowed after faxing a copy through from the Police H.Q. She added a further question : What Guard's uniforms were they ?

'Dark Blue Serge material with silver buttons on the pockets and epaulettes,' said the Met Officer's booming voice on the end of the phone Charlie Walsh was holding six inches away from his ear. 'And the proprietor remembers the bloke who hired them, a big, dark skinned, bearded individual; foreign looking but spoke perfect English. Left more than the required deposit. But, there's no doubt he's one of them, the address he left is that of the house in Hullbridge.'

'Good work. Get a good description and then get back here as soon as you can..... Ken, isn't it ?'said Walsh returning the handset to the cradle.

Andy Davison returned with the Commander who immediately enquired, 'Kathy gone Charlie ?'

'Yes, sent her off Chief, she's told us all she can remember. Has Andy told you about the barge ?'

'Only that Kathy says its being moved next week, or would have been if we hadn't rounded up those two Southall Terrorists. What do you make of it ?'

It only confuses matters more as far as I can see,' said the Senior Agent. 'I'll be interested to hear what Pete has to say as soon as he gets back this afternoon. That is, unless you want him to stay in the Southend area Sir.'

The trio discussed the most recent revelation together with the further information Walsh had accumulated since taking over from Richard Meade. He informed the Commander of the facts Meade had unearthed about the *Prince Sviatoslavl* being a Russian ship, currently at sea en route for the German port of Bremer-haven. 'I wonder if there's any significance in a German connection?' queried Davison. 'It was a tip off from the Germans in the first place. Per-haps the threat is returning to their own territory .'

'Crikey Andy, don't confuse us any more….sorry Sir,' interjected Walsh who went on to

tell them about the Met Officer's findings.
After ten minutes of *Brainstorming* , the Commander looked at his notes, reading out aloud. 'Targets: could be Canary Wharf, might be Bradwell Nuclear Power Station, and now we have the possibility of the Houses of Parliament. Or; it might be none of those.
What does seem certain is that the barge is prepared to be a huge bomb, lacking only a means of detonating it. That being the case, the link with Saleem and Southend appears to be only of providing suitable ordnance to make the explosion possible……by a boat called *Sprite* and by FOUR Terrorists ? No, that scenario is senseless. If bombs are to be transported from Southend to London why not just put them in the back of a van and drive up ? And, what on earth have Guard's uniforms got to do with it ?'
'Let's face it Sir,' Walsh said shaking his head, 'all we have at this time is some pieces of a jigsaw, none of which seem to fit together and still with plenty of pieces missing.
'And, don't forget, the timescale of everything we have is contradictory,' piped in Andy Davison. 'Sam says Saleem indicated something major was going to happen today and Kathy tells

us Hassam said the barge is being moved after the weekend.'

The Commander thought for a moment. 'Charlie, get Pete Jefferies and Callum back here; Sam too if you can get in touch with her. I called her a while ago and the Hotel maid answered her phone, said Sam had rushed off just as she came on duty and obviously forgot her phone which was lying on the bed. There is no major target in Southend, unless, however unlikely it may seem, they want to blow up the Pier. And, I think we can discount Bradwell, it's too far for the barge to travel without experienced boatmen which, we can conclude, the Terrorists are not. No; whatever is going to happen, it seems somewhere along the river in London is the most likely target.'

'It certainly won't be Southend Pier,' interjected Walsh. 'That's got a history of catastrophic fires and ships ploughing through it without the help of Terrorists. If we
are assuming that the barge is part of the operation we were warned about, should we increase the guard: there's only one of Superintendent Kimpton's officers on board now?'

'Don't worry for the present, it's not likely anyone would be so foolish as to attract attention to it in daylight hours; especially today. I see on the news that some whale has got lost and found its way up the Thames to London, there's crowds of sightseers along the embankment .If Saleem and his gang are involved, they will wait for darkness. We'll sort something out when Jefferies and O'Toole get back. ……if nothing happens meanwhile and we are not completely wrong about the barge,' said the Chief ominously.

'Barge in or you'll never get served,' said the seated figure of a bearded old boatman to Agent Samirah as she jostled with the throng of lunchtime drinkers at the bar of the Public House, where she first met Brad.

'I really only want a sandwich and fruit juice, and to ask the barman a question,' said Sam demurely.'

'Over here Vernon :serve the lady,' bawled the regular from his barstool. 'She wants to ask you something.'

'Hello again,' said the barman ignoring the pleas of other would-be customers to comply with the old-timer's request and serve Sam. 'If you're looking for Brad he's not been in for a couple of days. I think he said he had an angling party on Wednesday and then a couple of days charter for a film company. If it's important I'm sure he won't mind you calling him on his mobile....if he's remembered to charge it up,' adding with a grin, 'not that he ever does; usually tries to use it while he's in the middle of the ocean somewhere and then wonders why it doesn't work.'

Sam thanked him for the information, ordered her lunchtime snack, and asked him if he knew of the *Sprite;* the question, as the barman shook his head, bringing a retort from the old fisherman. 'Never been a boat of that name around here in thirty years miss. You sure you got the name right, is it important ?'

Unwilling to divulge it's real significance, Sam passed the question off with a lie. 'No, a friend wrote to me recently and said they were interested in purchasing a boat and had seen one called ....er, well, as the corner of the letter was chewed up by my vicious snapping letterbox as I pulled the letter out, S P R I and then nothing. I'm guessing at the missing letters.'

'Ha !' guffawed the old man. '*Sprite* be damned. I might be getting to be a senile old man but I bet it's the old *Sprinter* . That's up for sale; you should ask your friend Brad, it's his boat.'

The beautiful female Agent nearly fell off her stool at the fisherman's instant realisation of her Agency's mistaken guesswork, his surmise confirmed when the barman produced a business card and placed it on the bar in front of her. 'One of Brad's old cards before he got his Grandfather's old boat modified, repaired and up and running again.'

Sam's mind flashed to the vision of the charred card on Commander Beaman's desktop. There was no doubt: this was the complete version of the piece recovered from Hassam's house.

'I suppose I should phone Brad, after all I've got his number right in front of me' she said with a winning smile. 'But it will have to wait, I've left my mobile back at the Hotel.'

Half a dozen hands of the young men, who had, somehow, manoeuvred themselves close to the glamorous Agent, thrust phones at her; 'borrow mine' echoing from lips of at least three or four would-be suitors.

Although she recognised that she would not be able to ask too detailed questions in front of such a large audience, she decided to refuse the offers of assistance would be both churlish and unwise.

With a : 'Thank you,' demurely whispered to the nearest youth - who appeared to be hardly old enough to be in the bar - she took the proffered phone and dialled the number on the card.

Almost immediately an automated voice answered, 'This is the answering service for….,' Sam ended the call.

With a second, 'Thank you,' she returned the phone to the ,now, red-faced young man - embarrassed by his friends whispered comments while Sam was making the call .

'Switched off, but, at least, not a flat battery. I'll try later,' she declared to the interested gathering. 'Does anyone know if the *Sprinter* has got a new owner yet, or where it is now?'

'That's easy,' chimed in the old fisherman. 'He only advertised it three or four days ago, I shouldn't think it's sold yet. Most likely on his mooring over on the River Roach near his boathouse. He'll want to tart it up a bit I expect.'

Downing the last of her fruit juice and declining offers of another, Sam, anxious to get away and follow up the new lead, made her excuses and departed to a variety of wistful , sadly pensive and outright lecherous looks accompanied by a long, drawn-out , wolf whistle.

Chapter 8

The whistle of the boiling kettle outside the door in the galley woke Brad from his disturbed slumber, instantly reminding him that he was both thirsty and hungry. In the dim light of the cabin he looked over to his crewman and saw he was still asleep. A glance at his watch showed him he had slept for nearly six hours. Making sure the loosened panel was secure he knocked on the locked door.

Mohammad Sadat turned off the gas ring and poured himself a mug of tea before responding to the Skipper's knocking. Pulling the automatic pistol from his pocket ,he unlocked the door and stood back as Brad emerged; signalling him to go through into the wheelhouse.

'I trust you slept well Mr. Murray. How is your assistant ?' said the big Terrorist in a surprisingly friendly and quiet voice.

'He is still sleeping but is feeling much better thank you, no thanks to your boss. I should get him some refreshment and food, and I could do with something myself.'

'Help yourself Mr. Murray. Just be careful what you are doing with that boiling water, I wouldn't wish you to be tempted to throw it in my direction: my screams would undoubtedly awaken Saleem and give him the pleasure of setting off the explosives in Mr. Swift's house.'

Brad glanced at the transmitter he had disabled and noted, with satisfaction, that the "on" lamp was still illuminated. At least that one won't function he thought.

'No Mr. Murray. That's not the one you would wish to disarm. Saleem has that safely with him,' said Mohammad noting the interested look .'And remember, I am armed and will not hesitate to shoot you should you cause trouble. You could, if necessary, be considered "surplus to requirements". I'm sure your compatriot would be more than happy to follow our instructions to spare his wife and child. Do I make myself clear ?'

'Perfectly clear; but you are mistaken in thinking *Swifty* could replace me at present. He is hardly able to stand on his feet,' Brad lied. 'And, he does not have sufficient navigational knowledge or licensing to operate a craft of this size within the confines of this Estuary.'

Hopeful of keeping the Palestinian Terrorist talking and possibly revealing their plans, he continued, 'I am not a fool; once our usefulness to you is fulfilled all we can expect is a bullet in the back of the head so, what would you do in my place ?'

'That may have been the case before poor Latif died and forced Saleem to change our plans but now, who knows ? While there's life there's hope Mr. Murray .'

Despite further disguised enquiries included in a conversation about why the obviously intelligent man had become a Terrorist, Mohammad gave little away about the targets, simply stating: 'We are fighting a holy war, a Jihad. If that means I must sacrifice myself to inflict pain and suffering on the Western world, as they continue to do to my people, I am happy to die a glorious death. Only by bringing the war home to the people of Western Democracies will the voice of the Islamic people be heard.'

'Well stated, Mohammad,' said a dishevelled Saleem, stepping up into the wheelhouse. 'Listening to your questions Mr. Murray, it is clear you wish to discover where we intend striking for our cause. You will have to be patient for a few more hours and then, I promise you, it will become evident. Meanwhile, I suggest you return to the cabin and feed yourself and your patient while I discuss some arrangements with Mohammad.'

As soon as Brad left the wheelhouse, Saleem walked over to his coat, pulled his mobile phone from the pocket, and , signalling his subordinate to stand guard on the door to ensure the Skipper did not return, dialled Hassam's number. When he failed to get a dialling tone he tried Shauna's number. As soon as the message, " This is the…'started, he ended the call and punched the padded leather bench seat in frustration. 'Where is everyone ?' he cried dejectedly.
Recalling the almost forgotten number given to him by the spotty faced anaemic youth who visited him a week ago, he stabbed in the number which was answered immediately.
'Is that Cobra?' he asked the softly spoken voice of the recipient.
A verbal exchange of details confirmed their identification to one another before Saleem pleaded, 'I need to speak to Hassam urgently, I have his explosives.'
His face blanched as he listened to the speaker reveal that Hassam was dead.
Speechless at the shock news, he continued listening without interruption as Cobra detailed the events leading to the Al Qaeda man's demise at the hands of M.I.5 and the Anti-Terrorist squad

Chapter 8

,before enquiring; 'What do you want me to do ?'

The Terrorist Chief quickly recovered his composure , recognising his own plans appeared to be uncompromised and that the situation could, perhaps, be used to his advantage .With the loss of one member, Latif; and faced with a scale down of his original plan, Saleem fired a rapid series of questions to his listener, his evil smile getting larger with every affirmative response.

'We will rendezvous with you about 21.30 this evening. You are sure you can find the place and make it on time ?'

Receiving an assurance, he was about to ask one more question when the phone suddenly went dead. He pressed the recall button but realised the cause when he was rewarded only with silence. 'I thought I had made sure it was fully charged,' he murmured to himself. 'Mohammad,' he called: 'come in here and sit down I have some news and wish to discuss a change of plan with you.'

'Come on in Bill,' said Commander Beaman in answer to the knock ; continuing as the door opened to the touch of Superintendent William Kimpton of the Metropolitan Police, 'thanks for coming over. I know you must be busy, but you know how we are fixed on this Terrorist threat and I wanted to bring you up to date as we need all the help your boys can give us.'

'That's the trouble James. I don't see how we can help much. We're as short staffed as yourself and I've had to send a few of the usual constabulary down to the River to keep an eye on things. This wayward whale is the sort of visitor we could do without: there's hundreds of sightseers down there causing traffic chaos.'

'I understand ,but can I ask; could you continue to keep at least one of your lads on the barge for us. We need everyone on other tasks and, although we think we already have two of the suspect Terrorists under arrest, and that for now the vessel is no threat, we can't leave it completely unattended ?'

'Haven't you got one of my boys already on board ?' queried the Superintendent.

'Yes, but I did promise to send someone to relieve him; he's not had a break for twelve hours. But now I find I have nobody. Most of my lads are dead beat. All of us have not had much sleep in the past couple of days but this thing is coming to a climax soon and we must be ready to respond at a moments notice.'

Kimpton nodded in understanding. 'I'll get Robinson down there right away, that's the best I can offer at the moment. If this evening's sick call isn't as bad as it has been lately with this sickness bug that's about, I'll see if I can spare a second officer or WPC. Speaking of the barge: how's your female Agent by the way ?'

Before the M.I.5 Chief could reply, the slightest of taps on the door was followed by the entrance of a, bleary-eyed, Pete Jefferies who apologised for interrupting; the cause of his urgent intervention waving in his hand.

'Thought you'd better see this straight away Sir,' he said, proffering a six by four inch photograph of a man in a Guard's uniform. 'I'm told this is identical to , or remarkably similar to, those of the Bradwell Power Station personnel. We found it in Steven Hunter's house.'

'Good Lord, it gets worse. We thought that Bradwell could be discounted ,' sighed the Commander. 'At least, that is, if there's any tie in with the barge: there's no way that could get up there today. Still,' he continued turning to Bill Kimpton, 'it seems to confirm what I said about the vessel. It's now even more unlikely it is linked to Saleem's planned assault and be of little concern to us at present.'

'And there's something else Sir that, at first, we thought was an amazing piece of luck. Unfortunately it isn't; other than it tells us that Saleem is NOT a suicide bomber.'

The Senior Agent told the two Chiefs that he and Callum had just viewed a video tape recording of the Terrorists, at the BBC.'

'So we now know who they are at last,' snapped the Commander. 'How did the BBC get hold of this tape then ?'

'It was sent to them by Saleem for broadcasting tomorrow. They would not normally have got it until the postal delivery in the morning but the Corporation's News Desk had been enquiring at the Postal Sorting Office about a missing package that they should have received yesterday. During the search, Saleems's parcel was put with the other one that had been discovered, both packages being given to the courier who called to collect. The News Editor phoned us immediately after viewing just the first few moments. It shows Saleem , in an unidentified room, spouting a load of rhetoric about the Terrorist cause and boasting of their being responsible for yesterday's - that is today - attacks.'

Chapter 8

'So why are you saying Saleem is not a bomber ?' queried the Chief. 'And, can we get any identifiable pictures of the others ?'

Jefferies explained that only a brief piece of film showed the other Cell members, grinning, seated round a table ,gesturing towards a map of some description on the surface and throwing their hands apart to simulate an explosion .The images are not as good as we would have liked but possibly could be enhanced to give us reasonable recognition when we have the film in our hands.'

'What!' screeched Commander Beaman. 'Did you not bring it back in with you ? This is a matter of National security. You should have threatened the Editor with ....'

'I tried Sir,' interrupted the Agent defensively: 'but he wanted an undertaking that the tape would be returned to them for broadcasting if something major does happen. I was not prepared to do that without authority of yourself.'

The Commander excused himself and departed from the room leaving the others discussing the turn of events in his absence.

'Right, the film will be with us shortly. And, Peter, what you have just told us proves Saleem is most definitely a Bomber,' said the Chief re-entering the offices.

Jefferies, recognising his Senior had ,by use of his Christian name not intended any criticism, but was simply suffering the same frustrations they all felt at their failings to make any headway with the investigations, agreed enthusiastically. 'Oh; he admits to being a Bomber alright on the film. But, I said , NOT A SUICIDE BOMBER. From our artist's photo fits we have distributed, it is evident he is in disguise. If he was intending to blow himself up along with his victims there would be no need for him not reveal himself as he really is. No, our Saleem intends to survive and let others do his dirty work for him!'

'Survive, no. Be dead by morning,' said the doomsday merchant spectator alongside the watching eighth Terrorist on the embankment. 'Whales can't live in shallow water. You mark my words, you'll see on the morning's news that it's dead meat, especially the way it's heading. Be up in Chelsea Harbour before long the way it's going .'

Nodding acquiescence, Cobra moved away, concerned not with the creature's fate but by the sight just witnessed of the changeover of guard aboard the moored barge. The newcomer was extremely well built and could prove an obstacle not expected for the slender framed Terrorist. The skills developed at training camps on visits to the Middle East would undoubtedly be required for what Saleem had requested.

A rapidly darkening sky and first spots of rain, together with no sighting of the Whale for the past ten minutes, saw the crowd start to disperse. The Terrorist returned to a nearby parked , Scramble motorcycle and chained the machine to the railings before removing and pocketing : a pair of goggles; a small canister and ; a petit P32 Automatic from the pannier. The threatening squall chose that moment to unleash a torrential downpour, scattering the remaining bystanders as the Assassin sprinted back to the Waste Dispersal Station and slipped, unseen in the gloom and heavy rain, into Cringle Dock.

The small rowing boat, spotted earlier, was still there. A few moments later the black leather suited Terrorist had the craft released and, with a few strokes of the oars, nestling under the stern of the gently rocking barge . Looping the painter rope over a mooring post, Cobra climbed silently aboard.

Robby Robinson was still seated in the tiny cabin - from where both the river and short pier could be observed - having immediately made himself at home with a cup of tea and a newspaper.

Careful to avoid stepping into the light streaming from the cabin windows, Cobra donned the goggles and standing soundlessly upright, leant over the cabin roof with the canister directed into the rooftop ventilation cowl. Two quick squirts of C.S Gas, the hissing sound covered by the rain, produced the expected result.

The first Sergeant Robinson knew of anything amiss was when he felt a burning sensation in his throat and his eyes started to sting.

Bursting out of the cabin with streaming eyes, he vaguely registered a dark figure step up close, and hearing a soft cough-like sound, before a piercing, burning ,sensation stabbed his stomach's insides.

He attempted to grapple with his assailant, his large bulk smashing into the slight frame of Cobra and sending the pair tumbling back into the confines of the cabin where, despite his wound and tears streaming down his face, the Anti-Terrorist policeman managed to disarm the would-be Assassin.

Chapter 8

Alarmed at the unexpected counter-attack, and pinned back against the bulkhead by the sheer weight of the Sergeant, the ,now unarmed and disadvantaged, Terrorist grabbed at a pair of binoculars hanging from a hook on the damaged door: swinging on just one broken hinge.

Still blinded by the effects of the C.S. gas, and fighting the pain in his stomach, Robinson sought to hold his attacker with one brawny arm while feeling for his sub machine gun on the cabin floor.

His efforts were to no avail, the lithe figure escaped his grip and he suddenly felt a thin leather strap encircling his neck from behind, tightening as his clutching fingers tried to find leverage to alleviate the crushing pressure.

Harsh breathing on the back of his neck from his assailant ; indicating the struggle was far from over, gave him hope .Calling on all his remaining strength he abruptly raised himself from his knees, throwing off the Terrorist who was fortunate not to be catapulted out of the cabin.

As it was, the superhuman effort was his own undoing; his throwing off of the attacker causing an inadvertent swing of the binoculars which smashed into his temple, temporarily dazing him and giving Cobra time to; regain control; snatch up the silenced automatic pistol from the cabin floor; and snap off two shots in quick succession.

The first caught the Policeman over the left ear, the bullet furrowing a deep, but far from fatal, wound . It was the second that downed the Sergeant, burying itself just above his heart, the force of impact, although not great from the small gun, sufficient to propel him
backwards where he tripped over the door threshold and , with a drawn out groan, collapse unconscious onto the deck.

Confident that he posed no further threat, and was probably dead, Cobra stepped out of the cabin before removing the mask and taking in gulps of fresh air to counteract the after effects of breathing in the C.S. gas residue.

The Terrorist, refraining from breathing, reentered the cabin, switched off the light and slid back the side window , creating an airflow , before emerging to check both the river and embankment for any possible witnesses to the fight. Breathing a sigh of relief when it was evident the confrontation had been hidden by a combination of darkness and heavy rain, Saleem's recruit ran up the short pier and, five minutes later, returned wheeling the Scramble motorcycle which was soon lowered onto the barge.

'Bit too much water on the course,' joked a lone pedestrian witness to the loading, scurrying head down against the rain in the direction of the Chelsea bridge.

Lifting the corner of the cover of the nearest cargo hold, with a strength born of necessity , Cobra dragged the, profusely bleeding, comatose Policeman over to the compartment and tipped him, head first ,into the dark confines before releasing the mooring ropes tethering the barge.

The powerful diesel engine fired with a puff of smoke as the tide pulled the bow of the craft away from the pier and the vessel headed down-stream under Vauxhall Bridge for a rendezvous with the Terrorist leader.

'Just crossing Vauxhall Bridge Chief,' said the voice of Agent Scooter, Scott, en route for Has-sam's demolished house in Battersea. 'The traffic's bad; everyone's crawling along in this weather.'

'Well just get back as quick as you can Greg,' ordered Commander Beaman. 'Sam's phoned in with what looks to be a good lead: we could all be racing off down to north Essex once she's checked things out. If it's going to take you too long to get there I'll tell the Fire Chief to hold it until we can pick it up later. It's not likely to be of much help at this stage, after all he's dead,' he continued addressing the microphone link to his Agent sent to collect Hassam's passport ; discovered in the smouldering ruins.

'What's that about Sam Sir?' queried Pete Jefferies, entering the Chief's office with two cups of steaming coffee.

'While you were gone I had a call from her. It seems the name of the boat on that burnt business card found at the Hullbridge address is SPRINTER, not Sprite as we assumed.

And, of all things, it belongs to that new found boyfriend of hers, who, unfortunately, appears to be out of contact at present.'

'Does that help us ?'

'Only as much as she has been informed that the last known position of the boat was in the River Roach, which flows into the River Crouch. I don't have to tell you Peter, you've seen the chart, the mouth of the Crouch is just south of the River Blackwater where Bradwell Nuclear Power Station is sited !'

' Whew !' whistled Jefferies. 'So that could be the target after all. Uniforms, a sea approach by boat at night, they could be into the place and plant explosive charges before anyone even suspects their presence. Shall I get the lads armed and ready Sir ?'

'No, let's not jump the gun. Sam's on her way now to check if the Sprinter is gone. She says there is no way Bradley Murray is a Terrorist and can't believe he is in any way involved in this situation. We'll give her time to check: the worst thing we could do for now is go charging off when the threat may still be in London,' replied the M.I.5 Chief draining his coffee cup.

'Get that down you Miss. Got a drop of you know what in that,' winked the Landlord of the *Plough and Sail*, handing over a cup of piping hot coffee to Sam . 'You'll need that if you are going out in this weather. It will be a chilly walk along the sea wall to Brad's boathouse.'

Following the instructions given to her earlier, the female Agent had found her way to the riverside Public House where she parked her car and made herself known to the Publican; falsely claiming to be an Advertising Representative commissioned to take a photograph and details of the Sprinter.

'The light's going fast and there's another storm on it's way Miss,' said the proprietor before getting her the requested coffee.

Sam gulped down her refreshment, returned to her car for a pair of small binoculars and, following the directions given her, made her way to the sea wall; avoiding the worst of the muddy puddles. Standing on top of the embankment, she spotted the lone boathouse in the distance. A quick view through the field glasses revealed no sign of movement and a scan of the boats moored nearby was unrewarding: no names being easily visible.

'Here goes a good pair of boots,' she murmured heading along the wet sloppy conditions of the bank top. 'Bradley Murray, you can buy me some new footwear for not answering your phone.'

Ten minutes later she was standing alongside the deserted boathouse, a quick glance through a crack in the doors confirming the shed was empty. Turning her attentions to the river she saw a fishing boat anchored out in midstream, the name hidden by a small yacht barring a full view. Walking twenty yards further on, she raised the binoculars and focussed on the name emblazoned on the stern, SPRINTER.

Chapter 8

She swung her gaze over the whole of the vessel, confirming its identification with both the name on the bow and a large FOR SALE sign affixed to the front of the wheelhouse.

Both relieved and disappointed at the same time; happy that her new found boyfriend was not involved with the Terrorists but not so cheerful at imparting the news to Commander Beaman that the craft was obviously not involved with any attack, she morosely made her way back as the rain started to come down.

'Get in out of the rain Mohammad,' shouted Saleem from the wheelhouse cabin doorway. 'Quick; cover those satchel bombs up and come back in before you get drenched.'

Brad heard the footsteps overhead recede and heaved a sigh of relief. He and Swifty had spent the last two hours locked in the large cabin, taking it in turns to listen intently at the door to the Terrorists' conversation and activities in the wheelhouse.

Asif's excited comments had provided the majority of the information they had gleaned from the eavesdropping which, together with the sounds of the bomb packages being moved about, gave them some idea of Saleem's plans; the scale of which took their breath away.

'They can't be planning mass murder on such a scale, it's wholesale slaughter of innocent men, women and children,' whispered Trevor. 'They'll never get away with it, will they ?'

'It seems they may Trev. Who's to stop them ? I don't see hordes of police about to board us; it's probable the Authorities do not even know of any Terrorist attack. If only I could get hold of my mobile phone ?'

The usually talkative crewman was, for once, speechless; sitting on the edge of his bunk with his head in his hands for some minutes before looking up with a venomous hate in his eyes and threateningly stating, 'I will kill them all myself before I let them get away with it. They are not going to murder anyone, especially not my Nancy and Naomi.'

Brad grinned. 'That's just what I hoped to hear you say old friend. If stopping their plans gets me killed, that's the price I'm prepared to pay but, as a married man with a young child, I didn't feel I could ask you to put your life on the line.'

Chapter 8

'If they carry out what we think they intend to do, I won't have a wife and child…..there won't be ANYONE left alive on Canvey Island.'

'Our problem, as I see it,' said the Skipper, 'is when do we make our move against them? At the moment, although we could get out of here and on to deck, we have no way of getting assistance and we can't leave the boat ourselves. Even if we used the scuba diving suits in the locker in the forward cabin, the minute they discovered us gone Saleem would detonate your house bomb. I think for now, we had better play the compliant captives and see if we can find out any more details of how they intend to attack all the places mentioned. At some time, with only three of them, they are going to have to split up. That will probably give us our best chance to overpower them.'

'I'll be ready the minute you give the word Skip. I can't wait to get my hands on that vicious bastard Saleem.'

Having agreed their own intentions, Brad suggested he return to the aft engine room hatch to see what had happened to the armaments hidden beneath the tarpaulin on the stern deck. 'Perhaps I can sabotage some other items while they are otherwise occupied.'

'Hold it a minute boss,' said Swifty hammering on the cabin door and shouting: 'How much longer are you going to keep us locked up in here? We're thirsty and need to use the toilet.'

'Nice to hear you are back with us Mr. Swift,' said Saleem's smarmy voice through the door. 'We won't be much longer, ten minutes or so, then you can join us for our Thames cruise.'

With the confirmation of no immediate disturbance, the duo lifted out the bulkhead panel. Brad slipped inside the engine room and, using the pencil torch to avoid obstacles, made his way to the rear hatch. He was about to raise the cover when he detected approaching footsteps overhead and froze where he was, afraid to move a muscle or breath.

After what seemed an interminable wait, Brad heard a muffled voice calling the Terrorist on deck, the undecipherable communication resulting in a shuffling and scuffing above, before the sound of footsteps faded behind him.

Edging the cover up, he peered forward into the near darkness and, detecting no movement, poked his head above deck and shone his torch beam beneath the tarpaulin.

The packing crates were broken up and , packed together alongside the timbers were eight, dark blue, canvas satchels: some wired together in pairs and three with digital timers affixed.

Powerless to make the explosive bags harmless in the short time available to him, without his sabotage being evident, he, reluctantly, decided to leave them untouched ; a wise decision as he had only just returned to the cabin when the door opened and Mohammad's voice called, 'Come in gentlemen, it's time we made a move.'

'Shouldn't we be on the move Guv ?' said Charlie Walsh checking the magazine of his sidearm. 'The traffic at this time of the evening will be murder. Pete's arranged a chopper at City Airport but it will probably take as long to get there by car as it will for us to fly from there to Bradwell.'

'Yes, we can't wait any longer; we could be too late as it is. It's obviously taking Sam longer than she thought to check out this "Sprinter" boat. I think she's reluctant to use her mobile too much as she said, last time we spoke, that the battery charge was getting low.
I'll get Kate up from downstairs, she can mind the office in case Sam phones in while we're on our way.'

As the M.I.5 gang of Agents rose and made their way towards the exit, and before the Commander could pick up the phone to arrange the office manning, the outside phone on his desk uttered it's shrill beeping.

The Agents stopped in their tracks and watched their Chief listen briefly before they heard him respond: 'Okay Sam, keep trying. There's nothing you can help with back here for now. Keep digging, see if you can locate Mr. Murray, he may be able to tell us how his card came to be in the Hullbridge house and give us a lead to Saleem.'

'Are we still off to Bradwell boss ?' queried Agent Walsh .

'No; come back all of you. Sam tells me that the "Sprinter" is safely moored at a place called Paglesham and there's no sign of any activity of any sort. It looks as though we can discount that idea; we're back to........well, nothing,' said the Commander, the dismay reflected in his voice.

A rap on the door interrupted the silence, a junior officer entering ,on a: 'Come in,' command, with a small jiffy bag package in his hand.

'Sorry to disturb you Sir, but this package was just brought in to reception. I was told you were expecting it urgently,' said the young recruit, adding enthusiastically, 'It's a Video tape from the BBC. I brought the bag up too, in case it was important.'

The Senior Agents grinned at one another as the youngster left, remembering their own early days in the department.

'Put the TV and VCR on Andy,' ordered the Commander tossing the tape to Davison who was standing nearest to the set. 'Let's see what Saleem has to say, and what the others look like.'

'What does he look like ?' said Sam to the barman in the "Ship" pub. 'And is he likely to come in this evening at all ?

The barman, in answer to Sam's earlier probing about the whereabouts of Brad, had mentioned the best person to ask would be his usual crew-man, Trevor Swift.

'I can't say. Occasionally he comes in while waiting for Brad, but seldom on his own other-wise: they're quite inseparable that pair.'

'Oh ! Do you have an address then, it really is important that I get in touch with Mr. Murray before I go back to London ?'

'All I can tell you Miss is that Brad lives out Paglesham way somewhere but has a flat up the road that he often uses, somewhere off the Broadway but don't ask me the exact address. He could be in the phone book I suppose or, he might even be staying overnight with *Swifty* ; he sometimes does that when they get in late.'

Sam thanked the obliging barman as he returned to polishing the glasses, asking if she could borrow a telephone directory while awaiting the meal she had ordered. A study of the M's, revealed five B. Murray's but only one with a Leigh address. Checking the battery level of her mobile, she dialled the number.........it went unanswered. She tried Brad's mobile again, ...the same, 'You have reached' message. She rang off...... to save the battery. She thumped the table ....in frustration.

The pretty young waitress delivering her meal nearly dropped the plate in alarm. 'Is there something the matter Miss ?'

Sam apologised, excusing her actions as frustration that she had suddenly remembered something important. 'Perhaps you could help me though, I don't want to trouble your barman again as I see he's getting busy. 'Do YOU know Brad Murray ?'

The young girl blushed. 'You mean that good-looking one in the photograph on the wall over there ? All the girl's want to know him. You his girlfriend then ?'

The Agent looked closer at the picture of a bunch of anglers kneeling behind a display of some twenty or so Skate ; obviously caught by them. Standing to one side , smiling, and leaning with his hand on a mast was Brad with his other arm around the neck of a shorter, burly character with a mischievous grin on his face; obviously Trevor from the barman's description.

'That's him,' replied Sam ignoring the girl's personal intrigue. 'Any idea where I can find him ?'

'Hold on,' requested the waitress returning to the bar and speaking to a bearded, ruddy-faced drinker who, even that time of early evening, appeared to have difficulty in balancing on the barstool.

'If his boat is not moored out in the "Ray" , which it wasn't when I came into work, Jack says he will be either out on a charter or moored over at Hole Haven Creek on Canvey Island and staying at Swiftys'.

Making a mental note to leave the youngster a generous tip, Sam picked up the telephone directory and skimmed through the pages while picking at her meal. There it was: T. Swift with a Canvey number.

She tapped in the number on her mobile and was immediately rewarded with a lady's voice enquiring who was calling.

Sam asked for Trevor and was told, 'I'm sorry, you must have the wrong number, this is Southend……' The Agent apologised and rang off feeling foolish at not realising that Canvey obviously had a different code.

Obtaining the Canvey code from a couple on the next table, she rang the correct number. The receiver on the other end was just picked up when Sam's phone emitted a series of pips and went dead.

Careful to not let her frustration show this time, she finished her meal, made sure the girl got the deserved gratuity, crossed the road and over the railway bridge to a telephone kiosk she had previously seen. The effort was wasted: the vandalised booth had no handset.

'You have the choice of going back to the hotel and wasting time recharging the phone,' she said to herself. 'Or, getting in your car out of this wind and cold and driving over to the Canvey address.'

Chapter 8

Deciding a visit being the most sensible course of action, especially as it would allow her to check whether Brad's new boat was moored where it had been suggested it might be, she returned to her car and put the journey details into the vehicle's satellite navigation system before setting off.

'Time to set off Mr. Murray. Will you kindly take us round to Canvey Island, Hole Haven Creek I believe is the spot we wish to anchor.'

Brad was tempted to leave Swifty's security devices in operation but decided against the idea, fearful Saleem's instability would cause him to use the explosive transmitter, regardless of the consequences.

Trevor emerged from the cabin feigning unsteadiness and stumbling into the two Terrorists who, distracted for a vital few seconds, failed to see Brad snatch his mobile phone from the chart pouch alongside his left arm and pocket it.

'You are not, perhaps, as strong as you think Mr. Swift,' sneered the Terrorist leader.

'Mohammad will assist Mr. Murray. May I suggest you make us all a nice hot drink and then telephone your wife and tell her you will be in later than you first thought. We don't want her reporting you missing or anything do we ?'

Swifty would have loved to have swung one of his pudgy fists into the Terrorist's grinning face, restrained only by the sight of the signal unit being deliberately and provokingly displayed in Saleem's raised hand.

'Nancy knows I wouldn't phone around now, she'll be getting my daughter ready for bed soon. I'll phone later,' said the crewman; secretly hoping that his non-contact would indeed cause his wife alarm and start a hunt for himself and Brad.

To his surprise, the Terrorist accepted his excuse. 'As you say Mr. Swift, it can wait.'

The burly frame of Mohammad, streaming rain, returned from unhitching the *Whaleback* and Asif chose that moment to emerge from the forward cabin, rubbing sleep from his eyes to crowd the wheelhouse even further.

'Ah !' exclaimed Saleem. 'All together at last. Let's get the party under way shall we ?
Come Asif, let us get changed, it shouldn't be long before Mr. Murray drops us off at our first port of call.'

Chapter 8

'I'll make Hole Haven my first call,' said Sam to herself as she made her way over the Benfleet Creek bridge on to Canvey Island; suddenly laughing out loud as her headlights picked out a vandalised sign on the side of the road reading: Canvey **Is**, the rest of the notice having been torn away. Some wag had scrawled underneath in black felt tip pen:

In need of a new sign.

Five minutes later she was driving down Haven Road past the Oikos Storage depot, terminating her journey in the car park of the "Lobster Smack" public house.

Pulling the hood of her anorak up, she ran to the pub, already busy with regulars.

Having only recently eaten ,she avoided the Restaurant area and made her way to the bar, declining the offer of: 'What can I get you Miss ?' from the barkeeper.

'I'm actually in a hurry and am only seeking information for now. Could I ask you, do you know a Mr. Bradley Murray or Mr. Trevor Swift ? I'm told Mr. Murray parks his fishing boat around here sometimes.'

Amused at the term *Parks*, the bartender laughed; 'Everyone knows Brad and Swifty.

Trev lives just down the road and Brad often MOORS his boat over in the creek. It could even be there now; although if they're around here this evening they would normally call in for a quick one.'

'Can I look ? How will I know his boat if I can't see any names in the dark?'

The barman smiled. 'Brad's craft is a 60 foot long, old wartime, launch. You can't mistake it; nothing like the normal fishing boats you may have seen. If you climb up the bank to the sea wall just outside you'll be looking right into the Creek where Brad has his mooring. If it's there, you'll see it.'

Thanking the informative assistant, Sam went out into the now persistent rain and scrambled up the slippery grass bank to the path at the top. The force of the wind, as she lost the protection of the embankment, sprayed the fine rain directly into her face and temporarily blurred her vision.

The sight that met her eyes as normality returned, stunned her. Huge tanker ships were moored to short piers no more than a stone's throw away and, to the west, the Coryton Oil Refinery was lit up like a Christmas display.

Chapter 8

Such was the volume of illumination, the Creek itself was not as dark as she expected; the moored craft being easily visible. She scanned the choppy, turbulent, water, noting three squat sturdy looking Tugboats at the entrance to the Creek, a couple of thirty foot fishing vessels and some vacant mooring buoys with dinghies attached……but no sixty foot *Whaleback Swift.*

Dismayed, she hurried back down the slope out of the wind just as, unseen behind her, the bow of Brad's launch nosed its way past the stern of a Tanker into the mouth of the Creek. Starting her car, she headed out of the car park towards Trevor's house.

'Mrs. Swift ?' enquired the unfamiliar voice on the end of the phone.

'Yes, who is it calling ?'

Saleem smiled and , in his best dulcet voice, said; 'My name is Stevens, Hunter Stevens. I'm a Film Director aboard *Whaleback Swift* with your husband and Mr. Murray. Trevor asked me to give you a call and put your mind at rest. We have broken down and he and Bradley are endeavouring to carry out repairs. They are a little bit covered in oil and grease at the moment, hence my calling on Trevor's behalf. He says you are not to worry if he is quite late as we may have to get towed back in if the repair is unsuccessful.'

Ignoring the venomous look Swifty gave him as he rang off, the Terrorist leader, now dressed in a dark blue uniform, called out through the open door; 'Asif, is the dinghy ready ?'

Asif, similarly attired to his leader, appeared in the doorway with two of the blue satchels slung over his shoulder and the sniper's rifle in his hand. 'We are ready to go Saleem.'

Without speaking, he exited the wheelhouse after Asif, leaving Brad and his crewman alone with Mohammad and the ever threatening signal transmitter.

The dinghy settled gently alongside the wooden jetty and Asif jumped ashore , followed by Saleem. Securing the small boat , and ensuring the rifle and rocket launcher were completely covered in the bottom, the pair of *Thamesguard Security* guards made their way along to the "Lobster Smack" and entered the smoky interior.

'Hello Gents. What would you like? You're new are you ? I thought I knew all the guards around here.'

Chapter 8

'We'll just have a couple of coffees and sandwiches if you have them. You obviously haven't heard: there's a bit of a scare on, we've been drafted in for additional patrols. Daren't have anything stronger than coffee,' said Saleem with a smile. 'We go on duty soon. What can you tell us about the place ?'

Ten minutes later, having gleaned a great amount of information regarding the security arrangements of both the Canvey Petroleum and Calor Gas terminals, together with Coryton Oil Refinery, the Terrorists departed and made their way back to the dinghy.

'Asif,' said the Terrorist Chief, 'your role in our plan is changed now that Latif is already enjoying the rewards of his sacrifice. You will no longer be required to hide yourself in the Coryton complex and be the human bomb to explode one of the tanks. You are to have a larger role to play. We will content ourselves with secreting two satchel bombs alongside a couple of the nearest full tanks; they should set the whole complex ablaze. The timers will be set for eleven p.m. to coincide with our other attacks.'

After walking along the sea wall to confirm what they had been told about the Calor Gas Terminal, the duo returned to the dinghy and paddled their way over to a short jetty at the mouth of the Creek where they silently crept onto the structure. Pulling automatic pistols from their uniform pockets, they approached the building at the end of the jetty and threw open the door.

The surprised occupants, two men and a woman of the National Coastwatch Institution, faced with two armed Guards, offered no resistance.

'What's going on ?' said the Senior of the three recovering from his initial shock. ' 'You're Guards from the Oil Refinery aren't you . Why are you pointing guns at us ?'

Saleem did not answer the question, simply barking; 'When does the watch change, when are you to be relieved ?'.

The bewildered volunteer watch keepers, who usually keep both a visual lookout and local VHF radio Emergencies listening watch - to safeguard the dangers of shipping movements in the confines of Refineries and Gas storage area - sealed their own fate when their leader answered, 'Not until midnight.'

With their planned attack taking place at eleven, there was no danger of their presence being spotted by replacement watch keepers .

Chapter 8

'Kill them,' snarled Saleem as he pulled the trigger of his own automatic, the silenced projectile catching the Senior man directly over his heart and propelling him backwards into his companions. Asif, adrenalin pumping, and seeing the hapless volunteers as the first victims of revenge against all 'Westerners' for the death of his brother, needed no second order. His weapon belched flame and lead in a murderous fusillade until clicking empty. Even Saleem was amazed at how quickly the youngster had emptied the entire clip of bullets into the twisted forms of the three observers who now lay bleeding profusely on the hut floor. The young Terrorist's accuracy was, however, not as proficient as his leader; groans from the victims indicating at least one had survived the unsteady onslaught. Saleem casually leant over the crumpled forms and carefully placed a single bullet into the back of each of their heads before signalling Asif to leave, and slamming the door behind them. Ten minutes later, the Terrorists beached their dinghy by a bend in the Creek and crawled up the embankment to a high wire fence surrounding the Refinery. Hidden by deep shadows, they crouched and ran along the wire until they had a huge, obviously full, storage tank in front of them, where they cut a small hole in the fencing. Asif crept through the small opening with the two haversacks while Saleem viewed the surrounding area through the night sight of the sniper's rifle.

Spotting a security camera pointed directly at their location, he was about to pull the trigger when he noticed it moving away to cover an area to the right. He motioned to Asif who rose to his feet and sped across the open ground to the tank where he scooped a hole in the soft ground alongside the storage facility and pushed one of the satchels in as far as he could.

The surprising amount of light made it difficult to completely keep to the shadows, but gave him the advantage of being able to discern Saleem who signalled him to stay where he was. A few moments later his leader indicated for him to continue. With nothing to gain by running, he stood and boldly walked across to the next nearest tank where he crouched holding his breath; at any minute expecting a challenge. When no such summons came, he repeated his earlier actions before rejoining Saleem. Pinning the fence back to disguise any obvious interference, the two Terrorists returned to the dinghy and made their way back to the launch.

Chapter 8

'Leave the Launcher but put the rifle back on board Asif,' ordered the Chief Terrorist as they tied up and clambered aboard the larger craft. 'I will go and inform Mohammad of our success.'

The big Palestinian greeted him at the wheel-house door, anxious for news. Within minutes he was grinning and reassuring his leader that Brad and Swifty had been co-operative. 'I separated them just in case,' he told Saleem. 'Put the crewman in the front cabin out of the way and kept an eye on Mr. Murray here with me.'

Had he known, he may well have been a little less cheerful. The minute the cabin door slammed behind him, Swifty had lifted the bunk mattress and taken a small, but deadly looking ,harpoon gun from the locker beneath. Opening up the small hatchway through to the anchor rope stowage compartment, he had silently made his way on to the deck through the narrow opening. He was creeping back towards the cabin when he spotted Saleem and Asif returning as they approached through a patch of reflected light.

He slid the spear gun between the front of the wheelhouse and small stowage boxes, that were formerly ammunition lockers, out of sight from the cabin windows. Cursing his luck, he rushed back before the Terrorists boarded and was laying back on the bunk , eyes closed, when the door opened and the harsh face of Saleem filled his vision.

The sneering look in Saleem's eyes showed unquestioned contempt as he began to speak from the television screen in the Commander's office; the gathering of Agents hanging on every word for some clue as to the intended target.

'Anyone recognise any of the others ?' enquired the M.I.5 Chief as the tape ended.

'One thing is certain,' said Pete Jefferies, 'Saleem is still in disguise on the film if the description we got of Steven Hunter from his neighbours is any guide. And, the big guy with the beard is most certainly Mohammad; fits the description of the Costume Hire shop owner perfectly. But, the other two: unknown, brainwashed, bomb fodder will be difficult to trace unless we have time to go visiting every Mosque between here and Southend,' he added morosely.

'You can turn that off now Andy. There doesn't seem to be much we can glean from that; so where do we go from here ?'

Chapter 8

Having already stopped and rewound the tape, and returned the set to Television reception , Andy Davison continued staring at the TV screen as though he hadn't heard his Chief's instruction; and with a perplexed look on his face.

'Are you with us Andy ?' said the Chief sternly. 'We haven't got time to waste watching the antics of a wayward whale.'

'No Sir, but look !'

The commentator was saying: 'It seems the creature may be trying to make its own way back out to sea. It's no longer up at Battersea but has just been spotted in the Nine Elms Reach between Victoria Rail and Vauxhall Bridges. Scientists say the whale is, however, very w..........there it is surfacing again close to the far bank.'

'So what Davison ? What are you playing at, don't you realise we are trying to locate armed and dangerous Terrorists, not bloody great fish!'

'Sorry Sir, but don't you see: that's the spot where Hassam's barge was?'

'Don't you mean is?'

'No Sir, I don't. Look, it's GONE!'

9

'Come on in dear. Don't stand there in the cold and rain,' said Nancy Swift as Agent Samirah introduced herself on the doorstep as a friend of Brad, trying to locate him urgently.

'Sit down, let me get you a cup of tea, I've just made a pot for myself. Then we'll see if I can help at all.'

'Thank you Mrs. Swift. The man up at the "Lobster Smack" said your husband would almost certainly know of Brad's whereabouts,' said the Agent as Nancy disappeared into the kitchen to return, almost immediately ,with the offered beverage.

'I'm afraid Trevor isn't home yet ; he's on Brad 's boat with him. They've got a film crew on a charter. In fact I've just received a call from the Director, the boat has had a breakdown that Trevor and Brad are trying to fix. They have a radio so if they can't get going they will have to call for a tow home. Whatever, they are going to be late; Trevor didn't want me to worry.'

'Oh, so I could speak to Brad if I telephoned your husband's mobile. I have tried Brad a couple of times but his is switched off.'

'No, I'm sorry, that's no good. I've got Trevs' mobile here; he forgot it again. I expect that's why he asked the gentleman to phone and I didn't ask his number,' apologised the housewife.

Sams' elation disappeared with the revelation that she still had no means of contacting the Skipper. 'Do you know the name of the Director Mrs. Swift ?' she asked hiding her disappointment.

'I don't. If Trevor mentioned it I didn't take a lot of notice.'

'It wouldn't have been Hunter, or possibly Stevens, would it ?'

'I'm really not any help, am I ? Neither name rings a bell, I just cannot say. Is it so urgent that a few more hours matter? They are sure to be back by then. Trevor is an excellent mechanic; I'm surprised they broke down at all.'

The female Agent decided to tell Nancy a partial truth to elicit as much additional information as she could without unduly alarming the crewman's wife. 'Actually Nancy, if I may call you that, I'm with a Government Agency. We came across an old business card of Brad's in relation to an investigation we are carrying out. I met Brad in Leigh the other day but , at the time, was not aware that he owns a boat called *Sprinter* which we thought was involved ,or about to be, in unlawful activities.'

Seeing the shock of disbelief on Nancy's face, she hurriedly added; ' We now know Brad and Trevor are in no way involved, but they may have information vital to our investigations that they themselves are unaware of. So it really is urgent.'

Nancy apologised again, saying that there was nothing else she could think of herself and that, as she had never had reason to call her husband on the ship to shore radio, she wouldn't have any idea of how to contact them in that way. Even if she did, she told the Agent; 'Unless they are well out to sea, or they had reason to use it themselves, it is probable that even that will be switched off.'

Thanking the housewife for her time, Sam rose to leave, passing the open door of Naomi's play-room. 'What a magnificent Doll's House,' she exclaimed on spotting Trevor's handiwork.

'Reminds me of the type of toy I always wanted as a child.'

'Trevor made it for our daughter; let me show you before you go, he's really made a good job of it.'

Nancy opened up the front to display the minature furniture and decorations. 'We're hoping to get a real place like this one day, somewhere off this Island in the country, away from all this industry. Look, Trevor even put tiny lights in the rooms. They're battery operated on a switch inside the roof here,'she added opening up the mini-tiled lid.

The red L.E.D. encased in the small parcel, lying alongside the battery compartment, winked like a malevolent eye; startling both women.

'What's this he's put in now ?' questioned Nancy reaching down to pick out the package.

Sam's brain, initially mesmerized by the blinking lamp, snapped back to reason. 'NO !' she screamed. 'Don't touch that, it's a bomb. Quickly, go and get your daughter. Where's your phone?'

Bewildered, Nancy did as asked without question and, following Sam's instructions,
carried the sleepy youngster outside to the Agent's car.

Sam snatched up the phone and dialled Commander Beaman.

The telephone rang on the M.I.5 Chief's desk, interrupting the stunned silence of the gathered Agents still staring at the TV screen; seemingly willing the camera to refocus on the scenes of a few moments earlier rather than that of an Animal Wellfare expert explaining the problems the whale was facing.

'Yes !' snapped the Commander. 'Ah, Greg, just the chap. Where are you now ?'

Agent Scott reported he was just about to leave the ruins of Hassam's house and was enquiring if he had time to snatch a meal break on the way back, having not eaten since early lunchtime.

'No, Greg. Get back as soon as you can. I'll arrange sandwiches for all of us; someone appears to have moved the barge. We'll need all the manpower we can muster but, take a peek at the Waste Transfer Station jetty on the way to see if it's not a mistake.'

'Are we absolutely certain that view the cameras were showing us was where the barge was ?' queried Agent Callum. 'Haven't we got a direct contact with Kimpton's man on board ?'

Chapter 9

'Those pictures were definitely of the stretch of river where the barge was moored,' piped up Davison.

Commander Beaman grabbed the nearest phone and asked the operator to get hold of the Scotland Yard Inspector, and send some sandwiches up. 'We'll soon see one way or another,' he sighed. 'Let's hope Andy's wrong and we haven't now got another headache.'

A phone shrilled: the Commanders' hand was a blur as he grabbed the handset. 'Yes Bill, thanks……, oh; sorry Sam I'm waiting for Bill Kimpton to call, we've lost the barge.'

His normally florid complexion paled as he, patiently, listened to his Agent's words.

'Don't touch it Sam: get the woman and child out of harms way but keep everything under wraps for now if you can, we don't want to start a panic. Callum and Pete are leaving now, they'll meet you as soon as they can. Is your mobile okay now ?'

'Afraid not Sir, there's very little battery charge left until I can get hold of my charger and I'm reluctant to use it just in case Brad does try to get in touch. I'm using Mrs. Swift's home phone .'

'Then, they'll meet you outside . What's the address ?'
He scribbled furiously on the pad in front of him before ringing off with a final; 'If there are near neighbours, see if you can get them away somehow; even if you have to call on the local constabulary. But, be careful what you tell them at this stage, we don't want to show our hand if the Terrorists are in the area. I agree, it's too much of a coincidence for there to be no connection to the people we are searching for. The last thing we want is for them to disappear back into obscurity.'
Handing the scrap of pad to Pete Jefferies, he looked at the questioning faces of the room's occupants and announced; 'Sam has discovered a bomb in the house of Bradley Murray's crewman. We have no idea, yet, why it is there; but it seems there must be a reason that is tied in with our investigations. Pete, you've got the fastest car. Get down there as quick as you can and take Callum with you, there's not a bomb yet he hasn't been able to defuse. Keep in contact, we still have to discover the whereabouts of the barge.'

Chapter 9

Cobra cut the engine and allowed the barge to drift up to the dark, deserted, wharf at Purfleet; a couple of miles west of the Dartford Toll crossings. The journey downstream had been uneventful, navigation of the Estuary proving well within the capabilities of the Terrorist. Unthought of, however, was the problem of mooring the craft single-handed; each time the stern was secured the bow swinging out towards mid-stream on the current of the incoming tide.

Eventually, at the third attempt, Saleem's latest recruit overcame the problem by roping the barge to a jetty bollard by a single, midway, fixing: thereby preventing either end of the vessel swinging out without forcing the opposite end into the pier.

With no sign of an approaching launch, Cobra climbed onto the jetty and, keeping low, raced up to the shore end where the entrance was barred by a padlocked iron gate. A single shot from the silenced P32 Automatic blew the lock off , the soft pfhutt no louder than the gurglings of the tidal flow around the pier's stanchions; attracting no attention.

Minutes later the, ever cautious, Terrorist wheeled the Scramble motorcycle to the gate post, ready for a speedy getaway and panting in a whisper: 'Don't be late Saleem, come on.'

'Come on Mr. Swift,' ordered Saleem; 'we have an appointment to keep. The sooner we return from our cruise up river, the sooner you can get home to your wife.'

Trevor wasn't fooled by the Terrorist Chief's lies but, accompanied by Mohammad, made his way out on deck to release the ASR launch as Brad started the engines. The big Palestinian saw the emergency axe clipped to the foredeck and stood his foot on it while Swifty unhitched the mooring and dropped it back over the side; but failed to spot the hidden spear gun in the darkness.The crewman stepped back alongside his Skipper as Brad gunned the engines and headed out of the Creek towards London, quickly whispering a few words in his ear.

The three Terrorists sat huddled together, discussing their plans with little regard to Brad and Trevor who took advantage of the lack of concern to quietly talk over their own options.

A short while later - just after they had passed under the Queen Elizabeth 2nd Bridge at Dartford - the Skipper reached below the console shelf and quickly switched the fuel control lever on and off; causing the motors to splutter and cough.

Saleem looked up in alarm . 'What is happening? I warned you against playing any tricks,' he hissed venomously. 'You will keep this boat going, or else,' he added pointing to the transmitter in Mohammad's hand.

'It's a fuel supply problem we have been experiencing,' said the Skipper. 'Trevor will have to go down to the engine room or we could break down completely.'

'Then get down there Mr. Swift,' snapped the Terrorist Chief. 'We will be at the rendezvous in a few moments. In fact, Mr. Murray, if you look through these night glasses, you will be able to see, over to the right hand shore, a barge up ahead : take us alongside.'

Swifty opened up the engine room main hatch and disappeared below deck ,observed by Mohammad and Asif as they went out on deck to drag the remaining satchel bombs from beneath the tarpaulin cover in the stern.

The crewman switched on the main light and made his way between the gleaming motors, now purring sweetly at little more than idle revs as Brad throttled back to approach the barge. Rummaging in his Aladdin's cave tool box, he pulled out a hacksaw blade, which he secreted in a deep pocket on the leg of his overalls ; a long shaft, thin bladed ,electrical screwdriver, and a length of flexible piano wire; concealing both the tool and cable inside his sock. 'That's better. Now Mr. Saleem , let me see if I can ruin your plans and disable the other rocket launcher. And, just let me see you put that transmitter down for a second and you're a dead man,' he mouthed silently to himself as the first part of Brad's considered actions was successfully achieved.

Overhead, he heard the movements of the Terrorists and soft mutterings as, with a gentle bump, he realised they had come alongside the barge.

The main hatch opened a fraction and Mohammad threateningly called down; 'Stay where you are Mr. Swift and keep the engines running whatever you do......or else. Do not let any light show.'

Swifty made his way to the small rear hatch and, switching off the light, lifted the lid up an inch. The words of the Terrorists became perfectly clear and surprised him when he heard a new, unrecognised ,voice say; 'Where is Saleem, I am anxious to get back: I have a mission of my own.'

Chapter 9

'Here he comes now,' replied Mohammad, surprising the crewman even more.

'Surely they haven't left Brad alone ?' he mused. 'You could have made a bad mistake if you have Mr. Terrorist; Brad now has his mobile phone.'

Brad was, in fact, at that moment trying unsuccessfully to extract the instrument from his pocket, hampered by his wrists being securely affixed to the wheel. The first the Skipper knew of the Terrorist even having the handcuffs was when, as he slipped the engines into neutral, he felt the barrel of Saleem's gun pressed against his temple and the order to: 'Hold out your hands.' The evil grinning Terrorist made for the door, laughingly adding; 'Don't go away Mr. Murray will you, we haven't finished yet?'

Barely daring to breath, Swifty continued to listen as Saleem greeted the unknown Terrorist. 'It's good to see you again. Did you have any trouble ?'

The quietly spoken voice of the newcomer responded curtly. 'A little, but nothing that need concern you any longer. I assume you have overcome your own little problem. Now, you no longer need my assistance, I will leave you to your Destiny. If you have my package I have my own Agenda to follow. We will not be meeting again: may Allah be with you.'

The three Terrorists watched as the black clad figure, forgetting to mention Robby Robinson's whereabouts, skipped adroitly on to the pier. Peering out of the wheelhouse side window, Brad gasped as he saw the new Terrorist turn under the lone weak lamplight and give a cheerful wave to the watchers, before donning a helmet and driving off on a Scramble motorcycle.

Below deck, the eavesdropping crewman's blood chilled as he listened to the Terrorist Chief issuing his final instructions to the youngster Asif.

'From here you will easily see and hear the explosion of the wreck, which I will set off soon. That is your signal to move the barge into position where you will drop the two charges with timers set for five minutes on top of the Tunnels, just before the Bridge ,and set off your other linked charges, that Mohammad is placing in the holds at this moment, as you get under the Bridge itself. The resulting explosions will destroy the Tunnels and take out the central span supporting pillars of the bridge. Your actions Asif will surely cause many ,many, deaths and guarantee you a better life after death with your own virgin maidens.'

A sudden curse and thump overhead startled Swifty who was about to flee back to his beloved engines before hearing Mohammad groan; 'This cursed rain has made everywhere slippery. I've fallen on my injured arm Saleem. Help me up, I have no feeling in it.'

'Go and rest in the cabin with Mr. Murray ,' ordered Saleem with a degree of sympathy that Swifty had not heard from him before. 'Here, take this key and set him free; we are ready to go once I unhitch ourselves from the barge.'

A minute later the crewman, still crouched beneath the hatch cover, felt, rather than saw, the bows of the launch swing out away from the barge as the front hawser was released.

He listened as Saleem's footsteps returned to throw off the stern restraining rope; ready to leap out with his lethal screwdriver and settle the score with the psychopathic Terrorist before realising, however quick he was, he would not be able to throw back the hatch , extricate himself from the small opening, and attack the Terrorist leader before he was aware of the threat.

'Be patient Trevor my boy,' he murmured as the footsteps faded and he eased the hatch open to find himself at eye level with the, half concealed, butt of a rifle.
Throwing the tarpaulin back, he was dismayed to find himself looking at empty and broken launcher boxes, the object of his intended sabotage having been removed.
He picked up the rifle, recognising it as the most popular, Super Magnum L96 Snipers, silenced, weapon. Such an opportunity to lower the odds and scupper their murderous intentions quickly overcame the distaste of the thought that came into his head. He hesitated no longer. Slipping a 7.62mm shell from the 10 round feed box into the chamber, he pushed the bolt home and raised the infrared telescopic night sight to his eye. Focussing on the barge being left astern, he quickly sighted the figure of Asif making his way back to the vessel's tiny rear cabin. Trying to make allowance for the gentle rocking of the *Whaleback*, and calling on his experience with a similar weapon from his Special Boat Service past, he lined the sight up on the young Terrorist and squeezed the trigger; grateful that the attached Silencer did its job and left Saleem and Mohammad unaware of his assassination.

Chapter 9

The heavy bullet hit Asif in his right thigh, taking off the top of his femur before emerging out of his lower buttock and embedding itself in the cabin's lower window frame.

With a look of disbelief on his face, the teenager slumped to the deck as blood spurted from the wound. Feeling no pain, he made the mistake of reaching up to the cabin's hand rail and pulling himself upright in an attempt to make his way into the cabin, exposing himself to further damage.

A second remarkable shot, at almost extreme range and from the unsteady platform of the launch deck, missed the aimed for heart target but carried out an instant Appendectomy as the projectile slammed into Asif's lower abdomen. The impact spun the injured youngster into the cabin wall from where he rebounded into the knee high bulwark and, for an instant appeared to Swifty, viewing the result of his marksmanship, to be toppling overboard. However, the lack of any support from the shattered leg was already causing a loss of balance, saving the Terrorist from a watery exit from the world in favour of one through loss of blood as he slumped to the barge's deck and lost consciousness.

Swifty lowered the lethal weapon with no sense of elation, more one of sadness at having taken the life of the young man who had, undoubtedly, been led into his actions by
cruel indoctrination. He considered the possibility of returning to the wheelhouse with the rifle as a means of overcoming Saleem and Mohammad but rejected the idea , recognising the weapon was too large and cumbersome for the confines of the relatively small cabin area. 'I might be able to get one, but not both the bastards before one of them got off a shot or two.'

Another idea sprang to mind that, with Brad's assistance, would provide the opportunity to snatch the bomb controlling device and cancel out that threat; after which, he was certain, he and his Skipper would be more than a match for the remaining criminals.

He emptied the remaining shells from the box magazine of the rifle and stepped back down to the engine room, closing the hatch over his head and deliberately interrupting the fuel flow to simulate a continuing problem. Five minutes later he hid a small, tape bound, package with protruding match heads behind one engine and, just in time, scribbled a brief note to Brad that he folded in his hand.

Chapter 9

The main engine room door hatch swung open. 'Have you finished down there Mr. Swift ?' enquired Mohammad. 'Mr. Murray says to come up and change places; he has an idea the problem is cleared. He'll check it out himself.'

'Check it yourself Pete. Enough explosive here to take out the house on either side as well,' gasped Agent O'Toole, adding with a grin: 'but not now, Callum "Bomb Buster" O'Toole has performed his magic.'

Ten minutes earlier, Sam had heard Jefferies' powerful car minutes before the Agents arrived , the Senior Agent sensibly cruising the final approach to Sam's vehicle to avoid arousing the curiosity of near neighbours. 'You've made excellent time. I've taken Nancy and her daughter over to a friend's place a few miles away. She's going to make up some story of a gas leak to explain the sudden imposition. We have no worries there but I haven't moved anyone else out ,seeing as the next nearest property is some sixty yards away and I thought it best to avoid unwanted inquisitiveness.'

Within minutes of examining the doll's house bomb, the explosives expert exclaimed; 'No

problem, a simple device with no booby traps. Get out and give me a minute or two.'
Emerging in no time at all, he disconnected the detonator from the receiving device and crushed it under his foot before tossing the explosive package to Jefferies: inviting the Agent to inspect the bomb.

'We'll keep this and that trigger device you have there, see what forensics can get out of it,' said Pete. 'You can tell Mrs. Swift it's okay to return home if she wishes Sam.'

'I think we'd better report in first. There has got to be a good reason for a bomb to be planted in Trevor's home. It might be safer for the present to leave Nancy where she is.
If I had any sense I would have taken her friend's phone number and could have called her. As it is; I'll have to go back and put her mind at rest. Let's see what Commander Beaman has to say, shall we ?'

'Not much question about why the bomb was there,' interjected Callum. 'If , whoever put it there wanted to kill Mrs. Swift and her daughter, it would have been set off long ago. No, I think it's holding a gun to somebody's head in order to force them into doing something against their will........but what ?'

Chapter 9

The other two Agents voiced their agreement, Sam pointing out that, with Trevor being a crewman for Bradley, the **against their will** almost certainly involved the use of a boat.

'Perhaps I have been searching for the wrong vessel and it's the *Whaleback Swift* that's involved ;although I pride myself on being a good judge of character and would bet my life that Bradley is no Terrorist. '

'We'll get an update from the Chief,' said Jefferies. 'Someone, somewhere, has got to have discovered something, we just need a break.'

'Take a break for five minutes Greg,' ordered the Commander when the Agent returned with Hassam's tattered passport and confirmation that the barge was no longer at the Waste Station pier. 'Charlie, get on to Security at the Houses of Parliament: ask them to check there's no barge in their stretch and Andy, you try the Port of London Authority office at Baker's Hall in the Upper Pool near Tower Bridge. See if they can give any info on any barge movements. I'll contact the PLA's Gravesend offices, they're possibly our best bet with their radar and CCTV coverage of the river.'

'Trouble is,' said Agent Meade forlornly; 'we've no idea how long ago it left the pier. And why haven't we been informed if the Met boys moved it for some reason ? They had someone on board so, presumably, they are in touch with him.'

The question prompted Commander Beaman to change his orders. 'Yes, that's something else we should check out. Richard, you telephone Gravesend, I'll get hold of Superintendent Kimpton. First one clear of those calls, get hold of the BBC and ITV Newsdesks; see if they have any film of the whale in the Nine Elms Reach earlier this afternoon.'

Five minutes later each Agent reported their findings, the collective results proving unhelpful with no current sightings of the barge. Andy Davison's call to the Television stations proved a little more helpful, both networks confirming the existence of film taken in the area of concern between three and four o'clock. Unfortunately, the Commander's call, despite being put on hold for nearly five minutes, failed to get him through to the Metropolitan Superintendent; a call back being the best response he could get from the Duty Officer.

Chapter 9

'The Television news Editors both wanted to know what was up Sir, ' reported Davison. 'I've fobbed them off with a lie about someone reporting a midget submarine in the river. I got the impression neither believed me so we may get some unwanted enquiries coming our way.'

'I'll get on to them before then and make sure nothing, factual or surmised, is aired. The last thing we can afford at the moment is a panicking public as a result of an imminent Terrorist threat that we still can't be certain is even aimed at the Capital. For now.....,'

One of the phones on the desk buzzed impatiently.

'Yes! Oh, it's you Pete. Anything new ?' snapped the Chief, listening to Agent Jefferies' report on the bomb situation and Callum's theory as to its purpose.

'We have a description of the person who planted the device; Mrs. Swift gave us excellent details,' enthused the senior Agent. 'One thing for certain is, it is neither Saleem nor Mohammad: we have a third Terrorist who drives a British Telecom van.'

Before the Commander had time to comment, a second telephone rang .'Hold it a minute Peter, this could be Kimpton with news of the missing barge.'

It wasn't. The M.I.5 Chief listened intently for a few moments, slamming the receiver back in its cradle on completion of the call.

Speaking loud enough for Jefferies and the room's occupants to hear, he said with hopeful enthusiasm; 'That was Southend. A Rover car with Saleem's registration has been notified as being abandoned by the staff at a Hotel near Southend Airport. The driver matches Saleem's disguised description but settled his bill and left late yesterday afternoon ,after informing them that he would collect his vehicle this morning. They phoned Southend Police when he didn't come back all day, fearing something may have happened to him. Southend have already checked the registration and found it to be false.'

'Another little piece of the puzzle boss; but does it help any more than all the other snippets,' said Charlie Walsh. 'We've still got nothing of substance that tells us where the attack is coming from.'

Commander Beaman put the phone back to his ear and spoke directly to Jefferies. 'There's not much you can do to help locate the barge for now Pete. Go and take a look at Saleem's vehicle. Is Sam around ?'

'Yes, just about to go off back to Mrs. Swift and give her the good news. But we think it may be better if she didn't return home until tomorrow. Did you want her ?'

'No, but you had better tell her to meet up with you at the Airport. I'm sending Charlie and Greg down to the City Airport where we still have a helicopter standing by. If things start happening this end it could come in handy.....especially if Sam can get in touch with that boyfriend of hers.'

In the gloom of the engine room, Brad pressed the last number called recall button on his mobile, expecting a response from the last person he spoke to on HIS phone; Detective Constable Astley ; cursing when he obtained only the usual answer phone message.

Fearful of not getting a message through before the battery died, he spoke swiftly into the instrument. 'Dave, it's Brad. This is not a hoax message. We have been hijacked by armed Terrorists who plan to blow up an explosive laden barge beneath the Q.E.2 Bridge. Swifty may have stopped it but they have planted two devices alongside an oil tank in the Coryton Refinery, and have plans to attack other installations along the river. We are going to try and stop them ourselves as time is short. Most important though is you must get someone over to Swifty's house. They've put a bomb in it somewhere and have a detonating device on board that they threaten to use. We are motorin'.........beep, beep, beep: the phone went dead.

'Useless blasted instrument,' he murmured. 'I know I charged it up and now it fails just when I need it most. I just hope Dave picks up his messages frequently and gets what I said before it cut out.'

He reread the note Swifty had slipped into his hand as they passed one another at the entrance to the engine space. Where had he got iron and aluminium filings to combine with the rifle bullets powder to manufacture a smoke bomb, he wondered ? The crewman's plan seemed to be their best hope of getting their hands on the signal device with which they were continually threatened. 'Once that's no longer a problem, we'll get our chance to overpower them I'm sure.' He prepared a small container of oil and petrol soaked waste wadding to ignite with his crewman's "smoke device"; sufficient to simulate the start of an engine room fire without actually endangering the vessel.

'Get Mr. Murray up here for a minute Mohammad,' commanded Saleem. 'He will not wish to miss the spectacular firework display I am about to set off,' he added with a malicious grin.

The big Palestinian Terrorist called Brad back up just as he was about create the diversionary ploy. 'Leave that a moment; we are about to instigate a Thames Tsunami, albeit on a minor scale.'

'What on earth do you want to do that for ?' enquired Brad. 'It's nearly high tide but, from what I've read, exploding the Montgomery will, even if the whole lot goes up together, produce a wave of no more than a few metres high. There will be a lot of damage to property on the Isle of Sheppey and the Oil Refinery on the Isle of Grain will possibly be flooded but, by the time the wave gets a few miles up river, the effects will be almost negligible; certainly nothing like a Tsunami.'

'The object, Mr. Murray is to create panic and confusion, especially on the low-lying Canvey Island which was seriously flooded in 1953. Since that time the sea defences have, we realise, been strengthened but, not sufficient to withstand a two or three metre surge. Following the huge explosion I will have no difficulty in penetrating the defences of our primary target, and blackmailing the Government into conceding to our demands.'

From what he and Swifty had previously overheard, the Skipper did not, for one moment, believe the Terrorists' intentions were of simple blackmail; but refrained from confronting Mohammad on the obvious lie .

'Ah, Mr. Murray, just in time: are you finished below ?' asked Saleem slimily. 'Perhaps you would like the honour of pushing the button so we can witness the results of poor Latif's endeavours.'

'The answer to your question is NO. We have a problem with water in the fuel,' lied Brad. 'Another five minutes and I will have it fixed. And, I do not wish to do your dirty work for you,' he snapped.

'Then, I will enjoy the experience myself. If you look ahead everyone, I'm sure the darkness will not spoil a spectacular sight.'

The head Terrorist stabbed the glowing button, dropped the transmitting unit on the bench, and covered his ears.

Chapter 9

Surprise registered on his, and Mohammad's, face when only the sound of the wind and rain penetrated the cabin walls……no flash……no huge explosion.

Swifty winked at his boss and gave him a thumbs up signal, fortunately not witnessed by the psychopathic Terrorist leader who was furiously pressing and repressing the transmitter button.

Throwing the sabotaged unit down, he glared at Brad and Swifty, hissing: 'If I thought you had anything to do with this failure I would kill you with my own bare hands.'

'I'd like to see you try you cretin. Don't blame us for your own peoples' incompetence,' snarled Swifty, recognising, too late, that now was not a time to antagonise the furious Terrorist.

Saleem's foot lashed out at the crewman who stumbled back down into the cramped cabin space as Mohammad stepped between Brad and his leader, preventing the Skipper intervening when he saw the Terrorist chief raise his gun and fire through the doorway.

Swifty gave a groan and slumped heavily to the deck and, suddenly, Saleem's anger was gone. 'Your man was stupid Mr. Murray,' he said quite calmly. 'Close the cabin door, I have no wish to see anymore of him. Then, will you kindly finish what you were doing below while I talk to Mohammad.'

'You are nothing but a murdering swine Saleem, or whatever name you choose to be,' growled Brad, struggling to keep himself in check. 'Why should I do anything you say? No doubt my fate will be the same as Trev's.

'Mr. Swift was a foolish man; don't you do anything silly. I'm sure you do not wish Mrs. Swift meets a similar fate. Remember,' said the Terrorist uneasily, 'I simply have to press the button and ,' he threw out his hands and arms, ' Boombh !'

Glaring at his adversaries, Brad retorted, throttling back the engines to little more than idling, 'Take the wheel and keep it straight. I'll be back soon.' He returned to the engine room contemplating a plan of his own....get the two remaining Terrorists separated in order to tackle them one at a time.

In the front cabin, Trevor opened his eyes carefully from his faked demise , ensuring he was alone before rising to his feet and looking at the bullet embedded in the woodwork alongside the spot his head had been a few minutes previously.

Chapter 9

Careful to make no noise he pressed his ear to the door.

'We have experienced a number of unfortunate mishaps during the past couple of days, and now this failure my friend,' Swifty heard Saleem say solemnly. 'With no diversion to interfere with the guards' routine, I fear the chances of you penetrating the double wire fence and eluding guard dogs, will not be successful . So, I have no choice: we will do this thing together.'

'But Saleem, who will plan more attacks if you give your life now ? I will shoot anyone who gets in my way before I can get to the tanks.'

'It is possible the guards are armed themselves. I have not been able to establish exactly what security is in place, only that the locals in the Public House I visited with Asif say the Depot has a number of "Secret measures" to counter any Terrorist attack. I have, therefore, devised an alternative plan.'

Although the crewman and skipper had, from snippets of overheard conversation, formed the opinion that the Terrorists were planning an additional attack, it was only now that Swifty heard for certain the enormity of the final act of Saleem's plan. He almost gasped out loud on hearing the intentions, the scale of which was so murderous as to make the bomb transmitter with which Nancy and Naomi were threatened obsolete; their deaths assured unless the Terrorists were stopped.

With no way of letting Brad know he was unharmed, he sat back to consider his next move, realising, just as the Skipper had done, that separating Saleem and Mohammad was the first priority.

'I'm doing no good in here,' he murmured to himself ; still uncertain of his course of action. 'Better I get out on deck where I can see if either of them leaves the wheelhouse.'

A scuffling from outside the door as he was about to remove the cabin panel and make his way through to the anchor rope stowage compartment, caused him to press his head against it again - just in time to catch the final part of the Terrorists' conversation.

'I've put the launchers and rockets in the dinghy, ready to go as soon as Mr. Murray moors us up again,' said Saleem. 'He will be joining his crewman before we leave. Call him back up; we're nearly there, the engines will not be required for much longer.'

Chapter 9

'Will you be much longer ?' shouted Agent Jefferies from behind the cover of a large metal waste bin in the corner of the Hotel car park. 'Here comes Sam.'

'It's alright, you can come out, it's safe,' Callum called back. 'No booby traps and I've got the doors opened, but it seems to be as clean as a whistle. If this is Saleem's car I'd bet it's about as much use to us as all the other dead ends we've come up against.'

Sam's car came to a halt alongside her two compatriots. 'Anything ?' she enquired, squeezing herself from the driver's seat.

'Not unless I've missed something,' replied Callum

'Better tell the Commander on your phone Pete, mine's nearly out of battery charge; see what he wants us to do next,' said Sam. 'I'll give Brad one more try , should be okay for that.'

As the Senior Agent took out his mobile, Sam reached into her car, picked hers up from the passenger seat and turned it on. The instrument immediately buzzed to alert her of a missed call.

'Hold it Pete,' she called. 'This might be a message from Brad.' She pressed the *play message* button and held the mobile to her ear.

The two watching Agents stared as Sam's mouth dropped open in awe and her eyes widened in alarm. As the message ended in a series of, battery expired ,bleeps, she looked at the phone and realised it was not her own instrument indicating failure. Pressing the message repeat button, she handed the phone to Pete Jefferies with an ordered: 'Listen.'

'Who the hell is Dave; and how come you have a message for him on your phone ? No, don't bother explaining now, I have to tell the Chief immediately. This is the breakthrough we've been waiting for.'

Sam was pondering the same question herself as Agent Jefferies made the call back to the Commander.

'Thanks for the call back Bill, ' said Commander Beaman. 'That's worrying for both of us. We've confirmed the barge is no longer there and if you are getting no response from your man ,we really do need any help you can give us in finding the blasted boat. I underestimated its importance once we had the Southall Terrorists under lock and key.'

'I've already alerted our riverside patrols to be on the lookout for it, but with no particular identifying features one barge looks like another. There's plenty to choose from but, at this time of night, I've told the lads to concentrate on any on the move. I'll be in touch if anything comes up.'

'I could kick myself,' said the M.I.5 Chief to Andy Davison and Richard Meade. 'Where is Saleem; where is the barge; are they now both in the same place ?'

Neither Agent , sitting alongside silent phones - willing them to ring, answered.

'Richard, tell Walsh and Scott to get airborne and……' The loud ring of the Commander's phone interrupted his order.

As soon as he recognised Jefferies as the caller, he switched the phone to speaker. The room's occupants looked grimly at one another as the Agent relayed the news of Saleem's car and Sam's missed phone call.

'I won't waste time asking who Dave is,' said the Chief as Pete Jefferies finished with: 'What do you want us to do now boss ?'

'We still haven't located the barge yet but those bombs are our priority for now, at least we know where **they** are. I'll get on to the Refinery's security chief to get his men searching straight away; but you and Callum get there as quick as you can, his expertise is sure to be re-

quired. I just hope you make it in time, oil tanks like those will spread toxic smoke and fumes for miles if they go up. And, goodness knows how many casualties there will be unless you can stop the explosions. From my memory of the place there are
dozens of storage tanks containing crude oil and petroleum products.'

The two Agents wasted no time in speeding off whilst still conversing with their Commander. 'Sam's taken my mobile and has gone back to Canvey Island in case the *Whaleback* turns up there,' said Callum into the phone as Jefferies drove the car at breakneck speed towards the A13. 'There seems little doubt it is involved somehow and that her newfound boyfriend is being forced to ferry a bunch of Terrorists about. If you manage to locate either the barge or the launch ,you can get her on my phone. We'll be at the Refinery in twenty minutes,' he added with his arm out of the window ,placing a blue light siren on the car's roof.

'Good, I'll send Charlie Walsh and Greg Scott down to Dartford, it sounds like the barge is in the vicinity of the Bridge. There's plenty of light around the area of the River at that point, they might be able to spot it from the air .

They'll have to put down as near as they can and liaise with the local police. If they find any danger aboard, requiring your assistance, I'll tell them to call you. I'm leaving here now with Andy Davison to meet you at the Refinery ; we shouldn't be too far after you. Richard will be here as our control source for any further news coming in.'

Andy Davison disappeared into the next room and returned with two bullet proof vests. 'Better take one of these Sir, you never know if we are going to need them.'

'Thanks Andy, I think it's more likely that Luck is what we'll need.'

'Now, with a bit of luck, that should cause a bit of a panic and separate them,' said Brad to himself in a hushed tone as he lit the fuel-soaked string fuse to his incendiary device in the engine room, before returning to the wheelhouse.

'We are nearly back to Canvey Mr. Murray, the engines will only have to keep going another five minutes and your valuable assistance to our cause will no longer be required.'

'They could still cut out and in this weather: we could be swept ashore or into a collision by this wind so I would keep that bullet you have with my name on it in your gun for now.'

The Chief Terrorist grinned evilly, and even Mohammad smiled as Saleem sneeringly uttered; 'Oh no Mr. Murray, we are near enough to shore for a gunshot to be heard, I have no intention of shooting you.'

'You shot poor Trevor without a seconds' hesitation,' interrupted Brad.

'Yes; a mistake that we got away with, the sound obviously unheard or dismissed. And, Mohammad has a silencer but, I'm sure, having missed out on the firework display, you will appreciate the view of our man-made daylight dawning out of darkness when our final endeavours show that our brothers triumphant sacrifice of nine eleven in America can be emulated throughout the world. The American's financial institutions suffered a blip with little effect on their economy but, our deaths will bring about a huge impact on the industrial and domestic markets in Britain for years to come. You will be handcuffed here to your boat from where you will be one of the first to witness the holocaust our final attack will unleash.'

Below deck, Brad and Trevor's own *bomb* ignited as the spluttering fuse finally reached the exposed match heads. Almost immediately a huge plume of smoke poured from the open engine room hatch and billowed around the cabin.

'The engines are on fire,' screamed Brad. 'Quick give me that fire extinguisher under the radio and one of you follow me,' he ordered, exiting the cabin.

Surprise and anxiety overtook Saleem's normal caution, the Terrorist meekly complying with the Skipper's command : following him through the whirling smokescreen back to the engines trap door.

Brad pulled the safety pin from the extinguisher lever and aimed the nozzle into the hatch until a fierce spray was emitted. The timing was just right, the full force achieved just as Saleem emerged through the black voluminous smoke. Swinging the extinguisher around he kept the lever depressed ,sending a frothy foam jet directly into the Terrorist Chief's face.

Blinded by the mass of small bubbles; whether by intent or just momentum, Saleem blundered forward into Brad as he attempted to smash the extinguisher over the killer's head. The fire staunching device descended under it own weighty impetus to a spot where Saleem's head should have been, and was......... milliseconds before.

Meeting no resistance, the Skipper's own loss of equilibrium carried him forward over the bent over Terrorist to sprawl on the wet decking, and almost tumble into the modified well deck amongst the angling gear.

Springing to his feet ,he turned back to face the Terrorist leader who had cleared his vision and was reaching under his coat for a weapon.

'It's just you and me , and I saw your gun go flying overboard when you threw up your hands to protect yourself,' said Brad triumphantly . Saleem backed away from the narrow aisle between the hatch side and outer guard rail towards the open space at the boat's stern.

'You, me and my trusty knife,' hissed the recovered Terrorist, withdrawing a long-bladed dagger from his clothing. 'You will not witness my own death after all Mr. Murray, your meddling in my plans is at an end. If time were not pressing I would watch you suffer the agony of a thousand cuts before putting an end to your miserable existence. But you must DIE now !', he screamed, rushing forward.

Brad had never seen such hatred etched on the face of an enemy before, even the fanatical Sadam guards he had come up against in his Special Boat Service days showed less malevolence; but, he stood his ground and simply grinned at the onrushing Terrorist.

Letting out a roar of contempt, Saleem raised the blade to strike a fatal blow but found his descending wrist held in a vice-like grip and twisted away from his intended target.

The Skipper deliberately fell backwards using his assailant's weight and forward rush to propel him over his own body.....with the assistance of a well-placed foot.

Saleem thudded into the deck with a grunt of pain but quickly turned, crouching, to face his opponent. 'So, Mr. Murray, you appear to have some experience of unarmed combat,' he panted. 'It seems, under the circumstances, I must ask Mohammad to shoot you .'

He rose to his feet and turned to call for his companion as the Skipper bent to pick up the dropped knife.

Recognising the danger, he jumped forward and kneed Brad in the shoulder; sending him skidding backwards into the broken packing cases and tarpaulin: snatching the knife from the deck himself.

Brad found himself partly entangled in the canvas cover and splintered wood casing, swinging one of the loose planks in defence as the Terrorist approached for an easy kill.

The heavy lath struck Saleem's arm above the elbow, numbing the limb and causing the knife to drop from lifeless fingers. Brad hooked his legs around the killer as he scrambled free of the canvas but found himself again going backwards when Saleem threw himself down on top of him.

Winded under the Terrorist's weight , he felt his throat being crushed as Saleem's hands sought to strangle him; the weakened limb, however, unable to complete encirclement with sufficient pressure to cut off his air supply. Freeing his left hand from beneath his body, he jabbed at Saleem's eyes, forcing his opponent to jerk backwards and release his grip. He rolled free of the tarpaulin and pushed himself up on his hands to face his adversary.

When Saleem sprang away from the former SBS man's thrusting fingers, his hand fell upon a cold metal object as he pushed himself to his feet. In the flickering, unsteady, reflected glow from the Refinerythat the boat was gliding past, he saw it was the crowbar they had used to open the packing cases. With a roar of triumph, he grasped the solid, heavy, implement and leapt towards Brad who was still not on his feet.

Fate intervened to give Brad time to defend himself : the discarded fire extinguisher rolled down the deck, as the bow of the launch met a larger wave, and hit the back of the Terrorist's legs as he battled to retain his feet and deliver a killer blow on the Skipper's defenceless head. The unexpected knock momentarily stopped the killer who wondered what was attacking his ankles, realising the cause as the extinguisher continued its skidding passage, halted as it met the resistance of Brad's hands.

Lifting the metal cylinder between his hands and above his head as Saleem renewed his attack and sought to smash his skull, he braced himself against the wild downward swing.

"Clang", the metals clashed ,sending an *electric type* shockwave up the Terrorist's arm as Brad kicked his assailant between the legs and ducked beneath the dropped crowbar.

A lull in the wind and rain at the time allowed Saleem's loudly screamed, 'AAGHHH !' to penetrate the wheelhouse door and alarm Mohammad, who promptly put the engines into

neutral and poke his head outside to seek the cause.
He was just in time to see, through the now wispy smokescreen, Saleem disappear overboard when he stood on the wayward fire extinguisher as he sought to avoid Brad's assault with the sniper's rifle he had grabbed from the deck; the luckless Terrorist loosing his feet completely, falling on to the low guardrail and toppling over the side.

The big Palestinian reached in his pocket for his automatic handgun and raced down the deck to confront his leader's killer.

Brad was peering into the darkness astern of the launch and failed to see the arrival of Mohammad, the first he knew of his presence being a stunning blow to the side of his head.

With a groan he fell to the deck but did not lose consciousness; his swimming vision registering the blurred outline of the big Terrorist pointing a lethal looking pistol at his head. The indistinct figure focussed into an enraged Mohammad as a heavy foot pressed down on his chest.

'You have ruined everything!' he screamed. 'But you will not stop my mission. The time has come for you to die.'

Chapter 9

As full vision returned, Brad could see only the round black hole in the middle of the cylinder attached to the end of Mohammad's weapon, watching it raise to centre exactly between his eyes as the Terrorist's finger tightened on the trigger.

The flash of flame and thunderous roar was not as fearful as expected by the watchers crouched behind the embankment wall alongside the Pitsea Creek.

'And that was just the detonator charges,' said Callum O'Toole. 'Now they are out of the way I feel a lot happier at carrying satchel bombs about in the boot of your car Pete.'

'A good job done Callum; now I'm as relieved as the Operations Manager and the Guards at the Refinery,' said Commander Beaman enthusiastically. 'Those guards did well finding the bombs so quickly amongst all those tanks. I just hope Sam's message was right and there were only two. Can you imagine what might have happened if even one of them had exploded ?'

A short while before, the Commander and Andy Davison had arrived at the Manager's office in the Coryton Oil Refinery, nearly twenty five minutes behind Jefferies and the Agency's bomb expert, who had been immediately led to the tanks where, earlier that evening, Asif had partially buried his two bombs.

By the time his Chief arrived, Callum had disarmed both devices and was enjoying a cup of tea with his fellow Agent and the Office Manager, feet resting on the dirt-caked haversacks and nonchalantly munching a digestive biscuit.

'Safe as houses Chief,' chimed up the ordnance expert when he saw the Commander looking apprehensively at the charges beneath his feet. 'Just so long as the detonators are kept away from them and, you can watch for yourself their destruction when I set them off before we leave.'

The Manager's phone rang loudly, drowning out Jefferies retort of, 'Yes, but just don't go playing football with those bags.'

'It's a Richard Meade for you,' said the Manager, handing the handset to the M.I.5 Chief.

Quietly listening, without comment, the Commander handed the receiver back with a final: 'That's good news Richard, at last we are making progress. I just hope we're not too late.'

'Some light at the end of the tunnel,' he announced. 'Thanks to the Port of London staff we have located the barge, Charlie and Greg are there now. It seems there is no longer any danger from that source and there is a dead youngster on board with two bullet holes in him, thought to be one of the Terrorists. And, as equally important, the PLA lads at Gravesend tell us that the *Whaleback* was earlier seen travelling back towards Canvey Island. In fact, they tried calling Brad up on the radio but got no response. They estimate that, if it hasn't stopped anywhere, it will now be somewhere off Coryton itself.'

'So if we had gone down to the River after I diffused the bombs we may well have seen it ourselves,' said Callum despairingly. 'Although one boat looks like another to me so whether it would have been significant is doubtful.'

Pete Jefferies interceded, 'Murray's message said the Terrorists were going to attack other places along the River, and that they were motoring....unfortunately he was cut off at that point so we do not know to where. It seems strange to have turned round and come back. How sure are we that it is the right boat and that the Terrorists are not, at this very moment, on their way to one of the London target possibilities ?'

'Uhmm,' said the Commander thoughtfully. ' Is Sam still on the Island ? She could possibly check the area long before we can get there.'

The Senior Agent immediately called Sam using Callum's number, the response so quick he was taken by surprise.

'I was just about to call you,' answered Sam's voice. 'I've just taken Mrs. Swift back home; she insisted in case her husband tries to get in contact. I was going to stay here a while unless you need me to help with the Coryton bombs.'

'Thankfully that's already resolved,' snapped Jefferies, continuing to pass on the Chief's order

.

Sam grabbed her coat and was halfway out of the door as she replied, 'I'll get back down to Hole Haven, I'll easily see any passing craft from there, there's plenty of reflected light to help spot Brad's boat. I'll call you when I get there.'

'Hurry Sam, the Coryton fuel tank bombs were set to go off at 11p.m. so whatever else is planned is sure to be triggered around the same time. That leaves us just twenty minutes to capture, or kill, the remaining Terrorists. We have got to stop that trigger being pulled.'

Chapter 9

Brad watched , transfixed, as Mohammad's index finger pulled the trigger; milliseconds after the black hole of the Terrorist's silenced weapon, pointed directly on the bridge of his nose, suddenly raised itself above his head. Such was the efficiency of the quietening device, the Skipper heard only a soft report as the gun fired, even that almost drowned out by the gurgling sound emanating from the big Terrorist clutching at his throat with his free hand from which blood flowed profusely as he spun round to face the cabin.

The cause of the faint whoosh, that had preceded Mohammad's pirouette, then became obvious : Brad's eyes registering the slim metal shaft of a harpoon protruding from the back of his, would-be, killer's neck.

The Palestinian assassin took a pace forward and attempted to raise his gun in the direction of his attacker who jerked the spear rope causing him to drop the weapon and clutch both hands to the impaled, barbed, arrow.

A lesser built man would have tumbled to the deck under the sudden pull, but Mohammad managed to remain standing until the Skipper, clambering to his feet,
lashed out a boot into the back of his legs.

The Terrorist's knees buckled and he dropped to the deck with perplexed look at his attackers, before toppling on his side and staring at the night sky with sightless eyes.

'Yet again, you've saved my bacon old friend,' said Brad gratefully hugging Trevor as he put down the spear gun . 'I thought that bastard Saleem had killed you.'

'Your diversion gave me the chance to get my hands on that transmitter,' replied Swifty. 'Once Mohammad left it in the wheelhouse as he came after you, I took the opportunity to grab it and hide it away in case something happened to me. It was nearly too late when I saw he had you in his sights; the harpoon gun just happened to be handy,' he added with his usual impish grin.

A sudden look of alarm crossed Brad's face : he almost threw his crewman aside and rushed to the wheelhouse.

Turning back himself, Swifty saw the reason for his Skipper's panic; the launch, with engines disengaged and at the mercy of both wind and current, was rapidly drifting towards the rocks of "Scars Elbow" on Canvey Island.

The motors roared as Brad swung the craft away from danger and back towards his Hole

Haven mooring, where Trevor speedily hitched up to the buoy.

'Let's get ashore and get to a phone Trev,' said the Skipper. 'The Authorities are not going to believe what we've been through in the last twenty four hours, and you must check on Nancy as soon as you can. Get the dinghy, I'll lock up.'

Sixty seconds later the crewman rushed back as Brad emerged from the cabin. 'The dinghy's gone,' he gasped. 'The rope's been cut !'

Facing into the wind on the sea wall, Agent Samirah Ahmad, brushed her watery eyes and peered into the darkness, blinking away the moisture . No doubt about it; that must be the *Whaleback* that was just tying up out in mid-stream.

She yelled , 'Brad!', at the top of her voice, realising with dismay the futility of her actions as the wind tore at her clothing and carried her cry away. Two unidentifiable figures were faintly discernible through the fine mist of rain, but she could not be certain it was Brad and Swifty. In desperation she tried the Skipper's mobile phone again but, frustrated by the no connection signal, decided to return to her car for a lamp to signal to the vessel.

The wet grass of the sea wall embankment proved as slippery as an ice slope when she returned with the torch, her feet sliding from under her just as she reached the top.

Recovering her footing and grasping a few tufts of long grass to apprehend her slide caused her to loosen her hold on the portable lamp which tumbled to the bottom of the
embankment. She carefully picked her way back down, retrieved the torch and , bending over clutching bunches of grass to assist her climb, made her way to the top where, to her dismay, she was just in time to see Brad's vessel moving off round the stern of a moored tug at the Creek mouth. Brushing herself down, and pulling her jacket's protective hood over her head, she called up the Commander to report her findings. Following further instructions, she set off at a trot along the deserted sea wall in an attempt to follow the launch, but the bulk of a huge tanker hid the vessel from view. 'No sign of it. I hope I'm going in the right direction,' she muttered to herself within the folds of her hood.

Chapter 9

'Can't see anything yet,' Swifty called back from his position on the foredeck. 'We don't even know if we're headed in the right direction.'

'He's up ahead somewhere, I know he is,' said Brad emphatically.

Following his crewman's discovery, it took only seconds for the Skipper to realise that only one person could possibly have cut the dinghy loose........'Saleem', he blurted out with incredulity. 'You're sure the rope's been cut and not just come undone ?'

'There's no doubt about it,' responded Swifty. 'Saleem must have climbed into it when he went overboard and,' he added ominously; 'I overheard him telling Mohammad he had put the rocket launchers into it. It looks like he is still trying to carry out his attack !'

'Then let's get after him!' shouted Brad, re-entering the wheelhouse to restart the engines.

Trevor rushed forward and wasted no time unhitching from the mooring, resorting instead to a swing of the axe snatched from its deck holder, severing the rope and saving precious minutes.

The engines roared as the Skipper swung the craft round to motor past a tanker moored at the wharf of the Oikos Storage Depot with its array of a hundred tanks storing aviation fuels; lubricants; oils and petroleum products; an attractive target for Terrorists. But, Brad was certain, Saleem's audacious plan featured an even more potentially destructive target, the Calor Gas Terminal with its 40,000 tonne storage of liquid nitrogen and propane/butane gas tanks.

Sam halted as her phone rang. 'We're on the Island: where are you, we'll meet you soon?' snapped her Chief's voice.

The female Agent described her location as best she knew ,and was relieved to hear the Commander say; 'We know where you are headed, be with you in ten minutes. Just keep an eye out for that boat.'

Up ahead she saw the lights of a fast craft approaching close inshore, a stabbing searchlight beam suddenly piercing the night sky to settle on a figure climbing on top of the sea wall with a long cylindrical tube on his back.

That's the *Whaleback* for sure she thought to herself as the vessel slewed broadside on to the shore, before heading in a wide circle and slowing to wallow some fifty yards offshore . The wavering light beam sought to refocus on the silhouetted form ahead of her; the flashing ray

briefly illuminating a crouching man with the tube now on his shoulder.
She gasped as recognition of what she was seeing penetrated her brain……she started running, torch in one hand, gun in the other.

On rounding the bows of the tanker, Swifty switched on the Whaleback's powerful signal lamp and played the beam over the nearby rocky shoreline, almost instantly highlighting the Head Terrorist leaving the grounded dinghy and climbing the sea wall with a Rocket Launcher on his back. 'There he is !' he cried out joyfully, while attempting to keep the light on their quarry.
'Sorry Trev, the angle's all wrong: I've got a tank immediately in the background. If I miss , it could be catastrophic, the result just what Saleem is wanting. I'll back off a bit for a clear shot. Try to keep the light on him.'
'Hurry, for goodness sake boss, a few more minutes and we'll be too late.'
Brad picked up the Sniper's weapon, retrieved from the stern, and fingered the single remaining bullet that Swifty hadn't used for his smoke bomb.

Cutting the engines as he completed the boat's manoeuvre , he rushed out onto the foredeck, gun in hand.

Saleem, still drenched from his recent immersion, but oblivious to the discomfort, grinned as he raised the Launcher to his shoulder and aimed, point blank, at the nearest full tank behind the perimeter wire of the Calor Gas compound.
'You are too late Infidels,' he laughed squeezing the trigger, or attempting to; the firing mechanism failing to move despite urgent forceful jerking. Throwing the weapon aside he scrambled back to the dinghy and pulled out a second Launcher ,already loaded with a lethal projectile; and a spare rocket before climbing back to the embankment top.
He dropped to one knee as a wavering beam sought to steady on him, the illumination coming not from the sea but from just along the seawall in the hands of a running figure.
His night vision was temporarily destroyed when his eyes registered a violent flash of light followed by a sharp retort as he rose back to his feet. A solid thud against the Launcher, and instant searing pain across his shoulder focussed

his confused mind on the danger he suddenly found himself in.
And then the lithe figure was upon him, the barrel of a small gun pressed against his head as his assailant screamed: 'Do not move a muscle; drop the weapon and put your…….'
Sam didn't finish the sentence, the swiftly rising butt grip of the Rocket Launcher slamming into her chin and choking off her words as she fell backwards under the onslaught; semi-conscious.
In a haze of pain she felt Saleem's foot pressing down on her throat, and was vaguely aware of him raising the missile projector to his shoulder, powerless to do anything about it.

Commander Beaman, together with Agents Jefferies and O'Toole, climbed the embankment and immediately spotted Saleem against the background light of the Refineries; some hundred and fifty yards away. The Agents watched spellbound as the Terrorist raised a heavy weapon to his shoulder, too far away to witness the wince of pain from where Sam's, deflected, bullet had scored a deep groove that produced a steady stream of blood down the Terrorist's sleeve. Nor too could they see the prone figure of their fellow Agent slowly being blood-soaked with the result of her own attack.

Jefferies assessed the situation immediately and drew his gun. 'We're too late,' he gasped ,snapping off a long range shot with little hope of hitting his target but hopeful of unsettling the assassin until they could get within killing range. Saleem was untouched, the projectile not even passing close enough to disturb his concentration.

Swifty's searchlight steadied on Saleem as Brad flung himself to the deck and steadied the barrel of the rifle on the lower guard rail. The Terrorist filled his sights before disappearing again as the launch rocked, none too gently, in the onshore crashing waves.

'This is impossible,' he said dejectedly. 'What hope have I got of stopping him. I think we can say goodbye; the thought of all those people,' his words tailed off.

'Take the shot Skip, it's the only chance!' screamed his crewman.

Saleem's outline again came into his wavering gunsight, clearly defined in Swifty's unerring light beam.

Chapter 9

The soundless rifle bucked in the Skipper's grip and he almost jumped for joy when he saw his target stagger backwards and drop like a stone, disappearing completely from view down the other side of the embankment.

'You hit him Brad,' shouted Swifty; the incredulity showing in his voice. Did you see that flash of light along the wall just before you fired. I can't be certain but I thought I heard the sound of another shot.'

'Get the light back on the spot if you can,' ordered Brad. 'There seems to be some movement over there. I hope he wasn't just faking, or only slightly injured. We may still be in trouble.'

Agent Jefferies, racing ahead of the others, suddenly found himself bathed in light as he reached the spot where Saleem had fallen. He gasped on seeing Sam sprawled on the ground covered in blood. 'Oh no,' he groaned as the Commander and Callum joined him.

A click of a gun being armed down the embankment just behind them, momentarily froze the standing Agents; Callum recovering the quickest to swing round and raise his own weapon.

Fast as he was, he knew he was too late. The expected impact of the Terrorist's bullet never came. A soft report came, not from behind but from low down in front of them as Sam, on her knees, completed Brad's effort: a killing shot that instantly put their common enemy beyond medical aid as the bullet entered his brain via his right temple.

'Anchor up Trev. I'll get the inflatable and we'll go ashore,' said the Skipper as the figures on the embankment waved. 'I don't know who they are but it seems they're on our side.'
A few moments later they were shaking hands with the Commander and Agents as the M.I.5 Chief revealed who they were. 'I cannot express our gratitude and thanks enough for what you have achieved for the Country,' he said sincerely. 'How many lives your actions have saved is beyond anything I can envisage. Now, there is one member of our team that I think you know,' he smiled. 'Let me introduce Agent Samirah Ahmad. I think you know her as Shauna.'

Brad stared, open-mouthed at the spectacle of a bedraggled, blood-streaked, Sam as she stepped into the torch beams. Shocked beyond belief, he couldn't even think of anything to say, simply stepping forward and hugging her close.

'Here comes the cavalry to clean up this mess,' said the Commander. 'I suggest we all get in out of these conditions. Fortunately, our shenanigans do not appear to have attracted too much unwanted attention. Here is what we will do ,if it's okay with Mr. Bradley and Mr. Swift.'

Following the Commander's orders, the Agents turned to walk back to their vehicles while Brad and Trevor returned to the inflatable to take the *Whaleback* round to the Hole Haven mooring.

'One thing before you go off again Brad,' said Sam. 'We all want to know. Who is Dave? '

10

'Help yourself to coffee Brad…Trevor, I've ordered a full English for us all,' said Commander Beaman as the two boatmen joined the M.I.5 Agents at the breakfast table . 'I trust we all managed to get some sleep. I suppose we were lucky to get booked in so late at night but it gave us a chance of a few hours rest. I expect Mrs Swift was delighted to see you two turn up last night so I'm sorry that I've had to drag you away again.'

'Where's Shauna, sorry Sam ?' apologised Brad. 'She's okay I hope after last nights' ordeal.'

'I insisted she went to hospital to have her jaw checked. They kept her in overnight but she should be out later, apparently no permanent damage done, only bruising. Now, let's have a full run down on your involvement with this gang of Terrorists we have been after for the past week. Start from the beginning while we enjoy this excellent breakfast,' said the Chief eyeing the approaching waiter.

By the time Brad had related the events of the past couple of days, with the assistance of relevant reminders from Swifty, and the occasional interjected question from one or another of the Agents, the Commander was shaking his head in disbelief .

Pouring, unasked, another cup of coffee for the boat Skipper, the M.I.5 Chief thrust his hand across the table to Swifty. 'I thanked Mr. Murray last night but, rather remissly overlooked your contribution in thwarting what would have been the worst Terrorist atrocity this Country has ever been subjected to. On behalf of us all I sincerely thank you now.'

Brad grinned at his crewman who looked decidedly embarrassed as the Agents rose to their feet and clapped their hands.

'We must be getting back to London soon Brad,' said the Commander as the Agents reseated themselves. 'But, I have to say, before we go, that we suffered some pretty bad luck all the way through this investigation and there is no doubt in my mind that Saleem and his cell members would have succeeded but for the fact they came up against a couple of resourceful characters. Thank goodness you sabotaged that first Rocket Launcher, I hate to think what would have happened if that had fired.'

' I can tell you, we wouldn't be here now talking about it,' said Trevor. ' The complex would have gone up in the largest fireball imaginable, comparable to that of the atom bomb on Hiroshima. You probably don't know but the fire authorities carried out a test when the original fuel tanks were installed. Just about every Canvey Island inhabitant knows of it but it seldom gets mentioned, even now when there is talk of more tanks being sited there.'

'So what happened when they did the test ?' queried the now curious M.I.5 Chief.

'They took just a few ounces, a saucer full, of the liquid gas and put a match to it.
Unexpectedly it, at first, just burned a short surface flame, appearing pretty stable in the open air, but then burst into a fifteen foot high conflagration before dying away. A serious assessment of the experiment suggested that, even at that time, if the tanks were full and were accidentally, or deliberately, exploded, the resulting fireball would completely engulf the whole of

the Island and extend out as far as Southend and Basildon, or even further !'

Swiftys' revelation was met with a hushed silence as each of those seated around the table took in the enormity of the Terrorists' intentions, the silence finally being broken by Agent Pete Jefferies who whistled, ' Phew ! Thousands upon thousands would have been killed.'

The Commander snapped out of his reverie. ' We should try to keep this thing out of the press for now,' he said seriously. ' I need to speak to the Director General. Can I ask you gentlemen for your co-operation? It may be that your heroic actions should not be brought to public attention, we do not want to create any panic. I would like both of you to come into H.Q tomorrow if you can. We must see what our best actions should now be. And, thank you Brad for taking those Launchers back on board your boat out of the way of inquisitive eyes and minds. We wouldn't want them seen, I'll have them collected later.'

He rose to his feet to leave, stopping suddenly when Brad said, ' You've forgotten one thing Commander Beaman. There are still two armed bombs in the Montgomery wreck !'

'Thanks for the reminder Brad but I hadn't completely forgotten. In fact I phoned Richard Meade at the office earlier to ask him to arrange for Naval divers to be sent up from Portsmouth in the next few days.'

'That will be too late,' responded Brad. ' After today, the last of this batch of low neap tides, the forecast is for a week of strong gales. Unless we act today and recover the explosives it will probably be weeks before they can be made safe and I, for one, do not like the thought of potential detonating devices sitting in that, bomb-filled hulk.'

The Commander looked disconsolate at the Skippers' comments. 'What choice do we have ? An operation of the kind we are talking about takes time to arrange.'

' No problem,' interjected Swifty. ' It's a nice day for a swim during this lull in the gale force winds. Both Brad and I are trained divers and I do have some experience of handling explosives. We have our wetsuits on board so I suggest we take the old *Whaleback* out this afternoon and recover the bombs ourselves, low water is at 3.40 p.m.'

At first the M.I.5 Chief would not hear of it. ' You're civilians for goodness sake. I can't let you risk yourselves any further after your experiences of the past couple of days.'

' Me and Pete could go with them and help boss,' piped in Agent O'Toole. ' I agree with the Skipper, the threat of that wreck going up remains potent all the while Saleems' bombs are aboard.'

The combined efforts of the boatmen and Agents finally convinced the Commander to accept the plan, a telephone call from Richard Meade adding weight to their argument when he reported the Naval Divers Officer suggested the weather was likely to deter any recovery until the latter part of the following week.

'That's it then,' declared Brad as he made to leave. 'We'll pick you two gentlemen up from Southend pier head about 2.30 p.m. Perhaps,' he added addressing the Commander, ' You would be so kind as to inform the Port of London Authorities of our expedition to the wreck, they may well wish to keep shipping clear of the area in case of any accident.'

Mindful of the restriction of information, the Commander suggested that he did not tell anyone of the existence of the bombs, simply saying they were investigating a suspected hoax threat to blow up the wreck. ' We'll announce afterwards that nothing was found.'

'If that ship goes up while we're in it, they won't find much of us. I hate keeping things from Nancy but I don't want to worry her unnecessarily. Told her we'd be home for teatime,' said Swifty in a remarkably sombre tone as the *Whaleback* approached the Pier head slipway.

'Are you sure you're fit to dive ?' responded the Skipper noticing his crewman dragging out their diving gear. 'That blow on the head must still be troubling you.'

'Take more than a little tap on the head to give me water on the brain,' joked Swifty returning to his usual light-hearted banter. ' There they are,' he cried out on spotting the two Agents chatting to an old bearded angler on the lower deck of the Pier.

With the tide receded to a suitable level for embarking the Agents direct from the deck, the crewman, to the chagrin of some anglers, loosely tied the craft up to the front of the decking rather than taking it round to the slipway. Jefferies and O'Toole leapt aboard and Brad immediately gunned the engines to take the vessel away in the direction of the wreck.

Chapter 10

'Want a look around the old girl before we get down to work Gents?' enquired Trevor coiling up the mooring rope. ' Brad will take us down river a bit first to approach uptide.'
Leading the way, the crewman showed the Agents into the Wheelhouse where Brad grinned at them and said, 'Welcome aboard the Air Sea Rescue Launch 271 for another rescue in the boats' history.'
Seeing the perplexed look on their faces he briefly related the boats' former wartime exploits and his acquisition as Swifty descended to the galley to make them all a cup of tea.
Agent Callum picked up the original transmitter ,that Brad had sabotaged , from the bulkhead shelf where Saleem had thrown it in disgust. 'Technical piece of equipment for such a small unit,' he remarked as the Skipper took the printed circuit board out of his pocket.
'Not much good without this though,' he laughed. 'It was a pleasure to see Saleems' face when he pressed the button and nothing happened.'
'You mean like this,' replied Callum joining in the good-natured repartee by pressing the button and putting on a puzzled look.

THE WRECK OF THE S.S. RICHARD MONTGOMERY EXPLODED !

As the *Whaleback Swift* left Southend Pierhead, the ravages of the previous two days' gales, having scoured away part of the sandbank upon which the Montgomery wreck sat, caused the broken vessel to settle a further ten centimetres into the seabed . Small though the movement was, it resulted in additional strain on the rusty stays holding the protruding masts in position.

The sudden twang as a couple of cables parted under the increased pressure was unheard by any human, but seagulls floating around the sunken vessel took flight in alarm, narrowly avoiding a falling mast as it splashed into the placid sea.

Below the rippled surface, Latif Amin swung gently in the current as his encasing net trap released the lower half of his body when ropes were severed by the heavy mast .

His drifting legs caught the wire attaching the small surface buoy to the detonating device attached to the bombs, pulling the small box and bombs over on their side to nestle amongst the wartime munitions.

The tiny amount of encased water that had entered the device via the missing screw hole, dripped to the bottom of the casing, slowly rising until it finally short-circuited the battery connecting wires and sent the signal to the detonator that had been patiently waiting the command.

Thirty six year old shop assistant Colin Tremain was the first to hear the explosion, and the first to die that day. Off from work, supposedly sick, he had sneaked down to the boom pier, a few miles from his home on his Isle of Grain at the mouth of the River Medway, for a few hours angling.

His peaceful relaxation came to an end with what was, at first, a report no louder than a car backfiring. Seconds later, however, the dull sky in front of his eyes lit up with a degree of brilliance that was temporarily blinding , the flash immediately followed by the loudest thunderclap ever to bombard his eardrums. Deafened and blinded, he never saw the explosive column of water, mud, wood and shrapnel that soared over a kilometre high, the expanding blast wave physically propelling him off the structure and into the sea over twenty yards away.

A poor swimmer at the best of times, his fate was sealed by the heavy clothing and wading boots he was wearing. His feeble attempts to stay afloat quickly exhausted him as the outgoing tide swept him further from shore. By the time debris and muddy water started raining down on his head, hypothermia had already lowered his body temperature to below that of sustaining life, his last conscious thought before death overtook him being, 'The boss will kill me if I don't go in tomorrow.'

A close second to fall victim to Latifs' detonation was, sixty nine year old, Archie Harrison, his fishing expedition that day also resulting in his demise.

Regular Archie was a popular visitor well-known to the Southend pier staff, often requiring a little assistance in boarding the train for the return to shore, especially when he had finished his days' sport with a pint or two in the famous landmarks' Public House outside the tram station. Completely deaf since childhood when his parents house had been bombed in the blitz, the elderly fisherman heard nothing of the explosion but witnessed the blinding flash just as he was descending the wet, slippery, stone steps to his favoured fishing spot on the lower deck.

The incandescent flare of light, momentarily, completely destroyed his vision just as he made to step from the stairway to the deck itself, resulting in no platform being where he misplaced his foot. The forward momentum was impossible to stop, Archie literally stepped straight into the sea, complete with heavy tackle box and fishing rod. In the confusion and fear following the explosion, there was no witness to either the inadvertent error of judgment , or the anglers' flailing arms as the ebbing current swept him past the 'East Point'. His body was found a day later on the mudflats at Thorpe Bay by a yachtsman inspecting his boat in the aftermath of the previous afternoons' events.

Being only half an hour before the low water mark when the S.S. Montgomery finally discharged the remainder of its' wartime cargo, the explosive forces were hardly contained at all by the surrounding water, the explosion almost in 'open air'.
As a result, the erupting geyser of mixed water, mud and ship parts initially did little damage other than to the sea life but lethal fragments of munitions and ship parts were projected nearly two miles and, the nearest boats, including the *Whaleback* were suddenly splattered with glutinous mud and clay as a deluge descended from

the sky. There were no subsequent reports of any damage sustained by falling debris although some large sections of the ship were seen to splash back into the sea, one section of mast actually making a landfall two kilometres away on the nearby Kent coast. By a quirk of fate, the six foot by three foot sign warning, **DANGER UNEXPLODED AMMUNITION DO NOT APPROACH OR BOARD THIS WRECK,** survived the blast and landed intact on the mud-flats of Westcliff.
Although there was little water above the wreck when the explosion occurred, the surrounding sea was suddenly compressed as the tremendous forces sought to make a 'hole in the sea', resulting in a build up until a near three metre wave was produced in a stone ripple effect. This mini Tsunami was destined to add to the loss of life but was, fortunately short-lived.
By far the greatest cause of damage, death and injury was by the Flash 'Air Blast' created, the area affected extending well inland of the Medway and Southend coast.

When the sea and sky ahead of the *Whaleback* erupted into a combined flash of brilliant intensity, Brad immediately spun the ships' wheel away from the rising column of water and pushed the throttle controls to maximum in an attempt to 'outrun' it's return to earth with the dangers of destructive debris.

The violent turn and leap of speed threw the two 'landlubber Agents' to the deck in a tangle of arms and legs, the Skippers' apologetic, ' Sorry about that gentlemen,' lost in the roar of the explosion.

Scrambling to their feet, the two Agents, without thinking, rushed out on deck to view the aftermath of the explosion, their ears still ringing from the blast noise failing to hear Brads' warning, 'Keep inside, it will be dangerous for a while.'

The strong gust of heated air took their breath away and propelled them backwards into the safety guard rails. Jefferies managed to grasp a stanchion, saving himself from an unwanted swim as the , hurricane force, wind tore at their clothing and threatened to topple both Agents overboard. O'Toole was not quite so lucky, his frantically clutching hand meeting only fresh air as he felt his feet leaving the deck. The tornado picked him up like a leaf blown in the wind, depositing him in the wake of the speeding launch. Spluttering his way to the surface he was grateful to see the *Whaleback* turn back and sweep alongside where the willing hands of Jefferies and Swifty hauled him back on board just as a ten foot high wall of water reared up off their stern.

Doug Freeman , digging for ragworm on the sands three quarters of a mile out from the beach alongside Southend Pier, turned seawards as the flash lightened the sombre afternoon sky. The thunderous roar of the explosion and visibly rising column of water left him open-mouthed in awe before a tearing warm wind drove him back head over heels to leave him sitting confused in a pool of water left by the receding tide.

Looking over to where his pal had also been gathering bait, he was alarmed to find himself alone. He rose to his feet and rushed over to the spot where he had last seen him and found himself looking into a water-filled rivulet that had, previously, not been there.

A shout from his left interrupted his bewilderment. 'What the f…. was that ? '

Before he had time to respond, and as his friend lifted himself from the mini river, they found themselves cowering under a sudden downpour of watery mud and scattered metal pieces.

Chapter 10

When the deluge abated, Doug turned seawards and gasped, 'I think the wreck of the Montgomery blew up. We won't have to go fishing, they'll be plenty floating on the top of the water, we can scoop them up by the bucket lo…….' He stopped in mid sentence, eyes widening in sudden fear as a tidal wave of white, foam flecked water rushed towards them. Neither survived the tsunami, non swimmer Freeman was pummelled forcefully backwards as the wave hit, staggering before falling…..directly onto the sharp prongs of his friends' bait digging fork lying on the mud. Only one tine punctured his body, penetrating his right kidney, but the sharp searing pain produced a natural reaction of opening his mouth to scream in anguish. The muddy, grit laden, water lost no time in filling his mouth and lungs. His body continued to be carried shorewards with the inrushing sea which finally gave up its hold when it was repelled by the beach and promenade, leaving , by that time, only a lifeless corpse on the sand.
Dougs' friend Paul nearly made it. He too was bowled over by the force of the wave but managed to surface in the wake of the crest, finding himself almost alongside a moored boat that had survived the rolling wave. With a kick of his

legs he reached the small cabin cruiser and grasped the bulwark but was too exhausted to haul himself out of the water.
He never saw the bulk of the heavy yacht that, wrenched from its' mooring buoy by the force of the wave, smashed into his fragile body as it slammed into the smaller vessel, crushing his chest and head like ripe melon. Death was instantaneous.

Of the dozens of anglers and other bait-diggers caught up in the aftermath of the explosion, remarkably, those were the only four deaths 'at sea', despite a number of fishermen and pier walkers being almost blown off the structure. One afternoon stroller did find himself ejected over the railings as the blast hit him, falling twenty feet into the mud but amazingly escaping uninjured. Even the following tidal wave failed to claim another victim, the walker having climbed a metal ladder almost clear of the passing water that snatched briefly at his legs on its way to shore.

At the Isle of Sheppey, Isle of Grain and, over the river at Shoebury, Southend, Westcliff and

Leigh, inhabitants and workers were not so lucky.
Over ninety percent of the two Isles and, fifty percent of the northern shore towns' windows were blasted out of their frames or punctured by lethal fragments, the Terrorists' posthumous action accounting for over three hundred minor injuries - mainly by flying glass - a dozen or more serious casualties and a further twenty three deaths.

Three of the fifteen had no warning of their impending demise, one minute going about their business at the Oil Refinery on the Isle of Grain, the next finding themselves engulfed in flames. True, they certainly saw, and heard, the Montgomery explode, but never felt the shock wave that travelled beneath their feet to split open one of the storage tanks. Their ears were still resonating from the roar of the explosion, the sound of grinding metal plates unheard, as aviation fuel spilled from the ruptured tank and ignited from a spark caused by the friction. Their instant deaths were followed by that of another unfortunate victim, a visiting tanker driver who was sitting reading a newspaper on the step of his cab at the time the tank exploded in a ball of flame. He escaped injury from the explosion but was immediately overwhelmed by thick, choking, smoke that burnt his lungs and blinded his attempts to feel his way into his cab. His determination to escape the poisoning fumes succeeded as he wrenched open the door , swung himself up and slammed the door shut. He was just recovering his breath when the windows of the lorry disintegrated as the Air Blast reached land, the miniscule shards of fragmented glass peppering his face and hands. His screams only opened his lungs more for the invading smoke to replace the life-giving air he so desperately sought. There was no air in the black cloud, he never made it back out of the cab.

At the time of the explosion, in addition to the *Whaleback*, two other craft were in the immediate vicinity and directly affected.
The fishing boat, "Cockles" with a two man, father and son crew, out of Leigh was proceeding at a sedate five knots inshore but abeam to Brads' launch when the sky lit up.
Even as the thunder of the explosion reached his ears, Henry Dale Senior instinctively knew the ammunition ship was the cause and, one handed, turned the sturdy 38 footer into the wave he knew would be following grabbing the handset

of the ship to shore radio with his free hand. In some ways it was a mistake, the Air Blast catching the protruding overhang of the wheelhouse cabin roof and ripping it away complete with half the cabin itself. The long handset cable of the radio wrapped itself around Henrys' neck as the cabin was torn to matchwood, the radio still attached to part of the cabin bulkhead that
sailed over the side catching the younger boatman a glancing blow, in transit, and rendering him unconscious. Henry senior was dragged off his feet and found himself pinned with his back against the guardrail with a tightening cord about his neck. The "Cockles" passage through the water increased the pressure as the cabin wall trailed astern seeking to free itself from the restraining cord. Henrys' struggles got weaker while his son still lay comatose. The tidal wave struck the boats' prow and lifted it high as the compressed water passed underneath and hit the trailing board, snapping the radio cable........along with the fishermans' neck.

Garrison Point, Sheerness - at the mouth of the River Medway - fell astern of the eight hundred metre long, shallow water, small, grain laden, coaster "Grey Dawn" as the helmsman lined the ship up along the Medway channel. ‘ Looks like we may have seen the worst of the gales. Could have a pleasant run up the coast for once,’ said Captain Mcleod to his two fellow seamen manning the bridge wheelhouse.

‘Providing Collins and that new greaser lad keep this wrecks’ old engines going,’ responded watch keeper Stan Tully. ‘ About time it wen’……the whole of the surrounding sky lit with a brilliance of the strongest sunny day, stopping the sailor in mid sentence. ‘What in the name of ’….this time his final words, although spoken, were lost in a thunderous roar.

Before anyone had time to answer or comment, the whole of the bridge house disintegrated , the complete front windscreen section slamming back into the three occupants as the surrounding structure broke into matchwood.

Their feeble attempts to protect themselves, throwing arms up in a vain hope of warding off the heavy screens, were nothing more than a futile gesture, the thick Perspex windows snapping their limbs in contempt before crashing into their unprotected bodies.

Captain McLeod died instantly, his neck vertebrae snapped by one section of the lethal flying screen.

Chapter 10

Tully and helmsman Dimitrov survived a little longer, a spoke of the ships' wheel spearing the stomach of the luckless Polish seaman as he collapsed under the weight of another section of the windshield, leaving him trapped and slowly bleeding to death.

Seaman Tully would have considered himself even unluckier, fate saving his life after the initial Air Blast but then snatching it away in an act of malevolent cruelty.

He avoided serious injury, as the heavy screen hurtled towards him , when the rear of the bridge structure at his back collapsed in wooden fragments depositing his bruised, but otherwise, uninjured body on the empty poop deck. Winded, he sat up scratching his head in wonderment on viewing the carnage of the 'exploded' wheelhouse.

In something of a daze, with his Bosuns' instinct to examine the seaworthiness of the vessel, he started on a tour of the upper deck, immediately noticing a grain hold cover had been torn away leaving the compartment open to the elements. 'Must get that covered quickly,' he muttered to himself peering over the side at the cereal below.

At that moment the tidal wave reached the ships' side, catching it directly abeam and tilting it over to starboard. Tully was catapulted head first into the loose grain which, quicksand like, enveloped him completely within seconds as the vessel see-sawed in the explosions' sea disturbance, swilling the cargo back and forth and shuffling his body deeper and deeper. Embedded in the shifting mass and completely disorientated, the Bosuns' scrabbling hands only deepened his grave, his struggles quickly weakening as the air in his lungs became exhausted and non replaceable.

Below deck the remaining two crew members had problems of their own. Such was the volume of the detonation, even the ships' engines could not drown the sound as the Terrorists' bomb initiated the huge explosion.

'What was that ?' cried the youngster in alarm, the fear showing in his wide-eyed expression.

'Don't panic Eric, keep calm,' ordered Engineer Harry Collins.'Probably a wartime mine, they're still being dredged up from time to time. I'll ask the Captain on the intercom.'

A minute later, his attempted communication meeting no response, he suggested, ' No answer. We'd better go up and see what's going on.'

Chapter 10

The young assistant needed no second invitation, mounting the iron ladder two steps at a time ahead of the Senior sailor.

Neither made it to the top, the ship suddenly, and violently, heeling over, sending a dislodged Eric tumbling into the climbing Engineer, the pair crashing back to the Engine room floor.

Harry Collins let out a loud cry of pain as the boy crawled clear. ' I can't move, I've damaged my back. Get help !' He passed out.

Frozen in fear, the young second Engineer sat unmoving for some minutes before attempting to remount the ladder, a delay that was to eventually sink the ship. Just as he recovered some composure and stood at foot of the steps a loud rumbling and crashing sound came from above. His hands gripped the ladder rails so tight his knuckles went white as he started to climb. Reaching the top of the hatch, he stood in the short corridor listening before plucking up the courage to pull down the cold iron lever of the outside watertight door to the deck. He pushed the iron door forcefully….it opened an inch.

Outside, the wreckage of the bridge and toppled ships' crane jammed the opening with a solidarity that no human force could budge, the Engineers were trapped as the 'pilot less' vessel headed for the Estuary mouth. Torrents of water and mud descended on the wounded ship but only one piece of debris......a ,battered, gem encrusted, jewellery box that bounced on the foredeck before coming to a rest on the canvas cover of hold number one.

When the wall of turgid water swept under the *Whaleback* , lifting the stern and sending the craft into a bow-diving twist, Brad felt the wheel yanked from his grasp as the boat plummeted into the trough behind the wave. Attempting to remain on his feet he clutched at the nearest fixture, one of his grandfathers' old wartime shell cases that Swifty had securely glued to the windshield shelf. His questing fingers missed the shiny brass case but locked on to the bunch of keys hanging on the improvised hook. The saving handhold gave way as the tortured launch skidded sideways, tossed like a cork in the turbulent water.

Brad sprawled backwards, half on, half off the wheelhouse bench seat, dropping the keys as he pushed himself upright to throw himself at the wheel in an attempt to bring the boat back under control.

Chapter 10

The door burst open as *Swifty*, drenched, but grinning, stumbled in. 'Bloody steep hills out here boss, thought you might want a hand.'
'Should be alright now, are the others okay ?'asked the relieved Skipper.
'Well, they're hanging on for their lives out there but I'll get them back in shortly.'
Brad throttled back the engines as he took hold of the wheel, suddenly, with an alarmed look on his face, spinning the steering spokes violently anti-clockwise.
The grimace on his face, reflecting the failure of whatever manoeuvre he was attempting, was followed by a grinding crash that shook the vessel from stem to stern.
' That blasted wave took us into the Mulberry,' screamed Brad referring to the broken, World War Two, concrete caisson, built for use as a floating harbour for the D-Day landings, that had beached itself off Shoeburyness. 'Take a peek below Trev, see if there's any damage.'
The crewman disappeared outside as the two soaked M.I.5 Agents stepped in. 'Are we alright Brad ?' enquired Pete Jefferies. 'Did we hit something?'
'We had an argument with a block of concrete but don't worry, Trevor's checking at the mo-

ment and we've only got a couple of feet of water under us now.'
Swifty rushed back in grim-faced. ' We're holed on the starboard side near the stern Skip. I've jammed some rags in it and put the pump on but we need to do something better if we want to save her.'
'I'll run her up on the mudflats, the tide is still dropping, we'll be high and dry soon and be able to carry out a better repair before the tide comes back in. I'm sorry gentlemen but you'll have to get your shoes muddy. Better let your boss know the score. Tell him we'll be late for the meeting tomorrow. And Trev, you'd better phone Nancy, she's suffered enough trauma recently. She knows we were going to the wreck and must be worried.'

Stan Tullys' was not the only bizarre death that day, Barbara Elliot meeting her end in a manner bordering on an absurd farce. When the wreck exploded, barmaid Barbara was walking along Southend Esplanade on her way to work, actually just descending the steps to the below street toilets. The flash of light and explosive roar brought her running back to the pavement where she found herself one of only a half a dozen sightseers looking out to sea. Being a Friday afternoon in late winter, the promenade was sparsely populated but Barbara spotted a young police "special" heading her way with his radio intercom to his ear. He suddenly pocketed the communicator and yelled at the congregating bystanders. ' Get off the seafront immediately. There's been a huge explosion.....' Before he had time to complete his warning the 'Air Blast' reached land, knocking people off their feet and even toppling a few cars onto their sides before turning the seafront Amusement Arcades, Public Houses and Souvenir shops into a resemblance of a war-torn Iraq suburb.

Barbara, at the first warning words, had already turned back down the steps, avoiding the full force of the hurricane wind that skittled the pedestrians like nine pins. But, she heard the shouts and screams of terror.

Shaking with relief, she rushed into a cubicle and slammed the lock in a confused belief that the flimsy compartment would protect her from whatever was causing the panic and fear above her head. How long she sat on the loo pan with eyes closed and her head in her hands she would not have been able to guess, realisation of where she was only recognised when she felt her legs getting cold and looked down to see she was up to her ankles in water. Her first thought was that the toilet was leaking but, hypnotised she watched the water rapidly rise to her calves before the sound of rushing water outside prompted her rise and slide back the cubicle lock. The door slammed into her under a torrent of inrushing water. Struggling to regain any equilibrium proved impossible as the flood, in seconds, submerged her completely.

Remarkably, the Toilets lights remained on for a good two minutes, giving the drowning woman some hope of reaching the exit stairway before her lungs collapsed.

She might have made it but was suddenly plunged into a terrifying darkness and lost all sense of direction.

As Barbara's life ebbed away in her watery dungeon, so did the tidal wave that caused her death, leaving those still on the promenade wet but otherwise unharmed.

The *Whaleback* had 'surfed' the wave nearly all the way to the beach before running aground as the water shallowed. Ahead of them the crest of the rapidly diminishing wave spent most of it's force on the sea-wall but retained sufficient power to 'top' the defences and flood across the road into the open fronts of the Arcades. It was this overspill that cascaded down the steps of the underground toilet and took Barbara's life along with that of fourteen year old Simon Pallister, a schoolboy truant playing the seafront's slot machines to which he had become addicted.

Having survived, intact, the force of the blast that had upturned other vehicles, the Fiat Uno driven by an elderly, white haired, lady was suddenly hit by the wave that overwhelmed the promenade defences. Instinctively she attempted to turn away from the torrent and , in a state of panic, swung the small Italian car up the pavement straight into the Arcade. Young Simon, himself in an equally shocked state, was just wandering aimlessly out into the street. The impact as boy met metal was heard above the rush and gurgle of water before the car ploughed into the machines and stalled.

Injured, but not fatally, the youngster rolled off the bonnet into foot deep water. Remarkably, he felt no pain and sat up watching his favourite game machine topple slowly onto it's side. Flashing sparks and smoke turned the interior of the Arcade into a Hades hell as he reached out to

use the machine to pull himself to his feet, his body immediately arching rigid as he touched the metal casing.
As the water receded the power suddenly failed leaving the Arcade in semi-darkness and with a stench of burning flesh.
In all, seventeen vehicle accidents occurred along the stretch of seafront between Shoebury-ness and Leigh-on-Sea, two resulting in serious casualties but no additional deaths.
Across the Estuary, closer to the source of the calamitous explosion, the town of Sheerness bore the brunt of the Air Blast. Shattered glass and torn loose debris showered pedestrians and motorists alike, creating extreme panic, height-ened as a rain storm of water, mud, fish and shrapnel quickly followed.
As across the River, vehicle collisions and acci-dents were numerous when drivers lost concentration or control. Two elderly pedestri-ans were killed outright when one wayward car, swerving to miss another, cart wheeled on to the pavement before coming to a rest on it's roof. Benny and Martha Solomons never saw the ve-hicle that tumbled into them, cutting short their, pre-holiday cruise, clothes shopping spree….and their lives.

Chapter 10

A collision with a lorry left freelance reporter Steve Holton trapped in his car for nearly two hours before the over-stretched emergency services were able to free him, the delay proving to be fatal when his heart stopped on the way to hospital and failed to respond to resuscitation.

Trainee window dresser Sarah Harris was changing a window display when the plate glass shop front, seemingly in slow motion, disintegrated into a thousand razor sharp shards that peppered her body. Her screams of pain ,as dozens of pinpricks punctured her face, turned to screams of anguish when streams of blood started dripping from her chin to quickly pool at her feet. 'No ! Not my face,' she shouted at the mannequin she was dressing. 'What about my modelling career ?' she screamed in reference to a recent *photoshoot* she had attended. Discarding the model she was dressing and dropping to her knees in dejection amidst the shattered window, she continued, ' I might as well be dead!'

She got her wish when a large, dagger-like, sliver of glass, precariously holding in the frame above her bent head, chose that moment to detach itself, the heavy glass 'weapon' slashing through her carotid artery on it's descent as cleanly as a Surgeon's knife. Sarah slumped

forward in her own blood to become a second 'window dummy' unnoticed by befuddled pedestrians scurrying by.
A further seven of the town's inhabitants, workers and visitors lost their lives within an hour of Sarah's demise, crane driver Reg McKintyre being the final victim after suffering nearly sixty minutes of hopeless waiting. A hundred and ninety feet up in the air, manning his huge jib crane on a development site overlooking the mouth of the River Medway, he had a magnificent view of the explosion. He never really stood much chance of surviving the resulting 'Air Blast' which thundered into the metal lattice work of the tall crane, twisting and weakening crucial struts. The top-heavy crane structure partially collapsed in a grinding screech of tortured metal before jamming itself to leave the near hysterical operator trapped, still suspended over one hundred and fifty feet from the ground. Unable to open the cab door from the inside, he knew his chances of being freed from outside were pretty negligible, a synopsis confirmed when his mobile phone rang and the site manager informed him that, in view of the danger of the swaying crane collapsing , the area was be-

ing cleared. 'Hold on, I'll get help as soon as I can.'

Reg, with the condemned man's hope of reprieve, sat motionless trying to calm his nerves for over thirty minutes, fearful that any sudden movement on his part would be fatal. A stronger gust of wind caused the structure to sway alarmingly, convincing him he could wait no longer for rescue and that his only hope lay in getting out of the cab to descend the cage enclosed ladder. Too late he realised his half hour wait was wasted time as the girders slowly bent to leave him staring directly at the deserted site below. He knew then he was about to die and reached for his mobile phone to text a message to his wife, fearful that were he to attempt to speak to her his nerves would fail and leave her with a memory of him he had no wish to preserve. He never got to send the message, a long, drawn out squeal and clamour of metal against metal preceded a violent lurch as the projecting jib separated and fell to the ground taking the cab and Reg with it. Beneath the pile of twisted metal, a mobile phone rang.

The other six fatalities were more fortunate in that they did not suffer such an agonising death, their ends coming quickly and unexpectedly.

Doris Hadley was watching television at the time of the explosion, rushing out on to the small balcony of her eighth floor flat as the roar of it shook the room. She was still there staring open-mouthed in the direction of the sea wondering at the huge geyser of water, easily visible from her high viewpoint, when she sensed, rather than felt, she was flying.
She was but , not in an aircraft. Her landing, over fifty yards away from the take off point was anything but the gentle touch down of an aeroplane flight.
A floor above, at the same apartment building, lifelong pals, Derek Gemmell and Shane Budden were already outside when the wrecked ship 'went up'; engaged in a friendly argument about a question in the previous evening's "Question Time" television programme while cleaning windows from their precariously perched cradle on the side of the building. Their argument, ironically on the question of Terrorism, was brought to an abrupt conclusion when their cradle support suddenly plummeted. There was no question of them surviving the nine storey drop. Derek was immediately catapulted out of the breaking cradle, his safety harness no longer attached to any substantial support. Shane man-

aged to hold on by one hand for ten seconds longer, giving him just sufficient time to correctly think, 'I bet some bloody Terrorist caused this.'

Albert Thompson suffered a ghastly death within a few moments of the explosion. As an employee of the Kent Water Company he was in an underground sewer at the time, inspecting a suspected tunnel collapse. Little of the noise suffered by those above penetrated to his level but, the shock wave did. The walls of the tunnel appeared to shimmer before his eyes. He thought he might be suffering the effects of a build up of gases and turned back towards his assistant, twenty yards away, standing at the foot of the steps leading to the surface. Before he had time to call out, the wall on his left exploded in a shower of bricks as raw sewage water and solids burst through from an adjacent tunnel. One brick caught the luckless sewerman at the base of his neck pitching him, semi conscious into the evil smelling swill that quickly submerged his struggling form as the sewerage climbed the walls of the tunnel to two feet high. Albert never came up for air.

The following tidal wave caused the final two deaths, husband and wife Brian and Rita Collier, both recovering from the flu deciding to see the week out at home before returning to work after the weekend. In their case, home was a houseboat moored a mile upstream from the mouth of the River Medway.

Such were the reinforced defences surrounding Sheerness, the mini tsunami wave was rebuffed to an even greater degree than across the River in Southend. The sea wall facing the explosion on the Isle of Sheppey remained unbreached but the flood of rushing water sped up the River Medway, reaching the Colliers' river home just as they returned below decks to their galley kitchen after looking outside for the source of the tremendous explosion. ' Let's finish getting dinner then we'll get in the car and go down to town, see what it's all about.' said Brian.' I'm looking forward to a good fry up after not eating much all week.'

Rita lit the calor gas stove and poured some oil into a frying pan just as the wave hit, lifting the houseboat violently before dropping it back like a stone. The oil and pan went flying ,together with the oil bottle that broke on impact with the deck, splattering the surrounding cupboards and flooring. The gas bottle, insecurely fixed, flew out of it's cubby hole as the spraying oil ignited.

Chapter 10

Within seconds both Brian and Rita found themselves with parts of their clothing on fire. Brian's attempts , with nothing more than a wet tea-cloth, to extinguish both his own and his wife's burning attire was doomed to failure by the fact that the tap on the gas bottle was still in the open position. With a heat-searing whoosh the escaping gas ignited first the tiny window curtains and then the cabin walls and door. Their escape route blocked and the cabins' oxygen supply feeding only the ,now five foot high ,flames, the couple mercifully passed out as the cabin walls collapsed in on them.

Not all of the Kent coast escaped intact from the tidal wave, a breach occurring on the Isle of Grain resulting in a further Refinery employee narrowly avoiding a fearful death. Water poured into the Refinery complex adjacent to the fireball of the ruptured tank which, fortunately, remained the only one affected. Such was the heat emanating from the conflagration - and the danger of further explosions - all, except one, of the afternoon shift had retreated to a prearranged assembly point at the main gate. Unfortunately for Bill Maitland he was in the wrong position for a direct route to safety and was still in danger when the sea flooded in. Having just breathed a sigh of relief at having got around the flaming tank unharmed, he gasped in horror as he saw a three foot high wall of water sweeping towards him, much of the surface of which was covered by smoke and flames of floating aviation fuel.

When the water hit his legs he took a deep breath and threw himself headlong into the wave, holding himself under for as long as he could before surfacing. The flames had passed and the water depth was not increasing at all as he strode purposefully through the deluge towards safety, halting only briefly to turn and view the astonishing sight of a still fiercely burning tank protruding through a sea of surrounding water.

The rebuffed wave swept along the Sheppey coast where, small boat anglers, Denny Foster and Keith Smith were lucky to escape with their lives. Fishing in the sheltered offshore water for flatfish on the late ebbing tide, they had a clear view of the exploding Montgomery but were not touched by the Air Blast that followed. They were, however, frightened by what they had witnessed and already had the anchor up when the, diminishing but still powerful , wave caught them stern on and swept their fragile craft high

on to the beach at Warden's Point before continuing on it's way leaving the relieved fishermen wet but unharmed.
Not that the "Grim Reaper" had finished for the day, he still had the unfortunate trapped crewmen of the 'Grey Dawn' on his list.
Followed by clouds of black smoke from the burning petrol tank, the *driverless* coaster continued it's passage eastwards across the shallow waters of the Cant, heading directly towards the old wartime Red Sand Tower forts.
In the Engine room, Chief Engineer Harry Collins had recovered consciousness and ordered the frightened young Eric to strap his legs together. ' I think I've dislocated my hip boy,' he said through clenched teeth. ' You've got to get me up top if we're to get out of here. It seems we're on our own.'
With a strength belying his slender frame the youngster hoisted the Chief over his shoulder and climbed the steps up into the passageway above, sweating profusely from the concerted effort and collapsing in a panting heap as he dropped the Engineer to the deck. The white-faced old-timer groaned in agony before rolling over to push at the door hatch to the deck out-

side. Eric clambered to his feet and joined his superior's efforts. The door refused to budge.
'Let's think about this lad,' said Collins. 'There might be a....' his words were drowned out by screeching crash that shook the ship and continued for two or three minutes before suddenly ceasing. The Engineer was about to speak again when a further rumbling and screeching , this time from just outside the jammed hatch, caused the frightened youngster to scream out, ' What's happening Chief, are we sinking ?'
Before Chief Collins could reply the hatch door swung back on it's hinges letting a cacophony of noise penetrate their refuge. 'Get out there, see what the hell that noise is,' ordered Collins to the youngster who needed no second bidding.
Returning pasty faced a few minutes later, the apprentice Engineer gasped, 'We hit the Forts Chief. The crane's gone over the side but we're taking on water, the bows are almost under but there's a bloody great helicopter overhead.'
'What about the Captain and the others ?'
'There's no bridge or wheelhouse left, the Captain's 'ad it but I didn't see the Bosun.'
'Get me outside boy, 'grunted the Chief. 'We're going to need that helicopter. Then get below and see about stopping the engine.'

Chapter 10

Ahead of the 'Grey Dawn', Captain Silas, *Hooter*, Hobbs, so-nicknamed on account of his large red nose, replaced the handset of the ship to shore radio in the high bridge house of the **Hyundai Warrior** ,a Mega , Liquified Natural Gas, Korean -built, carrier anchored up in the Warp awaiting a pilot. The huge, distinctive domed -tank, 215 cubic metre capacity ship had been scheduled to move up to the Canvey Gas Terminal once the tide started to flood.
'That was Gravesend PLA, Mr. Mate,' he uttered in exasperation. As we already guessed, the old wartime wreck of the 'Montgomery' has finally exploded. We won't be moving from here until tomorrow, There's no Pilot boats available this afternoon, they've got their hands full with other things.'
'We might have to move ourselves Captain,' responded the first Mate dropping his binoculars. ' I've been keeping an eye on that coaster over by the Red Sands. I think it hit the Towers and appears to be out of control and heading this way. There's a coastal rescue helicopter overhead but I can't see what they can do.'
'It seems to be down by the head a bit but on it's present course it will certainly collide with us,' responded the Captain peering through his

own binoculars. 'I'd estimate it is only doing about four knots but there is no time for us to get the anchor up and out of the way. Signal the crew to stand by their collision stations. God help us if it hits us directly amidships.'

Eric returned to the Chief Engineer who had dragged himself upright against the port guard-rail peering ahead into the gloom of approaching dusk. 'We've been knocked off course by that collision lad, look we're heading directly for that LNG tanker . Have you shut the engine down?'

'No Chief, the engine room is partly flooded and there's no lights on. I'm scared to go down there.'

'That's it then boy, signal that chopper to pick us up before we hit that ship or sink.'

Aboard the helicopter, the rescue crewmen had already assessed the situation, signalling the pilot to maintain position on the ship while going lower. 'There only seems to be two crew,' one calmly told the pilot. ' Phil is going down to help.'

The rescuer dropped swiftly to the deck of the moving ship while the expertise of the pilot kept the helicopter immediately above. After a few brief words with the young Engineer, he looped Harry Collins into a harness and signalled for the cable to be wound in, while supporting the injured Engineer as the two of them were hauled to safety.

Left alone below, awaiting his turn to be rescued, young Eric looked apprehensively towards the bow of the ship which was now dipping deeply into the waves as the 'runaway' ship continued to forge ahead. It was then, in the gathering gloom, that he spotted the jewellery box when a rare gleam of the dying wintry sun briefly poked through the clouds, glinting off the gems directly into his eyes.
Fear temporarily forgotten, he left the relative safety of the poop deck and carefully picked his way down the now quite steeply inclined deck towards number one hold.
The coaster was constructed with movable hold bulkheads to accommodate various cargoes but, like the ill-fated *Titanic* the top of these 'dividing walls' did not reach the deck level. As the bows of the of the "Grey Dawn" sunk deeper, the flood of seawater spilled over the top of the forward hold into the next. This may not have been immediately catastrophic were the ship not

still underway and number two hold being the one missing it‘s cover. But, the driven ship forced it’s bow even deeper quickly filling the second hold which was more than sufficient weight of water to sink the stricken vessel.
Overhead, the helicopter crew could only look on helplessly as the coaster’s, still turning, screws came clear of the water when the ship suddenly ’nose-dived’ and disappeared within seconds beneath the waves.
As his hand reached for the jewelled casket, poor Eric found himself propelled into the same hold where the unlucky Stan Tully met his fate, only by now the solid mass of loose grain was a liquid quicksand that spilled around the boy as the upturned vessel continued it’s journey to the seabed six fathoms below. Drowning Eric’s last conscious, but inane, thought as he saw Tully tumble past him in a snowstorm of grain ,was, “The Chief is looking for you Bosun.”
The hovering helicopter continued to scour the area for half an hour in search of the missing crew member, finally conceding defeat and flying the rescued Engineer back to their Kent base and hospital.

Chapter 10

Watching the evolving spectacle of the ship's sinking, less than a hundred and fifty yards from his own vulnerable vessel, Captain Hobbs let out a sigh of relief, uttering to his awe-struck Mate, ' I never thought I'd ever hear myself saying I was glad to see a ship sink but, in this case, I'm happy to make an exception.'

Brad and Swifty watched the two Agents, socks and shoes in hand, pick their way across the mud towards the beach, Jefferies already with his mobile phone to his ear.

The rebuffed wave had speedily drained back to sea shortly after the *Whaleback* grounded, leaving the mudflats almost the same as before the bomb ship detonated. With the exception of a few 'beached' craft that had broken free of their moorings, it was like any other day out on the wide expanse of mud as the tide went out. Not so, however, on shore where the swamped promenade and blast damaged buildings resembled the aftermath of a hurricane, the sight shocking the M.I.5 men as they trudged up the beach to walk back to their car parked at the Pier entrance.

Brad's mobile rang, it was Jefferies. 'The car is undamaged. If you are okay we are going to get

back to H.Q. I've brought Commander Beaman up to date on what has happened - they heard the explosion in London. He is anxious to tie up any loose ends about your involvement before making a statement to the press. Can you still make it up to town tomorrow ?'
The boat Skipper confirmed they needed no further assistance and that they would report to Trafalgar House the following day. Putting his phone down on the windscreen shelf he noticed the splintered wood where his grab at the 20mm shell key hook had ripped it free
'Right Trev,' he said bending down to pick up the keys and shell case, 'Let's get to work on this repair before the tide comes back.'
As he stood up he noticed the caulking drop out of the brass case. Diamonds cascaded to the deck and rolled down the slight incline to lay against the side, glittering, in the cabins' lamplight.
'Are they what I think they are ?' queried Swifty incredulously.
'They certainly appear to be diamonds,' replied Brad bending to pick up the gems. Let's see if Grandfather's other shell case has anything in it.'

Chapter 10

The crewman tugged on the second hook which, after considerable leverage, finally came free in his hand. 'I certainly glued them on securely didn't I ?'

Unlike the previous container, the caulking in the second shell case was still firmly in place necessitating it's removal with a small screwdriver that Swifty magically produced from somewhere. 'Hold out your hand,' he said to Brad, tilting the brass cylinder.

More diamonds poured into the Skipper's palm. 'There's a small fortune here if they're genuine. Get a plastic bag from the galley Trev, we'll have them checked out later, we must get that repair carried out as a priority before the tide comes back in.'

Slipping the bagged up gems in his pocket, the *Whaleback's* Skipper led the way back aft of the engines to inspect the hull. 'Oh !, that's not bad at all, the old girl's a tough nut,' he exclaimed on seeing the impact damage. We'll put a patch on for now to take it round to the boathouse where we can renew what ever needs doing.'

'There's still some water in between the double skin we'll need to get out,' responded Swifty. ' If I poke the end of a hose down there and put the pump on, it will soon empty it. If you want to tidy up top Skip, I'll carry on down here.'

Ten minutes later the crewman called out. 'Skip, you'd better come down here and see this,'

Brad dropped back down to his crewman friend who, he found staring ,disbelievingly, at a small pile of jewelled earrings and necklaces on the deck at his feet.

'The pump suddenly appeared to be clogged. When I pulled the hose out this lot was sucked onto the bottom of it,' explained his friend.

Speechless, the Skipper shook his head in wonderment. ' You know what Trev, I think this is Grandfather's actual old boat after all. These jewels and the diamonds all tie in with the story he told us about the encounter with the U-Boat and that crewman Henry Martin who, he thought ,he'd heard mention jewels when he was lying injured. And, remember, when I was young I did find that old German Mauser pistol on board. I'll put this lot with the diamonds for now .'

Six hours later, after an uneventful cruise around the Maplin Sands back into the River Crouch, where he dropped the crewman off at Wallasea Island to collect his car, Brad tied the *Whaleback* up to the boathouse slipway in the

River Roach, locked the cabin and walked back along the sea wall in the dark to the Paglesham car park.

Trevor was waiting for him and half an hour later they were back at Swifty's Canvey home where Nancy prepared the exhausted duo a late supper while her husband related their traumatic experiences of the day.

'You know,' said Nancy sombrely, When we heard that tremendous explosion I didn't know what to think, I thought the worse. Thank goodness you had the foresight to phone and let me know you were safe . And, thanks to you two, Canvey's inhabitants are still sleeping safely in their beds tonight. The Terrorists may not have achieved their aim of thousands of casualties on the Island but, unfortunately, they did manage to take the life of poor Sheila Unsworth's husband Ted down the road. He was working on the roof of the Waterside Farm Sports Hall. After the explosion he just stepped off the edge and fell to his death. He had a hearing defect and wore a hearing aid. They think he had it up full and the roar of the detonation affected his sense of balance so that he just simply lost his footing. Poor Sheila is so shocked she's been taken to hospital herself.'

The trio went to bed ,each with their minds full of the days events and struggling to find the elusive peacefulness of sleep.

Chapter 10

11

EPILOGUE

It was gone noon when Brad and Swifty finally walked into Commander Beaman's office where Pete Jefferies greeted them cheerfully. ' Hello lads, all recovered from our roller coaster ride yesterday, no after effects I hope. The Chief will be back shortly, he's just finalising a few details with the D.G. I think they're preparing a brief for the P.M. The rest of the lads are in the main office if you want to wait in there. Help yourself from the coffee machine. Oh no, hold it, here he is now.'

'Glad you made it okay you two. Peter has filled me in on the events yesterday afternoon. I'm certain you realise, the detonator device that Callum picked up was completely disabled and was not the cause of the explosion,' said the Commander. 'At the time you could be forgiven for thinking it was, I know Callum did initially. We'll never know what happened but the best guess is that , either the detonator in the bombs was faulty or short circuited somehow, or Latif planted a timer device that went off late.'

'There was definitely no timer attached when Saleem and Latif left in the dinghy,' interrupted Brad, ' I would have seen it at the time.'

'Well, as I said, we'll never know,' continued the Commander. ' The only regret is that those particular two bombs did go off and cause a significant loss of life, we believe twenty seven people in all although there were, I understand, a number of other serious injuries, so the death toll could still rise.'

'According to this mornings' newspapers hundreds were killed and some are mentioning a Terrorist connection,' piped in Swifty. 'Just where do they get their information from?'

'Not from us, that's for sure, 'replied the M.I.5 Chief. 'I've just spent an hour with the Director General compiling an official press release. Let's go out to the General Office , I'll let you all know what the official line will be and what information MUST remain confidential.'

The gathered Agents, less Samirah - who, the Commander explained, had gone to collect Kathy Doyle - pushed their paperwork aside and listened attentively as their boss revealed the collective findings of the unit and his instructions from the top echelon.

'Some of you will know parts of the jigsaw we were trying to assemble this past week, but not all. We now think we can make reasonable assumptions about some of the missing pieces, some guesswork and some now firmly established,' he began.

The Commander continued, almost without interruption, to relate the full story of the Terrorists' intent and the sequence of events that eventually resulted in their failure and deaths, referring not only to their own bad luck but also to the misfortunes that befell Saleems' cohorts, without which, he said, 'There was a good chance the full plan would have been achieved resulting in the biggest act of Terrorism the world has ever seen.'

Much of the assumptions he informed them came from the snippets of conversations that Brad and Swifty had overheard and, from some scraps of paperwork recovered from the ruins of Hassam's house. These, he told the Agents, showed that it was Saleem's original intention to fire rockets at the stanchions of the Queen Elizabeth Two Bridge, causing the collapse of the entire central span and the bombs were intended solely for the other targets, the Montgomery wreck, the Dartford Tunnel, Coryton Oil Refinery and Canvey Calor Gas Terminal. 'The sabotaging of the ammunition shipwreck should have taken place around nine o'clock in the evening, at high tide. Saleem hoped the resulting tidal wave would create such panic on Canvey Island - where, at High water, flooding would have occurred - that Latif and Asif , dressed in their Guards' uniforms ,could have easily sneaked into the Gas Terminal and Oil Refinery undetected. The explosives barge was a bonus for him and gave him an alternative plan that was, in some ways superior to his original although it did mean Mohammad sacrificing himself along with Asif. I believe that Saleem himself was not intending to become a Martyr until Brad and Swifty's intervention left him no choice if his plan was to succeed. He was undoubtedly aware of the double fencing and guard dogs at the Calor Gas Terminal and, when his detonator failed to blow up the Montgomery, recognised the only way was for a suicidal rocket attack. Not much fences or dogs can do about that.'

'Shows how wrong our guesses of Canary Wharf, Bradwell and the Houses of Parliament as targets was then,' intervened Pete Jefferries. 'But how did Saleem know about the barge. Wasn't that part of some other operation Chief ?'

The Commander informed them that no evidence had been uncovered linking the two operations but it was thought Hassam had a hand in both and, therefore, it was possible Saleem had been contacted about the London Al Qaeda leader's death and saw the opportunity to utilise the barge full of explosives against his own targets .'Under the Q.E.2 Bridge, the barge would have not only have taken out the centre concrete piers but had sufficient power to destroy the huge underwater caissons , completely collapsing the whole structure and, probably, the two Tunnel crossings as well, without the need for additional bombs. Even at that time of night there would have been something like a thousand vehicles involved and the economic cost to the country would be unimaginable. It took eight years, at a cost of over 60 million, to build the two tunnels and the bridge took three years and cost 86 million pounds. What those figures would be at today's costs is anybody's guess and, the disruption to traffic, especially to the Channel ports via the M25 motorway would continue for years. The good news about the barge is that Superintendent Kimpton's man, Sergeant Robinson, who Charlie found aboard, is still in intensive care but is expected to pull through.'

'Has he been able to give us any idea who his attacker was Chief ?' enquired Callum. 'No, we assume the same Terrorist still at large out there who we don't have a clue about.

I was hoping Mr. Murray and Mr. Swift may be of assistance there,' smiled the M.I.5. Chief looking at the two boatmen.

'I caught a brief glimpse under a weak lamp-light and Swifty only heard the Terrorist speak so we may not be too helpful but, I think there is also something else that should concern you,' said Brad quietly. 'If I'm not mistaken I heard you say earlier that you had recovered a further seven bombs and they had all been made safe by Callum here.'

'That's right. Two, you say were put on the Montgomery , we picked up two from the base of the tank at Coryton , there were two linked with a timer on the barge and one in each of the three holds , nine in total.'

' That still leaves one to find. Swifty can confirm, there were TEN that were unpacked aboard the *Whaleback*. The motorcyclist I saw had a satchel bag, it's possible that contained the other bomb !'

Shocked silence met the Skipper's words, the significance of the revelation taking minutes to sink in.

'That makes it even more critical that we find this last Terrorist quickly,' said Commander Beaman vehemently.' Each of those bombs is capable of killing dozens of people. If detonated in an enclosed area the casualty numbers will be horrendous and there can be only one reason this particular elusive zealot took one, he intends to use it !'

'Ah, you're wrong there Commander,' interrupted Brad. 'When you say,' he paused as the office door opened and Samirah entered the room with a, ' Sorry we're late Chief, Kathy's just hanging up her coat and bag.'

'That's okay Sam, your new found friend here was just about to correct me on something,' said the M.I.5 Head with a grin.

' I was only going to say that,' again he was interrupted by the door opening behind him and a soft voice saying, ' Hello all, it's good to be back after my little problem.'

Chapter 11 – Epilogue

Swifty jumped to his feet as Brad turned to face the newcomer, instantly recognising the face of Kathy Doyle……last seen under the pale lamp-light of the pier at the deserted wharf near to the Queen Elizabeth 2 Bridge.

'I'd know that voice anywhere,' spluttered an angry Trevor. 'You were on the barge, you're a bloody Terrorist !'

For someone just recently out of hospital, the female Agent was unbelievably quick, evading the crewman's lunge and covering the room's occupants with a handgun that appeared by magic in her hand as she retreated back through the doorway.

Callum O'Toole disregarded the weapon and stepped quickly towards her. 'Give me the gun Kathy, we'll sort this out .'

The pointed gun spat flame with a deafening report, the bullet smashing into the centre of the Agent's chest and bowling him over backwards. Kathy ran and grabbed her bag from the coat stand, snapping open the clasp to reach inside as the others rushed along the corridor towards her.

A shot rang out shattering the rogue Agent's forearm and causing her to drop the shoulder bag, a second quieter report instantly following as she sought to bring her gun back to bear on the rushing Agents. The weapon dropped from her lifeless fingers when the lethal bullet entered her brain via a small neat hole in the centre of her forehead and she slumped to the floor in a widening pool of blood.

Pete Jefferies kicked the Terrorists' gun away and felt for a pulse. Looking back at Brad, with his hand still in his coat pocket from which the muzzle of a smoking gun protruded, and at Samirah with a small automatic in her hand, he shook his head. ' She's not going to give us any trouble now, better check that bag.'

'Leave that to Callum,' ordered the Commander from the doorway behind them where he stood with the 'shot' Agent.

'Still wearing my bomb blast protective jacket wasn't I ?' said the units' explosives expert with a grin. 'Didn't have time to change after checking those bombs out. I'll take the bag down to the Armoury's sandbagged area, it appears safe to move.'

The Commander beckoned the Agents back into the office and asked Andy Davison to arrange the removal of Kathy's body while everyone recovered from the surprise action they had just experienced.

Chapter 11 – Epilogue

’That was what I was going to say about you being wrong Commander. You said “he intends to use it.” I was going to correct it to “she”, the person I saw leaving the barge was distinctly female. I couldn’t believe it when I turned and saw that person.’

‘But Kathy, it’s unbelievable she was a Terrorist. She’s been with us for nearly a year and the Special Branch security checks would surely have looked into her background. I understood that her father was murdered by the IRA when they discovered he was an undercover informer for our forces in Ireland,’ said the Senior Officer with a questioning shake of his head. ‘I presume that is Mohammad’s gun you have in your pocket, luckily for us.’

‘I thought I had better bring it along and hand it in, it was missed by your “cleaners” when they took his corpse away.’

The Commander turned to Sam. ‘Have you any idea how she got that bomb into the building ?’ he enquired. ‘ The scanner should have picked that up.’

‘It’s Saturday Chief, the main doors are locked as only staff are usually in the building. We used the back entrance with our security coded cards to enter and access the lift direct to this floor

.Kathy said she had brought a packed lunch in as she was going to catch up on her paperwork after the meeting. She's done that before so I didn't think it anything unusual.'

'I think we can safely say she intended to destroy us and this building, wiping out the Country's main Anti-Terrorist Unit in one go,' continued the M.I.5 Chief.

'But not as a suicide bomber,' claimed Pete Jefferies. 'That bag of hers had a timer device inside, I saw it under the open flap when Callum took it away.'

Just then the explosives expert returned, signalling a Thumbs Up. 'Disarmed. A real powerful device that one. Had a timer with just ten minutes remaining, nobody would have got out of here alive had that gone off.'

'So much so for your theory it wasn't to be a suicide attack Peter,' said the Commander.

'I don't suppose anyone has any idea how she came to be a Terrorist, or why ? I guess we'll never know now.'

He was wrong, Kathy's true identity and association with the Terrorists came to light a few months later as a result of further papers discovered at Hassam's former residence , interrogation of imprisoned suspects and liaison with Israeli Intelligence. True, she was an Irish girl who had attended the same University as Kathy Doyle, studying Middle East languages and usually accompanying her on field trips abroad, but her real name was Colleen Brady - shortened to *Cobra* by her Terrorist instructors - and, both her Grandfather and Father had been killed by British Forces during the IRA troubles. Although she knew Kathy's parents were dead she had no idea of the association with the British Army . According to the Israeli Secret Police , on one of the trips she met, and commenced a romantic affair with a Palestinian militant ,Hassan Allami ,who was one of the two Southall Terrorists arrested by Special Branch.

Colleen held a hatred of the English and, when Kathy was killed in a motorboat accident while in Israel, it was Hassan - already in contact with Hassam in London - who noticed an application form for a job in M.I.5's languages section among Kathy's belongings and suggested Colleen take over the dead girl's identity in the hope of obtaining the position which would be very useful for any future Terrorist activity. Security checks on Kathy, given her family background, were considered faultless and Colleen's command of Middle East languages virtually assured her of the job. After a year in the section she applied for a 'field Agent's' position and excelled in nearly all the disciplines and training, undoubtedly assisted by her prior instruction in the Terrorists' camps abroad. She came to M.I.5 on excellent recommendation.

A partial explanation of Hassam and the barge incident also came forth when an early riser railwayman, living nearby , was questioned with others in the area about their Terrorist neighbour. He reported seeing the female Agent, carrying a case and assisting Hassam who was limping badly, from his bedroom window as he was preparing for work.

The case was assumed to be the one found aboard the barge, filled with Euros. The rest was speculation but it was thought that Kathy was not injured at the house, but the Al Qaeda man was, necessitating the Agents' help in eluding capture. Somehow, possibly by a fall from the pier to the deck of the barge, Kathy / Colleen sustained the head and neck injury, but why Hassam had raised his gun to shoot at Jefferies while he was carrying the injured female Agent remained a mystery.

Chapter 11 – Epilogue

'As you know, I had a meeting with the Director General earlier today,' resumed Commander Beaman when the Agents and boatmen returned to the office after a brief lunch break of sandwiches and coffee in the Headquarter's Restaurant.' Obviously, in view of the numbers of people involved over the past few days, although the D.G. would like to, we are not able to completely avoid a public statement about the Terrorists and Montgomery explosion, especially with the number of deaths and injuries incurred. However, in order to alleviate public fear, the statement being issued makes no mention of the Terrorists' targets, only that a Cell preparing an attack on London was successfully discovered by Special Branch personnel resulting in the arrest of some members and the deaths of others. As we are able to say these results were achieved before the bomb ship wreck detonated, we are saying the explosion was coincidental as it had been suspected for years that the munitions aboard had become unstable.'

Murmurs of approval from the Agents were summed up by Charlie Walsh saying, ' We know the score Chief. If the public got to know the extent of Saleem's plan there would be a mass exodus from places like Canvey Island. I would think all thirty six thousand residents would be putting their homes up for sale, if they could find anyone to buy them, and heading well away from the danger of the riverside industries. Or demanding such tight security it would be like a Police State. I think I can speak for us all when I say no word of any of this will leave this room.'

'Thank you. Now I'm sure you will all be wanting to catch up with some home life, we'll continue normal service Monday morning. Brad and Trevor, can you stay a minute?'

When the others had left, Samirah mouthing to Brad , 'Phone me', just Senior Agent Jefferies and the two boatmen remained.

'There is something else I have to say gentlemen that both the Director General and the Prime Minister agree with me over,' said the Commander solemnly. ' Much as your major contribution to foiling the Terrorist plot is recognised, we, and I hope yourselves, will make no further mention of it, especially when the press people start prying around as we know they will. This is in the best interests of all concerned, not the least yourselves. Such is the influence of the Politically Correct brigade these days, even proven Terrorists are deemed by them to have rights.'

'It's a pity they don't look at victims rights in the same way,' interceded Swifty.

'Yes, I quite agree but, what we certainly do not wish to see is yourself and Brad being accused of Murder, the sort of accusation you can expect if the PC mob get to hear of your part in the affair. The press release will simply state that the deceased Terrorists were killed by our own people in pursuance of their sworn duty. Latif will not even be mentioned as we will not make any association with the Montgomery.'

Both boatmen were more than happy to agree with the Commander's recommendations as he continued, ' It is recognised ,however, that your boat was damaged solely in an act of significant assistance to the welfare of this country and, as such, I am able to inform you that you will not find yourselves financially penalised by your actions, a generous sum of compensation will be provided from the Public purse.'

Brad grinned and reached into his pocket. ' That won't be necessary Commander,' he said withdrawing the plastic bag full of jewellery. ' The *Whaleback* itself has more than taken care of us and its own repairs.'

Jefferies looked amazed at the array of diamonds and jewels as Brad went on to explain their discovery aboard the old wartime launch and his intention to share the find with his long time friend and crewman so that he could attain his desired move off Canvey.

'So,' said the Agent, ' Some good has come out of your trials of the past couple of days.

Brad, ' he added thrusting out a handshake, 'It's been a pleasure to meet with the pair of you after the usual low-life we meet in the course of our work. You deserve your good fortune and I'm sure Swifty appreciates your generous gesture.'

Still stunned by what he had just heard his Skipper say, Swifty jubilantly piped in, ' If you'll excuse the pun , bearing in mind the huge spout of water from the Montgomery explosion resulted in the find of the jewels and Brad's offer to share the fortune, I would say you've just met a real " Diamond Geezer." '

Laughing at the crewman's wit, the Commander bid them farewell as Brad said, 'Come on Trev, you've got some house-hunting to do and I've got a launch to get back in the water.'

Chapter 11 – Epilogue

The launch disappeared into the gathering dusk as Sea Pilot Captain Harland climbed the long rope ladder to the deck of the ' **Hyundai Warrior**' and made his way to the tall Bridge house. Puffing from his exertions, he greeted Captain Hobbs, ' Hello Silas, nice to see you again. Let's get this monster of yours under way shall we? The sooner I'm off this floating bomb the better I like it.'

A mile ahead of the Carrier, the rusting, frayed, cable anchoring the old wartime mine to the seabed, having suffered further forceful tidal surges the day before, parted with a subdued twang. Released from it's sixty five year anchorage, where it had patiently waited to do its job, the horned iron ball shot to the surface and began a slow drift into the main shipping channel, directly in the path of the slowly approaching Liquified Natural Gas Tanker.

THE END